A Tender
Hope

Books by Amanda Cabot

Historical Romance

TEXAS DREAMS SERIES

Paper Roses

Scattered Petals

Tomorrow's Garden

WESTWARD WINDS SERIES

Summer of Promise

Waiting for Spring

With Autumn's Return

CIMARRON CREEK TRILOGY

A Stolen Heart

A Borrowed Dream

A Tender Hope

Christmas Roses

One Little Word: A Sincerely Yours Novella

Contemporary Romance

TEXAS CROSSROADS SERIES

At Bluebonnet Lake

In Firefly Valley

On Lone Star Trail

CIMARRON CREEK
TRILOGY · 3

A TENDER HOPE

AMANDA CABOT

Revell

a division of Baker Publishing Group
Grand Rapids, Michigan

© 2019 by Amanda Cabot

Published by Revell
a division of Baker Publishing Group
PO Box 6287, Grand Rapids, MI 49516-6287
www.revellbooks.com

Printed in the United States of America

Library of Congress Cataloging-in-Publication Data
Names: Cabot, Amanda, 1948– author.
Title: A tender hope / Amanda Cabot.
Description: Grand Rapids, MI : Revell, a division of Baker Publishing Group,
   [2019] | Series: Cimarron Creek trilogy | Includes bibliographical references and
   index.
Identifiers: LCCN 2018030588 | ISBN 9780800727581 (pbk. : alk. paper)
Subjects: | GSAFD: Mystery fiction. | Suspense fiction.
Classification: LCC PS3603.A35 T46 2019 | DDC 813/.6—dc23
LC record available at https://lccn.loc.gov/2018030588

This book is a work of fiction. Names, characters, places, and incidents are the product of the author's imagination or are used fictitiously.

19 20 21 22 23 24 25   7 6 5 4 3 2 1

For Mary Gillgannon and Joanne Kennedy,
fellow writers and the best of friends.
Your stories inspire me; your insights into human
nature continue to amaze me; your friendship
buoys me during those dark moments that seem
to be an intrinsic part of writing.
Thank you!

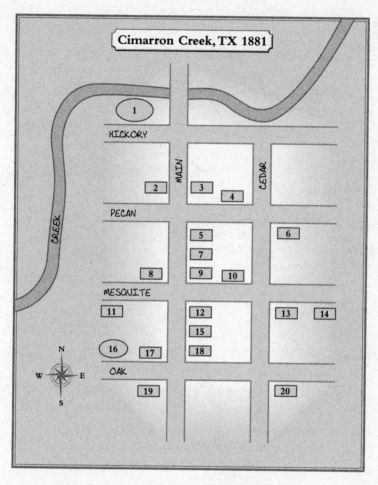

Cimarron Creek, TX 1881

HICKORY

MAIN

CEDAR

PECAN

CREEK

MESQUITE

N
W E
S

OAK

1—Town park
2—Silver Spur saloon
3—Livery stable
4—Thea's home
5—Mercantile
6—Lydia and Travis's home
  (a Founder's house)
7—Apothecary
8—Doc Harrington's home and office
9—Dressmaker's shop
10—Opal and Edgar's home
11—Patience's home

12—Sheriff's office and jail
13—Jacob Whitfield's home
  (a Founder's house)
14—Warner Gray's home
15—Mayor's office/post office
16—Cemetery
17—Church
18—Cimarron Sweets
19—School
20—Matthew Henderson's home
  (a Founder's house)

Descendants of Emil Henderson

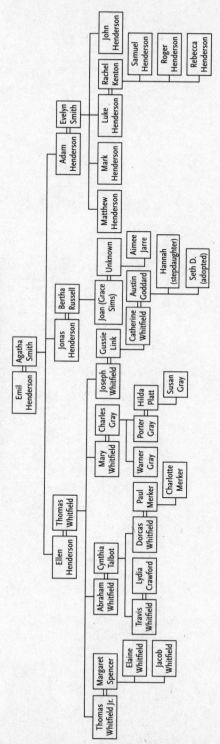

1

AUGUST 8, 1881

She was free.

Thea Michener smiled as she checked the harness, then climbed into the buggy. Within minutes, she would be leaving the only home she could remember. As much as she loved Ladreville, whose half-timbered buildings and Old World charm made visitors declare it to be one of the prettiest towns in the Hill Country, it was time for a change.

While others might have trembled with fear over the thought of leaving family, friends, and all things familiar, the prospect filled Thea with relief. A new town, new possibilities, a new life beckoned her. A year ago she would not have dreamt of leaving, but that was a year ago. So much had changed in the past year, most of all Thea.

"But you haven't changed, have you, Maggie?" Her smile widened into a grin as she looked at the bay mare that had carried her on countless journeys. The horse was the one part of her old life that she was taking with her, that and the tools of her trade. What she was leaving behind were the need for secrecy and the fear that someone would discover the truth she had tried so hard to hide.

Waving good-bye to the liveryman who'd cared for Maggie whenever Thea's business brought her into town, she set off down the street. It was time to be gone. The sun was already high in the sky, although a layer of clouds promised some relief from the heat of a Texas summer. Not for the first time, Thea was grateful for her buggy. The padded seat that some in Ladreville had considered an extravagance would make the long journey more comfortable, while the top—another extravagance according to the town's more frugal residents—would block most of the sun's rays.

"You sure you won't change your mind?" the mayor's wife asked as Thea passed her home. She had hoped to escape last-minute farewells, but a number of the town's matrons were outside their homes or strolling along the main street, apparently waiting to say good-bye to Thea or perhaps, like the mayor's wife, hoping to persuade her to remain.

Thea shook her head. Though she would miss the friends she had made, not to mention her sister, brother-in-law, and their children, she wanted—no, she needed—a complete change. Cimarron Creek would provide that.

Thea smiled as she waved at another woman, then smoothed a wrinkle from her skirt. Another change was coming. Tonight when she was miles away from those who would look askance at her action, she would remove her black garments for the last time. Just the thought brought a sense of peace, as if she'd shed a heavy burden. Thea knew she would never stop mourning her husband and son and the dreams that had died with them, but the outward trappings weighed her down, both literally and figuratively.

Not only did she hate black clothes, but the sight of them wasn't good for her patients. Women who were *enceinte*, to use the French word that sounded so much more genteel than the English "pregnant" with its harsh consonants, needed no reminder that not all babies were born healthy and that not all fathers lived to hold their children in their arms. They didn't need the reminder, and neither did she.

Thea closed her eyes briefly, trying to block the painful memories. She wouldn't dwell on what had happened. Not today. Today was a day to celebrate the beginning of a new life, a day to put the past behind her.

Less than a minute later, she reined in Maggie in front of the parsonage.

"*Bonjour, Aimee,*" she said as a blonde woman, only a couple inches taller than Thea's own five foot two, hurried from the building and stowed the modestly sized valise that contained all her earthly belongings in the back of the buggy.

Thea was surprised that Aimee, the woman who'd explained that her name was pronounced eh-MAY, not Amy, was alone. She had expected the couple who had been her hosts during her time in Ladreville to accompany her to the buggy. Evidently they'd said their farewells in private.

Aimee returned the greeting in the same language, then shook her head and said, "Good morning. We should speak English, though. I need to get in the habit." Her hazel eyes held a note of apprehension, perhaps at the prospect of going to a town where English was the only language. Cimarron Creek did not share Ladreville's history.

Though almost everyone in Ladreville spoke English now, the town had been founded by immigrants from Alsace, and when Thea and her sister had arrived almost a quarter of a century ago, most of the residents had spoken either French or German. As a result, Thea had grown up trilingual.

It was a skill she rarely needed now that her generation had adopted English as their primary language, but it had proven helpful the day Aimee Jarre arrived. The woman had been so exhausted from her journey that she had struggled to find more than a few English words.

"Are you certain you want me to accompany you?" Aimee

asked as she settled onto the seat next to Thea. While her English was practically faultless, when she was distressed or fatigued, Aimee struggled for words, and whenever she spoke, her accent belied the fact that she was a native Texan, born right here in Ladreville.

"Yes, of course, I am." Thea's heart ached for the painfully thin woman who'd traveled all the way from France to the heart of the Texas Hill Country in search of the mother who'd given her up for adoption. As heartbreaking as the past few months had been and as heavily as her fears weighed on her, Thea's life had been easier than Aimee's.

The day Aimee had arrived in Ladreville, it had been obvious to Thea that she had not eaten in days, for she'd practically fainted when she'd climbed down from the stagecoach. Fortunately, Thea had been passing by and had taken her to the parsonage. She had known Pastor and Mrs. Russell would care for Aimee, but it was only later that Thea realized that she had helped Aimee with her quest by leading her to the house where she had been born.

As the light breeze teased her bonnet strings, Thea smiled at her companion. If the breeze continued, the midday heat might feel less oppressive. Even if it did not, they were on their way, and that felt oh, so good. For Thea, it was a new beginning, a chance to forge a life where no one would learn what had happened. For Aimee, this could be the end, the final step that would reunite her with her mother.

"I'm glad you're coming with me," Thea told the young Frenchwoman. Though Aimee had been born in Ladreville, she had spent the rest of her life in a small French town and was, for all intents and purposes, French. It was virtually impossible to think of her as a Texan.

As they reached the town's limits, Thea continued. While she wouldn't share all her reasons for being grateful for Aimee's companionship, she wanted her to understand that they were helping each other. Aimee had already bemoaned her inability to pay her share of expenses.

"You came at exactly the right time. My sister was having a conniption at the thought that I might drive to Cimarron Creek alone. Sarah forgets that I'm twenty-seven and not a child any longer."

"Ancienne."

Thea laughed, both at the word itself and the fact that Aimee had already forgotten her resolution to speak only English. "There are days when I do feel ancient," she admitted, "but today's not one of them."

For far too much of the past year, her fears had made her feel older than Sarah despite the fact that Sarah was twenty years her elder. The need to escape those fears and put the past behind her was one of the reasons the position in Cimarron Creek had sounded so attractive to Thea.

"You seem happier this morning than I've ever seen you," Aimee said in lightly accented English.

"I am." The thought of a new life filled Thea with an almost unbelievable sense of freedom. "The announcement that Cimarron Creek needed a midwife came at exactly the right time."

"For me too." Aimee turned to glance back at the town where she'd been born. From this distance, it appeared peaceful, a place where nothing could go wrong. Thea knew otherwise, and so did Aimee.

"God's timing is perfect," Aimee continued. "He was looking out for me when he brought me to Ladreville and you."

He'd been looking out for Thea too. "I hope you find your answers in Cimarron Creek," she said, deliberately changing the subject, "but even if you don't, it will be wonderful having you with me. Travis Whitfield—he's the man who hired me—said the town would welcome me, but I'll still be a stranger for a while. I'm glad I'll have a friend with me."

Aimee had become a friend more quickly than Thea had

thought possible. The young Frenchwoman had arrived in Ladre-ville less than two weeks ago, but from the first hour she had spent with her, Thea had felt a connection between them. Though she couldn't identify the reason, she felt as if Aimee was the younger sister she'd always wanted, and when it had turned out that Aimee's mother had come from the same town that had hired Thea as its midwife, she had known that was no coincidence. They were meant to go together.

If all went as planned, Aimee would find her mother, and Thea would begin a new life, a life free from secrecy, fear, and worry. No matter what anyone said, no matter what anyone thought, she was not running away.

She was trying to run away from him. Jackson Guthrie scowled as Ladreville's sheriff told him the woman he'd tracked this far had left town only hours before he arrived. Somehow—and he didn't know how, since there'd been no sign of the rest of the Gang—she must have realized that he was searching for her. Admittedly, the story that she'd accepted a position as a midwife in another town sounded plausible, but the timing was suspect. It was more likely that with her husband dead, she'd decided to operate from a different location.

The Gang had done that before. That was part of what made finding them so difficult. They kept moving, and when they weren't robbing stagecoaches or trains, they simply disappeared from sight. Three men and a woman. The Gang of Four. And unless his hunch was totally wrong, she was one of them.

She was running. Jackson didn't doubt that for a minute. What she didn't know was that she couldn't outrun him. Texas Rangers always got their man, or in this case, their woman.

"C'mon, Blaze," he said as he swung into the saddle. "We've got a ways to go."

As the sun rose the next morning, Jackson yawned. The

journey was taking longer than he'd expected. When Blaze had stumbled and injured his fetlock, Jackson had had no choice but to slow their pace. He wouldn't risk further injury by pushing the gelding, nor would he do what some men might have and return to Ladreville to find another horse. He and Blaze had been together for five years. They were partners, and one partner didn't abandon the other.

And so, although he'd thought he would overtake his quarry before nightfall, he had not. When he'd realized how slowly he'd have to travel, Jackson had given up on the idea of apprehending the suspect along the way and had decided to head straight for Cimarron Creek. Rather than stop, he'd ridden all night. If there were no other delays, he should reach the town before Thea Michener and the Frenchwoman who was accompanying her did, for the sheriff had said they'd planned to stop at an inn along the way.

Arriving before her would give Jackson an element of surprise, a weapon of a sort. If he combined that with a plausible reason for being there—something other than his official reason—he might lull her into making a mistake and revealing her guilt.

He yawned again, then smiled at the realization that he was within hours of achieving his goal. The day was beautiful. Hot, of course, but at least it was cooler here in the Hill Country than it was on the plains. Blaze's leg seemed better than yesterday, which was little short of a miracle, and Jackson was filled with anticipation. By nightfall he would have met the woman who held the key to his brother's killers, and if she slipped up and admitted what he suspected, he'd have her in custody faster than a rattler could strike.

His smile widened into a grin at the thought that he would be in Cimarron Creek in little more than an hour. From everything he'd heard, it was a friendly town. Why, it might even have a hotel. A night or two in a bed sounded good right now.

Jackson didn't consider himself old—after all, thirty wasn't decrepit—but he had to admit that sleeping on the ground had lost its appeal. So had—

His thoughts were interrupted by the unmistakable sound of a baby crying.

He reined in Blaze as he surveyed the area. There was no one in sight, and he hadn't passed any houses in the last hour. What was a baby doing out here in the middle of ranch territory? Jackson tipped his head to one side, listening intently. There was no question about it. A baby, an unhappy baby, was nearby.

"C'mon, Blaze. Let's see what we can find."

It didn't take long to discover an infant lying beside the tallest prickly pear cactus in the field, its face red from crying and sunburn. The poor thing must be hungry. He took a deep breath, then frowned. Judging from the smell, the child was also in dire need of clean clothes.

Jackson rummaged through his saddlebags, pulling out a spare bandanna, and made short work of changing and cleaning the little boy. It had been years since he'd done that for his younger brother, but he hadn't forgotten how.

As he hefted the baby into his arms, the crying that had subsided momentarily resumed. Hunger, no doubt, and that was a problem. The boy was clearly too young for jerky or hardtack, but Jackson had no milk. He'd have to settle for drizzling some water into the child's mouth. That wouldn't fill an empty stomach, but it might help prevent dehydration.

Sure enough, as soon as he'd swallowed a little of the warm water, the boy's cries stopped, and he looked up at Jackson with eyes as blue as the summer sky. It might be his imagination, but Jackson thought the baby looked grateful for his rescue. The question was, why had he needed to be rescued?

As far as Jackson could see, there was nothing wrong with the child. He'd heard of parents abandoning babies with deformed limbs or faces marred by birthmarks, but this one had no defects. Even when parents abandoned children, they usually left them at a church or on the porch of a home where they knew someone would find the infant. Why would anyone leave a baby here where his chances of survival were slim?

As soon as he'd taken care of Mrs. Michener, Jackson would track down whoever was responsible for this baby's plight. It might not be official Ranger business, but what had happened to this boy was criminal.

"All right, son," he said as he mounted Blaze. "You're coming with me to Cimarron Creek." The boy wasn't his son, of course. Still, the name sounded right. He had to call the baby something.

"We'll figure out what to do with you there," he promised.

A smile curved his lips at the thought that had popped into his mind. "You may be just what I need—an innocent-sounding reason for meeting Thea Michener."

2

Oh, I love it!" Aimee flung both hands out, as if she wanted to embrace the whole town. "It feels like home."

Thea stared at her companion. Though she and Aimee had chatted as they'd ridden toward Cimarron Creek, this was the first time the Frenchwoman seemed exuberant. Admittedly, the town was prettier than Thea had expected. While it lacked the Old World charm of Ladreville with its half-timbered buildings, everything was well cared for, and the tree-lined Main Street provided welcome shade from the August sun. Still, she was surprised by Aimee's declaration that it felt like home.

"Did Maillochauds look like this?" To Thea's eyes, Cimarron Creek was Texan, not French, but she had no way of knowing what the town where Aimee had been raised looked like.

Aimee gave her head a vigorous shake. "Oh no—not at all. The buildings in France were older and . . ." She paused, obviously searching for a word, settling on "grayer." "It's simply that I feel as if this town is welcoming me."

Thea hoped that would be the case. Aimee had been through a lot in the past months—first learning that she had been adopted, then traveling halfway around the world and practically starving when the cost of transportation proved more than she'd expected. All she'd wanted was to learn the truth about her birth, but she'd uncovered more questions than answers. Cimarron Creek was her last chance.

"Do you mind waiting in the buggy?" Thea asked as she hitched Maggie to the post in front of what was clearly the sheriff's office. There hadn't been time to send a letter to Travis Whitfield, the man who'd been instrumental in hiring her, to say she was bringing a companion. Though Thea doubted he'd object, she didn't want Aimee to be embarrassed if he did, particularly when she seemed so taken with the town.

While Thea had to admit that Cimarron Creek had its share of charm, she refused to make a hasty judgment. She'd done that last year, let her heart overrule her head, and the results had been disastrous. She wouldn't make that mistake again.

"Of course I'll stay here." Aimee settled back in the seat, apparently content to watch passersby.

To Thea's surprise, the sheriff's office was locked. So much for the warm welcome she'd hoped for. She started to turn back toward the buggy when a man emerged from the building next door, his expression radiating curiosity.

"Are you Mrs. Michener?"

Thea nodded.

"I'm Matthew Henderson, mayor and postmaster for this fine town." The man straightened his shoulders as he continued. "Travis and his deputy are out chasing some cattle rustlers right now. Travis said to tell you Warner would give you the key to your house. That's Warner Gray. Mighty fine man if I say so myself. His ma was a Whitfield, you know."

Thea wasn't certain why that mattered, but she nodded as politely as she could. Both she and Aimee were tired of traveling and had been looking forward to a quiet afternoon in their new home, but it seemed that the self-appointed welcoming committee was not finished.

"It's a shame what happened to his family, but I guess what

my ma used to say about every cloud having a silver lining is true. If it weren't for the Grays' problems, you wouldn't have a house to live in."

Trying not to sigh at the realization that the man seemed to have a penchant for gossip, Thea raised an eyebrow. "Where might I find Mr. Gray?"

The mayor gestured to the right. "He's at the apothecary. It's the second building past Mesquite."

Rather than drive half a block, Thea walked the short distance. Five minutes later, having made the acquaintance of the town's apothecary who was, thankfully, less inclined to chatter than the mayor, although he'd given her an appraising look, she climbed back into the buggy, the key in her hand, directions in her head.

"We're almost there," she told Aimee. "Pecan's the second street. Mr. Gray said our house is on the corner of it and Cedar."

"I wonder what it looks like. I just know it'll be perfect." Once again, Aimee was filled with enthusiasm.

As they rounded the corner, Thea's eyes widened in surprise. It seemed Aimee's predictions were accurate. Thea hadn't expected a three-story house with a turret and a wide front porch, but that's what she saw on the corner. Instead of the simple cottage she had thought she was being offered as part of her pay, this house had more than enough room for her and Aimee. Why, she could invite Sarah and Clay and her nieces and nephews and still have plenty of space left over.

And then there was the house catty-cornered from it. That could only be described as a mansion. While the buildings they'd passed on Main Street had been attractive, nothing had prepared Thea for this grandeur.

Though the houses astonished her, what caught and held her gaze was the man standing on the porch of her new home. She might have believed him to be part of a welcoming committee had it not been for the baby in his arms. As a midwife, Thea was accustomed to women visiting her with their children in tow.

Occasionally a worried father-to-be would accompany his wife, but she'd never had an unaccompanied man seek her services.

A frisson of unease made its way down her spine. Who was this man, and why was he here? There was only one way to know.

"Looks like we've got a visitor," she said to Aimee as she climbed out of the buggy. Though Aimee looked as startled by the man's presence as Thea was, she followed Thea toward the house.

"Mrs. Michener?" The man's voice was deep and firm. While he did not raise it above normal speaking volume, there was no question that this was a man who was accustomed to giving orders. His posture spoke of both competence and confidence.

"Yes, I'm Thea Michener."

This close, Thea could see that the man was an inch or two taller than her husband had been, which made him at least six feet tall. Unlike Daniel, who'd had brown hair and eyes, the stranger had auburn hair paired with the most vivid green eyes she had ever seen. Right now, those eyes reflected both surprise and what appeared to be disappointment. How odd. Never before had a man or, for that matter, a woman had that reaction to her.

"I'm Jackson Guthrie," he said. "A Texas Ranger." He pulled a tin star and a folded sheet of paper from his pocket and handed them to Thea.

As she examined the page that established Jackson Guthrie's credentials as a Ranger, Thea felt the blood drain from her face. One of her questions had been answered. She knew who the stranger was. But that only raised a dozen more, including why he appeared to be watching her so carefully. She'd met dozens of men in her life, but none had ever subjected her to such scrutiny.

Did he know something about Daniel's death? Thea hadn't thought the Rangers involved themselves in a simple robbery and murder, but perhaps she'd been mistaken. And then there was the baby. Though she kept her eyes averted, she could not forget that the Ranger held a child.

Ranger Guthrie turned his gaze from Thea back to the infant in his arms. Though the child had not begun to squall, from the way it fidgeted, Thea suspected it would be only minutes before it let out a cry.

"There's no easy way to say this, ma'am, but this baby needs you. I found him abandoned next to a cactus about an hour out of town. There was no sign of his mother."

Thea heard Aimee gasp when the Ranger extended his arms, as if he expected Thea to take the baby from him. He had no way of knowing that what he'd asked her to do was akin to telling her to cut out her heart while it was still beating. It was one thing to deliver other women's babies—she'd managed to do that twice in the three months since her son's death—but caring for a child as if he were her own was far different.

"I'm a midwife, Ranger Guthrie, not a nursemaid," Thea said in a voice that was surprisingly even. Somehow, she had managed not to betray the way her heart had clenched at the very idea of holding this infant. "I deliver babies; I ensure that they are healthy; but I am not a nanny."

Though she should have known better, Thea darted a glance at the child in the Ranger's arms. Blue, not brown, eyes stared at her from a face that was sunburned, not waxen white. The baby's cheeks were full, his lips plump. He bore no resemblance to Aaron, and yet he was a baby—a baby boy probably the age Aaron would have been if he'd lived.

There was no way she could hold him, much less care for him, without being reminded of all she'd lost. She could not—she simply could not—let herself be so vulnerable.

"It looks like you need to make an exception this time, unless you're willing to let this boy die," the Ranger said, his voice as matter-of-fact as if he were asking Thea's opinion of a new kind of string bean.

At her side, Aimee gasped again. "You can't do that, Thea."

Aimee had heard the story of Thea's stillborn son and knew

24

that she had not recovered from the loss, that she doubted she ever would. Coming so soon after Daniel's death, the day Thea had held her baby for the first and last time had been the most painful of her life. The last of her dreams had died the morning when the midwife who'd trained Thea had placed the lifeless body in her arms.

"There must be someone else." There had to be another answer. While Thea had been in Cimarron Creek only a few minutes, she knew from her correspondence with Travis Whitfield that it was a friendly town. Surely one of the residents would be willing to care for an abandoned baby.

The Ranger shook his head. "This little one's going to need special care for a while. My guess is even the most well-meaning ladies won't have time to give him that."

"And you think I will?"

The reply came quickly. "Yes, ma'am, I do. At least for the next couple days."

He was probably correct in believing that Thea would have free time for a while. When he'd outlined the job's responsibilities, Travis had said that the first baby she'd deliver, the one he and his wife were expecting, wasn't due until late September.

Aimee touched Thea's hand and waited until Thea met her gaze before she said, "We can do it for a few days. If you show me what to do, I can care for him." She lowered her voice so that only Thea would hear her say, "I hate the idea that he was abandoned."

Thea nodded, realizing that the baby's situation reminded Aimee of what had happened to her. Though there were differences—Aimee's mother hadn't left her next to a cactus, and she had known her daughter would be adopted the next day—she had fled Ladreville in the middle of the night, leaving no trace. When Aimee had learned what had happened, she'd felt as if she'd been abandoned.

Thea nodded again. No matter how painful it might be for

Thea to hold a baby that wasn't Aaron, she would do nothing to cause Aimee distress.

"All right, Ranger Guthrie." She tried not to make her acceptance sound too grudging. "We'll take him for now, but I expect you and Sheriff Whitfield to do everything you can to find his mother."

"You can be sure of that, ma'am." The Ranger's green eyes darkened with an emotion Thea could not identify. Regret? Determination? Something else? The only thing she knew was that Jackson Guthrie appeared to be as affected by the child as she was.

As he placed the baby in her arms, Thea stared down at the tiny infant and bit the inside of her cheek to keep from crying. It felt so right—and so wrong—to cradle a child again.

"The baby's still asleep."

Thea nodded as she gazed at the infant curled up in a dresser drawer that Aimee had lined with soft flannel. "The salve Warner recommended seems to be helping his face."

It might have been the coward's way out, but Thea had left Aimee with the baby while she took Maggie and the buggy to the livery. Once they were safely boarded, she had returned to the apothecary for burn ointment and had stopped at the mercantile for bottles, diapers, and a few ready-made garments.

While she'd been at the pharmacy, Warner—he'd insisted she call him that rather than Mr. Gray—had explained that the house the town had given to Thea as part of her salary had once belonged to his brother. Though he did not mention the problems to which the postmaster had alluded, a shadow had crossed Warner's face when he'd spoken of his brother. A second later, he'd nodded briskly, as if shedding his unhappy thoughts, and told Thea that his sister-in-law had left some of her daughter's baby clothes and toys when she'd left Cimarron Creek and that Thea was welcome to anything she found in the attic.

Tomorrow would be soon enough to explore the attic. Before Thea had left to do her shopping, she and Aimee had taken a quick tour through the first and second floors of the house and, at Thea's suggestion, had chosen bedrooms on the opposite sides of the building.

"I'll keep the baby in my room," Thea had told Aimee. "He's likely to cry at night, and there's no need for both of us to be awake."

Aimee, obviously in awe of the grandeur of the house with five bedrooms, not to mention a parlor, formal dining room, and kitchen, had agreed. "Once you show me what to do, we can take turns," she had volunteered.

It was a kind offer, but by then Ranger Guthrie would have found the baby's family. That was the thought that had sustained Thea while she unpacked her trunk, leaving Aimee to watch the sleeping infant. Now she was back in the parlor where her new friend hovered over their young charge.

Aimee's smile was sweet as she touched the baby's forehead. "The salve may have helped him sleep, but a full stomach didn't hurt, either. I know I sleep better when I'm fed." Thea's first lesson for Aimee had been how to determine when milk was the proper temperature and how to coax a child to drink from a bottle.

"Is that a hint that we should start supper?"

"Maybe," Aimee agreed, "but there's something else we should probably do."

"What's that?"

"Give the boy a name."

Thea chuckled at the evidence that she and Aimee had been thinking along the same lines. "How did you know that I was going to tell you that? Even though it'll only be for a few days, we can't keep calling him 'the baby' or 'the boy.' What do you think of Stuart?" Though Thea couldn't explain why the name had popped into her head, once it had, it refused to be dislodged.

Aimee tipped her head to the side for an instant before grinning. "I like it."

"Then he'll be Stuart until the Ranger finds his family." Thea refused to consider the possibility that Stuart's family was either dead or had no intention of coming for him. Caring for him was a temporary measure. Strictly temporary. "Now, what shall we eat?"

They were washing dishes after a simple meal when Thea heard someone knocking on the front door. Seconds later she ushered a tall man with a star on his chest and a lovely blonde who was greatly with child into the house. Though they both smiled, the woman's eyes widened at the sight of Thea's clothing. In all likelihood, she'd been expecting widow's weeds.

"You must be Sheriff and Mrs. Whitfield," Thea said as she gestured toward the most comfortable seats in the parlor. One of the attractions of this house had been the fact that it came completely furnished, and while the elaborately carved horsehair settee and three side chairs would not have been her choice, they saved her from having to buy furniture.

"Please call us Lydia and Travis," the woman said as she settled into one of the chairs. "One thing you'll discover is that we're not too formal here."

Another thing Thea discovered was that Lydia spoke with a northern accent. Though she was curious about the reception Lydia had received when she arrived and hoped that her obvious acceptance by at least one influential person in town meant that Aimee would also be welcomed, this was not the time to ask Lydia about that.

"And I'm Thea." She decided to address the question of her clothing directly. "You both know I'm a widow, so you're probably wondering why I'm not in black."

Lydia inclined her head. "I didn't realize the people in Ladreville were as progressive as Aunt Bertha." When Travis laid

28

a hand on hers, Lydia explained that Aunt Bertha had been Travis's great-aunt and the original owner of the mansion across the street where Lydia and Travis now lived. "She was insistent that no one wear black in her honor. She claimed we should celebrate her life rather than mourning its end."

Thea couldn't claim that that was her reason for eschewing black clothing, so she merely nodded.

Travis filled the momentary lull in conversation by saying, "I apologize for not being in town when you arrived this afternoon."

Grateful that no one asked about Daniel, Thea gave the sheriff a questioning look. "I hope you caught the rustlers."

"We did." He started to say something else, but whatever he was going to say was interrupted by the unmistakable sound of a baby's cry. "I heard you had a surprise waiting for you."

"You mean Stuart?" News traveled quickly in small towns, and the fact that Travis was the town's sheriff meant that he was probably one of the first to learn when anything unusual happened in Cimarron Creek. In all likelihood, Ranger Guthrie had reported what had happened, which meant that Travis already knew about Aimee too. He didn't appear upset or disapproving, but Thea needed to be certain.

"Is that his name?" Lydia tipped her head to one side as if trying to decide whether she liked it.

"Temporarily." It was time to talk about Aimee. "I hope no one objects—" At the sound of footsteps, Thea turned toward the doorway. She had waited too long. Now Aimee would witness Travis's reaction. Thea could only hope it would be favorable.

"I hope no one objects," she repeated as Aimee entered the room, "but I brought a friend with me. This is Aimee Jarre."

A gasp echoed through the room, and the blood drained from Lydia's face so quickly that Thea feared the expectant mother might faint. Her eyes wide with shock, Lydia stared at Aimee. "You're Aimee Jarre?"

3

T ell me about her."

    Jackson glanced at the man who'd barged into Warner Gray's residence as if he lived there. An inch or so shorter than Warner, the man bore no apparent resemblance to Jackson's host. His hair was blond rather than Warner's light brown, his eyes a lighter blue than Warner's, his build more muscular. As he spoke, the aroma of mint filled the room, making Jackson suspect the man had been chewing mint leaves. Perhaps he suffered from dyspepsia the way Grandpa Guthrie had. One thing was for certain—he'd disturbed the peaceful evening Warner had promised when he'd offered his home to Jackson.

    That was just one more thing that hadn't gone the way Jackson had expected. By now, he should have had a member of the Gang in custody. Instead, all he had to show for his efforts were a baby who aroused painful memories and a woman whose appearance raised questions rather than answering them.

    He should have been on his way back to camp, not thinking about Thea Michener and the baby who did not look like Micah, despite the fact that the very sight of him reminded Jackson of his younger brother. Instead, he'd be staying in Cimarron Creek for at least a few days.

The town's apothecary had offered Jackson temporary lodging, claiming he would have peace and quiet, not a visit from a man who seemed almost belligerent.

"Rachel said she was supposed to arrive today," the intruder continued. "I want to know everything about her."

Warner chuckled as he picked up his coffee mug and took a long slug. Apparently, he was used to the man's brusque manner. "I suppose you also want a piece of the chocolate pie Mrs. Higgins made for me."

When the visitor's eyes widened, Warner gestured to one of the empty chairs. "It's yours once I introduce you." He nodded in Jackson's direction. "Nate, this is Ranger Jackson Guthrie. He's got some business with Travis, the new midwife—I assume she's the woman you're so interested in—and her companion."

With barely a glance at Jackson, Nate fixed his gaze on Warner, his excitement reminding Jackson of the time when his older brothers had begun courting the women who were now their wives. Five years younger than Quincy and Jefferson and at the age where girls were annoying rather than attractive, Jackson had found his brothers' antics silly. Today he found Nate's enthusiasm for a woman he'd yet to meet more annoying than silly.

"Two women? Rachel didn't tell me that."

While Jackson remained silent, trying not to cringe at the picture of Nate courting either Mrs. Michener or her friend, Warner's chuckle turned into a full-fledged laugh. "That's what your sister gets for being out on the ranch. She misses all the good gossip. Now, if you want some of the pie, you know where the plates and forks are."

As Nate opened a cupboard, Warner sent Jackson a look of amusement. "The man who's more interested in pie and finding himself a wife than displaying the manners his mother drummed into him is Nate Kenton. He raises the best goats and peaches in the area."

After plunking the now-filled plate onto the table along with a mug of coffee, Nate extended his hand toward Jackson. "Sorry. Warner's right. Ma raised me to do better than this." After they'd shaken hands, he settled onto the chair and raised an eyebrow. "What brings you to Cimarron Creek, Ranger Guthrie?"

A woman. Though that was the truth, Jackson would not admit it, especially since Nate would probably misunderstand. He had no more intention of telling Nate about the criminals he was chasing than he had had of sharing that information with Warner. He'd simply told Warner about the baby and that he hoped the new midwife would be able to care for him. As the town's sheriff, Travis Whitfield needed to know about Jackson's search for the Gang, but civilians did not.

"There's no need for formality," he said, trying to deflect the question. "The name's Jackson."

"And I'm Nate." Nate swallowed a generous bite of pie before adding, "It's not often we get a Ranger in town."

"It's not often I find an abandoned baby along the road." Jackson leaned back in his chair, trying to relax.

The kitchen was pleasant enough, with yellow curtains that matched the chair cushions, but somehow it lacked the warmth of his parents' home. Perhaps the absence of a woman explained that. Ma would have put a vase of flowers on the table, but Warner had no wife to add a soft touch. When he'd invited Jackson to stay with him, he'd explained that he'd lived alone since his parents' deaths and would welcome company.

"So, two women and a baby arrived on the same day?" Nate reached for his mug. "What's happening to our town, Warner? We haven't had this much excitement since Lydia stepped off the stagecoach last year."

"You think I know what's happening?" Warner forked his remaining bite of pie. "You ought to be asking Jackson. He's the one who found the baby. I talked to Mrs. Michener, but he's the only one who's met both of the women."

"What do they look like? I heard the midwife was a widow."

"That's true," Jackson confirmed. The most unusual widow he'd ever met. Though recently bereaved, she wore not a stitch of black.

"Her husband died a few months ago." The report of Daniel Michener's body being found had been the first big break Jackson had had on this case, because it had given him a name to put with the face he'd sketched.

"Do you think she might be looking for a new one?"

Jackson focused on the fact that Nate raised his left eyebrow when he asked a question rather than the idea that the woman he'd met only a few hours earlier might be eager to remarry. There was no reason he should care that her lack of obvious mourning might mean that one of the reasons Mrs. Michener had come to Cimarron Creek was to find a new husband, but there was also no need to share that information with Nate. Warner had also met the widow, and he hadn't commented on her clothing.

"Can't say," was all that Jackson would offer.

"What does she look like?" the farmer continued. "Is she pretty?"

This time Warner didn't wait for Jackson to respond. "She sure is. Dark blonde hair, brown eyes, and the prettiest face you've ever seen."

"Is that right?"

Jackson nodded. He'd seen all that and more the second Thea Michener had climbed out of her buggy. As it had then, disappointment warred with relief. Until that moment, he'd been certain that she was the woman he sought, but she wasn't. There'd been no need to question her, to find a way to get her to reveal where the others were hiding out, because while she may have been Daniel Michener's wife, Cimarron Creek's new midwife was not the female member of the Gang.

Although Daniel's had been the only face he'd seen, Jackson

had gotten a good look at all four of the bandits, and there was no doubt that each of them was almost as tall as he. Thea Michener was only a couple inches over five feet.

He couldn't explain it. He'd wanted her to be part of the Gang. He owed it to the Rangers, to the State of Texas, and, most of all, to his brother to put the remaining three members behind bars. Jackson knew that. But at the same time, once he'd met Thea Michener, he hadn't wanted her to be part of the foursome that had robbed countless travelers and stolen so many Army payrolls.

The woman intrigued him. It wasn't only her clothing that was unexpected; so were her reactions. As she'd approached him, Jackson had seen fear on her face. It wasn't the first time that had happened. Even innocent citizens sometimes feared Rangers, but his instincts had told him that Mrs. Michener's fear wasn't directed at him.

She hadn't known he was a Ranger when her eyes had dilated and she'd clenched her fists. It was the baby he'd held in his arms that had triggered her fear. For a second he'd been puzzled. That was hardly a normal reaction for a midwife. But then Jackson had recalled the sheriff in Ladreville mentioning that her baby had been stillborn. Perhaps seeing a live infant stirred the same painful memories that assailed Jackson whenever he saw a lanky youth with red hair.

"You're saying she's real pretty?" Nate appeared to need reassurance.

Once again, Jackson nodded. The memory of wide-set brown eyes, a classic nose, and a chin that hinted at stubbornness or at least determination was etched on his brain. "Mrs. Michener is good-looking, but so is the Frenchwoman she brought with her."

That got the farmer's attention. "A Frenchwoman? I've heard they're mighty pretty too."

Setting his now-empty mug onto the table, Warner wrinkled his nose at his visitor. "You're just hoping she won't speak enough English to understand that the last two women you set your sights on turned you down."

"Seems to me you didn't have any better luck with one of them."

"True, but I learned my lesson. You don't see me running after every single gal in town."

"And you're saying I do?"

Warner simply shrugged, his casual gesture appearing to irritate Nate more than a retort would have. Jackson tried not to smile. The two men sounded like squabbling brothers. How many times had Micah bickered with him, his voice holding the same annoyed note when Jackson refused to engage in a game of sibling rivalry? How many times had he tried to elude the little brother who wanted to follow him everywhere, even into a fight he had no chance of surviving?

If only . . . Jackson brushed the melancholy thoughts aside. He couldn't change the past. All he could do was ensure that those who'd killed his brother got their just deserts.

"Why the rush to marry?" he asked in an attempt to lighten his mood. Though Ma kept urging him to find the right girl and settle down, Jackson knew he wasn't ready.

Warner shrugged again, as if the answer should be apparent. "Nate here's an old man—almost thirty."

"Careful." Jackson held up a hand, as if to stop traffic. "I turned thirty a couple months back, but I'm not ready to call myself an old man."

"I'd have been married years ago if Warner's parents had seen fit to have a daughter." With his plate now empty, Nate seemed more interested in talking.

"Growing up, Warner and his brother were my best friends. The truth is, I spent more time with them than my own family. I always wanted to be an official part of the Gray family, so I told them they needed a sister for me to marry." He gave Warner a wry grin. "Since they didn't oblige, maybe the Frenchwoman is the right one for me. Warner can court the widow."

Acid bubbled in Jackson's stomach. It was none of his business, he tried to remind himself. He was only passing through town. There was no reason the idea of either of them courting Mrs. Michener should bother him, but it did.

Aimee stared at the couple, trying to make sense of what had just happened. The wonderful feeling she'd had from the moment she'd entered Cimarron Creek, the feeling that this was where she was meant to be, had dissipated at the sight of the woman's shock.

The star on the man's chest told Aimee this was Travis Whitfield, the sheriff who'd hired Thea. The woman must be his wife, Lydia. Aimee wasn't surprised that they'd come to visit Thea, but she was surprised that they'd recognized her name and even more surprised that her identity had triggered such strong emotions.

"Oui, je suis . . ." She broke off, embarrassed that she'd reverted to French. "Pardon me. Yes, I'm Aimee Jarre."

Something in her voice must have alerted Thea to her distress, because her friend rose and took the baby from Aimee's arms, practically pushing her onto the settee.

Lydia Whitfield's eyes moved slowly from the top of Aimee's head to her toes. "Your hair is the same shade as your mother's, but her eyes are green. The way you hold your head reminds me of your grandmother." She sounded bemused, as if this was the last thing she had expected.

Aimee swallowed deeply as the woman's words registered. Her mother. Her grandmother. Lydia Whitfield had met both of them! Her instincts hadn't been wrong. The unmistakable feeling of elation that had washed over her when she'd arrived here was not an aberration. This was indeed where she was meant to be, for even though Pastor and Mrs. Russell had thought it unlikely, Aimee's mother was here.

36

"You know my mother and my grandmother?" Somehow, she managed to find the correct English words when all the while her heart was pounding so hard that she could barely breathe.

Lydia nodded, her blue eyes radiating warmth. "Travis and I live in what used to be your grandmother's house. She left it to me when she died, but before that I lived with her. It's the one catty-cornered from here."

"The mansion?" Thea asked as she rocked Stuart to keep him from waking.

Travis chuckled. "That's one way of describing it. There are three of those huge houses in Cimarron Creek. Each of the founding fathers wanted to leave a legacy for future generations."

Lydia laid her hand on her husband's arm. "I don't think Miss Jarre is interested in the town's history. She wants to know about her mother."

"*Exactement.*" Aimee nodded rapidly. "Where does she live?" It didn't sound as if she stayed with Lydia and Travis, even though that was where she had grown up. "I want to see her— tonight if it's possible."

She looked at Thea, relieved when her friend nodded. No matter how tired they were, this was important. This was the reason Aimee had crossed an ocean and traveled thousands of miles by train and stagecoach.

Lydia exchanged an uncomfortable look with her husband. "I'm afraid it's not that simple. You see, your mother's on her way to France."

"France? Why?" Nothing was making sense.

"She's gone there to find you," Lydia explained.

As a wave of dizziness swept over her, Aimee leaned back in the settee. She wasn't certain whether it was caused by relief or shock, but the light-headedness made her grateful she wasn't still standing or holding Stuart as the impact of Lydia's words registered. Her mother wanted to find her! Even though she'd let someone else adopt and raise her, her mother was now searching for her. This was the best news Aimee had ever heard, and yet . . .

"*Quel gâchis.*"

"It is a mess," Thea agreed, "but we'll sort it out." She turned to Lydia and Travis. "Can you tell us what happened? Aimee's been searching for her mother ever since her parents died and she discovered she'd been adopted. The letters she found didn't reveal her real mother's name, just that she'd given birth in Ladreville."

Aimee nodded, confirming Thea's statements. It was good that her friend was making the explanations, because she wasn't certain she could have mustered enough English. Though her schoolmistress had insisted they speak only English each morning, telling them they might one day want to travel to London, when Aimee was anxious or tired—and she was both right now—her command of English faltered.

Thea continued her explanation. "When Aimee arrived in Ladreville and learned that no one knew much about her mother other than that she used to live here, I invited her to accompany me."

Lydia smiled at Aimee, almost as if she understood her confusion. "Your mother came back to Cimarron Creek a few months ago. That was the first time she'd been here in over twenty years. She was hoping her mother would know where you were."

"But Aunt Bertha—that's your grandmother—had already died." Travis confirmed what Aimee had already learned, that both of her grandparents were dead.

"Grace was devastated."

Thea's gasp echoed Aimee's. What was Lydia saying? Had she been mistaken about her mother's name?

"Grace?" Thea asked. "I thought Aimee's mother was Joan Henderson."

"It's a long story." Lydia turned so that she was facing Aimee directly. "When you were born and she was forced to give you up for adoption, Joan wanted to start a new life, so she fled to San Antonio and changed her name. She's been Grace—first Grace Brown, then Grace Sims when she married—ever since. It was only after her husband died that she came back here, hoping to reconcile with her parents."

"But they had died." Aimee's heart ached at the thought of what her mother had endured. She'd had a child out of wedlock, given her up for adoption, been estranged from her parents, and returned to Cimarron Creek too late for a reunion with them. No matter what Aimee herself had experienced, it had not been that heartbreaking.

Lydia nodded. "Grace wouldn't give up hope that she would find you, but it took months before she learned that the family who adopted you had moved back to France. Once she knew that, she wanted to catch the first ship to Europe."

"Meanwhile I was leaving France to look for her here." Though it had been a shock when she'd found the papers that proved she'd been born in the United States and had been adopted by Jean-Joseph and Denise Jarre, Aimee had also felt a sense of relief. So many things made sense once she understood her origins.

Lydia nodded again. "I'll send a letter to Paris tomorrow. Grace was planning to spend a few weeks there before heading to the town where she thought you were living. She's traveling with our new doctor, his wife, and their children. Once she learns you're here, I know they'll return immediately."

And then many of Aimee's questions would be answered. Grace—it seemed odd to think of her by any name other than Joan—would tell her why she'd given her up for adoption. Though Aimee had suspicions, she wanted to hear the words from her mother's lips.

"What about my father?"

Lydia and Travis exchanged another uncomfortable glance

before Lydia responded. "That's your mother's story to tell. What you need to remember is that Grace loved you dearly. She would have kept you and raised you if she could have."

Though Aimee had assumed that her father had died before he could marry her mother, Lydia and Travis's reaction made her wonder if he was still alive. But if he was, why hadn't he married Grace?

Aimee turned to Thea, seeking guidance. Though she wanted to press the sheriff and his wife for answers, it seemed they'd said all they would.

"I imagine there are others in town who could share stories about Aimee's mother and grandmother," Thea said as she tickled Stuart's nose. The infant had wakened but seemed content to remain in Thea's arms.

Once again, an uncomfortable silence fell as Lydia and Travis looked at each other. Finally, he spoke. "It's a complicated situation. Lydia and I would be happy to tell you everything we know, but until Grace returns, it would be best if you didn't say anything to others about being Grace's daughter."

There was only one reason Aimee could imagine for such a request. "They don't know she had a child, do they?"

"No."

4

Even if he hadn't seen the jail cell on the far wall or heard the two men currently incarcerated muttering curses, Jackson would have known this was a sheriff's office. It had the same spare look and smell of old coffee that seemed to characterize practically every lawman's office he'd entered.

"Sheriff Whitfield?" The man sitting behind the desk ignoring his prisoners' complaints matched the description Warner had given him—around six feet tall with dark brown hair, gray eyes, and a square chin.

"That's right. You must be Ranger Guthrie."

"I figured you'd know I was in town."

The man with the star on his chest nodded. "I would have stopped by Warner's house last night, but Lydia—she's my wife—said it was more important to welcome the new midwife, and by the time we were done there, she was pretty tired."

The smile that lit Travis Whitfield's face when he mentioned his wife left no doubt that he loved her. Jackson had seen his father wear the same almost-silly grin when Ma walked into the room. Quincy and Jefferson were less demonstrative with their wives, but Jackson knew they'd do virtually anything to make them happy.

"I never had a wife," he admitted, "but my pa said a wise man doesn't argue with his missus."

Travis chuckled. "I'll keep that in mind. Now, you want to tell me what brought you to Cimarron Creek?"

Straight to the point. Jackson appreciated that. Like the sheriff, he didn't have much patience for dithering. "It's confidential." He tipped his head toward the jail cell. While its current inhabitants didn't appear to be listening to the conversation, he had no intention of saying anything important in front of them.

"Of course. Let's go outside." Travis settled his hat on his head and led the way to the back of the building. "No windows on this side and no one close enough to overhear anything." Even so, he kept his voice pitched low. "I won't tell my deputy unless you want me to."

Jackson shook his head. "I'd rather you didn't. Just between us, I'm on the trail of the Gang of Four."

Narrowing his eyes slightly, Travis nodded. "It seems like every lawman in Texas dreads the thought that they might find their way to his town. When I hadn't heard of any robberies recently, I wondered if they'd hung up their spurs."

If only it were that simple. "I don't think so. One of them turned up dead."

"Not of natural causes, I'm guessing."

"Not unless a single gunshot to the heart is natural. It looked like a simple robbery, but my guess is that there was a falling-out among the Gang and that one of them shot him."

Jackson leaned against the back of Travis's office, then recoiled. The morning sun had left the stone hotter than he'd expected. "I don't have any proof yet, but I suspect the others are having problems trying to figure out how to operate as a threesome. At any rate, I got a lead that brought me to this part of the Hill Country."

He wouldn't mention either Thea or the fact that the man who'd been killed was her husband until he learned more, because he didn't want to make any false accusations. A woman's livelihood was at stake, and Jackson would do nothing to jeopardize it. He was all too well aware that once a person's reputation had been besmirched, it was difficult to repair it.

At this point, he didn't know enough about Thea Michener to make a judgment. The only thing he knew was that she wasn't part of the quartet that committed the robberies, but that didn't mean she was innocent. She might have been involved in the planning. She might even have been the brains behind the operation. If that was the case, she was as guilty as the outlaws who'd killed Micah. But Jackson had no proof, and until he did, he would remain silent.

"I need a place to use as a home base while I continue my search." His hope that a quick arrest would lead him to the rest of the Gang had disappeared. "Cimarron Creek seems like a good one." Especially since the enigmatic Thea Michener now called it home. Living here would give him a chance to observe her and learn what she knew about her husband's cohorts.

Travis nodded, though his expression told Jackson he suspected there was more to the story than he was admitting. "It's a mostly peaceful town. We had a rash of crimes last year, but that's over and things are on pretty much an even keel." The way he glanced at the sky, as if judging the sun's position, told Jackson he was anxious to return to his office. "Is there anything I can help you with?"

"As a matter of fact, there is." Jackson headed back toward the street. There was nothing confidential about the next subject. "I'm sure you heard about the baby I found yesterday."

"Stuart."

"Stuart? Is that his name?"

Travis shrugged. "That's what Thea Michener's calling him."

"Stuart." Jackson rolled the name across his tongue and discovered that he liked it. "I need to find his mother. I didn't see any signs of her on the road, but she's got to be somewhere.

The little tyke is months away from crawling, so he sure as shooting didn't wander off to that cactus patch on his own."

Travis clapped him on the shoulder. "Edgar and I can help you, but not today. We need to get those cattle rustlers out of Cimarron Creek and to the county seat to stand trial. We should be back tomorrow night, so we can start looking Friday morning."

"Fair enough. I'll send you a telegram if I find anything in the meantime." Though he hoped he would have good news to report, Jackson's instincts were shrieking otherwise.

"This is the first time I've bathed a baby." Aimee dabbed the wet cloth across Stuart's arm as gingerly as if she were trying to remove pollen from a rose petal. "I'm glad you're here to show me how."

Thea smiled at her friend. "It's not difficult. It just takes practice." Aimee had struggled to keep Stuart from squirming out of her arms when she first began to wash his face. Now she seemed a bit more comfortable, perhaps because he'd stopped screaming and was staring at her as if fascinated by her hair.

"I'm glad you're here to help," Thea continued. "I couldn't leave Stuart alone while I visit my patients, but I'm not ready to start taking him on my rounds." She'd been excited by the summons she'd received this morning, asking her to call on a woman named Belinda Allen. Her first patient! Thea had thought Lydia would be the first, but that appointment wasn't until later. Mrs. Allen would be her very first.

Smiling at the prospect, she turned back to Aimee. "God definitely had a good plan when he sent you to Ladreville."

Aimee dropped the cloth back into the basin and began to dry Stuart's arms and legs. "I still can't quite believe that my mother's been searching for me. It was all I could think about last night. Oh, Thea, I just wish she hadn't given me away. We've wasted so many years apart."

Thea heard the anguish in Aimee's voice and looked for a way to ease it. "She may not have felt as if she had any choice. It would have been difficult for her to raise you alone."

"You would have kept your son even though Daniel was gone."

Thea wondered if small towns in France were different from the ones in Texas. "A widow with a child is acceptable. Unmarried mothers have a much harder time. They and their children are often shunned."

There had been only one unwed pregnancy during the time Thea served as Ladreville's midwife, and the mother—little more than a child herself—had asked Thea to find a home for her baby. She had even refused to hold her son lest she grow attached to him. Three days later, in a story oddly similar to that of Aimee's mother, she had disappeared, leaving no word of where she'd headed.

"It won't be long before you know the whole story." Thea hoped that prospect would provide some comfort.

Aimee tipped her head to one side as she laid Stuart back into the flannel-lined bureau drawer. "You and I are quite a pair, aren't we? We were both raised by people who weren't our real parents."

When Aimee had first arrived in Ladreville, obviously distraught over the fact that no one in the town knew where her mother had gone, Thea had shared her own past with the lovely Frenchwoman, telling her about her parents' deaths when she was only two and how Sarah and Clay had become substitute parents.

"You're fortunate, Aimee. You're getting the chance to meet your mother. I don't even have a picture of mine." The one Sarah had brought from their home in Philadelphia had been destroyed in a fire.

"But you had Sarah and Clay's love."

The envy she saw reflected on Aimee's face startled Thea.

"Didn't your parents love you?" If that was the case, Aimee hadn't confided it.

"No. I never understood why, but I felt as if I was a burden." Aimee looked up from the now-contented baby. "If they didn't want a child, why did they adopt me?"

Thea thought for a moment, knowing that her answer was important. "Maybe they didn't realize what raising a child involved. I've seen parents like that. They believe they want a baby, but they're not prepared for the reality. It's hard work."

"Do you think that's what happened to Stuart?"

"I don't know. If I had to guess, I would say that his mother loved him, because he looked well cared for." But that didn't explain why he'd been abandoned next to a cactus.

"I hope you're right." Aimee pressed a kiss on Stuart's forehead. "Everyone deserves to be loved."

Aimee's words were still echoing through her brain as Thea turned the corner from Pecan to head north on Main Street. Everyone did deserve to be loved—by parents, siblings, spouses. The last thought brought a frown to her face.

"You look serious, Mrs. Michener. Is something wrong?" Ranger Guthrie asked as he led his horse from the livery.

Thea forced her lips to turn upward in what she hoped was a natural-looking smile. "I was just thinking about Stuart." That wasn't a lie; she *had* been thinking about him. It was simply that Stuart hadn't been the reason for her frown.

"Is he all right?" Concern shadowed the Ranger's green eyes.

"His face is starting to peel from the sunburn, but he should be fine. I can't imagine why anyone would have abandoned him." That was the thought that had haunted Thea as she'd fallen asleep last night, the one that had weighed on her so heavily as she'd made breakfast this morning.

"I've seen worse things." The Ranger's frown deepened.

"I imagine you have." Lawmen had the unenviable job of confronting the worst aspects of society. Not wanting to dwell on that, Thea gestured toward the handsome chestnut with the white blaze. "Are you leaving town today?"

The thought sent an unexpected pang to her heart. She shouldn't care, but somehow she did. Thoughts of the Ranger whose grim expression kept him from being conventionally handsome had mingled with worries about Stuart's mother.

Jackson Guthrie was a puzzle. He seemed as honest and dedicated as Rangers were reputed to be, and Thea's instincts told her that she could trust him. What bothered her was that it appeared he didn't trust her. She couldn't forget the way he'd looked at her yesterday, as if he believed her guilty of something. That was absurd, just as it was absurd to be disappointed that he was leaving. The only thing Thea was guilty of was trusting the wrong man.

As the Ranger shook his head, an auburn lock slid from underneath his hat, giving him an almost boyish look that contrasted with the solemnity of his voice. "I'm not going away permanently. I made you a promise, and I plan to keep it. The reason I'm leaving is to discover what happened to Stuart's mother."

Jackson's solemn tone of voice and the fact that he said "discover what happened" rather than "find" told Thea he did not expect a happy ending. "You don't think she's alive, do you?"

As his horse moved impatiently, the Ranger laid a reassuring hand on his neck. "I hope I'm wrong, but either way, I'll get the answers."

"I'm sure you will." Not only did the Rangers have a reputation for successfully completing their missions, but this man exuded confidence. "Thank you, Ranger Guthrie."

He touched the brim of his hat in farewell. "You're welcome, Mrs. Michener."

As he mounted his horse and headed in the opposite direction, Thea paused, remembering his final words. Surely it was her imagination that he appeared uncomfortable pronouncing her name.

Less than two minutes later, she reached the Allens' house. At first glance, the location across from the town park and close to the river seemed ideal, but as Thea approached the large stone building, she revised her opinion. The stains on the foundation told her the house was wet whenever the river flooded, probably every spring. No wonder a young couple could afford such a large home.

Seconds after she knocked on the front door, it was flung open. "Come in, Mrs. Michener. I'm Belinda Allen."

Thea's patient was a tall woman with eyes and hair several shades darker than Thea's. Though her pregnancy had not yet thickened her waist, her face bore the slight flush that Thea called "mothers' glow." Belinda Allen was *enceinte* and thrilled by the prospect of motherhood.

Patients like her made Thea's job easier, because they seldom complained about the less pleasant aspects of pregnancy—queasiness, swollen ankles, even labor pains—but accepted them as part of the process. In the instant it took her to make her assessment, Thea knew she would enjoy having Belinda Allen as her patient.

"I'm so happy you've come to Cimarron Creek," Mrs. Allen continued. "This is my first baby, and Hank and I are worried that something will go wrong. The ladies at the church remind me that having a baby is natural and that women since Eve have been doing it, but . . ." She glanced at the doorway that she was still blocking and flushed. "Listen to me, standing here prattling. Come in, come in."

As Belinda Allen waved her arm to usher Thea into the house, Thea's optimism shattered. Once again, she'd made a snap judgment. Once again, she'd been wrong. Would she never learn?

Thea took a shallow breath, trying to ignore the fragrance that Mrs. Allen's expansive gesture had released. *No. Not now.*

Not here. It couldn't be. But, though she tried desperately to repress them, memories flooded through her, sweeping her back to the day she had opened Daniel's valise and discovered the truth about her husband.

He'd just returned from his first trip to San Antonio after their wedding and, declaring he couldn't wait another minute to see her, he'd stopped by their house to kiss her and drop off his valise before delivering the goods he'd bought for the mercantile.

It was the moment Thea had been waiting for, her bridegroom's return. Relieved that their first separation—four days that had felt like a month—was over, she'd checked the roast, then decided that a good wife would unpack her husband's clothes.

It should have been an ordinary task, but as Thea had pulled out his spare shirt, intending to inspect it for loose buttons, the unmistakable scent of a woman's perfume had assailed her. A perfume she had never worn or even smelled before that day. The same perfume that Mrs. Allen was wearing.

"Are you all right, Mrs. Michener?"

Her patient's worried tone brought Thea back to the present. "Yes, of course." Many women must own bottles of that particular scent. There was no reason to believe that Mrs. Allen was *that* woman. After all, Daniel had gone to San Antonio, not Cimarron Creek. As far as Thea knew, he'd never been to the town that was now her home. And surely if Mrs. Allen had known Daniel well enough to mark his clothes with her scent, she would not have wanted his wife to attend her. This was simply an unfortunate coincidence.

As she entered the house, Thea made a show of looking around the parlor, mentally cataloguing the furnishings in an effort to control her emotions. Though the room was large enough to have accommodated twice as many chairs and settees, the ones that flanked the stove were of fine quality, and the way they'd been arranged left no doubt that Mrs. Allen had a flair for decorating. "Your home is lovely," Thea said, meaning every word.

Belinda Allen smiled. "Thank you. It's still a little empty, but Hank insisted we buy quality. Sometimes he's extravagant, like with this perfume." She raised her hand, sending another wave of the noxious scent in Thea's direction. "I was shocked when I learned how much he'd spent on it and the things he bought for the baby, but he said nothing was too good for me or our child." A blush accompanied her words, as if she feared she'd been boasting.

Thea forced a smile to her lips, though her heart ached at the contrast between her life and her patient's. Daniel had said that he wanted to shower her and the baby with luxuries, but he hadn't. He had said he loved her, but if he did, why did he always return from his trips with a shirt smelling of someone else's perfume?

As she motioned Mrs. Allen to a chair and began rummaging through her bag for the instruments she would use for her examination, Thea's thoughts continued to race. Sarah had cautioned her not to marry so quickly, saying Thea hardly knew Daniel, but Thea had been adamant. She loved him; he loved her; there was no reason to delay.

It was only after their vows had been spoken that the doubts had crept in. Though he'd told her it was nothing more than her imagination that reading the newspaper sometimes made him short-tempered, Thea knew she had not imagined those perfumed shirts.

Aimee was right. Everyone deserved to be loved. The question that haunted Thea was whether Daniel had loved her or whether what he felt for her had been nothing more than infatuation. Unfortunately, she would never know the answer.

5

At last! Aimee smiled as Stuart's eyes remained closed and his breathing became slow and regular. Though he'd been close to falling asleep after his breakfast, he'd turned fussy the moment Thea left. Aimee knew it was unlikely, but she couldn't help wondering whether he feared being abandoned again. Surely a child this young would not have any real memories.

She certainly had none of her mother, but, thanks to Lydia, she was beginning to form a picture of the woman who'd given birth to her. It was a picture that caused happiness to bubble up deep inside Aimee. Joan or Grace—the name didn't matter—loved her. Far from being a mistake, coming to Texas had been the right thing to do, for in a matter of weeks, she would be reunited with her mother.

Aimee's life was on the verge of becoming everything she had hoped for. She only wished she could say the same for Thea. Though her friend tried to disguise it, Aimee sensed a sorrow too deep for words, a sorrow she suspected was connected to her marriage. The speed with which Thea had shed her widow's weeds surprised Aimee far less than the way she deflected questions about her husband. Though it could be that Thea's grief was still too raw for her to speak of it, Aimee doubted that was the case. Something had been amiss in Thea's marriage. Aimee could only hope that she'd find healing in Cimarron Creek.

Confident that Stuart would remain asleep if she laid him down, she placed him in the wicker basket that she'd decided would be his downstairs cradle, then opened a cupboard, looking for ingredients for the midday meal. She'd pulled out flour and a tin of peaches, planning to make a cobbler, when she heard a knock on the front door.

Aimee glanced at Stuart, then, satisfied that he was still asleep, hurried to greet the visitor.

"Mrs. Michener?" The woman was three or four inches taller than Aimee, with light brown hair, blue eyes, and an engaging smile.

Aimee hated to disappoint her. "Mrs. Michener is with one of her patients right now. I'm Aimee Jarre, her friend."

As discreetly as she could, Aimee inspected the woman's midsection. There was no sign of thickening, but the visitor could still be in the early stages of pregnancy. "Would you like to wait, or shall I have Mrs. Michener call on you when she returns?"

"Oh!" The woman seemed startled, then laughed as the direction of Aimee's glance registered. "This is a social, not a professional call. I wanted to welcome her to Cimarron Creek."

"Then you must come in and wait for her, Mrs. . . ." Aimee let her voice trail off.

"It's Miss. I'm Patience Kenton, the new schoolteacher."

"Could I offer you some refreshments, Miss Kenton?" Aimee asked as she led the way into the parlor.

The woman shook her head. "No, thank you, but please call me Patience. I hear 'Miss Kenton' often enough from my pupils, and school has yet to start."

She took a seat on one of the spindly legged chairs that flanked the low table. "Isn't Cimarron Creek the prettiest town you've ever seen? Rachel—she's my cousin—said it was, but I thought she was exaggerating. I just love being here."

Patience paused to take a breath, then shook her head again. "Oh, there I go again, talking too much. I do that when I'm nervous."

Aimee could not imagine what had made the schoolteacher nervous. "Is something wrong?" she asked.

"No. Not really. It's just . . . Well, I heard you came all the way from France. I've never met anyone from France before. What brought you here?"

"Curiosity." That was one way to describe her reasons, and it sidestepped the fact that the woman everyone knew as Grace Sims was her mother. "When my parents died, I learned they'd once lived in America and wanted to see it."

Patience appeared satisfied by the explanation. "What do you think of it?"

"It's very different from France. So much bigger." Aimee gave Patience a conspiratorial smile. "As a teacher, you probably know that Texas alone is larger than all of France, so you can imagine how big America seems to me. It's also newer and much friendlier."

She couldn't imagine residents of her hometown in France treating a stranger as well as she'd been treated in Ladreville and here. Of course, she had a connection to both towns, but she suspected that wasn't what made the difference. Texans were simply friendly people. Friendly folks, to use an expression she'd heard in Ladreville.

"Texans are friendly," Patience agreed. "They'll be especially friendly to you. You're so pretty, and your accent only adds to your attractiveness. Mark my words, you're going to have every single man in town wanting to court you. Rachel said they're always interested in newcomers."

The schoolteacher leaned forward slightly before she added, "I hope I can trust you not to tell anyone, but that's one of the reasons I came here. I want to find a husband."

Aimee was surprised at both her candor and the fact that

Patience, who she guessed was a few years older than herself, was still unmarried. While Patience wasn't beautiful by the usual standards, her enthusiasm infused her ordinary features with appeal. "Weren't there any eligible men where you used to live?"

"Half a dozen," Patience admitted. "The problem was, I wasn't interested in any of them. They were boring." And Patience was far from boring. She was energetic and vivacious, leaving Aimee with no doubt that she would find more reserved men boring.

"What about you?" Patience continued. "Did you leave a beau behind?"

"No. Like you, I had some suitors, but none that I wanted to marry." Though Aimee hadn't been able to explain it, she'd always felt as if she were an outsider, despite the fact that Maillochauds had been the only home she'd known. Then, when she learned the truth of her birth, she had realized that it hadn't been her imagination that she was different.

"You've come to the right place," Patience said firmly. "I predict you'll be married before the year ends."

"That's not why I came." While Aimee had dreamt of marriage and children, she had never dreamt of finding them anywhere other than France.

"Maybe not, but it would be a good reason to stay. Oh, I hope you do. I just know we're going to be good friends." Patience flashed a smile at Aimee. "A girl can never have too many friends, can she?"

Aimee shook her head. "No, she can't." Nor could she deny that she felt a kinship with the schoolteacher. While it wasn't as strong as the one she shared with Thea, it was still more than she'd experienced with any of the young women in France. Was this another of God's signs that she was meant to be here? Aimee felt hope, as tender as a shoot of grass in the early spring, take root within her.

"How did I miss it, Blaze?" Jackson knew his horse didn't understand him, but that didn't stop him from talking to him. Long hours of solitude meant that his vocal cords would tighten if he didn't exercise them someway, so he had frequent one-sided conversations with the animal who was as much a partner as Leander had been.

He'd been on this stretch of the road yesterday when he left Cimarron Creek. It was the same road he'd traveled when he'd first come to the town, and while he hadn't seen any sign of Stuart's mother that day, Jackson reminded himself that he hadn't been looking for anyone until he'd found the baby. Afterward, though he'd seen the countryside as he'd ridden, his primary thought had been getting Stuart to Cimarron Creek so that he could be fed and cared for properly.

When he'd begun his search for the missing woman, Jackson had believed it logical that this was the road the baby and his mother had been traveling when Stuart had been abandoned. While he'd acknowledged the possibility that the boy had been taken from his mother somewhere else and abandoned under the cactus when his abductors grew tired of his crying, that was a more convoluted scenario.

If there was one thing Jackson had learned from his years with the Rangers, it was that the simplest answer was often the correct one, and so he'd scoured the sides of the road he'd taken two days earlier, looking for evidence a young mother might have left.

He'd also stopped in each of the towns he'd passed before he found Stuart, asking if a woman and a baby were missing, all to no avail. There was no sign of anything unusual. When he'd finally decided that he was literally on the wrong track, he'd turned around, planning to retrace his steps until he reached the next intersection. Then he'd head west.

Jackson was perhaps three hours from Cimarron Creek when he saw the buzzards circling, some of them landing, others keeping watch from the air. It was not a good sign. Though there had been other birds soaring and chirping as he'd ridden through here yesterday, there had been no vultures. The sinking feeling in the pit of Jackson's stomach told him his search was over. While the scavengers could have been attracted by a dead steer, his gut said otherwise.

"C'mon, Blaze. Let's see what's going on." He tightened his grip on the reins as he turned the gelding into the field. The birds ignored him until he was only a few yards away, then scattered, their raucous cries leaving no doubt of their displeasure.

It was as he had feared. This was no steer, not even a large rabbit. The body of a young woman lay on the ground. Jackson dismounted, forcing himself to remain calm, though the sight set his senses reeling.

It was far from the first time he'd seen death. It was far from the first time he'd seen the result of violent death. But it was the first time he'd seen . . .

Jackson wasn't one to shrink from reality. He didn't consider himself a coward. But his mind refused to admit what his eyes saw. There was no question that the woman was dead. There was also no question why he hadn't seen her yesterday. The fact that rigor mortis was only beginning told him that her death had been recent, that Stuart had been left by the cactus more than a day before his mother died. The condition of the body left no question about the cause of death.

"Steady, Jackson," he said, voicing the words aloud. "This is your job." Though his brain continued to catalogue the details, his heart ached at the realization that the woman who was most likely Stuart's mother had been tortured. She had not died easily. That much was clear. And so was the fact that Jackson had trouble accepting, the one that made his gut clench.

The dead woman bore a striking resemblance to Thea.

"The poor woman." Travis's eyes flashed with fury as he stared at the body that was now lying on the cot in the town's sole jail cell.

When Jackson had arrived back in Cimarron Creek, he hadn't wanted to leave the woman strapped to Blaze and had carried her into the sheriff's office. Though he knew she was beyond caring, it still seemed wrong to leave her outside where she'd be subjected to the curious looks of passersby. Even though he'd wrapped her in a blanket, no one would have any difficulty identifying the form as a human body. Besides, Travis needed to see what had happened.

"Whoever did this deserves to be skinned alive."

The intensity of the sheriff's reaction surprised Jackson. His own feelings had seesawed between grief and anger, but Travis's appeared to be unmitigated anger. "I agree."

The thought of inflicting the kind of agony the woman had endured had an undeniable appeal. Death had come so slowly and painfully that when the killer had finally slit her throat, it must have been almost a relief.

"What do you make of it?"

Jackson clenched his fists, then forced himself to relax. "Someone wanted her to talk. That's usually the reason for torture. What surprised me is that the killer didn't touch her face. If I wanted to threaten a woman as pretty as this one, I'd tell her I was going to slice open her face."

"But this killer didn't."

"Nope." And that puzzled him as much as the fact that Stuart had been abandoned well before his mother was killed. Threatening a woman's child was normally more effective than threatening the woman herself.

"Any clues?"

"None. The vultures were already there by the time I arrived.

She'd been dumped in a field, but the lack of blood around her made it obvious that she'd been killed somewhere else."

Travis nodded. "The first thing we need to do is find out who she is." He looked at the woman's body again, shaking his head in either disbelief or dismay. "It's uncanny how much she looks like Thea Michener."

"It could be a coincidence." Jackson ventured the idea that he'd considered and dismissed simply to see the sheriff's reaction.

"You don't believe that." Travis didn't bother making it a question.

"No." Jackson had learned a long time ago that there were few coincidences. "I hate to do this to Mrs. Michener, but I want to see if she can identify the body."

Travis ran a hand through his hair, his frustration obvious. "I don't envy you that task. You're right, though, that it needs to be done. If Thea doesn't recognize her, I'll send telegrams to all the nearby towns to see if they know who she is."

While it was a logical step, Jackson doubted it would accomplish much. "You might be wasting your time. I asked in each of the towns I passed through, but they all claimed no one was missing."

"The difference is we have a description now. That might trigger some memories. It's worth another try if Thea can't help us." Travis pulled the blanket back over the woman's face. "I have to say that the resemblance bothers me."

"Me too." More than he was willing to admit to Travis. Though he'd told him about his search for the Gang, he hadn't mentioned Thea's connection to it. This woman's death changed everything.

If the resemblance wasn't a coincidence and if the woman had been killed because of that likeness, it increased the probability that Thea had some involvement with the Gang beyond being married to one of its members. Though he had no proof,

Jackson believed the Gang had killed her husband, and now, if his suspicions were correct, they'd killed the woman they believed was his wife.

He frowned as the thoughts whirled through his brain. Daniel Michener's death had been merciful compared to this woman's. A single gunshot had ended his life, but the woman's final hours had been fraught with pain, the torture indicating her killers believed Michener's wife had something they would do anything to get. But what?

The only thing that made sense was that the rumors that one of the Gang had taken all the gold from their last heist were true. Jackson nodded as his thoughts began to coalesce. The fact that Michener had been killed pointed to him as the one who'd stolen the loot. This woman hadn't led them to it— Jackson was certain of that—and that meant they'd try again.

That was an idea he didn't like. Not one bit.

6

Thea knew something was wrong the moment she opened the door and found Ranger Guthrie standing on her front porch. Though he tried to smile, she could see the concern in his eyes. Today, instead of being as bright as spring grass, they reminded her of a murky stream, its water darkened by submerged vegetation.

"Did you find her?"

"Possibly." Though Thea gestured for him to enter, the Ranger remained stationary. His lips flattened, the visible effort he made to control his emotions confirming her assumption that what he had found was unpleasant. "Do you have any family near here?"

Thea felt her eyes widen with surprise. She had expected further explanations, not this odd question. Still, though she had no idea how it related to Stuart's mother, there was no reason not to answer honestly. She shook her head. "My only family is in Ladreville—my sister, brother-in-law, and their children. Why?"

A songbird warbled to its mate, but the Ranger appeared oblivious to the melodic calls. He stood a foot away from Thea, his face as solemn as if he were a judge about to pronounce a death sentence. "I hate to do this, but I need you to come with me to Doc Harrington's."

Despite the grim air that clung to Ranger Guthrie, a glimmer of hope flitted through Thea. Perhaps she'd misread him. Perhaps Stuart's mother was still alive. Why else would he want her to go to the doctor's office?

"Is she very ill?" Although the Ranger's expression said otherwise, Thea hoped whatever it was wasn't serious enough to need the doctor's care.

When she'd made her first professional call on Lydia yesterday, Lydia had echoed Belinda Allen's relief that she'd come to Cimarron Creek, saying that the town's doctor was old-fashioned and used techniques that often did more harm than good. Unfortunately, until Austin Goddard, the new physician who was currently in France with his family and Aimee's mother, returned, Doc Harrington was Cimarron Creek's only source of medical care.

The Ranger's eyes darkened even more, and creases formed at the corners of his mouth. "There's no easy way to say this. She's dead. The doctor also serves as the town's coroner."

Dead. The word echoed through Thea's brain. It was as she had feared: Stuart was motherless and most likely an orphan. Though she'd believed she was prepared for this possibility, having it confirmed wrenched her heart, and tears sprang to her eyes. Blinking to keep them from falling, Thea looked up at the man who'd delivered the unwelcome news. "Where did you find her?"

When he shook his head and said, "That's not important," Thea realized he was trying to spare her what were undoubtedly unpleasant details.

"Thank you, Ranger."

A flicker of surprise crossed his face, momentarily lifting the shadows that had clouded his eyes. "You're thanking me? For what?"

"For trying to shelter me." It wasn't the first time that had happened. Because Thea was shorter than average, men often thought she was also fragile. She wasn't.

"I'm stronger than most people realize," she told the Ranger, "but I appreciate your concern. Let me get my hat and gloves." Even though it was only a few blocks to the doctor's office, she would not go farther than her front porch unless she was properly dressed.

"I don't doubt that you're strong, Mrs. Michener, but this could be difficult. I want to do everything I can to make it as painless as possible."

"Thank you again, Ranger."

His mouth puckered as if he'd bitten into something sour. "Would you do me a favor? Would you call me Jackson?"

Thea gazed up at him, startled by the request. It was turning into a day for strange questions, but perhaps this was part of his attempt to defuse the tension that accompanied thoughts of death. "All right, and I'm Thea."

For the first time since he'd knocked on her door, Ranger Guthrie—Jackson—appeared to relax.

Less than ten minutes later, he knocked on another door.

"Come in." Doc Harrington was younger than Thea had expected, probably in his mid-fifties, a heavyset man with gray hair and brown eyes that looked as if he'd seen too much misery. He barely glanced at her when he opened the door, but then his head jerked, and his eyes widened with what appeared to be shock.

The doctor stood silent for a moment before muttering, "You must be the new midwife."

Did he think she was too weak to do her job? That was the only reason Thea could imagine for the way he gazed at her. "Yes, I'm Thea Michener." She started to murmur that she was pleased to meet him but stopped, realizing that the words would be meaningless. Thea was not pleased to meet the doctor under these circumstances.

At her side, Jackson shifted his weight from his heels to the balls of his feet, his impatience obvious. "Where is she?"

"The back room." The doctor tipped his head to indicate the direction. "You don't need me. Stay as long as you want."

And so Thea walked toward the room where she'd be forced to confront what remained of Stuart's mother. She'd seen dead bodies before, but Jackson's obvious concern and the doctor's unexplained reaction to meeting her made her apprehensive. This was no ordinary death, her instincts told her.

To Thea's relief, Jackson laid his hand on the small of her back, as if he sensed that she needed that measure of comfort. When they arrived at the end of the short hallway, he reached in front of her and opened the door, revealing a room that held a desk, three bookcases, and what must be an examination table.

Jackson gestured toward the sheet-covered body that lay on the table. "Are you ready?"

Though Thea doubted she'd ever be ready, she nodded.

Carefully, Jackson pulled the sheet back, revealing only the woman's face and throat. "Do you recognize her?"

Thea gasped as she took a step closer. No wonder the doctor had been shocked to see her. It wasn't quite like looking in a mirror. The other woman's nose was longer than hers, her chin a little less firm, but the woman who lay so cold and still on the table looked more like Thea than her own sister.

Instinctively, Thea's hand moved to her own throat. There was no red gash there, no lifeblood spurting out the way it had from this woman. Thea's instincts had been correct; this was no ordinary death. Stuart's mother had been killed.

Still reeling from the evidence of violent death, Thea turned to Jackson. "I don't understand. Who is she?"

"I hoped you'd be able to tell me."

She stared at the woman again, a shiver making its way down her spine as she registered the similarities in this woman's appearance. It was uncanny and deeply upsetting to realize that a woman who looked so much like her had been murdered.

"I've never seen her before," Thea said, her voice wavering despite her best efforts to steady it. "I don't understand how it's possible, but we could be twins."

Jackson nodded. "My older brothers are twins, and they look less alike than you do."

"I'm sure she's not my sister." Sarah would have known if their mother had delivered two babies, and if Mama had, she would never have given one away. But that did not help explain the obvious resemblance between this woman and Thea.

"I once heard someone say that everyone has a double, but I didn't believe it. Now I do." It was the only explanation Thea could find.

Though Jackson was no longer touching her, he stood close enough to catch her if she fell. She could feel the warmth radiating from his body, and it provided a measure of comfort as her mind tried to make sense of what her eyes had seen.

"Are you sure you don't have any relatives in Texas?" he asked. "Cousins, maybe?"

Thea started to shake her head, then reconsidered. "I can ask my sister Sarah, but as far as I know, the only relatives we had were in Pennsylvania, and they've all died. Both of our parents were only children with few cousins."

Jackson nodded and covered the woman's face again. After a brief good-bye to the doctor, he escorted Thea outside.

"What about your husband?" he asked as they descended the porch steps. "Was his family from this area?"

Thea turned her face toward the sun, trying to dispel the chill that had settled over her when she'd seen that too-familiar face. "You're confusing me, Rang . . . Jackson. What does my husband have to do with that poor woman?"

"Probably nothing."

"Probably!" Though Thea knew her outrage was out of proportion to his comment, she couldn't help it. Seeing a woman who could have been her sister looking like a piece of marble left her trembling inside. It was almost like seeing her own death, and that was deeply disturbing.

Thea had heard that President Lincoln had had a dream about his own death a few days before he was killed. Was this how he had felt—both incredulous and frightened?

She clenched her fists, then released them as she tried to quell her fears. "Daniel's been dead for more than three months. He couldn't have killed her."

"Of course he couldn't have, but that's no reason not to answer my questions, is it?" Jackson spoke slowly, his tone conciliatory.

To Thea's surprise, his gently phrased question helped dissipate her fears. "I suppose not." She paused, collecting her thoughts. "I don't know much about his family, because Daniel was an orphan. His parents died when he was an infant, and he grew up in an orphanage near Boerne."

Though Jackson's eyes widened as if something in her statement had startled him, he asked only, "How did you meet him?"

Thea darted a glance at him as they turned onto Main Street. What a strange conversation. Perhaps this was Jackson's attempt to keep her from thinking about the woman who was most likely Stuart's mother. If so, it wasn't succeeding—not totally—but it was helping.

"Daniel was a traveling salesman. He was trying to sell some new items to the owner of the Ladreville mercantile one day when I was there. We met, we fell in love, and we married."

There was more to the story, of course, but Thea was not ready to tell anyone about the doubts that had crept in after she'd discovered the perfumed shirts. She would never admit how confused she'd been when she'd learned of Daniel's death, how an inexplicable sense of relief had mingled with her grief. And so she shared only the barest details of her marriage.

Jackson slowed his steps and looked at her, concern radiating from his eyes. "It must have been difficult for you if he was always traveling."

"But he wasn't." Thea shook her head, remembering how adamant Daniel had been about ending his old life once they married. "He started working at the mercantile so he didn't have to travel so much. The only times he'd leave were when he went to San Antonio to buy supplies." And to meet the woman who wore the same perfume as Belinda Allen.

"I see."

The skeptical expression that flitted across Jackson's face suggested he didn't believe her, and that made no sense.

7

This is where my mother grew up?"
        As Aimee looked around in astonishment, Lydia
        reached for Stuart. "Here, let me hold him," she said,
smiling as she cradled the baby in her arms.

When she'd invited Aimee to visit her, Lydia had insisted that
she bring Stuart, claiming that she wanted to practice caring for
a baby before hers was born. Practice was one thing, but the fact
that Lydia had practically grabbed the infant as she opened the
door told Aimee her shock was evident. Perhaps Lydia feared
that she'd drop the baby as she stared at her mother's home.

"I thought I knew what to expect, but this is so . . ." Words
failed her.

While it was obvious that no expense had been spared on
the exterior of the house with the massive columns and large
windows, that had not prepared Aimee for the interior. She
had seen other Texas houses, but none had been this elaborate,
this elegant.

Un palais. She shook her head slightly, dismissing the idea.
This was not a palace. Instead, the polished stone floor and
the curving stairway leading to the second story reminded her
of the chateau that had dominated the hill overlooking Maillochauds. Though she'd never been allowed inside, Aimee had

ventured up the hill one day and had peered into the windows before a groundskeeper had chased her away, declaring that commoners had no business there.

Amazingly, that building, which her parents had told her had been built more than three hundred years ago and which was the pride of the region, was no grander than her own mother's childhood home.

"It's a bit overwhelming, isn't it?" Lydia asked as she rocked the now-cooing baby.

Overwhelming was a good adjective, but not the one Aimee would have used. As her eyes continued to adjust to the relative darkness, she studied the interior. Open doorways on both sides of the expansive hallway revealed a parlor and a dining room, each tastefully furnished and large enough to accommodate several dozen people.

"I doubt I'll ever forget my first sight of it," Lydia continued. "I'm not sure what intimidated me most—the house itself or your grandmother. She was like a whirlwind."

"Domineering?" Aimee tried to picture the woman who'd forced her daughter into exile so that no one in Cimarron Creek would know she was expecting a child.

"No, although she certainly knew how to get her way. She did it so nicely, though, that no one seemed to mind." Lydia led the way into the parlor and gestured toward one of the comfortable-looking chairs. "I wish you could have known Aunt Bertha. She would have loved you."

Though Aimee wanted to believe that, it was not easy. "She sent her daughter away."

Lydia nodded. "You need to understand. Things might be different in France, but in a town like Cimarron Creek, unwed mothers are shunned. Aunt Bertha believed she was protecting Grace by sending her to Ladreville."

"Thea said the same thing." Maillochauds may have had unwed mothers in the past, but Aimee wasn't aware of any.

What she remembered were rushed marriages and babies born six or seven months after the vows were exchanged.

"The important thing is to remember that Aunt Bertha loved her daughter, and she loved you, even though she never met you. I know that may be difficult to believe, but I grew very close to Aunt Bertha during the time I lived with her, and I can assure you of that."

"Thank you for telling me." The warmth that infused Aimee told her Lydia was speaking the truth.

"I wish Grace hadn't taken your grandparents' wedding portrait with her. You'd be amazed at how much you look like Aunt Bertha." Her smile broadening, Lydia looked down at Stuart. "I don't know which parent he resembles, but he's the cutest baby ever."

"I won't tell your son or daughter you said that."

The smile turned into laughter. "You're definitely Aunt Bertha's granddaughter. That sounded exactly like something she would have said."

Lydia tipped her head to one side, her expression saying she was considering something. "You must have inherited her sense of humor, but you certainly didn't inherit Aunt Bertha's tendency toward long speeches. I used to have trouble getting in a word when she was talking, and Grace is the same way."

But Aimee was not. For as long as she could remember, she'd been quiet. Because her parents hadn't liked noise, she'd spent most of her time at home reading. Even when she'd laughed at something she found amusing, she'd learned to do it quietly to avoid criticism.

As if she realized that Aimee needed something to dispel less than pleasant memories, Lydia rose. "Let's go upstairs. I want to show you your mother and grandmother's rooms. Grace's hasn't been used since she went to Ladreville, because she lived with Catherine when she returned, so it looks the way it did more than twenty years ago, but Aunt Bertha had her own room repapered after her husband died. She told me she needed a new look for the next phase of her life." Lydia chuckled. "It must be contagious. I'm starting to ramble on the way your grandmother did."

The distraction worked, and before she'd reached the second story, Aimee was laughing again. She admired the well-appointed bedchambers, although she couldn't dismiss the tinge of disappointment that rose when she felt no connection to either her mother or her grandmother as she stood in the same places where they'd spent so much time. The rooms were lovely, but that's all they were—lovely, empty rooms.

It hadn't been like that in Ladreville. When Pastor and Mrs. Russell learned who she was, they'd insisted that she stay in the room that had once been her mother's, the room where Aimee had been born. And while she'd been there, Aimee had dreamt of a woman great with child, a woman who'd cupped her abdomen as if she cherished the life growing inside her. Her head had been bent, leaving Aimee unable to see her face, but she had had no doubt that the woman was her mother. That dream had buoyed her with the hope that she'd been loved, a hope that Lydia's stories had transformed into reality.

As she crossed the street several hours later, Stuart once more cradled in her arms, Aimee smiled. Her second full day in Cimarron Creek had been even better than the first. While she had made a new friend in Patience yesterday, today not only had she cemented her friendship with Lydia, but she had gained some insights into her mother and grandmother. What a wonderful day!

Jackson rubbed his hand across his eyes, trying to dislodge the grit that accompanied fatigue. The combination of a night with very little sleep, finding the body, and seeing the murdered woman's resemblance to Thea had left him exhausted.

He could—and probably should—return to Warner's house and sleep for a few hours.

Jackson blinked again as he thought of the comfortable bed awaiting him. Though the pharmacist had told him to make himself at home, he was reluctant to do that without at least stopping by the pharmacy to say that he was going to the house.

His decision made, Jackson turned right and headed back to Main Street. Thea was safely inside her home, and while he did not doubt that she was disturbed by what he'd been forced to show her, there was nothing more he could do for her right now. He needed time to think about what she'd told him and to choose his next steps, but first he needed rest to clear his head.

As he entered Warner's store, Jackson was surprised by the number of customers. When he'd come to Cimarron Creek two days ago, Warner had been alone, making Jackson wonder if business was slow. It appeared that had been only a lull, because today six women stood in line at the main counter, while two others studied the contents of one of the tall glass-fronted cabinets.

Unwilling to bother his host, Jackson waited until he caught Warner's eye, then moved to the far side of the pharmacy. Feigning an interest in the multicolored bottles of patent medicines displayed behind the glass doors, he kept his head turned slightly so that he could observe the town's apothecary at work. Though his customers made little attempt to hide their impatience, Warner remained unflappable.

"That's the Ranger over there," one of the two women who stood in front of a second cabinet announced to her companion. "I heard he's the one who found the woman's body just outside of town." Though she did not shout, her words carried clearly, causing a sudden silence in the room.

Her companion, a stout woman with unnaturally black hair, shuddered. "It makes me think we ought to start locking our

71

doors. What if this turns out to be like last year, only more serious? Killing people is worse than stealing a few things."

The first woman laid a reassuring hand on Black Hair's arm. "The sheriff will keep us safe."

"But it's only him and his deputy." Black Hair wasn't easily mollified. "What if we need more protection?"

"Sheriff Whitfield will call for help if he needs it. He's promised to keep Cimarron Creek safe."

"I suppose you're right." The words sounded perfunctory rather than heartfelt. "Now, which of these tonics do you think is the best?" As she pointed toward two bottles, the other women resumed their conversations.

Jackson took a deep breath and let it out slowly in a technique he'd learned would calm him. He wasn't surprised at how quickly the news had spread or that the facts had been distorted. The body hadn't been close to Cimarron Creek, but saying that it had been discovered hours away was less dramatic than claiming that the townspeople were in danger. Active grapevines thrived on sensational news, and people being put in jeopardy was definitely sensational.

Though he wished he could assure the women that Stuart's mother's death had no impact on them, that everyone in Cimarron Creek would be safe, Jackson could not. He didn't have all the facts yet. He frowned as he realized how few facts he actually had.

The more time he spent with Thea, the more convinced he was that she hadn't been involved with the Gang. If she was telling the truth—and his instincts told him she was—she had no idea what her husband had done under the cover of being an itinerant salesman. Jackson had to admit that it had been a good cover, yet another indication of just how canny the Gang was. Going from town to town was an excellent means of learning when wealthy people would be traveling and when shipments of gold and silver were being transported.

Jackson took another breath, trying to tamp down the frustration of knowing he was no closer to finding Micah's killers than he'd been four and a half months earlier. And, as if that weren't bad enough, now he had another killing to solve.

As weariness settled over him, he stared out the store's front window. Days like today made him wonder if he was becoming too old for this life.

"I don't suppose you'd like a new job."

Jackson turned, startled by Warner's words. He'd been so caught up in his thoughts that he hadn't noticed that the store was now empty of customers.

"Were you reading my mind?" he asked. There was no question of leaving the Rangers before Micah's killers were behind bars, but once he'd accomplished that, perhaps he should consider a change. The Rangers were changing—had, in fact, changed dramatically since he'd joined them. Maybe it was time for him to change too.

Warner shook his head and clapped a hand on Jackson's shoulder. "I was just feeling a bit desperate. Business seems to be picking up, and I could use an assistant."

"You don't want me." Jackson raised his hands in mock surrender. "I can't tell arnica from bay rum. And if that's not enough to convince you that I'm the wrong man, I need to tell you that while I might be good with a weapon, my mother wouldn't let me carry any of her china or glassware. She claimed I was the clumsiest of her boys." He gestured toward the cabinets filled with bottles of expensive tonics. "You wouldn't want me to touch those."

"You can't blame a man for asking." Warner returned to his position behind the main counter and leaned on the wooden top. "I heard you found a woman's body."

"I think she was the one I was looking for, but I sure wish the circumstances had been better."

Warner nodded, his expression solemn. "Sounds like the rumors that she was hurt pretty badly are true."

"Unfortunately, yes." What was also unfortunate was that someone—probably Doc Harrington—had divulged that information.

"Between you and Travis, I have no doubt you'll find whoever's responsible."

He would, Jackson vowed silently. Defeat was not part of a Ranger's vocabulary.

"I don't know what your plans are," Warner continued, "but you're welcome to stay at my house for as long as you'd like."

"Are you certain?" Though it was a generous offer and one that had the added appeal of keeping Jackson close to the intriguing Thea Michener, he didn't want to take advantage of his host.

"Absolutely. Living alone isn't all it's cracked up to be."

"I know what you mean." Jackson's job had been easier when he and Leander had traveled together. They'd shared responsibilities; they'd protected each other; most important, they'd kept loneliness at bay. Being a lone Ranger wasn't fun. No fun at all.

"What's wrong?" Furrows formed between Aimee's eyebrows as she entered the kitchen, cradling a now-sleeping Stuart.

Thea tried not to frown. She'd thought she'd hidden her distress, but obviously, she had not. "Jackson found the woman he thinks is Stuart's mother." As much as Thea would have liked to have spared Aimee the unpleasant details, she knew the story would soon be common knowledge.

"Jackson?" To Thea's surprise, Aimee fixed on the name Thea had used, not the story she was telling.

As a flush colored her face, Thea said as calmly as she could, "He asked me to call him that." It was downright silly to be so flustered, and yet she couldn't help it.

Her friend gave her a long, appraising look. "I see." She

turned to the baby in her arms and stroked his forehead. "And the reason you're upset is that Stuart will be leaving us."

Thea shook her head, shuddering as she remembered the scene in Doc Harrington's back room. "I wish that were the case. The woman is dead."

She wouldn't tell Aimee about the stranger's resemblance to her. Jackson had insisted that information was best kept confidential, and both the doctor and the sheriff had agreed. They had also agreed that if Jackson and Travis couldn't find the woman's family, they would bury her in the Cimarron Creek cemetery. In the meantime, she would rest in a simple closed coffin, protected from curious eyes.

Aimee tightened her grip on Stuart, waking him with her protective gesture. "It's all right, little one," she murmured. "But it isn't all right, is it?" she asked, her hazel eyes filled with distress. "What will happen to Stuart now?"

"Jackson and Travis are going to search for his family. I hope they'll be able to find them."

"And if they don't?"

That was the question that had weighed heavily on Thea's heart from the moment she'd seen the woman lying on the table. As she and Jackson had walked back from the doctor's office, even though he'd been questioning her about Daniel, she'd been unable to forget the motherless infant. While Jackson had no proof that the woman who could have been Thea's twin was Stuart's mother, Thea had no doubts. She'd caught the faint smell of spoiled milk when Jackson had lifted the sheet to reveal the woman's face. That had told her that the stranger was a nursing mother. It couldn't be coincidence.

"Travis said Reverend Dunn would see whether anyone in Cimarron Creek is willing to adopt Stuart." Though she knew that was the second-best choice for him, the idea was surprisingly distressing. Perhaps it was because the woman looked so much like her and she felt a connection to her because of that resemblance. Perhaps it was simply that Stuart was such a lovable child. Thea wasn't certain of the reason. All she knew was that her initial reluctance to even hold him had vanished.

"If no one steps forward, I'll keep him." The words popped out of Thea's mouth, surprising her. And yet, though she hadn't intended to say them, they felt right. Stuart wouldn't replace Aaron—no one could do that—but he might fill one of the empty places in her heart. The question was whether it would be fair to Stuart, whether she could be both mother and father to him.

"Would you mind?" she asked Aimee. While the thought of keeping Stuart was appealing, Thea wouldn't be able to do it without assistance.

"Of course I wouldn't mind. I've already learned to love this little one."

As had Thea. "Are you certain? It would mean that you'd have to care for him when I'm with patients."

Aimee pressed a kiss on Stuart's forehead before looking back at Thea. "That won't be a problem. Stuart's easy to care for. He and I had a good day today."

But Thea had not. In addition to seeing the woman who looked so much like her, she could not forget the questions Jackson had asked and how they reminded her of the day she'd met him, when he'd looked as if he didn't trust her. Why was he so suspicious?

8

There had to be something she could do to help Thea, Aimee reflected as she dried the last of the supper dishes. It was understandable that learning about Stuart's mother's death had distressed her—Thea had experienced more than her share of death recently—but Aimee knew that something else was weighing on her friend. Unlike the underlying sadness that she'd sensed from the first time she'd met Thea, this seemed to be more recent.

Perhaps it was the prospect of adopting Stuart. Though Thea obviously loved the boy at least as much as she did, perhaps she also feared that he would be a constant reminder of the son she'd lost. Aimee didn't know whether that was the problem. What she did know was that Thea needed a distraction.

"Let's take Stuart for a walk," she said as she hung the dish towel from a peg. "I'd like to explore the town, and it'll give us a chance to see if he likes the buggy." While Thea had been gone, Aimee had ventured into the attic and found a baby carriage. After only a bit of cleaning, it was ready to use.

Thea appeared dubious. "The shops are all closed."

"That's the best time. I won't be tempted to spend any money." Not that Aimee had much. The journey from France to Texas had cost more than she'd expected, leaving her funds severely depleted. She'd have to find a way to earn some money soon, but first she needed to help her friend. "C'mon, Thea. It'll be fun."

"All right." It was a grudging acceptance, but at least she hadn't refused.

Aimee rolled the buggy onto the porch and down the front steps, then took Stuart from Thea, laying him carefully in the blanket-lined body of the carriage. To her relief, the baby did not protest but looked up at her with wide eyes, as if trying to determine what was happening. He appeared content and, surprisingly, so did Thea.

Their progress was slow as they walked west on Pecan and turned to head south on Main, because she didn't want to jostle Stuart too much, but Aimee didn't mind. How could she when Thea was smiling again and commenting on the beauty of the live oaks and the flower-filled window boxes that reminded her of Ladreville? The day's heat had dissipated a bit, making it the perfect evening for a stroll.

They were standing in front of the mercantile, admiring the high-buttoned shoes in the front window, when Aimee heard a familiar voice. She turned, her eyes widening at the sight of the couple who were now crossing the street.

"I'm so glad to see you!" Patience used her best schoolmarm voice, the one that carried over children's squabbles, as she hurried toward Aimee and Thea. "I was debating whether we should stop by your house, but now we don't have to."

Aimee barely heard her friend's words, for her gaze was snared by the young man who accompanied her. He was . . . As had happened when she'd entered her mother's childhood home, words failed Aimee. Though she searched, she could not find the proper words—either French or English—to describe this man and how he made her feel.

Patience had no such problem. She gestured toward her companion. "One of the reasons we're here is that I want you to meet my cousin." Without giving anyone a chance to respond, Patience turned to Thea. "You must be Mrs. Michener. I'm Patience Kenton, the town's new schoolteacher, and this is my cousin, Nate Kenton."

"The town's *old* peach and goat farmer," the blond-haired man who smelled faintly of mint said, his lips curving upward.

He could speak. Aimee could not. But she could look, and look she did, trying to hide the fact that she was staring at Nate Kenton. She had grown up hearing *Maman* talk about the *coup de foudre*, the attraction she'd felt the moment she'd met Papa, and how in that instant she'd known he was the man she would marry. At the time, Aimee had believed it a fairy tale, but now she knew that love at first sight was possible. How could she doubt it when she'd felt the same lightning bolt that her mother had?

Nate Kenton was not the handsome man Aimee had always dreamed of, but when he smiled, his ordinary features became oddly appealing. Perhaps it was those blue eyes, so different from her own. Perhaps it was his broad shoulders or those muscular arms. She wasn't sure what caused it, but her heart had accelerated at the sight of that smile, and it was refusing to settle down, leaving her tongue-tied and more than a little confused.

"You don't look old to me." Thea, who was obviously not afflicted with Aimee's inability to utter a coherent sentence, made a show of inspecting the farmer, as if searching for wrinkles and gray hair.

"Ah, but I am." His smile widened, and Aimee's heart faltered. What was it about that smile that made her insides turn to mush? The man had barely glanced at her, telling her that he had not felt the *coup de foudre*.

"In three months, I'll be thirty." Nate kept his gaze fixed on Thea. "That's old!"

Older than Aimee had thought, but far from ancient. Still,

he was almost nine years her elder. Was that why he wouldn't look at her? Did he think she was a child?

"Nate's sister tells him he's wasting the best years of his life by not being married." Patience rejoined the conversation, and—unlike her cousin—she did not ignore Aimee. Instead, she gave her a conspiratorial smile when Nate's smile turned into a frown.

"Stop telling all the family secrets."

"That's not a secret," Patience insisted.

Thea laughed. "If I didn't know better, I'd say you two were siblings. You're acting just like my nephews did when they were three and four."

Clasping his hand across his heart and feigning agony, Nate groaned. "A direct hit. And here I thought midwives were supposed to be kind and gentle."

"We are," Thea told him, pausing for emphasis before she added, "with our patients."

"I'm cousin to Patience. Doesn't that count?"

"Bad pun, Nate. Shame on you." Patience shook her finger at her cousin, then turned to Aimee. "Where were you two heading when we interrupted?"

At least someone hadn't forgotten her existence. Aimee shrugged. "Just giving Stuart some fresh air and wandering around town." Now that she was not looking at Nate, Aimee had no problem speaking.

"May we join you?"

Aimee looked at Thea, waiting for her nod of approval before she said, "Of course."

"Perfect." Patience linked her arm with Aimee's for a second, then settled at her side, leaving Thea and Nate to follow them. And, in typical Patience fashion, she kept the conversation bubbling as they strolled down Main Street, stopping occasionally to admire the contents of a shop window or adjust the blanket that Stuart continued to tangle around his legs.

Aimee knew it was foolish to be upset that Nate Kenton had barely acknowledged her existence. She also knew it was rude to try to eavesdrop on Thea and Nate, particularly since it meant not giving Patience her full attention, but Aimee couldn't stop herself. While she couldn't make out any of the words they spoke, there was no ignoring the laughter that punctuated almost every sentence.

That was what she wanted, wasn't it? Somehow Nate Kenton had dispelled Thea's morose mood, leaving her lighthearted. That was good. That was what her friend deserved. It shouldn't bother Aimee that Nate had hardly spoken a word to her, and yet it did.

"I wish I had more positive news," Travis said as he riffled through the telegrams on his desk, "but so far no one has any missing women, and they don't know of anyone who looks like our victim."

Jackson nodded. "I'm not really surprised." Disappointed, but not surprised. His instincts had told him this would not be easy.

"There's still another half dozen towns. I imagine we'll get their responses tomorrow. Maybe one of them will be what we're waiting for."

Though he said nothing more, the way Travis glanced at the clock told Jackson he wanted to be home with Lydia. It was early evening, past the time when Travis was normally in his office, but he'd suggested they meet here after supper to see what telegrams had come in.

Time to leave and let the sheriff go home. Jackson grabbed his hat and rose. "There's no reason to keep you here any longer."

Travis gave him a grateful smile and reached for his own hat. As he approached the door, Jackson glanced out the window, his attention snagged by an approaching quartet. While it wasn't unusual to see pedestrians on Main Street at this time of day, it was unusual to see four together.

His gaze flitted over Aimee and the other woman who formed the vanguard, pushing a baby carriage that undoubtedly contained Stuart, then settled on the couple behind them. There was no mistaking their identities. Thea and Nate Kenton were laughing about something.

Jackson took a quick breath as the scene registered. They weren't touching. There was nothing unseemly about their conduct, and yet . . . He focused on Thea and the way she gazed at Nate. She looked happy and carefree. That shouldn't bother him, and yet . . . Jackson couldn't explain the sour feeling that had lodged in his stomach.

He forced the bile down and turned back to Travis. "I'll see you in the morning."

"Right. Good night."

But it wasn't a good night, Jackson realized as he strode north on Main. His temporary home was in the opposite direction, but Jackson knew he was in no mood to talk to anyone right now. As he passed the livery, he toyed with the idea of saddling Blaze and going for a ride, then dismissed it. Blaze deserved a rest.

"What's eating you?" Warner asked as Jackson entered the kitchen half an hour later. Warner had insisted there was no need for formality, that Jackson should consider this his home and forgo knocking. He'd chosen the side door tonight, thinking he could escape conversation, but instead he discovered his friend seated at the kitchen table with a cup of coffee in front of him.

"Nothing," he lied. "I'm just tired and discouraged. I had hoped someone would have claimed the dead woman by now."

The shadow of a smile tilted Warner's lips. "My ma would have said you need to be patient."

"That's something I was never good at."

Before Warner could respond, the door opened with such

force that it bounced against the wall, and Nate strode inside, his eyes gleaming.

"Why didn't you tell me?" He stopped in front of the table, fisting his hands on his hips.

"Tell you what?"

Nate dismissed Warner's question. "Not you. Him." He pointed a finger at Jackson. "Why didn't you tell me she was so beautiful? She reminds me of one of those princesses in the storybooks my sister used to insist on reading to me."

A princess? That was not the way he would have described Thea, but Jackson wasn't about to say that. This was a time to keep his mouth shut.

"I tell you, fellas," Nate continued, seemingly unconcerned by Jackson's failure to respond, "today was the best day of my life. I can't believe how fast it happened. One minute I was talking to my cousin. The next minute I saw her. One look was all it took for me to know she's the woman I'm going to marry."

9

"We need to get out of town," Jackson told Blaze as he led him from the livery the next morning. There was nothing for him here—at least not right now. Thea didn't need him, especially since Nate planned to court her. Jackson had done what he'd promised: he'd found Stuart's mother. And while he wished the circumstances surrounding his discovery of the woman had been different, he couldn't change them.

Travis had received word from the remaining towns, and—as Jackson had feared—no one recognized the dead woman. She'd be buried tomorrow in a grave with a simple wooden cross. Later, if they could locate her family and learn her name, some- one might erect a stone marker, but for now she would be known as the Unidentified Woman.

Travis had arranged for the minister to offer a graveside ser- vice and had assured Jackson there was no reason for him to be present. All that remained for him to do in Cimarron Creek was to give Travis the sketch he'd made.

"Looks like you're an artist as well as a Ranger," Travis said two minutes later when Jackson had hitched Blaze in front of the sheriff's office and entered the building.

"Hardly. It's just something I do occasionally." He thought

of the sketch he'd folded and slid inside his Bible. That was one piece of paper he didn't want to lose. "I thought you ought to have more than a description in case someone comes looking for her." It would be awkward to involve Thea in identifying the woman.

Though Travis nodded, his words were not optimistic. "We both know it's unlikely anyone will come, but I'm still glad to have the sketch." After he'd spun the dial on the safe and opened it long enough to stash the drawing inside, he turned back toward Jackson. "Where are you headed today?"

"I want to check on my partner. He was badly wounded in a shootout with the Gang." Jackson marveled that his voice remained calm. While months had passed, his insides still roiled at the memory of how he'd lost both his partner and his little brother that night. It wasn't the first or the last time that the Gang had killed, but that night had been different. As painful as it was to admit, Jackson held himself responsible for what had happened to Leander and Micah.

"You're coming back, aren't you?"

He met the sheriff's eye and shrugged. "I'm not sure."

He was gone. Travis had told Lydia, and Lydia had told Thea. The story was simple: Jackson had left town and didn't know whether he would return.

"I suspect both he and Travis doubt they'll ever find the woman's family," Lydia had explained as she offered Thea another of her chocolate creams. "That means there's no reason for Jackson to stay here."

Thea knew that was true, but she couldn't help feeling—she struggled for a word, settling on "hurt"—that he hadn't said good-bye. It wasn't as if he owed her an explanation. He did not. It wasn't as if they were friends or even close acquaintances. They were strangers who'd been thrust together by extraordinary circumstances. It wasn't as if she had any logical reason for wanting the man who sometimes appeared to distrust her to remain in Cimarron Creek. She knew all that, and yet his departure bothered her far more than it should have.

As soon as she could without being rude, Thea had left Lydia's house and come back here, determined to put Ranger Jackson Guthrie out of her mind. Pulling a sheet of paper and a pen from the small desk in her room, she nodded. Writing a letter to her sister would do the trick.

Dear Sarah, you can stop worrying now.

But Thea couldn't stop worrying about what Jackson was doing and why he'd left so abruptly.

Yes, I know you were worrying about whether Aimee and I would arrive safely. We did, and we're getting settled into Cimarron Creek. Fortunately, everyone is friendly.

Except for Jackson. He was a puzzle. He'd been kind and seemingly caring when he'd taken her to see Stuart's mother's body. There'd been a gleam in his eyes that seemed friendly—maybe even more than friendly—when he'd asked her to use his first name. But she couldn't forget the way he'd watched her when she'd answered his questions about Daniel. It was almost as if he were testing her, wanting to see whether she was telling him the truth.

Thea hadn't lied. What she'd told him was the truth. If she hadn't told him everything about her marriage, it was because Daniel's infidelity was no one's business except hers. Even Sarah, her sister and closest confidante, did not know about the perfumed shirts.

Thea stared at the wall, trying to compose her thoughts. The reason she'd started this letter was to keep herself from thinking about Jackson, but she hadn't succeeded. Instead, everything she wrote reminded her of him.

It was ridiculous. The man intrigued her more than anyone she'd met. He kept her off balance, seemed to challenge her, and made her want to know more about him. All that was dangerous. Hadn't she learned her lesson with Daniel? Of course it was good that Jackson was gone.

Thea picked up her pen, resolving to concentrate on the letter and nothing else.

The town is attractive. Oh, Sarah, you should see the house catty-cornered from where Aimee and I live. It's one of three enormous homes the locals call Founders' Houses. I'd call it a mansion. As big as you might think some of the houses in Ladreville are, they're small in comparison to these buildings. This one has columns on three sides, tall windows, and a porch big enough to host a square dance.

She paused, tapping the end of her pen against her cheek as she thought of her sister's reaction.

Yes, Sarah. I exaggerated. Just a little.

The town itself is quite different from Ladreville. More American is one way to describe it, but there's a touch of Europe here too. Most of the stores on Main Street have window boxes filled with flowers. Lydia said to tell you she got the idea when she visited Ladreville last fall. She also sends her greetings and Travis's.

Thea laid the pen back on the desk. Had Lydia realized how upset she was by the news of Jackson's departure? Oh, how she hoped that wasn't the case. She didn't need anyone speculating on her feelings for the Ranger, especially when she couldn't identify them herself.

Resolving to banish thoughts of the auburn-haired man, Thea dipped the pen in the inkwell.

I already have two patients. Lydia's less than six weeks from delivering. The other one—one who wears a perfume that makes me want to gag—is in her first trimester. That's not enough to keep me busy, but Lydia says that will change once the women on the outlying ranches hear that I've arrived. In the meantime, Aimee and I are caring for an abandoned infant.

Thea smiled, picturing her sister's expression when she read that.

You can imagine how surprised I was to find a man—she wouldn't tell Sarah he was a Ranger; that might alarm her—*standing on my front porch with a baby boy in his arms. We aren't sure what happened to him, but his mother is dead.*

Thea wouldn't give her sister any details lest she worry. Sarah was definitely a worrier.

At least for the time being, he'll stay with us. Don't frown. It's all right, Sarah. Honestly, it's all right. When I first saw Stuart, I didn't want to hold him, because I was afraid he would remind me of Aaron, but that didn't happen. When I looked at him, all I saw was Stuart.

He's not a replacement for the son I lost. No one could take Aaron's place in my heart, but even though it's only been a few days, Stuart is finding his own place. I wonder if he's the reason God brought me to Cimarron Creek.

Thea stopped, startled by the words she'd just written. She hadn't been aware of thinking that Stuart was part of God's plan for her, and yet there was such a sense of rightness to the idea. Although Aimee believed she'd been led to Cimarron Creek because it was where God meant her to make her home, Thea wasn't certain this was her final destination. But as she thought of the future, wherever it might be, she pictured Stuart at her side.

A smile lit Thea's face, and as she penned the final paragraphs of the letter, her heart felt lighter than it had in months.

"You look like you got caught in a stampede. Either that, or you tried to ride a bucking bull and lost."

"That's a fine way to greet your partner." He'd ridden all night, and while that always took its toll, Jackson doubted he looked as bad as Leander claimed. Still, there was nothing to be gained by arguing. In all likelihood, Leander was trying to deflect attention from himself, following the adage that the best defense was a good offense.

"You look better than I expected," Jackson told his partner. The man had always been heavyset, but five months of inactivity had added a few pounds to his middle and new creases to his face. Despite that, he looked remarkably good for a man who'd almost died. The bullets that had hit Leander had done serious damage. One had torn up his insides, the other shattered his right hand.

Leander leaned back in the rocking chair that, judging from the collection of empty bottles, crumbs, and cigarette butts next to it, must be where he spent most of his days. When they'd ridden together, Leander had joked about retiring to his front porch. It appeared he'd done that.

"The doc said I was plumb lucky to have lived, but you know that." In the aftermath of the gunfight, there'd been nothing Jackson could do for Micah, but he'd stayed with Leander during those first critical days when his hold on life had been so tenuous.

The Gang had already disappeared, along with the gold that had cost Micah his life. Though Jackson's captain had disagreed, he'd known there was no point in trying to pursue the outlaws. By the time he'd mounted Blaze, they'd disappeared without a trace the way they always did.

Jackson hadn't been able to save Micah, but he wasn't about to let his partner die, and so he'd carried him to the closest town, summoned the doctor, and watched while the man tried to repair what the Gang had destroyed.

"I can't say that I feel lucky." Leander held out his hand, displaying the mangled fingers. "There was nothing Doc could do to fix this. I'll never be able to shoot a gun again." As if anticipating Jackson's response, Leander continued. "Don't tell me I could learn to use my left hand. We both know that'll take years. By then I'll be too old to ride with the Rangers."

There was more than a grain of truth in that. The Ranger life was not for old men.

Leander shook his head. "I don't reckon talkin' about what ails me is what brought you here. What's bothering you?"

Jackson smiled. Leander had never been one to mince words. "The Gang. I keep hitting dead ends. I thought I had a chance when the bandanna slipped and I saw one man's face." He reached into his pocket for the sketch that he'd transferred from the Bible, holding it out for Leander's inspection.

"Good likeness. Looks just the way I remember him. You should have been able to find him with this."

"Turns out the man's name was Daniel Michener. I found him, but someone else got there sooner. He was dead."

"And not of old age." Leander reached into his pocket for the package of tobacco that had been as much a part of his uniform as his Colt and began to roll a cigarette.

"Nope. A single shot straight to the heart. I can't prove it, but I suspect there was a falling-out in the Gang. Daniel Michener could have been a liability once his face was seen. He also might have been the one who kept all the gold."

"Stands to reason. What's next?"

"That's why I'm here. I want your opinion. You always told me two heads are better than one." And if there was one man whose judgment Jackson trusted, it was Leander Carlton.

Leander tapped his forehead. "At least that part of me is still functioning. What have you learned about this Daniel Michener?"

As Jackson recounted the story, his partner listened carefully, his expression turning thoughtful at times, amused at others.

"What are you finding so funny?" Jackson demanded. "The way I see it, there's nothing amusing about what happened."

"But there is. I knew it would happen sometime. I just never figured it would be in the middle of a case."

Jackson stared at the man who'd been almost as close as a

brother. He was making no sense. Had Leander's brains been scrambled along with his gut? "What are you talking about?"

"You." Leander chuckled. "You've fallen for a woman."

Jackson blinked in astonishment. "What woman?" He tried to recall everything he'd told his partner. "Thea? You think I've fallen for her?"

"She's the only woman you mentioned other than the one who's dead." Leander took a deep drag on his cigarette, watching Jackson as he blew smoke rings. "I gotta say, it's downright amusing to see the way your face changes when you talk about her. You've fallen, my friend. Fallen hard."

"But . . ." The word trailed off. Jackson had no idea what to say. It was true that he couldn't dismiss his thoughts of Thea. But that didn't mean he was smitten, did it?

His partner gave him a smug smile. "She's the key, Jackson. The key to this case and your future."

10

"What's wrong, little one?" Thea lifted Stuart into her arms and began cooing to him as she walked around the parlor. "I know you're not hungry, and you don't need to be changed."

The baby continued to whine. Stuart was cranky, and so was Thea. Though she hated to admit it, she had been out of sorts for days. She'd tried not to let it show, but the way Aimee had looked at her when she'd asked if Thea needed a tonic from the apothecary had told Thea she hadn't succeeded. Even the time she'd spent in church on Sunday hadn't given her the peace it normally did.

She'd met more of the town's residents afterwards and wasn't surprised that they were as welcoming as her first acquaintances had been. Travis hadn't been exaggerating when he'd told her that Cimarron Creek was a friendly town, but there were limits. While many of the parishioners had greeted Thea with warm smiles for both her and Stuart, no one had expressed any interest in adopting the baby.

"It wouldn't be fair to my other children," one woman had said.

"I believe God wants you to keep him," another declared.

Thea had nodded slowly. The absence of anyone willing to

take Stuart into their home seemed to confirm her conviction that God meant this baby to be hers. Even though she'd once cringed at the very idea, now that thought filled her with happiness.

So did the conversations she'd had with other members of the congregation. When several women who'd spoken to Thea on Sunday had murmured that they hoped to need her services soon, she'd felt her spirits rise. It wasn't so much that she needed the fees she'd earn—the fact that she had free lodging meant that she could go quite a while without being paid—but she needed more patients to keep her busy and make her feel complete.

Thea pressed a kiss on Stuart's forehead. "I love you, little one, and I love being a midwife."

Even Sarah hadn't understood how important her profession was for Thea, how it was more than what she did. It was a calling, an essential part of who she was. Thea needed to help expectant mothers as much as they needed her. But right now, she needed to find a way to stop Stuart's crying.

She patted his back and bounced him ever so slightly. Yesterday that had eased his tears. Today it did not. Today it seemed as if nothing would comfort him.

"What's wrong, Stuart?" His only response was a shriek that threatened to puncture her eardrums.

If it weren't for Stuart's incessant crying, Thea would have been happy. Today marked a week since she'd arrived in Cimarron Creek, and though she hadn't thought it would happen so quickly, the town was already beginning to feel like home.

Part of the reason might have been Aimee's enthusiasm. She kept talking about how comfortable she was living here and how much she was looking forward to meeting her mother. Aimee practically bubbled over with happiness, and although she'd seemed a bit subdued the evening they'd met Patience and her cousin, the next morning she'd once again been cheerful.

The cheerful side of Aimee was such a dramatic change from

the apprehensive woman who'd stepped off the stagecoach in Ladreville that there were times Thea could not believe this was the same Aimee Jarre, and she gave thanks for the transformation. Cimarron Creek had been good for Aimee. It was also good for Thea.

She stroked Stuart's cheek, hoping the gentle touch would soothe him. It did not. Thea closed her eyes for a second, trying to focus on the positive parts of her life. Just this morning she'd realized that she'd gone two days without thinking of Daniel and wondering whether he'd been honest in claiming that he had not broken his marriage vows, despite the evidence to the contrary.

Not thinking about Daniel was good. What wasn't good was the way thoughts of Jackson popped into her head so frequently. It didn't seem to matter what she was doing, there appeared to be no way to stop wondering where he was and why he hadn't said good-bye. That was the reason she was cranky.

Stuart's problem was more difficult to diagnose. The baby let out another yell, his face turning red with the exertion.

"I wish you could tell me what's wrong," she said, raising her voice to be heard over his screams. Far from soothing him, that only caused him to intensify his cries. The wailing was so loud that Thea almost didn't hear the knock on the front door.

Though she was tempted to ignore it, she did not. It might be a new patient needing to consult her. And so she opened the door, but instead of the young woman she expected to see, a tall man filled the doorway, the same tall man who'd filled so many of her thoughts. Thea's heart skipped a beat at the sight of Jackson standing only inches from her. She no longer had to wonder and worry about where he was. He was here.

"It looks like you've got a mighty unhappy baby there." A hint of something that sounded suspiciously like amusement colored his words and caused Thea's hackles to rise. Her annoyance grew as he added, "Want me to calm him?"

Was that all he was going to say? No "hello"? No "sorry I left so abruptly"? As quickly as it had erupted, Thea's anger faded. The truth was, she was happy to see Jackson. He'd come back to Cimarron Creek. More than that, he'd come to see her. Life was once again good.

She wouldn't tell him how relieved she was to see him again. A lady didn't make such admissions. Instead, she focused on his offer. "Do you think you can do better?" Thea asked, not bothering to hide her skepticism. "Go ahead." She stepped onto the front porch and placed Stuart in Jackson's arms. The baby let out a howl, then opened his eyes, stared at Jackson, and grew suddenly quiet.

Jackson shrugged as if he'd expected that reaction. "You've got her wrapped around your little finger, don't you?" he asked the infant in his arms. "You know that if you cry, she'll hold you. I'm giving you fair notice that I'm not so easy to manipulate."

"Aren't you?" Thea chuckled at the sight of the big Ranger with the tiny boy. She shouldn't be acting like a schoolgirl, becoming giddy over Jackson's return, but while she knew it was foolish to trust another man so quickly, she could not stop herself from smiling. "It appears to me that you're holding him too."

The smile that accompanied Jackson's response was almost a smirk. "The difference is, if I lay him down, he'll stay quiet. Want me to prove it?"

"All right. I'll call your bluff." This was a lighter side of Jackson than she'd seen, and Thea liked it, just as she liked the fact that when he smiled, the right side of his mouth rose a fraction of an inch higher than the left. Somehow, the minor imperfection made him seem less formidable and reminded her that underneath the Ranger's slouch hat was an ordinary man.

"It's not a bluff. Where's his bed?"

Thea led the way inside the house and pointed to the buggy she'd positioned in the parlor. "We let him sleep there during the day." It was easier than climbing the stairs multiple times to place him in the makeshift cradle, particularly when she and Aimee were occupied with cooking or cleaning.

"That's a good idea. This way you can move him when you need to." Jackson touched the baby's nose. "It's time for you to sleep." He laid the child on his stomach, and to Thea's amazement, Stuart remained quiet.

"How did you do that?" she asked, her voice little more than a whisper. Not for anything would she waken the now-sleeping child. "I tried the same thing, and he only screamed louder."

Jackson feigned innocence. "I've probably had more experience than you."

"Just how did you gain that experience? I thought you'd never been married." Lydia had mentioned Jackson's single status, and while Thea wasn't certain where her friend had learned that, knowing that Jackson was unmarried had made Thea's pulse race.

"I may not have a wife, but I had a younger brother." His eyes darkened, and a shadow crossed his face as he spoke. "I was fifteen when Micah was born. By then, my older brothers were married and had families of their own, so it was only Ma, Pa, and me on the ranch. Ma didn't talk about it, but I guess Micah was a surprise."

Thea nodded. She'd had several patients with later-in-life babies, and while the mothers had been happy about the prospect of a new child, they'd also worried about whether they still had enough energy to handle a toddler's demands. That was, however, something they would not have shared with a fifteen-year-old boy.

"Ma had a hard time delivering him, so I wound up caring for him when he was first born." Jackson took a step toward the buggy, his expression relaxing when he saw that Stuart was still asleep. "That's one of the reasons I'm here, to see if you'd like me to help you take care of him for the next few weeks. Travis said no one in town has volunteered to adopt him."

Thea wasn't ready to admit how torn she was by that fact. As much as she loved Stuart and believed that God wanted them to be together, she couldn't dismiss the worry that as a single parent she would be unable to give him everything he needed. It was one thing to care for an infant, another to guide a young man into adulthood.

"I know you and Travis have done your best, but I keep hoping Stuart's family will come forward. My husband's experience showed me that children are best raised by family." What Aimee had shared about her adoptive parents had only confirmed that belief.

Jackson shook his head, as if disagreeing. "Family or people who love them." He amended her statement. "Whoever ran the orphanage probably loved children—I can't imagine doing it otherwise—but they wouldn't have had a lot of time to spend with any single child."

Which was one reason Thea was determined Stuart would never suffer that fate. "Stuart deserves better than that. I'll keep him and love him if you and Travis can't find his family, but what he really needs is both a mother and a father."

"Then you'll let me help." Jackson made it a statement, not a question. "I can be his temporary father."

While it was a tempting thought for many reasons, Thea could foresee problems. "How do you propose to do that? I can't afford to shock anyone." And having Jackson spending time in this house would shock at least some of the townspeople.

While Thea had more freedom as a widow than she would have if she were still single, she did not want to test Cimarron Creek's sense of propriety. She started moving toward the front door, knowing Jackson would follow. They'd already been in here unchaperoned long enough to start tongues wagging.

"When do you normally call on your patients?"

"Mornings." Travis had told her that she could arrange office hours whenever it suited her, and she had chosen mornings.

Jackson nodded. "Fine. I'll plan to take care of Stuart during the morning. I'll pick him up each day around eight or nine—whichever is better for you—and will bring him back at noon."

"But what about your work?" A Ranger's life was a demanding one and one that would not accommodate an infant's needs.

"I'm not making a lot of progress on my current case, so my captain agreed that I could stay here for the next month."

Thea suspected there was more to the story than he was telling. While she wouldn't pry, she couldn't deny that she wanted to learn everything she could about him. She gestured toward the swing and chairs that filled one corner of the front porch. "Would you like some coffee or perhaps some buttermilk? We could sit here without scandalizing anyone."

"I wouldn't turn down a glass of buttermilk." Another of those engaging crooked smiles accompanied his words.

Two minutes later, they were both seated on the swing, Jackson's foot moving it slowly as they sipped glasses of buttermilk.

"Tell me about your brother," Thea urged. The way his expression had changed when he'd spoken of Micah—grim at first, then softening as he'd talked about caring for him—made her want to know more. "Does he want to be a Ranger like you?"

Jackson's face darkened, and for a moment, Thea thought he was going to refuse to speak. "He did," he said at last, the firm line of his jaw telling her he was attempting to compose himself. "He's the one who gave me my badge." Jackson withdrew the tin star that he'd shown Thea the day they'd met, holding it almost reverently. "Micah made this."

Thea gave the five-pointed star that reminded her of the one on the state flag a closer look. Though the metal was not costly, the workmanship was finer than she would have expected from a boy.

"Your brother's quite an artist."

Jackson nodded. "Ma always said he was the most talented

of her sons. Quincy and Jefferson whittled, and I sketched, but our efforts were amateur compared to Micah."

As Jackson slid the star back into his pocket, Thea posed one of the questions it had raised. "I don't understand why a civilian was making a Ranger's badge."

"That's simple. The state doesn't believe we need anything more than the papers I showed you, so they don't issue badges. If a Ranger wants one, he buys one or makes his own. Some men's badges are shaped like shields. Others have stars made from Mexican coins. Still others are tin like mine."

"I can't imagine a silver star would be any more beautiful than yours. It was obviously made with love."

Jackson's lips thinned. "Lots of youthful idealism too. I tried to tell Micah that being a Ranger wasn't as exciting as he imagined, that a lot of time is spent waiting, not to mention sleeping on the ground and eating hardtack, but he wouldn't listen."

"That sounds typical for a boy his age. My nephews went through a stage where they were convinced they knew more than anyone, especially their parents."

"Micah should have listened." Jackson's voice resonated with anger, confirming Thea's suspicion that the story Jackson was obviously reluctant to tell was not a happy one.

"What happened?"

He took a long swallow of the cool liquid before he spoke again. "Leander—he's my partner—and I were chasing a gang of thieves. There were four of them, so we called them the Gang of Four." Jackson turned slightly to face Thea. "Have you heard of them?"

She shook her head. While Ladreville wasn't insulated from news, she had paid little attention to anything outside the town.

"They have two specialties," Jackson explained. "Robbing wealthy travelers of their money and jewels, and capturing Army payrolls. Like most outlaws, they wear bandannas over their faces and keep their hats pulled low so no one can identify them. Once the heists are over, they disappear."

"It sounds like a story from a dime novel." Thea's nephews had entertained her with tales from the popular books.

Jackson shook his head. "I wish it were nothing more than a story. The Gang is more elusive than any of the other desperados we'd dealt with, but Leander and I were sure we'd catch them eventually."

"Rangers always do, don't they?"

A wry smile lightened the seriousness of Jackson's expression. "That's the Ranger legend. A lot of things have changed since '74—now we're peace officers instead of citizen soldiers—but our goal hasn't changed. We're determined to catch outlaws and ensure that justice is served."

Jackson took a shallow breath, the almost imperceptible tightening of his jaw telling Thea he'd reached the critical part of his story.

"When Leander and I heard about a major shipment of gold, we knew it would be irresistible to the Gang. It seemed almost too good to be true. The stagecoach was passing not far from my parents' home, which meant that I knew the area better than any other place we'd tried to catch them."

Jackson looked away for a second, then continued his story. "There's a spot where the road narrows that would be ideal for them to ambush the coach. What I was betting on was that they wouldn't know about the back way into the narrows. I was so sure of success that I didn't see any harm in visiting my family, since we'd be so close." Jackson looked almost sheepish as he added, "A home-cooked meal holds a lot of appeal."

"But something went wrong." Thea cringed inwardly as she replayed their conversation. How had she missed the fact that he'd used the past tense when referring to his brother? While she'd thought that talking about Micah would bring Jackson pleasure, she'd actually caused pain.

Jackson gave a short nod before placing his glass on the small table that stood between the two chairs. "You could say so. If I could redo one day of my life, it would be that one. I should have realized that Micah was at an impulsive age, but I never thought he'd decide to play Ranger."

The lump that had settled in Thea's stomach grew as she watched the play of emotions across Jackson's face. Anger, grief, and something else warred for dominance.

"The stagecoach ambush took place right where and when Leander and I thought it would. We were set to capture our quarry, but then Micah rode in. He must have thought he could help us, but instead . . ." Jackson shook his head, his sorrow evident in the darkening of his eyes.

"The confusion he caused was just what the Gang needed." Jackson closed his eyes for a second, perhaps trying to hide his emotions. "Micah's shotgun was no match for the Gang's revolvers. They shot him and Leander, then escaped. The only good thing that happened that night was that one of the outlaws' bandannas slipped enough that I saw his face."

Jackson paused again, his visible anguish leaving no doubt that the worst part of the story was yet to come. "I'll never know whether I did the right thing, but I didn't pursue the Gang. Instead, I stayed with Micah. When I saw where he was hit, I knew he had no hope, but I couldn't let him die alone."

Thea didn't bother brushing aside the tears that streamed down her cheeks. That wouldn't stop them from flowing. "You did the right thing, Jackson. You'll have another chance to capture the Gang, but you won't have another chance to be with your brother."

"My captain doesn't agree."

"He's wrong," Thea said as firmly as she could with tears still falling. "No one should have to die alone."

Though Jackson's eyes softened, he pursed his lips, making her wonder if he too was struggling with tears. When he spoke, his question startled her.

"How did your husband die?"

"Someone shot him. A man Daniel had done business with in San Antonio found his body by the side of the road." Those were the facts. It shouldn't hurt to recite them, and yet it did. "Either it was a lucky shot or the killer was a skilled marksman, because the bullet hit Daniel's heart." Almost without her volition, Thea's hand covered her own heart. "Clay assured me that he would have died instantly."

Her brother-in-law, who was also the town's physician, had examined Daniel's body when it was brought to Ladreville and had been able to give her that small measure of comfort.

"Micah didn't last much longer. I didn't think he'd be able to speak at all, but with his dying words, he gave me a clue to the Gang."

Jackson's eyes darkened, and Thea knew he was remembering his beloved brother.

"What did he say?"

"He told me one of the Gang was a woman. Leander and I'd been close to capturing them half a dozen times, and we never noticed that, but Micah did."

Desperate to do something that would provide at least some measure of comfort, Thea said, "It sounds as if he would have been a good Ranger. I imagine he would have been happy that he was able to help you."

"He would have."

As if to signal that the discussion was over, Jackson reached for his glass and swallowed the last of the buttermilk. "Do you have any idea who would have killed your husband and why?"

His voice was steady, telling Thea he was once again Ranger Guthrie, ferreting out information about a crime. While Daniel's death wasn't connected to the Gang any more than Stuart's mother's was, Jackson was a lawman, and as such he wanted to resolve a murder.

Thea shook her head. "As far as I know, everyone liked Daniel.

It appeared to have been a robbery, because when they found him, he had no money on him, and his watch was missing."

Her voice broke as she remembered how distraught she'd been when she'd gone through Daniel's belongings and discovered the watch was gone. Even now, months later, the loss brought tears to her eyes. "Isn't it silly? My husband was killed, and I'm upset that someone stole his watch."

Jackson did not appear to think she was foolish. His green eyes radiated warmth and compassion, and the way he said "It's often the little things that trigger grief" made Thea wonder which memories of his brother were the most poignant. "Was the watch valuable?"

Thea shook her head. That was part of what bothered her. While the watch had been taken, whoever had killed Daniel had not touched the wagonload of supplies he'd bought in San Antonio. Those supplies were worth far more than Daniel's timepiece.

"It wasn't especially costly, but it was my Christmas gift to him. All it was was a simple gold watch with Daniel's initials on the cover and my portrait inside."

She wouldn't tell Jackson why she'd included the portrait, that she had wanted Daniel to have a reminder of her when he was with the other woman. She had hoped it would keep him from straying. Perhaps it had—Thea would never know the truth about that—but nothing had kept him alive.

11

"Do you have any . . ." Aimee opened the paper Thea had given her and read, "Mrs. Davis's salve? Thea says it's good for diaper rash." Stuart had begun to develop a mild case of the common ailment, which was one of the two reasons Aimee was standing at the counter of the pharmacy. She'd finished the rest of her shopping and would return to the house that had quickly become her home once she had the salve and the answer to her other question. The first was easy, the second far more difficult. Fortunately, the store was now empty, so no one would overhear.

Unaware of her internal turmoil, Warner Gray shook his head as he pulled a tube from one of the cabinets behind him. "I don't carry that brand, but the ladies tell me this one works well." He handed it to her, encouraging her to read the glowing endorsements printed on the label. If the fancy print was to be believed, the ointment cured everything from thinning hair to sunburned skin.

"I have to trust you about that." Aimee tried not to stare at the pharmacist. That would only make the next part of her mission more difficult, and yet she couldn't help wondering why he seemed so familiar to her. There was something about the way Warner held his head and the way his nose wrinkled when he spoke that sparked memories. It was almost as if Aimee had known him for a long time, but that made no sense. She'd met him for the first time less than a week ago.

"Is there anything else I can help you with?"

There he went again, tipping his head to the side ever so slightly in a gesture that reminded her of . . . Aimee's brain refused to complete the sentence. This was silly, silly, silly, and she needed to stop. She'd come here for two reasons, and she'd accomplished only one. It was time to ask the important question.

"Perhaps. You know I'm staying with Thea."

Warner's smile faded, replaced by concern. "Is something wrong with the house?" He leaned forward ever so slightly, as if by bridging part of the distance between them he could resolve whatever was troubling Aimee.

"No, not at all." The last thing she wanted was to worry the man who'd so generously offered his brother's house to Thea. "It's a wonderful house." She wouldn't tell him that it felt more like home than the one where she'd spent most of her life. "I appreciate your letting us use the things we found in the attic. That's been a godsend for Stuart."

"Then, what's wrong?"

If she were still in France, Aimee would have found a diplomatic way to phrase her question, simply hinting at the problem, but Thea had told her that Americans were more direct. That was why she'd tried to rehearse her next sentences.

"I need to earn some money," she said bluntly. "Thea insists I don't owe her anything, but I want to at least pay for my expenses. I wondered if you knew of anyone who might need help."

There was a moment of silence, and the expression in Warner's blue eyes suggested that he was shocked by her plea. A second later, shock transformed itself into a broad smile. "God was listening to me," Warner said, his voice reflecting his pleasure.

"What do you mean?"

He gestured around the store. "It's rare for the store to be this empty. Most days I've got people lined up in front of the counter."

Aimee knew that was true. Those crowds were one of the reasons this was her last stop. Each time she'd passed the apothecary, there had been at least half a dozen customers. She'd delayed coming inside, waiting until she would have privacy.

Furrows formed between Warner's eyes as he continued, "Normally pleasant people become impatient when they have to wait too long. That's bad enough, but some of the ladies aren't comfortable asking me about certain remedies." He tipped his head toward a cabinet filled with patent medicines.

"They don't want to talk about female problems with me. That's why I've been praying for God to send someone to help me. And he did." Warner leaned forward, his expression earnest. "It's no coincidence that you're here. Would you like to work for me?"

It was more than she'd expected—much more. Aimee had thought she might find a family that needed someone to help care for children or perhaps perform household chores. She hadn't dared hope that she would find a position in a store, even though that was what she knew best.

"Truly?" She couldn't mask her incredulity.

"Truly. Do you want the job?"

"*Mais oui!*"

"I'm glad you're here." Lydia tried to hug Thea but settled for squeezing her hand when her increasing girth made a hug awkward. "Travis wouldn't have agreed to the party otherwise." She waved her hand in the direction of the parlor, where Travis was moving furniture. "He's such a worrier. When I told him I wanted everyone to come for an evening of fun and games, he was certain that would harm the baby. Believe it or not, my worrying husband was adamant that this was a bad idea until I reminded him that you'd be here to look after me."

Thea studied her patient and friend for a moment. Although Lydia's face was slightly flushed, perhaps the result of being in an overly warm kitchen, Thea saw nothing of concern. "You look like you're doing well without help."

"Of course I am, but now Travis can relax a bit. I assured him there's nothing strenuous about charades." Lydia frowned, as if assailed by an unpleasant thought. "Do you suppose Aimee knows how to play?"

"I most certainly do know how to play charades," Aimee assured them when she entered the kitchen a minute later, announcing that the rest of the guests had arrived and Travis needed his wife to act as hostess. "*Maman* used to claim the game was invented in France. I don't know whether that's true, but we played it often." She glanced at the doorway. "*Allons-y.*"

"She's telling us we need to go with her," Thea explained when Lydia raised an eyebrow. Aimee must be more nervous than Thea had realized if she was reverting to French. She'd done that the first few days in Ladreville, but since they'd arrived in Cimarron Creek, her lapses had been infrequent.

"Let's go." Thea gave Aimee's words a literal translation.

As she entered the parlor, she looked around, trying to see it from Aimee's eyes. Was she still in awe of the beautiful house where her mother had grown up? Even though there were now ten people in the room, it was not crowded. As Thea had told Sarah, this was a mansion. In addition to Lydia and Travis, there was one other married couple—Opal and Edgar Ellis. Thea had met both of them briefly and had learned that Opal was Lydia's partner at the candy store, while Edgar served as Travis's deputy.

It was thanks to Opal that Stuart had a place to stay tonight. When she'd heard about Stuart, she had assured Thea that Widow Jenkins, who cared for Opal and Edgar's son, would be happy to watch both children tonight.

Aimee's new friend Patience had been invited, along with her cousin Nate, who was also Travis's childhood friend. Nate's sister and brother-by-marriage, Rachel and Luke, had been unable to come, but Lydia had declared that they still had enough people for a good game. Rounding out the group were Travis's cousin Warner and Jackson, who now made his home with Warner.

"It's a combination of Travis's oldest friends and our newcomers," Lydia had explained when she invited Thea and Aimee. "We want to welcome you two and Patience to Cimarron Creek."

And so here they were, dressed in their Sunday best as befitted an evening in one of the town's mansions.

"All right, everybody. Let's get started," Lydia said when she'd greeted her guests. She picked up two small baskets, each with five pencils and a number of slips of paper in it.

Travis winked at the group. "The sooner we finish, the sooner you can have some of my wife's candies." His gaze moved from Thea to Aimee and then to Patience. "You ladies who are new to Cimarron Creek may not know this, but there was almost a fight over some of those candies last Founders' Day."

"We won't fight tonight," Nate promised, "as long as she and Opal made enough for all of us." He smiled at Lydia and Opal, then extended the smile to include Thea and Patience. Oddly, when his gaze would have reached Aimee, he turned away, his expression telling Thea something about Aimee bothered him.

Could it be that she was a foreigner? Lydia had admitted that the townspeople had been wary of her when she'd arrived, but so far Thea had seen no evidence of prejudice against Aimee. Perhaps she'd been mistaken about Nate. Thea hoped that was the case.

"You don't need to worry, Nate." Opal flashed him a conspiratorial smile. "I made a batch of mint fudge just for you."

Nate may have been a simple farmer, but the bow he gave her was worthy of a courtier. "You have my undying gratitude, Mrs. Ellis."

Aimee, who'd been watching the exchange with unconcealed curiosity, raised an eyebrow. "*Menthe?* I've never tasted *chocolat avec menthe.*"

Thea hadn't tasted the combination of chocolate and mint, either, but that was of no interest to her. What intrigued her was Aimee's second reversion to French and the way her hands trembled. This was more than simple nervousness. Aimee was clearly upset by something, but what?

"I thought we'd play ladies against gentlemen," Lydia said as she handed one of the baskets to her husband.

"Wonderful! We'll win for certain!"

Patience's enthusiasm was not shared by her cousin. "Don't be so sure," Nate cautioned her. "I don't like to lose."

"Nor do I," Aimee said, her face flushing ever so slightly as she looked at Nate. Though the man glanced at her, he averted his gaze as quickly as if he'd laid his hand on a hot stove.

How odd. Aimee couldn't have helped notice the gesture, which verged on rudeness. Was Nate the reason for her uneasiness? Thea resolved to ask her friend once they returned home.

"Tonight's theme is book titles," Lydia announced, seemingly oblivious to the undercurrents between Aimee and Nate. "Each team needs to choose five for the other team to act out. We'll give each team two minutes to figure out the title." She placed a small hourglass on the table separating the two groups. "The team with the most wins gets to fill their plates first."

"Now I know we're going to win." Nate slapped Jackson, his closest teammate, on the back. "We've got a real incentive."

Five minutes later, the game began. There was good-natured ribbing as Warner had difficulty getting his team to guess *Tom Sawyer*, but they succeeded with only a few grains of sand to spare.

When Aimee chose the first clue for the ladies' side, she smiled and held up five fingers, indicating that the title consisted of five words. She wasn't smiling two minutes later when the sand had run through the hourglass and no one had guessed the correct title.

"*A Tale of Two Cities*," she announced when Travis declared the round over, leaving the women's team with no score.

Patience didn't bother hiding her annoyance. "I should have guessed that one. It was only yesterday that I decided to have my older pupils read it this year."

"Better luck next time," Warner said as he handed the basket to Jackson. "I hope you're not too hungry, ladies, because my partners and I have mighty big appetites."

"But you're gentlemen," Patience protested, her eyes flashing with what appeared to be anger, although Thea could not imagine anyone becoming truly angry over a mere game.

"It sounds like you've already admitted you'll lose," Warner taunted her.

"Never!" Patience turned toward Thea and the other women. "We'll show them next time."

When Thea looked up, she was surprised to see Jackson looking at her. He winked slowly, then unfolded the piece of paper he'd chosen. Though Thea had thought this title might stymie the other team, Jackson had no difficulty in getting the men to guess *Moby-Dick*.

When the game ended in a tie, with each team guessing four titles within the time limit, everyone moved to the dining room, where Lydia had arranged a collation of ham sandwiches, potato salad, an assortment of cakes, and four varieties of candy from Cimarron Sweets. Though it was not a formal dinner, Lydia had provided place cards, explaining that she wanted to be sure everyone had a chance to get acquainted.

Thea was grateful to find herself between Jackson and Warner, because it gave her a chance to tell the pharmacist how excited Aimee was about the prospect of working for him.

"Her parents owned a small shop in France," Thea explained, "so this will be perfect for her."

"And for me." Warner flashed a smile that seemed somehow familiar to Thea, then turned to Patience, who was seated on his other side, leaving Thea no option but to talk to Jackson.

There was no reason to feel awkward. She'd seen him several times since the day they'd spoken of Micah, and each time she'd managed to keep the conversation light. She could do that again.

"You did well," she told him.

Jackson's lips curved into a smile. "It was pure luck. I've never played before."

"Really?" The skill with which he'd portrayed the whale had convinced Thea that he was well acquainted with the game, and she'd found herself wondering if he'd whiled away rainy days playing charades with Micah, the brother who'd died so tragically.

"Really."

She stared at him for a second before the words slipped from her. "You're amazing."

12

Amazing. It had been five days since Thea had called him that. Jackson scraped the last whisker from his face and stared at his reflection. The word had shocked him then, and it still did. The only thing that was amazing was that he hadn't confronted her with the sketch he'd made of her husband. He'd had every intention of doing that, and yet he hadn't.

"Breakfast is almost ready."

At the sound of Warner's reminder, Jackson toweled his face and descended the stairs to the kitchen. Though the house boasted a formal dining room, the day Jackson had arrived Warner had explained that he never ate there. Not his style, he'd said. Not Jackson's either. The kitchen with the table that sat six was fine with him.

"Have I told you lately how glad I am you came to Cimarron Creek?" Warner frowned as he dished slightly blackened scrambled eggs onto two plates. It wasn't the first time he'd burned them. While the town's pharmacist might be adept at mixing prescriptions, his culinary skills were lacking.

Jackson bit back a smile. "You're glad because I cook breakfast half the time?"

"That's a bonus," Warner agreed. "Your bacon and eggs

are definitely better than mine, but that's not the best part of having you here." He pulled four slices of perfectly browned toast from the oven and smiled at the evidence that he could cook at least one thing. "You've taken the pressure off me."

Once they were seated and had given thanks for the food, Jackson raised an eyebrow. "What do you mean about relieving pressure?"

Warner picked up an overly crisp piece of bacon, studying it as he might an herb that he was prepared to grind with his mortar and pestle. "It's pretty simple. Ever since my parents' deaths, the town's matchmakers have been trying to find me a bride. You'd think they'd realize that I'm still mourning them and leave me alone, but—no—they're convinced that every single man needs to be married. They even quoted Aunt Bertha—she was Cimarron Creek's matriarch—and how she despised the outward signs of mourning."

Jackson wasn't certain where all this was leading, but he found himself intrigued by the town's somewhat unconventional attitude toward mourning. Was that why Nate was ready to pursue Thea? The thought shouldn't rankle, and yet it did.

He forked some of the overcooked eggs, choosing not to comment until Warner had finished whatever it was he planned to say.

When he'd swallowed his bite of bacon, Warner fixed his gaze on Jackson.

"Nate and I haven't made the matchmakers' jobs easy. There hasn't been anyone who caught my eye, and Nate—well, you know Nate—everyone catches his eye."

The feeling of relief that washed over him at the thought that Nate's infatuation with Thea was nothing more than a passing fancy surprised Jackson with its intensity. Warner had alluded to Nate's fickleness before, and he certainly knew the man better than Jackson did, so it was likely that Nate wasn't serious about courting Thea.

Jackson realized that Warner was waiting for a response. He wouldn't talk about Thea. Instead, he said, "Seems like every town has its matchmakers."

"Ours are pretty determined. Fortunately, you've taken the pressure off Nate and me."

"How?" This conversation was becoming stranger by the minute.

"The matchmakers have changed their focus. They want to ensure that you become a resident of Cimarron Creek."

"I'm a Ranger. Rangers don't get to pick where they live. Besides, Cimarron Creek already has two lawmen. They don't need another. And why would the matchmakers care about that, anyway?"

Warner crushed a piece of bacon and stirred the bits into his eggs. "It's not you they're worried about. It's Thea. From what I've heard, they think that if Thea marries again, she'll be less likely to look for a position in another town. Making certain that Cimarron Creek keeps its midwife is at least as important to them as finding husbands for every bachelor."

Jackson tried not to frown at the thought of Thea with a new husband, though he told himself that anyone in Cimarron Creek—even Nate—would be better than Daniel Michener. As far as he knew, Nate had no criminal background.

"Just how do I fit into this picture?"

"The matchmakers see your marrying Thea as killing two birds with one stone . . . or something like that. One less bachelor plus a permanent midwife. That's why they're happy you're courting Thea."

Jackson nearly spat out his coffee. It might be true that he was intrigued by Thea, but he wasn't courting her, and he certainly had no plans to remain in Cimarron Creek.

"I'm not courting Thea," he said firmly.

Warner merely smiled. "So you say."

Though Jackson wanted to wipe the smirk off Warner's face,

he realized that he'd accomplish nothing by that. Warner was only the messenger. Instead of responding to the smirk, Jackson seized on another part of the story, wanting Warner to confirm what he'd said about Nate.

"I'm surprised the matchmakers are picking on me. I thought Nate had met the woman he was going to marry. You were here when he said that, same as me."

Warner shook his head and lifted a forkful of eggs toward his lips. "Nate says that at least once a year. I've learned to discount those declarations, and I suspect the matchmakers have too."

"He sounded pretty serious."

Warner shrugged. "He always does, but either he falls out of love or the lady falls in love with someone else. I'm not saying he's fickle, but he does change his mind." After he'd taken another slug of coffee, Warner continued. "I figure you're different. I can't picture you being fickle. You wouldn't court a woman unless you were sure she was the one."

Which brought them full circle. "I'm not courting Thea."

A skeptical look was Warner's first response. "What else would you call taking care of Stuart? The surest way to a woman's heart is through a child." Warner spread jam on a piece of toast and waved it in Jackson's direction. "Three different ladies told me that."

That might be true, but it wasn't Jackson's motivation. "The next time you see those ladies, you can tell them they're wrong. The reason I'm spending time with Stuart is that I feel responsible for him. I'm the one who found him."

Jackson knew he'd never forget the sight of that squalling, sunburned baby lying next to the prickly pear or the way the child's plight had touched his heart. He hadn't been able to save Micah, but he was determined that the abandoned child would live.

"Caring for Stuart can't be easy for Thea. No matter what

she says, he must remind her of the baby she lost." As he pronounced the words, Jackson realized that he'd never heard the child's name. Perhaps Aimee could tell him. While it would be easier to simply ask Thea, Jackson didn't want to do anything that would cause her more pain.

Warner appeared unconvinced. "You can say what you want, but I saw the way you were looking at her at Travis's house the other day."

"And how was that?"

"The same way a man who's dying of thirst looks at a pitcher of cool water."

"That's ridiculous!" Jackson couldn't believe how this conversation had deteriorated. He'd believed Warner was his friend, but friends didn't make each other this uncomfortable. Did they?

"It's not ridiculous. I know what I saw."

Jackson raised the coffee mug to his face to avoid saying something he would regret. It was true that he'd watched Thea that evening, but the reason wasn't what Warner thought. He kept remembering Leander's declaration that Thea was the key to finding the Gang. While he no longer believed she was involved with them, he was convinced she knew something, even though she might be unaware of it. That was the only thing that made sense, the only way the clues fit together.

The worries that had begun when he'd seen Stuart's mother's resemblance to Thea had only increased when she'd mentioned that the missing watch held her portrait. Jackson wouldn't believe that was coincidence, and if it wasn't, it could mean that Thea was in danger. That was the reason he'd watched her. The only reason.

He drained the mug, then refilled it. He could tell himself that his sole concern was keeping Thea safe, but that didn't explain why he hadn't shown her the sketch and told her what he knew about her husband. There was no explanation—at least no good explanation—for that.

Surely it wasn't because he was attracted to her and didn't want to distress her. Surely it wasn't because, despite what he'd told Warner, he'd begun to entertain thoughts of courting a woman like Thea. He was a Ranger, not a lovesick boy. He was simply biding his time. That was all.

"You must be Miss Jarre." The woman smiled at Aimee as she entered the apothecary. "I've heard so much about you."

Aimee tried to return the smile. In the short time she'd been working here, she'd learned there was a rhythm to the day's business. Customers came in waves, followed by quiet interludes. Normally, she spent the lulls talking to Warner and planning ways to modernize the pharmacy, but today Warner was not here, and the time had dragged. Though it was good to have a customer, Aimee was apprehensive about this particular one, especially since she claimed to have heard about her. What had Nate said?

"How can I help you, Mrs. Henderson?"

The woman's eyebrows rose. "How did you know who I am?"

"You look a lot like your brother." Not only did Rachel Henderson have the same straw-blonde hair and light blue eyes as Nate, her face had the same shape. The physical similarities ended there. While Nate was muscular, his sister was not. And while he was of average height for a man, Mrs. Henderson was a taller-than-average woman, standing five or six inches higher than Aimee.

Aimee's customer's laugh brought back memories of the day she'd met Nate and how he and Thea had laughed as they'd walked through town. Rachel's was higher-pitched, of course, but there was the same little hitch that Aimee had noticed when Nate laughed.

Stop it! Stop thinking about Nate! She'd been telling herself that regularly and had increased the frequency of the admonitions after Thea had asked her whether she'd been upset about something at Lydia and Travis's party. Aimee had denied that anything was wrong, but she suspected that Thea had not believed her.

"If you ever have a problem, I'm a good listener," Thea had assured her. "I may not have an answer, but sometimes talking helps."

Aimee had nodded, though she had no intention of telling anyone how foolish she felt whenever she was around Nate. And now she had to wait on his sister.

Rachel Henderson laid her reticule on the counter and leaned forward, as if she was about to impart a secret. "You mean Nate looks a lot like me. I'm not ashamed to admit that I'm his older sister." She laughed again. "I won't tell you how much older unless you agree to call me Rachel, and maybe not even then. But I do hope you'll let me call you Aimee. After everything Patience has said about you, I know we'll be friends."

Patience. Naturally, it was Patience who'd spoken about her. Once again Aimee had been foolish, thinking that Nate might have at least mentioned her to his sister.

"Of course you may call me Aimee." It took an effort to keep the smile fixed on her face when inside she kept wondering why Nate had obviously said nothing about her. There was only one reason she could imagine: he had never really noticed her. That hurt.

"What can I do for you, Rachel?" Aimee adopted her most professional tone.

"I hope Warner still has some calamine lotion. The third of my children has chicken pox, and they're itching like the dickens." Rachel pretended to scratch her arm. "What a time to run out of lotion. I hated to miss church and Lydia's party, but I didn't want to leave the boys alone. Rebecca's a bit better— she won't scratch too much, because I told her that might leave scars. Still, I need to get back."

It wasn't difficult to believe Rachel and Patience were cousins, the way they both chattered, but Nate didn't seem to fit into the family, at least not when he was around Aimee. He was as silent as the proverbial stone then.

"Will one bottle be enough?" she asked as she turned toward the cabinet.

"I hope so, but you'd better give me two. Luke—he's my husband—doesn't believe he had chicken pox when he was a boy." Rachel shuddered. "I don't want to think about what kind of patient he'd be."

Aimee retrieved the bottles from the glass-fronted cabinet and placed them on the counter. "Do you need anything else?"

"I don't think so. Would you ask Warner to put this on my bill?" Rachel looked around the shop, obviously searching for something. "Where is Warner, anyway? I've never known him to leave his store."

"He's making a delivery to a ranch north of town."

Rachel's eyes widened. "Warner makes deliveries? When did this start?"

"I didn't know it was something new. He's been doing it all this week."

As she placed the bottles of lotion into the cloth bag she'd brought, Rachel's expression turned pensive. "He used to use one of the boys for deliveries. To be honest, I was surprised when I heard he'd hired you. Warner's always been a bit of a loner, especially where women are concerned. The matchmakers have tried their best, but no one's succeeded."

Rachel looked up, smiling, and declared, "This is good news. It means Warner's changing. First, he hires you, then he trusts you enough to leave the pharmacy in your hands." Her smile broadened. "You could be just what he needs," Rachel said as she began humming Mendelssohn's "Wedding March."

"You're wrong, Rachel." The very idea was preposterous. Aimee wouldn't deny that she enjoyed working with Warner, but there was nothing romantic about her feelings for him. In the few days she'd known him, he'd become a friend, perhaps even a good friend, but he didn't make her skin tingle or her pulse race. There was only one man who made her feel like that. Unfortunately, that man had no such feelings for her.

"Warner's my boss."

"So?" Rachel's expression was that of a woman trying to explain a simple concept to a stubborn child. "That doesn't mean he couldn't become something more. The man needs someone to love. He deserves happiness after what happened to his family."

Unwilling to indulge in gossip, Aimee refused to ask what Rachel meant, but even without prompting, Rachel continued. "First his brother died, then his parents. He has no one left. That's one of the reasons the matchmakers are so eager to see him married. If there was ever a man who needed a wife, it's Warner Gray."

Poor Warner! Aimee's heart ached at the thought of all that he had endured. She remembered how bereft she'd felt after her parents' deaths. It had been a difficult time, but Warner had lost more than parents. He'd also lost a brother.

Aimee's thoughts whirled over the revelation. Perhaps the fact that they were both alone was why she felt a special connection to Warner. There was a difference between them, though. She had hope, the sweetest of hopes, to help her through the dark moments. When Grace returned from France, she would have a family. Warner was not so blessed. Still . . .

"Being alone is not a good reason to marry," she told Rachel.

Nate's sister did not agree. "Warner needs a wife. He needed one even before he lost his family. Now he needs one even more."

"Maybe so"—though Aimee wasn't convinced, she saw no point in arguing with Rachel—"but I'm not the one for him." Marriage should be based on more than a mutual need. There should be respect, attraction, and love. While she respected Warner, there were no sparks between them. As for love, there were days when she wondered whether she truly knew what it was.

Warner's story lingered in Aimee's mind for the rest of the morning while she served other customers. She wasn't a matchmaker—heavenly stars, no!—but if she could find a friend for Warner, perhaps he'd smile more often, perhaps he'd discover the sweetness of hope. Everyone could use another friend, but who was the right one for Warner?

Aimee was rearranging the display in one of the cabinets when a face popped into her mind. She grinned, thinking about all that she'd observed. They could be friends, but maybe, just maybe, they could become something more.

There was definitely attraction, at least on the woman's side, because she'd spent most of her time at Lydia's party darting glances at Warner. And, if Aimee wasn't mistaken, he'd displayed more than casual interest in her. If it was true that opposites attracted, they were the perfect couple—quiet, reserved Warner and effervescent, gregarious Patience. Perfect! Now all Aimee had to do was find ways to get them together.

She chuckled. Maybe she was a matchmaker after all.

<hr />

"Twins? Are you sure?"

Thea coiled her stethoscope and replaced it in her bag while her patient swung her legs over the edge of the bed and rose. "No, I'm not certain, but it's a possibility. Even though I could only hear one heartbeat, you're larger than normal for this stage."

Lydia laid a protective hand on her abdomen as she stood, then wrinkled her nose. "I feel as big as a horse."

"I can assure you you're not quite that big."

"At least a good-sized pony, then." She tipped her head to one side, as if considering the possibility that she was carrying two children. "If you're right about twins, it would explain why there's so much kicking—four legs, just like a pony."

Thea couldn't help laughing at the image. "One thing I've

learned from my patients is that a sense of humor never hurts, especially during the birthing pains. You'll do all right, Lydia, and before you know it, you'll have the baby—or babies—in your arms."

The mother-to-be simply smiled and led the way downstairs to the kitchen, where she'd arranged an assortment of candies on a silver platter. As she poured two cups of coffee and placed one in front of Thea, she said, "I'm so glad you'll be here to make sure everything goes right with the baby. I thank God every day that you and Aimee came to Cimarron Creek."

Though Thea couldn't promise that there would be no problems with Lydia's delivery, she would do her best to ensure the safety of both the mother and her offspring.

Thea smiled, grateful that Lydia had mentioned Aimee. As she spooned sugar into her coffee, she asked the question she knew was foremost on her friend's mind. "Have you heard anything from Aimee's mother?"

"Not yet. Catherine mailed a letter before they boarded the ship, telling me their plans, but that's the last I've heard." Lydia took a sip of coffee before she continued. "If there were no delays in the crossing, they should have reached Paris either yesterday or today. My letter about Aimee will probably take another week to get there, but it should arrive before they leave. They were planning to spend a couple weeks in Paris before going to Maillochauds."

Lydia took another sip. "As anxious as Grace is to meet her daughter, she told me she wasn't going to deprive Catherine of that time. You haven't met Catherine, but walking along the Seine has been her dream for years. When Grace started talking about going there, Catherine joked that she'd borrowed her dream."

Though Thea didn't know what Aimee dreamt, she did know about her concerns. "Aimee doesn't talk about it much, but I know she's anxious about the reunion."

Lydia nodded as if she understood. "She won't be once she meets Grace. Her mother is a remarkable woman. She's strong and brave, and she loves her daughter."

"Aimee's stronger than she realizes. She's stubborn too." Thea hadn't realized that when she'd first met Aimee, but the stubborn streak—perhaps it was simply determination—had become evident since they'd arrived here. "I told her she didn't need to pay me anything, but she insisted on getting a job."

"From everything I've heard, that's working out well. Warner told Travis he doesn't know how he got along without her." Lydia picked up a chocolate cream and raised it to her lips. "We're all hoping the three of you will stay in Cimarron Creek permanently."

"Three?" They'd been discussing Thea and Aimee. That was only two.

"You and Aimee and Jackson. Travis says you're just what the town needs. The matchmakers are even saying you and Jackson belong together."

As the traitorous blush rose to her cheeks, Thea lowered her head, hoping Lydia hadn't noticed it. If she had, perhaps she would think it was caused by the praise Travis had given her. No one needed to know that she'd become flustered by the mention of Jackson's name or the fact that the busybodies of Cimarron Creek were linking her name with his. That was silly, downright silly, and it needed to stop now.

13

Jackson couldn't explain why he was so restless. He'd had a good morning with Stuart. Not wanting to remain indoors, he'd taken the boy for a walk along the creek, strapping him into the quilted carrier Widow Jenkins had given him this week.

When she'd presented it to him, she had claimed that holding a child close to a man's heart was better than letting him ride in the baby carriage. Jackson wasn't convinced. Stuart appeared to like the buggy and frequently fell asleep while riding in it. But since the carrier had the advantage of letting Jackson travel over rougher terrain without jostling the baby and would be convenient when he took Stuart for rides on Blaze, he'd accepted the gift gratefully.

Though there wasn't a lot of water in the creek at this time of the year, the burbling had seemed to soothe the boy. It should have soothed Jackson as well, but it didn't. Talking to Thea when he'd brought Stuart back at noon was another thing that should have soothed him, but it didn't, either. So here he was, wandering aimlessly along the streets of Cimarron Creek and feeling decidedly out of sorts.

The most logical reason for his uneasiness was that he'd made no progress in either catching the Gang or learning the identity of the woman who looked so much like Thea. None of Travis's inquiries had turned up any leads about Stuart's mother, and though he'd been reluctant to abandon the search, Travis had told Jackson there was nothing more he could do.

That bothered Jackson, but not as much as the fact that all he had were questions. Why hadn't the Gang struck again since that night in February when Micah had been shot? Why had Daniel Michener been killed? And why couldn't Jackson find the answers? The questions reverberated through his brain.

He and Leander had speculated that the lack of robberies since February was connected to Michener's death. Since then, there'd been several Army payrolls transported through areas where an ambush would have been easy, but though Jackson had been there waiting to apprehend them, the Gang had not attempted a robbery. Why not? It seemed difficult to believe they'd simply grown tired of the chase.

Leander had agreed with Jackson's hypothesis that if Michener was the brains behind the operation, the remaining three might not be able to plan and execute another heist. But if he was the brains, why had he been killed?

Though he had no proof, Jackson's instincts told him that Michener's death had not been a random robbery, particularly after Thea told him that the wagonload of supplies had not been touched. A thief might not have wanted to carry away bolts of fabric or a place setting of china, but the cargo could have included pieces of jewelry or even a watch like the one Michener had been carrying.

The fact that the thief had not searched the wagon made Jackson believe that Daniel Michener had been the target, and that led him back to the Gang. If, as he suspected, another member of the Gang had pulled the trigger that night, why? Was it related to the missing gold or simply an argument gone wrong? Had Michener been killed in a fit of anger, or was it a deliberate act of someone who wanted to take over as leader?

It was time to talk to Thea. She might not know anything

about her husband's criminal activities—and Jackson believed that was true—but she could tell him whether Michener had been crafty enough to plan a series of daring robberies.

Jackson glanced down the street, grinning when he saw her walking toward Main Street with Stuart in her arms. This could be the opportunity he sought.

"Is the carriage broken?" Jackson had never seen Thea take Stuart outside without it.

She shook her head. "No. We're only going as far as the livery. A woman on one of the ranches sent a message that she needs to see me. It sounded too urgent to wait until tomorrow, so I'm taking Stuart with me. Aimee's working today, and I didn't want to bother Widow Jenkins."

The opportunity had just gotten better. Though he could have offered to care for the boy this afternoon, Jackson wasn't about to give up the chance to talk to Thea without interruptions. There was only one possible glitch. If the matchmakers heard he and Thea had left town together, they'd see it as proof that he was courting Thea.

He wasn't. Of course he wasn't. This was business, a chance to learn more about her husband. And, if there was some pleasure involved once they'd finished discussing Daniel Michener, well . . . a man couldn't work all the time.

"Would you like some company? I could watch Stuart while you're with your patient."

Thea gave him one of those sweet smiles that somehow managed to make his pulse beat a bit faster. "Are you certain you don't mind? I'd hate to take you away from whatever you were doing."

What he'd been doing was walking aimlessly around town, thinking about the Gang and about her.

"I have nothing planned, and a ride in the country sounds good. Would you like me to drive?" Jackson asked as they approached the livery.

Thea shook her head again. "Thanks, but Maggie is used to me. She doesn't like others to handle the reins."

Jackson wondered why. The bay mare had seemed docile when he'd passed her in the livery, making him think she'd tolerate multiple drivers, but Thea obviously knew her horse better than anyone.

"In that case, I'll come along for the ride."

Within minutes, they were headed out of town, Thea with the reins wrapped around her hands, Jackson with the now wide-awake Stuart in his arms.

Thea turned toward Jackson, furrows forming between her eyes. "Are you sure you don't mind my driving?"

"Why would I?" Though Andrew Henderson, the cousin Warner had hired to run the livery after his brother's death, had looked askance at Thea's not handing the reins to Jackson, it didn't bother him. Admittedly, this was the first time a woman other than his mother had driven him anywhere, but there was a first time for everything.

Besides, not having to watch the road meant that he could spend more time observing Thea's reactions when he asked her about her husband. Even if he didn't question her, he'd have the undeniable pleasure of looking at a pretty woman. Who would complain about that?

Apparently, someone had. "My husband always had to be the one who drove."

As they headed up a small hill, Thea shifted so that Jackson was once more treated to a view of her profile. She might not be the most beautiful woman he'd ever seen, but she was the only one who stirred his senses, making him feel both protective and more than a little possessive. The second thought caused Jackson to swallow deeply. He had no right to feel possessive of Thea. He looked straight ahead, trying to calm his suddenly unsettled thoughts.

Oblivious to his inner turmoil, Thea continued her story.

"Daniel didn't mind if I drove when I was alone, but when we went anywhere together, he insisted on being the driver. Maggie wasn't happy about that. She's used to a lighter touch."

Jackson nodded slowly, filing away that insight into the man Thea had married. While it might not mean anything, Michener's need to be in charge dovetailed with the supposition that he'd been the leader of the Gang. The heavy touch on the reins could mean anything or nothing at all. Jackson hoped it did not mean that Daniel Michener had been an abusive spouse.

He had no reason to believe that had been the case, but he could not dismiss the possibility, given the man's violent history. A man who thought nothing of killing innocent travelers might not have shied away from using his fists on his wife if she displeased him.

"Did your husband mind that you continued to work after you were married?" Jackson knew that many men did, wanting to be the breadwinner in their families, and that sometimes frustration led to anger.

Thea appeared surprised by the question, her brown eyes widening ever so slightly. "Daniel worried about having enough money to buy a house and everything our baby would need, so he was happy to have my earnings."

Another insight, but one that contradicted what Jackson thought he knew. With all the successful robberies the Gang had conducted, money should not have been a problem. Even split four ways, it was a small fortune.

That was another part of the puzzle that had surrounded the Gang of Four for the past two years. Why did they continue to rob coaches and trains when they had enough money to retire from crime and live comfortably? The only theories he and Leander had developed were that either the Gang craved the excitement of outwitting the law or they'd developed a taste for expensive items. Jackson wouldn't pursue either possibility now. Instead, he'd turn the conversation to Thea herself, then gradually return to her husband.

"What made you decide to become a midwife?"

The smile that lit her face told Jackson this was a much happier subject than her late husband. "It started when I was a little girl. I idolized my brother-in-law, Clay. You need to understand that he was more than my sister's husband; he was like a father to me."

When Jackson nodded, silently urging her to continue, she did. "Clay was also a doctor, and sometimes he'd let me tag along while he visited patients. I thought the way he made people healthy again was wonderful and decided right then that I was going to be a doctor too."

Thea's smile widened, and she reached over to touch Stuart's fist as he tried to push it into his mouth. "Being a doctor was my dream until Priscilla, the town's midwife, took me with her one day. It was supposed to be a routine checkup. The baby wasn't due for another month, but by the time we arrived, the mother was in the final stages of labor."

Stuart giggled and batted at Thea's hand, making her smile again, although the subject was a serious one. "It was a difficult delivery, and Priscilla needed help. Unfortunately for Priscilla but fortunately for me, I was the only one there. Seeing what she did opened a whole new world for me, and when I held that newborn baby in my arms, I knew that was what I wanted to do with my life."

The flush on Thea's cheeks told Jackson as clearly as her words how much she enjoyed her profession and how much satisfaction it gave her.

"Why did you leave Ladreville? It sounds as though you had a good life there."

"It was a good life," Thea admitted, "until Daniel and Aaron died. After that, I knew I needed a change."

Jackson nodded, more because he'd learned Thea's son's name than because he understood her experience.

Her voice was firm as she said, "The advertisement for a midwife in Cimarron Creek felt like a sign from God."

Jackson wished he'd been given a sign. Ever since Micah had been killed, he'd felt like a rudderless boat, floating aimlessly.

"It must be nice to be able to bring life into the world. I see too much death."

Thea turned again, her smile fading when she saw his scowl. "But you're saving others' lives by bringing criminals to justice."

As two birds flitted by, Maggie's ears twitched, signaling the mare's disapproval. Jackson couldn't blame her. He didn't like animals coming too close any more than he did the direction the conversation had taken.

"That's what I used to believe. Now I'm not so certain. If it weren't for me, my brother would still be alive."

Thea's gasp told Jackson his last sentence had shocked her. It had shocked him too. He certainly hadn't meant to say that. Not even Leander knew how much he blamed himself.

"You didn't kill Micah."

Jackson knew Thea was trying to comfort him. It wouldn't work. "Maybe not directly, but if I hadn't gone home that day, he would not have tried to be a hero. He'd still be alive."

Thea shook her head. "You don't know that for a fact. He might have tried to tangle with a javelina. He might have hit his head falling off a horse. Life is fragile. Believe me, Jackson, I know that. You're not to blame for what happened to your brother."

Her voice was fierce, as if she were using it to erect a protective shield around him. Though the idea that Thea wanted to protect him was oddly comforting, she was wrong.

"If I hadn't been a Ranger, none of that would have happened."

This time Thea did not try to contradict him. "Why did you join the Rangers?"

Turnabout was fair. He'd asked her about her profession; she had a right to ask him about his.

"I wanted to do something very different from my other brothers. I think I told you that Quincy and Jefferson are twins. They're five years older than me, which meant that they were old enough to consider me a pest, not a playmate." Jackson closed his eyes, remembering how they'd refused to let him join their games.

"I grew up resenting them and decided that whatever they did, I'd do something else. I liked ranching as much as they did, but when they bought the ranches on either side of our parents' spread, I knew that wouldn't be the life for me. When I heard about the Rangers, it sounded like something I could do. I always was a good shot. Now I'm not sure it was the right decision."

It was the first time Jackson had voiced those doubts, but for some reason it felt right to tell Thea.

"Are you thinking about leaving the Rangers?" She sounded both shocked and concerned, as if she cared enough to worry about whether or not he was making a hasty decision.

Jackson wished he could give her a definite answer, particularly since it might reassure her, but he had to be honest.

"I don't know."

14

Thea frowned as she looked down at the sleeping baby. She ought to have started supper, but instead she was sitting in the parlor, watching a child who needed no watching, and thinking thoughts that were best forgotten. She had no business being fascinated by a man—any man. Hadn't she learned her lesson with Daniel? Other women might be good judges of character, but Thea was not. She had believed that Daniel was the right man for her and that they'd have the kind of marriage Sarah and Clay did, but she'd been wrong.

She'd been fooled, and she'd paid the price with months of anguish when the scent of perfume—any perfume—made her cringe. And then there'd been the day the sheriff had brought Daniel's body home and she'd realized that she would never know the truth about her husband. That was the day she'd vowed she would never, ever put herself in that position again. She would never again open her heart to a man. Yet, no matter how often she scolded herself, Thea couldn't stop thinking about Jackson and all that he'd revealed on their ride.

Rangers had the reputation of being big, tough men. Jackson was big, at least compared to her, and she didn't doubt that he could be tough, but there was a gentle side to him too. Few men would have volunteered to care for Stuart. And while he was only the second Ranger she'd met, Thea suspected few spent much time questioning whether they'd done the right thing, whether the killing was justified. It was simply part of the job. They did what they had to without a lot of introspection.

Jackson was different, and it wasn't difficult to find the reason. Thea suspected that few other Rangers had had their brothers die in their arms as a result of their job. That was bound to change a man, just as Daniel and Aaron's deaths had changed her.

"But you're alive, Stuart." She stroked the baby's cheek and inhaled the sweet fragrance that was his alone.

"Of course he is. Were you worried?"

Thea spun around, realizing she'd been so caught up in her thoughts that she hadn't heard the door opening.

"No . . ." She paused, trying to decide how much to share with Aimee. "It's just sometimes . . ."

Aimee nodded as if she understood. "You think about your husband and son. That's only normal."

There'd been more to it than that, but that was enough of an explanation for today. Aimee didn't need to know how deeply Jackson's story had touched her.

Aimee untied her bonnet strings and laid the hat on one of the tables. "How was your new patient?"

"Perfectly healthy." The urgent call that had summoned Thea to the ranch had been a false alarm. "This is her first baby, and she's nervous."

The expectant father had been even more worried than her patient, a fact that had warmed Thea's heart. Some men paid little attention to their wives' condition, but this one had been refreshingly concerned and protective of his bride, telling Thea they'd been married less than six months and that he couldn't bear the thought of anything bad happening to her. Daniel had been solicitous when she'd told him she was expecting their child, but not to that extent.

"It turned out she had a case of indigestion and was afraid it would harm the child," Thea said as she laid Stuart in the buggy. "It took me a while to reassure her and her husband, but once I convinced them that babies could survive much more than that, she seemed fine."

A slightly mischievous smile crossed Aimee's face as Thea settled into the chair across from her. "I heard Jackson went with you."

Though Thea knew she shouldn't have been surprised, she was, as much by the speed with which the story had spread as the gossip itself. "Lydia told me there are few secrets in this town, and it seems she's right. Cimarron Creek has an efficient grapevine." Thea raised an eyebrow. "Do you know who started it?"

Aimee nodded. "Patience. She saw you leaving the livery and couldn't wait to report what she'd seen." Her narrowed eyes said there was more to the story. "She's been coming into the apothecary almost every day."

"That's good, isn't it? Lydia mentioned that business declined for a few weeks after Warner's parents died. I would imagine he's glad to have additional customers."

"It is good. Warner told me more women would come in if I were there, and that's happening, but I don't think I'm the reason Patience comes." Aimee flashed a wry smile. "The truth is, I was going to encourage Patience to stop by, but I didn't have to. She keeps coming without an invitation."

Remembering the way the new schoolteacher had stolen looks at the pharmacist when they'd been playing charades, Thea wasn't surprised. "To see Warner." She made it a statement.

Aimee nodded. "I think so. Her face takes on a special glow when she talks to him. I never thought I'd be a matchmaker, but I can't help hoping they see how right they are for each other. Patience gets Warner to laugh, and he talks more when she's there, not like—"

"Like who?" Though Thea believed she knew the answer, she wanted Aimee to confirm her suspicions.

"Never mind. It doesn't matter."

Thea laid her hand on Aimee's. "If it bothers you—and I can see that it does—it matters. I can't force you to tell me, but I'd like to help you."

Aimee bit her lip, and for a second Thea doubted she would reveal anything. "I'm so confused," she said at last. "Do you know what a *coup de foudre* is?"

"Love at first sight." As she pronounced the words, a lump settled in Thea's throat. If there was one subject she did not want to discuss, it was that.

"Exactly." Aimee's enthusiastic response left no doubt that she did not share Thea's distaste for the lightning bolts of love. "My mother claimed that's what happened to her and my father. I didn't think it was real, but it is."

No, no, no! The lump grew, threatening Thea's ability to swallow. Though she wished it weren't so, it appeared that her friend was making the same mistake she had.

"You love Nate?"

As Aimee nodded, her mood changed. While her face glowed the way she said Patience's had, she was not smiling. "It should be perfect. *Maman* said falling in love was the best time of her life, but that's because Papa loved her. It's not that way with Nate and me."

Aimee let out a deep sigh that could have signaled frustration. "I feel wonderful when I'm around Nate, but he hardly seems to know I exist."

Thea had not had that problem, for she and Daniel had both been smitten from the day they'd met. She had believed they'd shared true love—a deep love that would last forever—but she had been wrong.

Thea's heart ached for her friend. As dangerous as her first love had proven to be, she knew that unrequited love was equally painful.

"What does Nate do?" Thea said a silent prayer for the words to comfort Aimee.

"It's what he doesn't do." Aimee practically spat the words.

"Every time he comes into the store, he greets me, but that's all. It's like the words freeze up inside him when he talks to me." She shook her head in obvious frustration. "It doesn't make any sense. He talks to everyone else. You've seen that—he talks to you. Why am I different?"

Thea made a show of checking Stuart while she gathered her thoughts. She didn't want to encourage Aimee to make a mistake, but she also didn't want to see her suffer. "There are a couple possibilities. He could be afraid of you."

"Afraid? Why? I can't imagine Nate's frightened of anything, much less me." Aimee shook her head, setting her blonde curls to bouncing. "That can't be it. What's the other possibility?"

Though it was one that worried Thea, she owed her friend an honest answer. "It could be that he's attracted to you. I've seen men become tongue-tied when they're near a woman they want to impress."

Aimee's eyes brightened as some of the tension that had gripped her began to dissipate. "Do you think that's the case?"

"It could be."

Today was going to be the day. Jackson clenched his fists and relaxed them, repeating the exercise that rarely failed to calm turbulent thoughts. He wouldn't do that on the street, lest someone think he was belligerent, but there was no one here in Warner's home to see him, and he definitely needed calming. As distressing as it might be, today was the day he would show Thea his sketch and discover what she knew about her husband's involvement with the Gang.

Jackson flexed his fingers, annoyed that fisting his hands had failed to calm him. He knew Thea was seeing Mrs. Allen this morning. He'd talk to her when she returned home. Flex, flex, flex. Clench, relax, clench, relax. It did no good. He might as well give up and admit that he wouldn't relax until he'd spoken to Thea.

Why wait? He could take Stuart out again, meet her at the Allens', and walk home with her. The town had gotten used to him walking up and down the streets with Stuart most mornings. No one would comment on a second excursion.

It didn't matter whether Jackson wheeled him in the baby buggy or placed him in the quilted carrier. The boy seemed to enjoy being outside as much as Jackson did. Jackson relished the activity, and Travis claimed it saved him and Edgar from having to do a morning inspection, because he knew Jackson would spot and report anything unusual.

"You don't stop being a lawman just because you're carrying a baby," Travis had said. "I know you're always looking for anomalies."

"Guilty as charged." Even though there'd been no sight of the Gang, Jackson was constantly vigilant. He tried to be circumspect about it, but he continued to worry about the Gang and its connection to Thea.

"We ought to put you on the town's payroll," Travis said.

He might be joking, but Jackson was taking no chances. "That's not for me." If he left the Rangers, it would be for something very different. But until he caught the Gang, there was no question of resigning. The fact that he needed to step up his search was the reason he needed to talk to Thea today.

There she was. Jackson lengthened his stride when he saw Thea emerging from the Allens' front door, then paused. Something was wrong. Even the day he'd taken her to view the body of Stuart's mother she hadn't looked this discouraged. Today Thea's shoulders drooped, and her step was slow.

"What's wrong?" It wasn't much of a greeting, but he couldn't help it. Seeing Thea's distress made Jackson forget the social niceties. He needed to learn what had happened so he could fix it.

Thea looked up, clearly surprised to see him. "Nothing."

It was a lie. A bald-faced lie. If nothing was wrong, she wouldn't look like this. Even more telling, she hadn't peered into the buggy to check on Stuart.

"I'm not buying that," Jackson said firmly. "You look like you lost your best friend." Perhaps she was worried about her patient. "Is Mrs. Allen all right?"

"Yes." Thea's lips moved as if she wanted to say something else, but no words emerged. Finally, she spoke, her voice so soft that he had to take a step closer to hear her. "It's silly. I know that, but I hate her perfume."

If it had come from another woman, Jackson would have agreed that the declaration sounded silly, but Thea was not a silly woman. She must have a good reason why her patient's scent had her on the verge of tears.

"What's wrong with Mrs. Allen's perfume?"

Thea shuddered and laid a hand on the top of the baby buggy, as if to steady herself. "Daniel used to travel. When he came home, his shirts smelled like that."

Jackson felt the blood drain from his face. He had no difficulty believing that Daniel Michener was a robber and a member—perhaps the leader—of the Gang of Four, but the idea that he might have been unfaithful to Thea left him speechless.

How could any man look at another woman if Thea were his wife? It was unthinkable, truly unthinkable. And yet Thea was standing there, her shoulders shaking with emotion, more vulnerable than Jackson had ever seen her. He had to say something. But what?

"Did you ask him?"

She nodded. "He said it was nothing for me to worry about."

Of course she worried. Anyone would have. "It might not have been what you're thinking." They were empty words. Jackson knew that, but he had to offer them.

"What else could it have been?"

"I don't know." As much as he tried, Jackson could not conjure an innocent reason why a man's shirts would carry the scent of another woman's perfume.

15

Thea took a deep breath, trying to calm her nerves as she poured a bit of boiling water into the teapot, then swirled it to warm the pot. She still couldn't believe she'd told Jackson her fears. She hadn't told anyone, not even Sarah, about the perfume on Daniel's shirts, but somehow the words had slipped out. Now Jackson knew her humiliating secret: her husband hadn't loved her. The trips to San Antonio to purchase merchandise were merely a ruse, an excuse that allowed him to meet the woman with the distinctive perfume. Daniel had lied to her.

She took another deep breath and gave thanks that Stuart had fallen asleep as soon as she'd brought him home. The boy was remarkably attuned to her moods. If he'd been awake, he would have fussed, as if to share her distress. For she was distressed.

As much as she hated to admit it, Thea knew that Daniel wasn't the only liar.

She had lied by not telling Jackson the whole truth. She'd claimed that Daniel and Aaron's deaths were why she'd left Ladreville. While that was true, it was only part of the reason she'd come to Cimarron Creek.

The most important reason was that she needed a new home,

one where no one had met Daniel, one where no one knew that anger outweighed her sorrow over his death. In Ladreville she would have had to pretend to be a grieving widow. In Cimarron Creek she could begin a new life, if only she could put the past behind her. But that was no simple matter, which was why she was making tea.

After she emptied the now-warmed pot, Thea inserted the tea ball, then filled the pot with boiling water. In five minutes, she'd have perfectly brewed tea. And maybe, just maybe, the soothing beverage would help her make sense of what had happened.

Until today she had believed that the way to rebuild her life was to pretend that the unhappy parts of the past had not occurred. If Sarah had known about Daniel's infidelity, she would have tried to comfort her, but Thea knew that the comfort would have been mixed with pity, and she didn't want that. It was better that no one knew, or so she'd believed. Now she was not so certain.

As the clouds that had obscured the sun moved and a ray of sunshine spilled across the table, Thea managed a smile. She hadn't planned to tell Jackson that she believed Daniel had been unfaithful, and yet now that she had, she couldn't regret it, for his reaction had not been what she had expected. Thea wasn't surprised by his shock and apparent sadness, but, to her immense relief, there had been no pity. Instead, there'd been something else in Jackson's expression, an emotion she couldn't identify.

He hadn't said much; he hadn't offered any platitudes, but somehow he'd made her feel better, and that was unexpected. Though Thea hadn't thought anything could ease her feeling of betrayal, the tenderness she'd seen in Jackson's eyes had done that. He didn't pity her; he didn't blame her; he simply cared that she'd been hurt.

She'd said it before, but now she knew just how true her words had been. Jackson Guthrie was an amazing man.

Thea was sipping her second cup of tea when Aimee arrived home, her slower-than-normal gait signaling fatigue.

"A hard day?"

Aimee nodded and sank onto one of the chairs. "A busy one. We had more customers than ever."

Thea rose and pulled another cup and saucer from the cupboard. Normally Aimee would have helped herself, but today she appeared too tired for even that small effort. When she'd filled the cup and placed it in front of her friend, Thea tried to lighten the mood. "Including Patience?"

Aimee shook her head. "Surprisingly, no. But Rachel came. She wanted one of the new tonics." A wrinkled nose told Thea what Aimee thought of the patent medicines that claimed to cure everything from balding to dyspepsia but did little more than dull a patient's senses with their high alcohol content. "I convinced her she didn't need it, that all she needed was rest. The poor woman's been run ragged caring for three children with chicken pox, and now her husband's caught it."

"He's probably the worst patient."

"That's what she said." Aimee took a sip of tea, then placed the cup back on the saucer, turning the cup ever so slightly until the handle was parallel to the edge of the table. The precision of her motions told Thea something was bothering her.

"Rachel said another thing that puzzled me. She claimed I remind her of Warner. I thought it was because I was honest with her about the tonic—he told me to always do what was best for the customer, not the store—but she said that wasn't it. She says I have some of the same mannerisms."

Thea couldn't imagine why the thought disturbed Aimee, but apparently it did. "You spend a lot of time with him. I suspect it's only natural that you might mimic some of his gestures and expressions."

Aimee's relief was palpable, and she flashed Thea a smile as she picked up her cup again. "That's what I hoped you'd say.

I don't know why the idea of being like Warner bothered me, but it did. Maybe it's because the last time she came in, Rachel wanted to play matchmaker for us."

Thea couldn't help laughing. "She did? I thought Patience was interested in Warner."

"She is, and I couldn't be happier. I just wish Rachel would stop meddling."

Aimee finished her cup of tea, then blinked. "I almost forgot," she said as she reached into the reticule she'd placed on the floor next to her chair. "You have a letter from your sister."

As a shiver of concern made its way down Thea's spine, she accepted the envelope. "It's awfully soon for another letter." Sarah had a schedule for almost everything, including writing letters. "I wonder if anything's wrong."

"There's only one way to know. I'll check on Stuart while you read."

Thea slit the envelope open and withdrew two sheets of paper covered with her sister's distinctive handwriting.

Dear Thea,

You're probably surprised to receive a second letter from me this week, but something odd happened and I wanted you to know about it. Yesterday two strangers came to Ladreville. They entered the mercantile and claimed they were considering moving to town, but they wanted to meet the midwife before they did.

Madame Rousseau was suspicious. This is the first time anyone's asked about our midwife, and the woman did not appear to be expecting. Madame also said they didn't act as if they were married. When she explained how to find Priscilla, the way they looked at each other made her even more uncomfortable. They said someone had mentioned a midwife with a different name.

Apparently, another customer overheard the conversa-

tion, gave them your name, and told them you'd moved to Cimarron Creek. When they heard that, Madame Rousseau said they reacted as if they'd discovered a gold mine. It felt wrong to her, so when the other customer left, she told them you'd thought about Cimarron Creek but decided you wanted to live in a big city and had gone to Austin instead.

It could all have been innocent, but Madame Rousseau was so concerned that I wanted to tell you to be alert. They didn't give her their names, but she said the woman was unusually tall with medium brown hair and eyes. The man was about the same height with the same color hair and eyes and a prominent scar on his forehead.

The letter continued for another few paragraphs, recounting some amusing anecdotes of life in Ladreville. Though Thea tried to interest herself in the news, questions whirled through her mind. Why would anyone be looking for her? It wasn't as if people outside Ladreville knew she was a midwife. The only possibility Thea could imagine was that these were people Daniel had met and told about her profession, but she doubted that. Surely Daniel would have mentioned them to her. Or would he? The man had obviously kept secrets.

Thea returned to the letter.

Oh, one more thing, Sarah added in a postscript. *Madame Rousseau said the woman wore strong perfume.*

Thea shuddered. Was it possible? Was the woman that Daniel used to meet searching for her? Why?

Jackson sat in the kitchen, nursing a glass of buttermilk while he waited for Warner to come home from work. Normally he enjoyed the cold beverage, but today it seemed almost tasteless, its flavor masked by his concerns. Poor Thea! The woman had endured more than he'd realized. Jackson's head was still reeling from the almost incredible revelation that Daniel had been unfaithful. How could any man even consider straying if he were married to Thea? But Daniel had.

Jackson couldn't forget Thea's stricken expression or the way her shoulders had slumped with defeat. She'd reacted the way any woman would have under the circumstances, being hurt by her husband's actions and perhaps fearing that all men were like Daniel. They weren't. Jackson's father and older brothers had never strayed, and he knew he would not break his vows if he married.

The story of Daniel's betrayal had left Jackson speechless. He'd wanted to reassure Thea, but the words wouldn't come. Instead, he'd fingered the sketch that he'd planned to show her, then dismissed the idea. He had waited this long to tell Thea her husband had been an outlaw; he could wait a bit longer. Thea needed time to recover from the obvious pain that came from discussing the wounds Daniel Michener had inflicted before she absorbed another blow.

Jackson took a slug of buttermilk as he considered his next steps. As much as he hated leaving Thea when she was so vulnerable, he needed to get some answers about Thea's husband. Instead of staying in Cimarron Creek, waiting for the Gang to make a move, he would do what he'd been trained to do—start at the beginning. In Michener's case, that meant the orphanage near Boerne.

If there was one thing Jackson knew, it was that childhood experiences shaped the rest of a person's life. He might not find all the answers he sought there, but he was confident he'd find some.

As renewed energy flowed through him, Jackson grinned. This was what he needed: something positive to do.

The back door swung open, and Warner entered, followed by Nate. "I hope you don't mind, but when I told Nate Mrs. Higgins made chicken and dumplings for us, he practically begged me to let him come."

Nate shrugged. "What can I say? I'm a desperate man. Every time she brings her chicken and dumplings to a potluck dinner, they're gone before I can get a taste." Nate feigned a look of deep despair that brought a smile to Jackson's face.

"I told him we'd let him have a *small* serving," Warner explained.

"And I agreed as long as Warner considered a gallon a small serving."

Jackson's smile broadened as his friends continued their normal bantering. "It's easy enough to set another place."

Half an hour later, Jackson had to agree with Nate's assessment. Mrs. Higgins's chicken and dumplings were the best he'd ever eaten.

"Thanks, fellas," Nate said as he sopped up the remaining juice with a piece of bread, "but food's not the only reason I wanted to see you tonight. I need your advice."

"About what?" Warner leaned back in his chair, his expression inscrutable.

"Women. What else?"

"You still thinking about the same woman?" Warner asked the question that had been on the tip of Jackson's tongue. He wouldn't ask, though, because he wasn't certain he would like the answer.

"Yep. She's the one for me. I know it, but now I'm worried that I might not be the one for her."

"Why not?" As far as Jackson could see, Thea would be perfect for any man. She was smart, caring, and generous with everything she had. If Daniel hadn't appreciated her, the man was a fool. Of course, Jackson reflected, he'd already proven that by getting mixed up with the Gang.

Nate's expression said the answer should be apparent. "I'm a farmer, and she's a princess. I keep trying, but I can't picture her as a farmer's wife. It's hard work, and it can be lonely. I'm not sure she's strong enough for that."

Those weren't the reasons Jackson had expected. Though she was small in stature, Thea was the strongest woman Jackson had ever met, not that he planned to tell Nate that. If the man hadn't figured that out on his own, he didn't deserve Thea. But when Warner remained silent, Jackson knew he needed to speak.

"I think you're wrong about that, Nate. Strength is more than muscles. Some ladies have more inner strength than any man." Thea must have to have survived her husband's betrayal followed by his death and their son's.

"Jackson's right." Warner rejoined the conversation. "There are all kinds of strength. If she loves you, that inner strength will help her overcome any loneliness."

Nate was silent for a moment as he drained his coffee mug. "How do I know if she loves me?"

Jackson couldn't help laughing. "You're asking two bachelors? Why don't you talk to Travis or your brother-in-law? It seems to me they'd know a lot more than Warner and I do."

"I can't ask them." Nate appeared horrified by the mere thought. "They'll laugh and think this is like every other time and that I'll lose interest. I won't. This time is different. She's different. I'm different."

It was clear that Warner wasn't convinced, even though Nate sounded sincere to Jackson's ears.

"Does she know how you feel?" Other than the one evening when he'd seen them walking on Main Street, Jackson hadn't seen Nate and Thea together.

"I don't know."

"What do you mean, you don't know?" Warner sounded outraged. "Haven't you told her how you feel?"

"Nope."

"That's a problem." Even a bachelor like Jackson knew that. "The only way you'll know if she cares about you is to tell her

146

how you feel." If a man who'd never courted a woman knew that, why didn't Nate, who had wooed at least half a dozen women?

"You make it sound easy, but it isn't. What if she laughs at me?"

Jackson could not imagine Thea being so cruel, but before he could say that, Warner spoke. "Then you'll have your answer. It may not be the one you want, but at least you'll know."

Nate nodded, then fixed his gaze on Warner. "You gonna tell your gal how you feel?"

Jackson stared at the man whose home he shared. Though they'd talked about almost everything else, Warner had said nothing about courting.

"What do you mean?" he demanded.

Nate looked as if he'd expected Warner's question. "I saw the way you looked at Patience when we were at Travis's. You had the same look on your face when you saw her after church. You're smitten, my friend, so when are you gonna start courting her?"

Warner's expression was that of a man who'd just swallowed a dose of bitter medicine. "I can't do that to her."

"Why not?" Nate was nothing if not persistent. "Rachel said she can't stop talking about you. According to Rachel, that's a sure sign a lady's interested."

Jackson rolled that information around in his brain. The only male he'd heard Thea talk about was Stuart. Did that mean she wasn't interested in Nate? Nate was a good man. He deserved a wife like Thea. But if Thea wasn't interested . . . Jackson wouldn't deny the relief that flowed through him at the idea.

"Who'd want to be saddled with my family?" Warner was still talking.

Though Nate's expression sobered, he shrugged as if Warner's family history was of no import. "They're all gone."

"Precisely. Three violent deaths. That's got to make anyone believe there's something wrong with the Gray family."

Nate had no response, but Jackson did. "For a smart man, you're not making much sense, Warner. If a woman loves you, she won't care what your family did. She's marrying you, not your family." Jackson didn't care what Daniel Michener had done. All that mattered was Thea.

"Listen to the man," Nate urged his friend. "He's right. You need to talk to Patience."

Warner gave him a short nod. "And you need to talk to your princess. Agreed?"

"Agreed." The two men shook hands and grinned at each other before turning to Jackson.

"What about you?" Warner demanded.

"What do I need? I need to leave town." Not only did he owe it to Thea to get some answers, but he didn't want to be here when Nate began his courtship. There was only so much a man could take.

16

He was getting soft, Jackson realized as he scraped the last of the bristles from his chin. A couple weeks of sleeping in a real bed had spoiled him. As beautiful as the stars were, especially with only a sliver of a moon as competition, he had not enjoyed making his bed on the ground. Rocks had dug into his back, and the rustle of nocturnal animals had seemed sinister rather than soothing. It could have been because Leander wasn't here to commiserate, but Jackson knew that wasn't the real reason he was out of sorts this morning. He could deny it no longer. The Rangers' life had lost its appeal.

Looking back, he realized that his discontent had begun last winter even before Micah had been killed. That had crystallized his feelings as anguish and anger warred for dominion, and he'd known that he could not continue to travel the same road. Like Thea after her husband and son's deaths, he needed a change, but in Jackson's case, it would be more than a change of location.

He hadn't told his parents or Leander, but ever since the night Micah died, he'd been searching for the answer to "what next?" and in the last few days, he believed he'd found it. Oddly enough, the answer was the one thing Jackson had sworn he would not do.

It couldn't be coincidence that he'd begun to feel as if Cimarron Creek was his home. It couldn't be coincidence that Travis had mentioned that Austin Goddard, the rancher who'd turned out to be a doctor, was planning to sell his ranch and live in town. It wasn't coincidence at all. It was an answer, or at least a possibility.

Jackson rinsed the razor in the stream, then stowed it in his saddlebag as he prepared to break camp. He knew from his childhood that there was satisfaction to be found in ranching. If it hadn't been for his desire to be different from his brothers, he might never have become a Ranger, and Micah might still be alive.

"You don't know that for a fact." Thea's words echoed through his brain. She was right. He didn't know that. What he knew was that buying a ranch near Cimarron Creek had a definite appeal. But first he had a job to finish. Jackson mounted Blaze and headed southeast.

An hour later as he approached Boerne, the sound of church bells pealing reminded him that it was Sunday. With a rueful look at his clothes, he shrugged. They weren't his Sunday best, but God wouldn't mind and, if he sat in the back of the church and left quickly, he might not offend the parishioners.

When a small stone church that reminded him of the one in Cimarron Creek caught his eye, he looped Blaze's reins over a hitching post and headed inside. It was time to give thanks to God for bringing him this far.

As he rose for the final hymn, Jackson's heart felt lighter than it had in weeks, and he knew why he'd been led to this particular church. Pastor Goehle, as he'd learned the minister was named, had expounded on Matthew 7:7. "Ask, and it shall be given you; seek, and ye shall find; knock, and it shall be opened unto you."

It was not the first time Jackson had heard that verse, but it was the first time he'd heard it used as the focus of an entire sermon. Pastor Goehle had claimed that far too few asked God for anything. They simply expected him to give them whatever they needed, but the parson pointed out that in this verse Jesus emphasized the need for action, urging his followers to ask, seek, and knock. Jackson planned to do exactly that.

"That was a powerful sermon," he told the minister as he shook his hand and prepared to leave the church. Tall and thin, Pastor Goehle had brown hair lightly peppered with gray, and faint lines etched the corners of his eyes, though he was probably only five or six years older than Jackson. Despite the other signs of age, his gray eyes twinkled with youthful enthusiasm.

"Believe it or not, I had a different one planned, but as I was entering the sanctuary this morning, I knew that today was the day for Matthew 7:7. I had no idea you'd be here, but you looked as if it touched you."

The minister's words surprised Jackson. He'd never heard of a preacher making a last-minute substitution like that. "It did."

Though other parishioners were waiting to speak to him, Pastor Goehle did not release Jackson. "I haven't seen you before. Are you new to town or just passing through?"

"I'm a Ranger, and I'm seeking some information." Jackson emphasized the verb, causing the minister to smile.

"Let's see if I can help you find it," he said, stressing the word "find." "What is it you're seeking?"

"I understand there's an orphanage somewhere nearby. I was hoping someone could give me information about a boy who lived there fifteen or twenty years ago."

Pastor Goehle's smile faded. "I wish I could help you, but the orphanage has been closed for more than ten years. That occurred before I came here. From what I've been told, the boys were causing so much trouble that the town insisted they leave."

Though that was not what Jackson wanted to hear, it was consistent with the picture he'd formed of Daniel Michener. "Was it relocated?"

"I believe so." The minister stared into the distance for a

second. "I tell you what. Why don't you join my wife and me for dinner? Sally may have more information."

It was probably silly to spend so much time on her toilette. Aimee knew that, but it didn't stop her from heating the curling iron to try to frame her face with sausage curls. Though they weren't the latest fashion, *Maman* had assured her that they flattered her, giving some needed width to her thin face.

Would Nate notice? That was the question, and there was only one way to learn the answer. She would have to muster every bit of courage she possessed.

"You look especially pretty today," Thea said when Aimee entered the kitchen. "I like that hairstyle. It's fancy, but not too fancy for church."

Aimee had hoped that would be the case. While she wanted Nate to notice her and perhaps say more than "good morning," she did not want to offend the town's matrons. They had definite ideas of what was appropriate clothing and behavior for the Sabbath.

Though Thea's expression suggested that she knew exactly why Aimee had curled her hair and worn the green dress that highlighted her eyes, she said nothing, instead discussing her schedule for the week and what they should wear to next Saturday's square dance.

Half an hour later, as she and Thea approached the church, Aimee forced her thoughts of Nate aside. She was here to worship, not to think about the goat farmer who'd caught her imagination. She succeeded until Pastor Dunn gave his weekly call for prayer requests.

The rustling of skirts told Aimee a woman several rows behind her had risen to her feet. "Please pray for my brother," Rachel Henderson said. "Three of Nate's goats have taken ill, and he's worried about them. That's why he's not here today."

Aimee said a silent prayer for Nate and his goats and another for forgiveness for her frivolous thoughts. Never again would she try to use the Lord's Day for her benefit.

"That was a mighty fine meal, Mrs. Goehle." Jackson couldn't remember the last time he'd eaten such succulent pot roast. The vegetables were tender, the gravy savory, and the biscuits . . . ah, the biscuits. Not even his mother, whose biscuits had won ribbons at the county fair, could surpass these. The apple cobbler that the minister's wife had served for dessert was equally good. Now the three of them sat in the parlor with a pot of coffee on the table between them.

"Thank you." Though Sally Goehle's smile was as welcoming as her husband's, that was the only similarity between them. The minister's wife was a short, plump blonde with deep blue eyes. Right now, those eyes were focused on Jackson. "Edward said you had questions about the old orphanage. The building's still standing, even though it's been vacant for years."

She stirred a teaspoon of sugar into her coffee as she added, "I know a bit more about it than Edward does, because my quilting circle talked about it one day. When I mentioned that it was a shame no one bought it after it was abandoned, they explained that the interior was in shambles. It seems the matron wasn't able to control the children."

"I'm surprised." Jackson was more than surprised. He was shocked. "I thought matrons were chosen based on their ability to maintain discipline."

Mrs. Goehle nodded her agreement. "I haven't had any first-hand experience with orphanages, but I thought that too. From all that I've heard, the previous matron was a good disciplinarian, but she retired a year or two before the orphanage was closed. You'd probably like her. Miss Millie's quite a character."

The fact that the former matron was still alive was the first encouraging news Jackson had had about the place where Daniel Michener had spent his childhood. "You know her?"

"She's one of our parishioners," Pastor Goehle explained, "although she rarely comes to services. She says I have too many newfangled ideas."

Jackson couldn't help grinning at the picture that was beginning to emerge of a stern disciplinarian with rigid opinions about the proper way to deliver a sermon and no compunction about expressing those opinions. Mrs. Goehle's description of her as a character sounded accurate. "I'd like to talk to her. She may be able to help me."

The minister nodded. "If Miss Millie knows something about the boy, you can be sure she'll tell you. I've never known her to mince words. There's only one problem. You'll have to wait until tomorrow, because Miss Millie spends her Sundays in prayer. She wouldn't answer the door if you knocked on it."

"That's right." Mrs. Goehle seconded her husband's comments. "But Edward shouldn't call it a problem. I see it as an opportunity to get to know you better. You're the first Ranger I've met, and I'd like to hear more about your life. Since you'll be here until at least tomorrow, I hope you'll stay with us."

Even if the bed was lumpy, which Jackson doubted based on the fine cooking he'd enjoyed, it would be better than sleeping on the ground, and while he was not anxious to discuss his life as a Ranger, he would not insult the Goehles by refusing their hospitality. "Are you certain I wouldn't be an inconvenience?"

"Not at all." Pastor Goehle drained his cup. "If you'd like to take a Sunday drive, we can show you the old orphanage."

"I'd appreciate that." Even abandoned and derelict, it might still hold clues to why Daniel Michener had turned to a life of crime.

Once the dishes were washed, the minister harnessed the horse and helped his wife into the buggy, his pleasure at driving apparent as they left the town.

"I'm out and about visiting parishioners alone almost every day," he explained, "but it's a treat for me to take Sally with me."

Jackson settled back and tried to relax, though his brain continued to whirl with questions about what he might find.

"Here it is," Pastor Goehle said a few minutes later as he pulled the buggy onto a rutted road that led to the former orphanage.

Built of native stone, the exterior of the large two-story building itself showed few ravages of time, but many of the windows were broken, the front porch had gaping holes from rotted boards, and the door hung open.

"Do you want me to go with you?"

Jackson shook his head, declining the minister's offer. "It doesn't look too safe. I'd rather go alone. Besides, this will give you more time with your wife."

Jackson hopped down from the buggy and picked his way across the porch to enter the place where Daniel Michener had spent much of his childhood. It was difficult to tell what it had looked like then. Now the only adjective Jackson could find was "sad."

The rooms were empty except for a few rodents' nests in the corners and some piles of dried leaves that the wind had blown inside. Cobwebs and peeling paint were the walls' only décor, while the ceiling bore the unmistakable signs of a leaking roof. Though Jackson wouldn't use the word "shambles" to describe the interior, he knew it would take substantial effort to make it once again habitable.

The grounds had fared better, or perhaps it was only that the grass had grown enough to hide whatever damage active children had inflicted. A few strands of rope still hung from a live oak's massive branch, telling Jackson the orphanage had had at least one swing, while the presence of two wells suggested that one had not been dug deep enough to provide water year-round.

"Did you find what you were seeking?" Pastor Goehle asked as Jackson climbed back into the carriage.

"No, but it was a long shot."

"There's always tomorrow." When Mrs. Goehle infused her words with encouragement, Jackson nodded.

After evening services with the Goehles, a good night's rest, and a hearty breakfast, Jackson said his farewells and prepared to meet Miss Millie. She was his last hope for learning about Daniel Michener's time at the orphanage. When he knocked on the door of the small but well-maintained house, the slow footsteps he heard approaching confirmed that this was the home of an older person.

The footsteps stopped and there was silence, as if the resident was debating whether to open the door. Seconds later, Jackson heard the snick of a lock and the door swung open, revealing a tall, stern-faced woman with gunmetal gray hair and piercing blue eyes.

"Miss Fielding?"

The former matron nodded. "No one's called me that in years, but yes, I'm Millie Fielding. What can I do for you, young man?"

It had been a while since someone had called him a young man, but Jackson suspected that he appeared young compared to this woman's seventy or eighty years.

From what he'd learned about Miss Millie, Jackson knew there was no need for social niceties, and so he said bluntly, "I wondered if you might remember one of the boys who lived at the orphanage while you were the matron."

She bristled. "My bones may not be as strong as they once were, but my mind is still sharp." She glanced around. "I don't discuss business outside where just anyone can overhear."

Though there were no pedestrians in sight, Jackson could not disagree with her desire for privacy.

"Come in, young man." She gestured to him to enter, then closed and locked the door.

Jackson couldn't help wondering about the lock. In his experience, few people felt the need to secure their houses. Perhaps Miss Millie feared some of her former pupils might wreak havoc here.

When they were both seated in the parlor whose intricately crocheted antimacassars fit the image Jackson had conjured of a spinster's home, Miss Millie leaned forward ever so slightly. "Now, who is it you're seeking?"

"Daniel Michener."

Though she pursed her lips, obviously trying to place the name, when she spoke, her voice was firm. "I'm sorry that you came all this way, but we never had a Daniel Michener at the orphanage."

17

Thea smiled as she guided Maggie out of town and headed toward her new patient's ranch. She was thankful for the summons, grateful for the opportunity to think of something other than Jackson and his absence.

It had been two seemingly endless days since he had left. The note she'd found slipped under her door Saturday morning said he had business to attend to and didn't know when he'd return. Though it wasn't much of an explanation, at least she knew he planned to return. That was better than the first time he'd left town; still, his absence left an unexpected void in her life.

Thea hadn't realized how much she looked forward to seeing Jackson every morning. Even though they spoke for only a few minutes when he picked up Stuart and again when he brought him back, those times had become the highlight of her days. It didn't matter what they spoke of—Stuart's antics, Thea's patients, the weather—Jackson always managed to find a way to make her laugh, and the memory of his crooked smile lingered in her mind long after he'd gone.

She missed that, and so, it seemed, did Stuart. The child continued to look around, as if searching for Jackson, and he'd been crankier than normal since Jackson left.

It wasn't only Jackson's smile that Thea missed. It was also the help he gave her caring for Stuart. Fortunately, she hadn't had any patients on Saturday, and Jackson never cared for him on Sunday, but today she could have used his help. The Harris ranch was more than an hour southwest of Cimarron Creek, farther than she wanted to take Stuart, especially since this was her first visit with Mrs. Harris. A baby could be an unwelcome distraction.

"Don't worry," Aimee had said when Thea explained the problem. "I'll see if Widow Jenkins can watch him. If not, he can go to the pharmacy with me."

And so, Thea was on her way, eager to meet her new patient. The directions the woman had sent with her request were excellent, leading to an obviously prosperous ranch. Two friendly barking dogs greeted Thea as she approached, while the well-fed cat sunning itself on the front step did not deign to acknowledge her presence.

Thea was hitching Maggie to the porch railing when a heavyset woman with dark brown hair and brown eyes emerged from the house. Her face brightened, and her lips curved into a welcoming smile.

"Helen! Where you been? I expected you weeks ago."

Thea stared at her patient. Why was she calling her Helen? Was she touched in the head? But as Mrs. Harris rushed down the porch steps toward her, a sinking feeling filled Thea. There was another reason why the woman might have mistaken Thea's identity. The unwelcome memory of a sheet-draped body forced its way into her brain.

"Good morning, Mrs. Harris. I'm Thea Michener, your midwife," she said firmly.

The woman stared at her, cataloguing her features. "You're not Helen?" She appeared unconvinced.

"No, I'm not." Knowing Mrs. Harris had just sustained a shock, Thea took her arm and led her back up the steps. "Let's go inside. You shouldn't be standing when you're this distraught. It's not good for you or the baby."

159

The woman kept her gaze fixed on Thea's face for a long moment, then opened the door and led Thea into her parlor. "I don't understand. You look like Helen." She tipped her head to one side, obviously considering something. "You're not as tall."

Thea nodded. Stuart's mother had been at least four inches taller than Thea. Thea swallowed deeply, trying to control her emotions. It wasn't only her patient who had sustained a shock. She had come here to call on a patient, not to solve the mystery of Stuart's mother. But she shouldn't jump to conclusions. Helen might not have been Stuart's mother.

"Who is Helen?" Thea wouldn't use the past tense. Not yet.

"Helen Bradford. She's my cousin what lives near Leakey. I oughta say what *lived* there. Poor dear."

It sounded as if Mrs. Harris was aware of her cousin's death, and yet that made no sense, given the way she'd greeted Thea. She was obviously still expecting Helen to come here.

"Helen's husband died three or four months ago," Mrs. Harris explained as she sank onto the horsehair settee. "The man just keeled over, leaving Helen alone with a baby on the way."

Thea shuddered. Not only had Helen Bradford looked like her, but their stories were eerily similar. The only difference was that Helen's son had lived.

"Helen din't know what to do. Her bein' family and all, I tole her she could live with me and Angus fer a while. She was gonna come once she had the baby." Mrs. Harris frowned. "I expected her more than a month ago."

Thea's patient stared at her again, then shook her head in amazement. "I cain't get over how much you look like her."

All the pieces fit. There was no doubt that Helen Bradford had been Stuart's mother, but still Thea asked, "Do you know whether her child was a girl or a boy?"

"A boy. I don't rightly remember what she named him, though." She frowned. "I cain't figger out where she went. She oughta been here by now."

Thea wished there were an easy way to tell Mrs. Harris that she would never see Helen again. She'd never been comfortable delivering bad news, but sometimes there was no alternative. She took a deep breath, exhaling slowly before she began. "I'm sorry to be the one to tell you this, but your cousin is dead."

Though Mrs. Harris's eyes widened, she said nothing.

"She and her son were found outside Cimarron Creek earlier this month. The baby's doing well, but Helen died." Thea wouldn't tell Mrs. Harris that Helen and Stuart had been separated or how brutally her cousin had been killed. "The sheriff and a Ranger tried to learn who she was, but none of the towns they contacted knew anything."

Mrs. Harris appeared perplexed. "Helen and Hiram din't have no other family, and they kept purty much to themselves 'cepting for goin' to church. They done that every Sunday. I woulda thought the minister woulda remembered them."

Thea summoned a mental picture of the state map and tried to calculate distances. "It could be that the sheriff's inquiries didn't go as far as Leakey." She had never asked Jackson or Travis how wide a circle they'd established for their search.

Her patient was silent, digesting the news. When she spoke, it was to say, "I hope somebody done give her a Christian burial."

At least Thea could reassure Mrs. Harris about one point. "They did. She was laid to rest in the Cimarron Creek cemetery. Now that we know her name, the town will have a headstone carved." Travis had assured her that he and Lydia would pay for that.

"Good. Now, what can you tell me about this baby of mine?"

What about Helen's baby? Thea wanted to shout the question. According to Mrs. Harris, she was Helen's only living relative, yet she displayed no curiosity about her cousin's child. What kind of woman was she?

Though Thea had told herself she wanted to find Stuart's family so that he could be raised by relations, now that she had, she was no longer convinced that uniting him with this cousin would be a good thing. If Mrs. Harris didn't care about him enough to ask where he was and who was ensuring that he was fed and clothed, how would she treat Stuart if she became his foster mother?

Thea bit the inside of her cheek to keep from spewing angry words. Family was important for children, but love was even more critical to their happiness. Perhaps she was overreacting. Perhaps this was nothing more than another example of her poor judgment of people, but Thea could not imagine Stuart being happy here. She wished—oh, how she wished—that Jackson were here so she could ask his opinion, but Jackson was gone.

Jackson stared at Miss Millie. That was not the answer he'd expected, but perhaps the story of having been raised in an orphanage was yet another of Daniel Michener's lies. He'd obviously lied to Thea—if only by omission—because he hadn't told her of his activity with the Gang, and then there were the perfumed shirts and the probability that he'd been unfaithful to her. It was possible that he'd never lived here, and yet Jackson's instincts told him that much of Daniel Michener's story had been true. He'd try another tactic.

Pulling the sketch from his pocket, Jackson unfolded it and handed it to the former matron. "Are you sure you don't remember this man? He would have been younger, of course."

She gave the paper a cursory glance. "I most certainly do remember him. He and those two scalawags were always getting into trouble."

Jackson blinked as he tried to absorb Miss Millie's words. "I thought you said he didn't live there."

Though he hadn't thought it possible, the woman's spine stiffened. "Young man, you asked me about Daniel Michener. This is Danny Klein."

Another lie. By now Jackson ought to be used to that. "He must have changed his name." Honest men rarely did that, but Thea's husband had not been an honest man.

Miss Millie's lips thinned with what appeared to be contempt. Though Thea had found the man charming enough to marry, the boy had not fooled his teacher.

"He never did like being called Klein. Once someone told them that *klein* was the German word for small, the other boys began to torment Danny about being little. He was thin and shorter than normal until he was about fourteen."

The former matron pushed her glasses back onto her nose. "You said he's calling himself Michener now. It's not difficult to figure out why he chose that name instead of Klein. I told you there were three scalawags. The other two boys were Micheners—Will and Rob."

She shook her head, as if trying to dislodge unpleasant memories. "The three were thick as thieves and caused more trouble than all the other children combined. I don't mind telling you, Ranger, that every night I prayed they would come to their senses before it was too late and they ruined their lives. The way they were acting, they were headed for a bad end."

If what Jackson believed was true, Miss Millie's fears had been justified. It seemed likely that Daniel and the Michener boys were the three men in the Gang of Four.

"What did they do?"

She pursed her lips as if she'd bitten into a lemon. "What didn't they do? It started with harmless pranks like tying bootlaces together so another boy would trip, but then it escalated to setting fire to the schoolroom and dropping a dead armadillo into the well."

Jackson nodded. While some might consider those typical boyhood shenanigans, he shared Miss Millie's opinion that they were serious. "Was there anything else?"

She fixed her gaze on him and shrugged. "I could never

prove it, but I believe they were responsible for Violet Baker's death."

Jackson's breath escaped in a whoosh. Death, even if accidental, was a whole different order of magnitude than fires or well poisoning.

"Was Violet another orphan?"

"Yes." Miss Millie's gray eyes flashed with remembered pain. "She was a year younger than the three scalawags and the prettiest girl living there. The only time I saw those boys fight among themselves was when Violet came to the orphanage. They turned from friends to adversaries as they all vied for her attention."

Jackson could picture the scene. Adolescent boys were not noted for their rational behavior. "How did she die?" Though he hoped it was nothing more than a prank gone wrong, Miss Millie's expression told Jackson that was not the case.

"I found her with her throat slit."

Just like Stuart's mother. A shiver of dread made its way down Jackson's spine. Though the Gang had never killed that way during their heists, only a fool would ignore the probability that they were behind Stuart's mother's death. Jackson was not a fool.

He looked at Miss Millie. "But you had no proof that they were responsible."

"No," she admitted, "but I don't know who else would have done it. Two days later, the three of them ran away. I alerted the sheriff, and he looked for a while but could find no trace of them." She hesitated for a second before adding, "I probably shouldn't say this, but I'm not certain he searched very hard. He may have figured we were better off without them."

The orphanage might have been, but the State of Texas would have been a more peaceful place if the trio had been caught and somehow set on the right track all those years ago. There was, however, no point in speculating over what might have been. Jackson needed to deal with what the Gang had done and what they might continue to do if he didn't catch the remaining members.

"Do you remember when they left?"

Miss Millie nodded. "I certainly do. April '65. That dreadful War Between the States had just ended. Everything was topsy-turvy as folks speculated what that would mean to us. No one could believe that General Lee had surrendered."

She pursed her lips again in what Jackson was beginning to believe was a characteristic gesture. "We might not have missed the boys right away if they hadn't taken so much food. Cook was beside herself when she discovered a whole ham missing. That's when I started looking for Danny. The boy's favorite food was ham."

The former matron closed her eyes for a second, as if remembering something less than pleasant about Daniel Klein and his fondness for ham. "You didn't come here to listen to an old woman reminisce. Why were you looking for Danny?"

There was no point in lying. "I have reason to believe he was involved in some robberies." And some killings, although Jackson would not burden Miss Millie with that piece of information.

Apparently unsurprised, she inclined her head in a regal nod. "I can see that happening. As I told you before, I was afraid he and the others would come to a bad end. And robbery? Definitely. I can still remember him telling the Michener brothers they were well named—Will and Rob. I recall Danny laughing as he called out, 'Will Rob, Will Rob.'"

It seemed they had done just that. Jackson gave a silent prayer of thanks for Miss Millie's reminiscences. He'd been correct in thinking that he'd find some answers here, and he had. Thanks to her, he knew the names of two of the three remaining Gang members.

"I've been tracking a group called the Gang of Four," he told Miss Millie. "They specialize in robbing wealthy travelers and

Army payrolls. I know that Daniel was one of them, because I almost caught them one night. His bandanna slipped enough that I could make the sketch I showed you."

He'd done that while he waited for the doctor to patch up Leander as best he could. "I didn't see the others' faces, but from what you've said, I think it's likely that the Micheners were his partners."

Jackson paused in case Miss Millie had any questions. When she didn't speak, he continued. "The fourth member of the Gang is a woman. It might have been someone they met later, but I wondered whether any of the girls left the orphanage around the same time."

Miss Millie pursed her lips. "I don't believe so." She paused, then nodded. "No, that's not right. There was one, but I can't believe there's any connection. Charity James was a model child. She was never in trouble, and I never saw her with those boys."

If that was true, it was unlikely she was part of the Gang, but Jackson needed to be certain. "Do you remember where Charity went when she left the orphanage?"

Once again Miss Millie closed her eyes for a second. "As I recall," she said when she opened them, "she found a position with a couple in Comfort. I doubt she's still there, but someone might remember her."

But no one did. When Jackson reached the small town late that day, he discovered that not only had no one ever heard of Charity James, but no strangers had come to Comfort in '65.

Another dead end.

18

Thea settled into the chair and picked up the book she'd started reading the day before, hoping it would distract her. Perhaps she should have gone with Aimee when she took Stuart for his evening walk, but there was only one person she wanted to see today, and he wasn't in Cimarron Creek.

Thea wished she knew where Jackson had gone and when he would return, and so she sat here, wondering when the handsome Ranger would ride back into town and what he'd say when he heard what she'd learned today. Although it had assured her that his absence was only temporary, Jackson's note had given no details.

Like so many men, he was sparing with his words. The single sheet of paper said very little, and yet she kept it, because it was the first and only piece of written communication that she had from Jackson. That was silly. Thea knew that, but she also knew she was not ready to throw it away.

As she had feared, the book did not hold her attention. She had been staring at the same page for minutes, unable to recall a single word. Instead, her mind whirled with memories of what had happened at the Harris ranch. Mrs. Harris's shock, her own shock, Helen's story, Mrs. Harris's lack of concern for Helen's son—the pictures rotated through Thea's brain, overlapping and changing like the colors in a kaleidoscope.

At times, she felt as if everything had changed today, as if the ground had shifted beneath her feet, but at other times, it seemed that nothing was different. Oh, how she wished Jackson were here to help her make sense of what she'd learned. When she'd stopped at the sheriff's office to tell Travis that Stuart's mother had a name, she'd found it locked tight.

"He's at the county seat, testifying against the cattle rustlers he and Edgar caught," Lydia had explained. "Do you want to leave a message?" But Thea did not. Her news could wait until tomorrow, and maybe by then Jackson would have returned.

She looked around the parlor and wondered if she'd made a mistake in not accompanying Aimee. There was no way of knowing how much longer Stuart, the boy she'd come to love like a son, would be allowed to remain in Cimarron Creek. He now had a family, people with legal ties to him. Thea didn't know what the law said and whether, once Travis learned about Stuart's connection to the Harrises, he'd be forced to give them custody of the boy, even if they were not eager to accept him.

Though Thea's instincts told her that was not the best alternative for Stuart, she had to acknowledge that she might be wrong. It could be that shock over Helen's death had colored Mrs. Harris's reaction. She hadn't had a chance to meet Stuart, to hold him in her arms.

Once the Harrises saw Stuart, they might love him as much as Thea did. She doubted anyone could love him more, but if the Harrises adopted him, Stuart would grow up in a family with two parents. That was something Thea could not offer him.

She rose and walked to the window, hoping the simple act of moving would help settle her thoughts. The street was empty, the evening peaceful, but Thea's brain continued to whirl.

Questions about Stuart's future troubled her; so did what she'd learned of Helen Bradford's past. Though she'd never met her, Thea felt a connection to the woman whose face and story had such an uncanny resemblance to her own. There were many similarities, but there were also differences. They'd both lost husbands, although Helen's had died of natural causes. They'd both given birth to sons at almost the same time, but Helen's son had lived. They'd both left their homes, planning to settle in or near Cimarron Creek. Thea had arrived safely; Helen had not. And that brought Thea to the question with no answer: Why had Helen Bradford been killed?

Jackson might know. Perhaps he'd learned something about Helen Bradford, and that was why he'd left Cimarron Creek. If only he'd return.

As she looked out the window for what felt like the hundredth time, Thea let out an exasperated sigh. Pacing was accomplishing nothing. She might as well sit down instead of wearing a track in the carpet. Maybe this time she'd be able to focus on the book. Everyone had told her that *Jane Eyre* was such a compelling story that they could not put it down.

But instead of worrying about what would happen to Jane and Mr. Rochester, Thea found herself thinking about two very different men. It wasn't merely appearance that distinguished Jackson from Daniel.

She frowned at the realization that although she had loved Daniel, she had never had the same sense of certainty that she felt about Jackson. Wasn't that odd? Daniel had been her husband, while Jackson was . . . Thea didn't know how to finish the sentence.

Sighing, she closed the book. There was no point in continuing the charade of reading when her mind refused to concentrate on it. She needed to find something else to occupy her. She rose and looked around, trying to think of something that might settle her turbulent thoughts. Now might be the time to bake a loaf of bread. Sarah had once told her that kneading dough was a good way to release frustrations, and Thea had more than her share of frustrations tonight.

She was on the way to the kitchen when she heard a knock on the front door. Though she tried to steel herself for disappointment, she couldn't help hoping it was Jackson. She flung the door open and smiled, her heart beginning to pound with excitement at the sight of the Ranger. His clothing was dusty and his face bore lines of fatigue, but Thea was certain she'd never seen anything more wonderful.

"You're back!" It might be an unconventional greeting, but Thea couldn't help it. She had prayed for Jackson's return, and her prayers had been answered.

His lips curved into one of those smiles that lingered in her memory long after he'd gone. "I'm glad to be back. I've got so much to tell you."

"And I've got things to tell you too. But first . . ." Thea studied him, wondering if his fatigue was heightened by hunger. "Have you eaten supper? I have some leftover ham and could make you a sandwich if you don't mind eating on the porch." She wouldn't risk the townspeople's gossip by inviting him inside.

"Ham?" Jackson's eyes narrowed for an instant, leaving Thea wondering what about the food concerned him. A second later, he nodded. "That sounds good, if it's not too much trouble for you."

"No trouble at all." Less than five minutes later, she returned to the porch carrying a tray laden with two sandwiches, a piece of cake, and two mugs of coffee. "We'll talk after you've eaten," she said and picked up one of the mugs.

As Jackson took the chair opposite her and leaned forward to reach for a sandwich, a piece of paper fell from his pocket, fluttering to the ground.

"I've got it." Thea grabbed the paper before the evening breeze could whisk it away. She started to hand it back to Jackson but stopped, riveted by what she saw.

"Where did you get this?" This was not a letter but a sketch. More than that, it was an unmistakable likeness. Though the expression was one she'd never seen, hostile and fierce, there was no question that the man staring at her from the piece of paper was her husband. "Where did you get this?" she asked again.

Maybe it wasn't Daniel. Maybe there was someone who resembled him as much as Helen did her. But even as the possibility flitted through her brain, Thea knew it was unlikely.

Jackson laid the sandwich back on the plate. "I drew it."

Thea blinked in confusion. "I don't understand." Surely if Jackson had met Daniel, he would have told her before this. "When did you see Daniel?"

Jackson's lips thinned, and he took a deep breath before responding, his reluctance to answer the question obvious. "It was the night Micah was killed. I told you one of the robbers' bandannas slipped and I saw his face." He pointed at the drawing. "This was the man I saw."

It was probably foolish to be walking this way. Just because Patience had said she and Nate were going to be in town this evening to bring some goats' milk to Reverend Dunn didn't mean they'd be strolling down Main Street as they had the day she met Nate. Most likely they'd already come and gone.

But as she pushed the buggy and tried to pretend there was no special reason she'd chosen this route, Aimee knew she was being silly, just as she'd been silly to try to impress Nate with a fancy hairstyle and a pretty dress on Sunday. She was acting like a lovelorn schoolgirl hoping for another glimpse of the boy who'd caught her eye. The problem was, Nate wasn't a boy and she was no longer a schoolgirl. She ought to be behaving like an adult.

"Good evening, Miss Jarre." Widow Jenkins crossed the street and peered into the buggy. While she might pretend that she'd come to greet Aimee, Aimee knew better. The widow was as fascinated by Stuart as Aimee was by Nate.

"It's good that you bring Stuart outside most days. Others might disagree, but I believe fresh air is important for a child." She chatted for a few minutes, her attention clearly focused on the baby inside the buggy. When Stuart responded to her coos with a blink of his eyes, the widow grinned. "He recognizes me."

How sad it was that Stuart paid more attention to Widow Jenkins than Nate did to Aimee. There had been times when she'd caught him looking at her with what, if she were fanciful, she would have called yearning, but he never acted on it, if indeed it was yearning. Instead, he offered her the briefest of greetings when he entered the apothecary.

Just as frustrating, when she tried to engage him in conversation, asking about his farm and his goats, Nate's answers were stilted. If she hadn't known better, she would have thought he was speaking a foreign language, searching for the correct word. Aimee almost laughed at the irony. Though she was the one conversing in something other than her native language, she was not tongue-tied.

"Don't forget that this little one is welcome at my house anytime you need someone to care for him," the widow said as she bade Aimee farewell. "He reminds me of my Ambrose when he was that age." Ambrose, Aimee had learned, had lost his life during what Thea called the War Between the States.

As Widow Jenkins turned to resume her walk northward, Aimee continued south on Main, pausing to admire the new clothing in the dressmaker's window. She should probably take Stuart back now, but that would be admitting defeat. When she reached the end of Main, she'd cross over to Cedar and return home that way. And if she happened to glance down Mesquite toward Warner's home, well . . . no one would know that she was hoping Nate was visiting his friend and that he would be outside.

Silly! Aimee shook her head as she scolded herself. This was more of that schoolgirl behavior she'd forsworn.

As she approached Oak Street, Aimee heard the unmistakable sound of Patience's laughter and the deep timbre of a man's voice coming from the schoolyard. She'd found them! The route she'd chosen had been the right one. Aimee quickened her pace, smiling at both the prospect of seeing Nate and the fact that Stuart appeared to be enjoying the faster ride, then stopped abruptly as she neared the schoolhouse.

Patience was with a man, but it wasn't her cousin. The couple—that was the only way to describe the two who stood much closer than casual acquaintances—were next to the swing, gazing at each other. Patience had her face tilted toward the man, as if waiting for something, while he tipped his head to one side. As Warner lifted his hand to touch Patience's cheek, Aimee turned, blinking away her tears.

It was a tender scene, not a reason for tears. Aimee shook her head, wishing that the sight of her friends didn't remind her of what was lacking in her life. She was happy for Patience and Warner. This was what she'd hoped for, what she'd prayed for, but that didn't assuage the emptiness inside her, the longing to be loved. She brushed the errant tear from her cheek and hurried down Oak Street. The sooner she reached home, the better.

You didn't come here to find a husband, Aimee reminded herself. *You came to America to find your mother. When Grace returns, you'll have your answers. And maybe, just maybe, her love will fill the emptiness.*

Thea could hardly breathe. Her heart was beating at twice its normal pace, her hands were clammy, and she knew her legs would not support her if she tried to rise. She stared at Jackson, hoping beyond hope that he'd deny what he'd just said. But he did not.

"You think my husband was an outlaw?" The words came out in short bursts. "One of the Gang of Four?" It couldn't be true, and yet the likeness was excellent. Other than the expression, Jackson's sketch had captured the image of the man Thea had married.

"I do."

She shuddered, then wrapped her arms around herself to try to ease her trembling. Daniel was a robber. The thought reverberated through her brain, causing her to shudder again. A robber. Maybe worse. He might have been the bandit who killed Jackson's brother and wounded his partner. Her husband had been a true desperado, and she had had no inkling.

Thea's trembling intensified as she remembered the day she'd met Jackson and the way he'd looked at her. At the time, she'd thought he suspected her of something, but she'd quickly dismissed that as improbable. Now . . .

"You believed I was one of them. That's why you came to Cimarron Creek, isn't it?"

He took a swig of coffee before he responded. "Yes," he admitted, his reluctance obvious, "but the moment I saw you, I knew you weren't part of the Gang. They were all tall, including the woman."

Relief and anger warred within Thea, and anger won the round. "I can't believe you didn't tell me this before." She'd known Jackson for more than three weeks, and yet he hadn't told her the truth about her husband.

Jackson nodded, accepting her anger. "I should have told you. I came close on several occasions, but it never seemed like the right time. I knew it would hurt you, and you'd already suffered so much loss that I wanted you to have a bit longer to recover." There was no questioning his sincerity. As misguided as he may have been, Jackson had been thinking of her.

"I'm not sure I'll ever recover from this." Thea stared across the street at Lydia's home, remembering all the secrets that house had held. Now it seemed that hers did too. "I had no idea what kind of man my husband was. I was shocked that he'd broken his marriage vows, but even knowing that, I would never have imagined that he was a criminal. What does that say about me?"

Thea shuddered again as she raised her eyes to meet Jackson's. Only a coward would continue staring into the distance, and Thea was not a coward. She owed Jackson the courtesy of a direct look. To her surprise, instead of the pity she'd expected, she saw warmth. He didn't pity or condemn her. Instead, it seemed he was offering compassion.

"It says you're an honest, trusting woman who sees only the best in others."

"But how could I have been so wrong?" Thea turned away again, feeling unworthy of the confidence Jackson had placed in her. "Sarah told me I was being too hasty. She thought I should wait longer before I married Daniel, but I wouldn't listen. What a fool I was! Everything he told me was lies."

Jackson reached across the table and laid his hand on Thea's. It was warm and comforting, more than she deserved.

"I never spoke to Daniel, so I can't be sure of this, but I imagine he truly loved you. That's the only reason he would have settled in one place."

"What do you mean?"

"From what we can tell, the Gang traveled between heists, looking for new targets but never staying anywhere too long. The fact that Daniel married you and planned to raise a family in Ladreville says that something changed."

"I still can't believe it." A mirthless laugh escaped from Thea's lips. "If I could believe that he broke his marriage vows, why can't I accept the proof that he was a thief? Why do I want to believe that he was what he claimed to be, nothing more than a traveling salesman who wanted to find a permanent home?"

For a moment, the only sounds were the soft soughing of the breeze and the chirping of a bird settling into its nest. Then Jackson spoke. "I suspect he was very good at showing you only what he wanted you to see. Some people are like that—they change depending on the circumstances."

"Like those lizards that change color to blend into their surroundings." Thea had read about them.

"Exactly." As if he sensed that she was becoming calmer, Jackson lifted his hand from hers and reached for his sandwich. "I need to ask you a few questions," he said when he'd swallowed a bite. "Did Daniel ever talk about two men named Will and Rob?"

Thea shook her head.

"What about a woman named Charity?"

She shook her head again. "Who are those people?"

"I learned about them when I spoke to the matron of the orphanage." Jackson took another bite, his hunger seeming to outweigh his need for answers.

"Is that where you went, to the orphanage where Daniel grew up?"

"Yes. I'll tell you more about that later, but what's important is that those people—Will, Rob, and Charity—might be the other members of the Gang. I believe Daniel was the leader." As Thea started to protest, Jackson continued. "It would explain why there have been no heists since he was killed, if he was the one who planned everything."

Thea drained her cup of coffee and placed it carefully back on the tray. "I can't picture Daniel as a leader. He never seemed like one to me, but what do I know? He obviously fooled me."

She pushed the piece of cake toward Jackson, silently urging him to eat it. When he'd taken his first bite, she spoke again. "Did you learn anything else at the orphanage?"

He nodded. "His name wasn't Michener. It was Klein. Daniel Klein."

19

Poor Thea. Jackson tried not to stare at the woman on the opposite side of the small table, knowing that would only deepen her distress. Instead, he shot brief glances in her direction. Though he wished there were something he could do to help her, he was the last person she'd want to comfort her when he'd been the one to deliver the news. She sat there, her face almost as pale as buttermilk, those brown eyes that often twinkled with amusement now filled with anguish.

What must it be like to know that your marriage had been based on lies? Jackson doubted he'd ever forget Thea's expression when he had told her that even the name she bore was false. Horror, disbelief, and sorrow had flitted across her face as he'd shattered the few illusions she'd still held about her husband. Now she appeared almost paralyzed, unable even to speak.

It was probably only a few seconds, but it felt like an eternity before she shook her head slightly, perhaps trying to deny the reality of his revelations. "I'm sorry, Jackson. I can't—" Thea lurched to her feet, her normal grace absent as she rushed into the house without another word.

Belatedly, Jackson rose. He had no idea what she'd meant to say and probably never would. Right now, Thea was like a wounded animal seeking its lair, her instincts telling her to put as much distance between them as she could. For, though he was only the messenger, Jackson had been the one who'd inflicted the wounds. While he wished it were otherwise, there was nothing more he could do here today.

He descended the steps and stood in the street, his thoughts whirling like autumn leaves before a storm. The fastest way back to Warner's was down Cedar, but Jackson needed time to ponder his next move before he was forced into ordinary conversation. His decision made, he turned right and headed for Main Street. A second later, a man barreled around the corner.

"Did you see her?"

Jackson tried not to grimace at the enthusiasm in Nate's voice. There were times when the man reminded him of an exuberant puppy, and while that could be amusing, tonight it was simply annoying.

"Yes," he admitted. "She just went inside."

Nate slapped his head in dismay. "That's the way my day's been. I'm always too late." He stared at the empty porch, not bothering to hide his longing. "I had hoped to catch her while she was out walking, but Pastor Dunn talked longer than normal, and then Widow Jenkins stopped to tell me what a wonderful woman she was." Nate's lips curled in disgust. "I know that. It's just my luck that I finally got up the courage to talk to her, and then I'm too late."

If circumstances had been different, Jackson might have felt sympathy for Nate. One thing was certain: while she may have questioned the depth of her husband's feelings, Thea wouldn't have to wonder whether this man loved her. Nate made no attempt to hide his feelings, and Jackson's instincts told him they were sincere.

Nate was an honest man, and unless Jackson was sadly mistaken, he would never betray Thea. Unlike Jackson's, Nate's future was secure; his past was not filled with regret. Even the matchmakers couldn't find a man better suited for Thea.

She deserved a man like Nate, but tonight was not the night for him to declare himself. Jackson was hardly an expert on the female of the species, but even he knew that a woman who'd sustained the blows Thea had would not be in the mood for a suitor.

"You could knock on the door," Jackson pointed out as Nate continued to gaze at the house, "but I wouldn't suggest doing that tonight. Thea's had a worse day than you."

Nate's head snapped back, and he stared at Jackson as if he'd suddenly lost his mind. "Thea? Why would I want to see her? I was looking for Aimee."

Lies. They were all lies. Thea stared at the wall, her eyes focusing on the almost imperceptible gap between two strips of wallpaper. It was easier to think about the room's tiny imperfections than the grand deceptions of her life with Daniel. The man who'd wooed and won her heart was an outlaw, possibly a murderer, and had even lied about his name.

Daniel Klein. That meant that she was Thea Klein, not Thea Michener. Thea shook her head. No! That wasn't true. Michener was the name on her marriage certificate, and Thea Michener was the name she'd carry unless she . . .

She rose to gaze out the window. How could she even think about marrying again when her first marriage had been such a disaster? And how could she face Jackson again, knowing that the man whose name she bore might have been the one who killed his brother?

"What's wrong?" Aimee turned her attention to her friend and away from the bacon she was frying. Though she'd hoped that Thea's normally even disposition would have been restored, that did not appear to be the case.

Thea had been in her room when Aimee had returned home

last night and had refused to emerge, claiming she was coming down with something and didn't want Stuart to catch it. Though Aimee had pretended to believe her, the thickened voice told her Thea had been crying. On another day, Aimee might have tried to coax her out of the room and encourage her to talk about whatever was bothering her, but her own mood had been so dismal that she hadn't even tried. Now, though, she could not ignore the shadows under Thea's eyes nor the pain reflecting from them.

"It's nothing I want to talk about." Thea busied herself pulling plates from the cupboard.

"Are you certain? You're the one who encouraged me to talk when I had problems, and you were right. It helped."

Thea shook her head. "Some things are too awful to put into words." She glanced at the clock and pursed her lips. "Jackson's back, but I don't know whether he's going to come for Stuart today. Would you take him to Widow Jenkins? I promised Mrs. Coulter I'd call on her first thing this morning before she and her husband leave for Austin."

"*Naturellement*. Of course." Aimee corrected herself, reflecting that it was a measure of how upset she was that the French word had slipped out. Between her own problems and Thea's, today was not beginning well.

Aimee. Aimee—not Thea—was Nate's princess, the girl of his dreams, the woman he wanted to marry. It had been more than twelve hours since Nate had stared at him as if he had bats in his belfry when he'd talked about Thea, and Jackson was still grinning. He'd been so shocked at first that his jaw had dropped, but then he'd grinned at his own foolishness.

Thinking back, he realized that Nate had never mentioned his lady love's name; it was Jackson who had assumed that Thea was the one who'd caught the goat farmer's eye. A valid assumption, at least from Jackson's perspective. While Aimee was a nice enough girl, she couldn't compare to Thea. No one could. But Nate didn't see that, and Jackson couldn't be happier.

He still hadn't caught the Gang. He still didn't know who Stuart's mother was and why she'd been killed. He still didn't have a firm plan for the future. But right now, none of that mattered. What mattered was that Nate had no intention of courting Thea. And that made Jackson a happy man.

"God was looking out for me when he sent you to Cimarron Creek."

Aimee looked up at Warner, not certain what had precipitated his comment. He'd seemed more cheerful than normal today, a fact that Aimee attributed to his having spent time with Patience yesterday. Though he hadn't mentioned Patience's name, he'd worn a satisfied smile all day. It could have been because they'd had a busy morning, but Aimee doubted that.

Now that the store was empty, Warner was leaning on the counter, looking at her, his expression as enigmatic as his comment. While she believed that God had led her to Cimarron Creek, she hadn't realized that Warner felt the same way.

"You mean because people like the way I arrange the cabinets?" Aimee had stayed after closing hours on three different nights to remove all the bottles from the glass-fronted cabinets and replace them in what she believed to be a more pleasing order. Since then, sales of those items had increased dramatically. As she'd expected, women were drawn to the colorful displays and rarely left the store without at least one bottle, whether or not they truly needed its contents.

Warner chuckled as he shrugged. "That's part of it. You have an artistic eye, and I don't."

"But you know how to blend medicines. I'm a failure with your mortar and pestle." Aimee's one attempt at grinding a tablet into powder had ended with dust everywhere but where it was supposed to be.

"Exactly. We complement each other. God knew that I needed a helper, and he sent the perfect one."

As a blush warmed her cheeks, Aimee made a deep curtsy. "Thank you, kind sir. Your praise overwhelms me." It was also exactly what she needed. Though there was nothing romantic between her and Warner, she knew that being able to work with him was another of God's gifts.

She enjoyed the work. More than that, she enjoyed being with Warner. He was right: they did complement each other. More times than she could count, they would finish each other's sentences, then laugh at the fact that they were so in tune. Other times, they'd disagree, neither willing to back down until, almost as if they'd choreographed the moment, they'd both begin to apologize at the same time.

Aimee couldn't explain it. All she knew was that her feelings for Warner were unlike those she had for anyone else, and they made her time at the apothecary more enjoyable than she'd believed possible.

She was still basking in the glow of Warner's praise when Lydia entered the shop, her expression radiating excitement.

"The mail just arrived," Lydia said, brandishing an envelope. "It's a letter from Catherine." She paused and laid a hand on her abdomen, as if to assure the baby that she was done rushing. "I couldn't wait to share it with you."

Warner tipped his head toward the back room, which boasted two chairs. "You'd better sit down. I don't want you delivering that baby here." Winking at Aimee, he added, "Take your time. If a customer comes in, I can handle it. Lydia needs to rest."

Aimee shared Warner's concern. The mother-to-be did look flushed. When they were both seated, Lydia handed Aimee the envelope with familiar French stamps. "You haven't opened it," Aimee said, surprise tingeing her words.

"I thought we could read it together. My guess is that it's about you, because Catherine should have received my letter telling her you're here. Why don't you open it? This baby is having a kicking match right now, and that's making it hard for me to talk."

Though she knew the letter would probably contain good news, Aimee felt apprehensive as she slit the envelope and withdrew a single sheet of paper. Would her mother have included a message for her? What would she say? There was only one way to know.

Dear Lydia,

France is beautiful, what I've seen of it, that is. When we disembarked at Le Havre, both Austin and I could see how anxious Grace was, so we changed our plans. Instead of spending two weeks in Paris, we traveled directly to Maillochauds. We wanted Grace to be reunited with her daughter as quickly as possible.

Lydia frowned. "They didn't get my letter."

"It appears not." That meant there would be no note from Grace. Aimee bit back her disappointment and returned to Catherine's missive.

I wish you could have seen how excited Grace was as we approached the small town where the Jarres lived. The only way I can describe it is to say she was glowing with happiness. Unfortunately, her happiness was short-lived. We soon learned that Mr. and Mrs. Jarre had died and that Aimee had left. No one knew where she'd gone.

Oh, Lydia, my heart broke for Grace. Her hopes were crushed, and so was her spirit.

Aimee closed her eyes, her heart aching as she pictured her mother's distress. She knew she would never forget how devastated she had been when she'd arrived in Ladreville only to learn that no one knew where Grace was. The unexpected and unwelcome news had left her on the verge of collapse. It had been hours later when the Russells had ventured the possibility that someone in Cimarron Creek might have the answers Aimee sought, renewing her hope.

Grace had no leads, and that was Aimee's fault. When she'd left France, she hadn't considered that someone might search for her, and so she hadn't told anyone that she was heading for America. If only she had! If only she'd mentioned Ladreville, Texas. But she hadn't, and nothing was gained by regretting what she hadn't done.

Resolutely, she continued reading.

Austin and I decided the best thing was to return to Cimarron Creek immediately. Grace protested, of course, reminding me of how long I'd dreamt of walking along the banks of the Seine, but I knew I wouldn't enjoy Paris when she was suffering. I'm not sure how long it will take us to find passage on a ship, but we're heading back to Le Havre. We'll be home as soon as we can.

Tears glistened in Lydia's eyes. "If only they'd gone to Paris, Grace would have been spared this agony."

Aimee couldn't let her friend shoulder the blame. "You did the best you could. The fault is mine. I should have told someone what I planned to do, but I didn't."

Lydia's expression said she wasn't relinquishing her regrets. "I could have sent a letter to Maillochauds as well as Paris."

Laying her hand on Lydia's, Aimee waited until Lydia met her gaze before she said, "But we didn't do those things, and we can't change that."

Lydia nodded. "The only good thing I can say is that they'll be back sooner than we expected. Before you know it, you'll meet your mother."

And then her questions would be answered.

20

Thea smoothed the fingers of her gloves, then checked her reflection in the small mirror by the front door of the Coulters' house. Though her insides were still knotted from the revelation that nothing she believed about Daniel, including his name, was true, that was no reason to be less than well-groomed when she stepped outside. Somehow, she'd managed to retain her composure when she met her new patient, but now she wondered whether her legs would support her. Of course they would. She had a job to do, and she would do it.

She bade Mr. and Mrs. Coulter good-bye, keeping her head high as she walked home. As she'd paced the floor last night, she'd realized there was no reason to believe Jackson blamed her for what Daniel might have done. He'd been nothing but kind, trying to protect her from the unpleasant news. She was the one who'd overreacted, believing that he would view her as tainted by her husband's crimes. Deep in her heart, she knew Jackson was a fair man, and though his brother's death weighed heavily on him, he would not condemn her for it.

It was time they talked. Once she'd dropped off her bag, Thea would find him and tell him what she'd learned about Stuart's mother. Then perhaps she'd be able to relax.

She was heading south on Cedar toward Warner's house

when she saw Jackson approaching. His gait was steady, and there was nothing in his demeanor to suggest she'd been mistaken about his reaction to Daniel's crimes.

"How are you?" Jackson asked once he was within speaking distance. The furrow between his eyes underscored the concern in his voice.

"All right, I guess." Thea wouldn't tell him that she'd slept only a few minutes at a time last night, her rest disturbed by dreams of Daniel wearing a mask, shooting a boy that she knew instinctively was Jackson's brother, then grinning as if killing someone was nothing more than a lark. "I feel as if my world was turned upside down."

Jackson nodded as he crooked his arm and placed her hand on it. "That's understandable. I'm sorry I had to be the one to tell you."

"You were simply doing your job." Thea had told herself that dozens of times during the sleepless hours, reminding herself that it would have been even more painful to have learned the truth from someone else.

He shook his head. "Hurting innocent people is never part of my job, but you needed to know what I'd learned."

Thea's heart lightened at his use of the word *innocent*, because it confirmed her belief that Jackson did not blame her. The second half of his sentence gave her the introduction she'd sought. "And you need to know what I learned while you were gone."

Jackson lifted one eyebrow as if puzzled, then nodded. "That's right. You said you had something to tell me last night, but you never had the chance." He gave her a long, appraising look. "Do you need to sit down while you tell me, or should we walk?"

Though it had been only a few minutes since Thea had felt as if her legs had turned to rubber, being with Jackson had revived her. "Let's walk. I heard there's a path along the creek, but I haven't explored it yet."

They walked slowly up Cedar, leaving her bag at the house, then continued past the end of the street until they reached the creek. Calling it a path, Thea soon realized, was an exaggeration, but there was a faintly visible track that paralleled the water.

"Will you be all right here?" Jackson glanced at her shoes.

Thea nodded. "They're sturdier than you might think." And since there'd been no recent rain, she did not have to contend with mud.

They walked for a few minutes, each step taking them farther from the town and, though Thea hadn't expected it, from her worries. "It's so peaceful here," she said, gesturing toward the gently flowing creek. "It's hard to believe there are murderers and thieves in the world when I'm in a place like this."

Jackson nodded as if he understood the respite she'd found. "Everyone needs a special place, a sanctuary. Did you have one in Ladreville?"

Thea smiled, remembering. "It was a small garden. Sarah used to call it her secret garden. I'd go there whenever I was sad, and it never failed to make me feel better. What about you?" The way Jackson had spoken of a sanctuary made her believe he'd had one of his own.

"We have an old oak tree on the ranch. I used to climb it and pretend I was in a different world."

Thea gazed at the water, watching as a small fish tried to fight the current before it decided to change direction and be carried downstream. Was that the right approach, letting stronger forces determine your path? Thea wasn't certain. What she knew, though, was that it was time to tell Jackson what she'd learned.

"I wonder if Helen had a special place."

"Helen?"

"Stuart's mother. That's what I needed to tell you. I learned who she was and why she was traveling to Cimarron Creek."

As quickly as she could, Thea recounted what Ethel Harris had told her.

Jackson listened intently, his face darkening. "And she lived near Leakey."

"That's what Mrs. Harris said."

"That explains why Travis's telegrams and my inquiries didn't reveal anything. Neither of us thought she would have come from that direction. I found both Helen and Stuart east of here. Leakey's southwest."

"Then why were Helen and Stuart on the other road?"

When a bird squawked its displeasure at having humans disturb its habitat, Jackson took a breath and exhaled slowly. "There's only one possible explanation: their abductors found them before they reached Cimarron Creek and the Harris ranch and took them somewhere else to question Helen."

The way Jackson said "question" told Thea that Helen had endured more than questioning. "Where were they taken?"

Jackson shook his head. "I'm not sure it matters. I doubt we'd find any answers there, but there may be some in Leakey. I'll go there next week to see what I can learn."

Thea had expected him to do that. What she hadn't expected was that he'd delay his departure. Perhaps he was tired of traveling. Perhaps he knew that a few days would make no difference. Whatever the reason, she was glad that Jackson would be in Cimarron Creek a bit longer.

She still needed to tell him about Ethel Harris's apparent reluctance to have anything to do with Stuart, but that could wait. Now that Jackson knew Stuart's mother's identity, he would tell Travis, and they'd initiate the necessary legalities. In the meantime, Stuart would stay with her.

Thea looked up at Jackson, knowing he would do what was best for the boy. Perhaps, despite what Ethel Harris had said, someone in Leakey knew of another family member. If not . . . Thea didn't want to complete the sentence.

"Could you make a sketch of Helen's house when you find it?" she asked.

"Certainly, but why?"

Though the thought had just popped into her mind, it felt right. "I think Stuart should have a connection to where he was born. He may never want to visit it, but he should know what his first home looked like."

Jackson was silent for a moment. When he spoke, his question surprised her. "You've grown to love him, haven't you?"

"Yes." Thea wouldn't lie, but she couldn't stop herself from adding, "That's part of the problem."

21

"I'm not in the mood for a square dance." Aimee's frown matched her words, not the lace collar and cuffs she'd added to her frock to make it more festive. "I keep thinking about Grace and how awful it must have been for her when she learned I'd left Maillochauds and she had no idea where I was."

Thea continued braiding Aimee's hair. Though her friend had protested attending tonight's event, she had agreed to let Thea try a new hairstyle, one that would be better suited for dancing than her usual style or the one she'd worn to church on Sunday. "She'll be here in a few weeks—maybe even by the end of the month."

The prospect did not appear to cheer Aimee. "I'm worried about her. It's odd, Thea. When I first learned that she had given me up for adoption, I was angry. I almost hated her. Now all I feel is sorrow that she's hit another . . ." She paused, searching for the correct word. "What is it you call them? Dead somethings."

"Dead ends." Thea coiled the braid into a knot at the base of Aimee's head, then stepped back to admire the effect. "I'm glad your anger has faded." She wished hers would. She had believed she had gotten beyond her anger over the perfumed shirts, and she had. Even her visits to Belinda Allen no longer triggered unhappy thoughts. But the revelation that so many things she had believed about Daniel were false had set off an avalanche of destructive emotions.

How could he have robbed and killed people? How could he have lied to her by claiming that he was going to San Antonio to buy supplies when he was probably holding up a stagecoach? And why hadn't he told her his real name?

The questions whirled through her, eroding the hard-won peace she'd begun to find in Cimarron Creek. The truth was, Thea wasn't certain whether she was angrier at Daniel for the deception or at herself for being so gullible. All she knew was that anger churned her stomach and woke her in the middle of the night.

There was nothing to be gained by dwelling on that now. Her friend needed encouragement.

"It's wonderful that you'll be able to meet your mother." Thea wouldn't lament that that was something neither she nor Stuart could do. While Aimee's life had not been easy, at least she would have one parent.

Aimee rose from the dressing table stool and studied her reflection in the cheval mirror. "I like this look," she admitted. "It makes me seem older."

While someone twice her age wouldn't appreciate that, Thea had thought that Aimee might gain confidence from appearing more mature.

"I hope Grace will tell me about my father." Aimee's distraction had lasted only a few seconds.

"It won't be a happy story," Thea cautioned her. The reasons a woman had a child out of wedlock were not pleasant ones. Admittedly, some were worse than others, but none would fill Aimee with joy.

"I know that, but I don't want to live with secrets, and I don't want to go to this dance."

The emphasis Aimee put on the last part of her sentence made Thea suspect that her reluctance was fueled by more than concern about her mother. Grace was a convenient excuse for Aimee to avoid a gathering where she was sure to encounter Nate.

"You can try staying home, but you know Patience will come knocking on the door and will insist you go with her."

At Patience's instigation, Rachel had arranged a square dance to be held in the town's park. Though she claimed it was to celebrate the end of summer—not that summer had yet ended—Thea suspected it was part of Rachel's matchmaking.

Lydia had told her that Rachel was determined to find Nate a bride this year. According to Lydia, Rachel had begun to despair of her brother settling down and had decided to take matters into her own hands, but Lydia had no idea which women Rachel had identified as potential candidates. Thea only hoped that Rachel's matchmaking did not interfere with what she believed was Nate's genuine attraction to Aimee.

"We don't have to stay too long," she told Aimee as she straightened one of the ruffles on her skirt. "An hour or so should be enough."

When she'd proposed the dance to Thea, Rachel had pointed out that it would be another opportunity to meet potential patients and had urged her to make an appearance, even if she did not remain for the whole evening. According to Rachel, families who rarely got into town were coming for the dance and staying for church services tomorrow. Some of the women would be eager to meet Cimarron Creek's new midwife.

Though she looked as if she wanted to protest, Aimee nodded. "You're right. We should go for a short time. I don't want to waste the hours I spent practicing."

When Patience had learned that Aimee had never seen a square dance, much less performed the steps, she'd insisted on giving her a lesson. That evening, Aimee had been embarrassed by how awkward she'd felt and had wanted to practice with Thea until she was comfortable with the basic steps. While Thea doubted any of the men in Cimarron Creek would notice if she missed a step or two, Aimee wasn't convinced, which was why she'd continued to practice.

"Patience assured me I would not be a wallflower." Aimee wrinkled her nose. "How can there be any wallflowers when there are no walls?"

Relieved that Aimee had regained her sense of humor, Thea headed for the front door.

Though the dance had not yet begun, the park was crowded by the time she and Aimee reached it. Aimee appeared surprised by the number of strangers and, instead of joining Patience even though her friend beckoned her, she remained at Thea's side, once again the fearful woman who'd stepped off the stagecoach in Ladreville.

Thea kept a smile fixed on her face as they headed toward the center of the park, greeting acquaintances along the way. She told herself she wasn't searching for anyone in particular, but she couldn't deny the way her heart skipped a beat when she saw Jackson coming toward her. It would be wonderful to talk to him, even if only for a few minutes, and the fact that Nate was at his side meant that Aimee would have a companion, if they could break through Nate's discomfort around her.

"Good evening, ladies," Jackson said when he reached them. His gaze moved from the top of Thea's head to her toes, the approval in the smile that lit his face making her grateful she had chosen a new dress for tonight. Dark blue was not a color she'd worn in Ladreville, but when she had seen it in the dressmaker's window, the gown had caught her eye. To Thea's delight, it had proven to be a flattering hue, and the dress itself needed only a few minor alterations.

Though both she and Aimee returned Jackson's greeting, Nate said nothing, the flush that colored his face making Thea wonder if he was ill.

Jackson clapped his friend on the shoulder. "It looks like a fine night for a dance, doesn't it, Nate?"

The goat farmer remained silent, although the perspiration that beaded his forehead and the way he continued to clear his throat left no doubt that he was nervous. "I want . . . um, that is . . . I would like . . . um, that's not right . . ."

Though the scent of mint that accompanied his words was pleasant, Thea found the long pauses painful and suspected that it was far worse for the man who was having such difficulty communicating. Since he'd had no trouble speaking on the few occasions when he'd met her in town, Thea knew that she was not the problem. Aimee had claimed that Nate was tongue-tied around her, but this was more than tongue-tied. The man appeared almost petrified.

"Just spit it out, Nate."

Thea heard Aimee gasp at Jackson's command, but she kept her eyes fixed on Nate. He'd glanced at Aimee, then turned his gaze to the ground, as if the words he wanted to say were carved on his boot tips.

At last Nate raised his eyes and stared at Aimee. "Would you dance with me, Miss Aimee?" he asked, the words coming out in a rush.

At last! Thea wanted to crow with relief, but she remained silent, waiting for her friend to respond.

Shock, then pleasure flitted across Aimee's face, and for a moment Thea feared that she had been stricken with the same silent malady that had afflicted Nate. Finally, Aimee spoke. "There's nothing I would like more."

As she took a step toward Nate and placed her hand on the crook of his elbow, he grinned, his face as radiant as if he'd been crowned the victor in a Roman chariot race.

"I can't remember when I've seen a man so nervous."

Thea nodded in response to Jackson's comment as she looked at the couple who were moving so slowly that she wondered if they'd reach the makeshift dance floor before the music began. "Aimee didn't want to come tonight, but I'm sure she's glad she's here now." Nate's head was bent toward hers, his expression that of a child on Christmas Day who'd been given the one thing he wanted most.

Jackson smiled. "I'm glad Nate's so happy. If he could just get over being nervous, I think he and Aimee would suit each other."

Though Thea had been thinking the same thing, she was surprised to hear Jackson say it. "Be careful, Jackson. You're starting to sound like a matchmaker."

"Me? Never!" He feigned horror. "No one in the company would believe that."

Thea was puzzled for a moment until she realized he was speaking about the company of Rangers. "You mean you can't be both a Ranger and a man? Surely some of the men have sweethearts or wives."

The subject appeared to make Jackson uncomfortable. He cleared his throat and looked around. "It sounds like the fiddlers are getting ready." There was the slightest of pauses before he said, "I would be honored if you'd be my partner." The wink he gave her surprised Thea. "That's how Travis told Nate and me we were supposed to ask a lady to dance."

Though she recognized the formal invitation, having heard it a dozen or more times, and knew how she should respond, Thea hesitated. "I wasn't planning to dance at all," she said softly.

"Why not?"

"It doesn't seem appropriate when I'm so recently widowed." While it was true that she no longer wore mourning clothes and that the town's former matriarch would have approved of her shedding her widow's weeds, Thea wasn't certain most residents would be so lenient about dancing. Society had firm ideas of what was acceptable behavior after a bereavement.

"Not dancing won't bring Daniel back."

Thea felt the blood drain from her face. Jackson was mistaken if he believed she wanted Daniel to be raised from the grave like Lazarus. While it was true that she had far too many unanswered questions and that if Daniel could miraculously return, she would demand answers, Thea did not want her husband back. She could forgive his infidelity, because that hurt only her, but she could not forgive him for the innocent people he'd robbed and killed.

Mourning Daniel was not the reason she was hesitant to dance. The only reason not to accept Jackson's invitation was to placate Cimarron Creek's more conservative residents.

The almost wistful expression she saw reflected from Jackson's eyes told Thea that he wanted to dance. More than that, he wanted to dance with her. Fears about propriety fled in the face of Jackson's request.

Making a deep curtsy, Thea gave Jackson the formal reply she'd been taught. "I'd be honored to be your partner."

The smile and the virtually imperceptible relaxing of his shoulders confirmed the rightness of her decision. As Aimee had done with Nate only a few minutes earlier, Thea placed her hand on Jackson's arm and walked toward the music. Moments later, they were dancing.

Thea had expected a pleasant interlude. What she hadn't expected was that dancing with Jackson kept her from thinking about the past. While they were following the caller's commands to bow, promenade, and allemande, all she thought about was how good it felt to be here at this moment in time with this man. It was without a doubt the most enjoyable experience she'd had since she'd arrived in Cimarron Creek.

Though the dance steps separated them frequently, each time they were reunited, Jackson's smile broadened, and the gleam in his eyes said more clearly than words that he was savoring every minute of the dance. So was Thea. Ladreville had had its share of dances, and she'd had her share of partners, but no one had made her feel as energized—as alive—as Jackson did. His crooked smile, his sparkling eyes, his dry comments attracted her with the force of a strong magnet.

When the set ended and Thea found herself breathless, she knew that the cause was being close to Jackson rather than the dance steps themselves.

As the caller announced the formation of a new set, Jackson turned toward Thea. "I don't know about you, but I could use some lemonade." He gestured toward the table where Lydia was serving lemonade, cookies, and candies from Cimarron Sweets, then bent his arm and placed Thea's hand on it. "I vote we get some."

"I second the motion." As the words registered, Thea clapped her free hand over her mouth. "That came out wrong, didn't it? I don't think you second votes." She laughed, as much from the sheer joy of being with Jackson as from her error.

He shrugged and continued walking toward the refreshment table. "Who cares? I know what you meant. You wanted to wet your whistle."

"I wouldn't have phrased it exactly that way."

"But you knew what I meant. That was my point."

Thea laughed again. It felt so good to be talking about silly things rather than worrying about why someone had killed Helen Bradford and what other criminal acts Daniel might have perpetrated. She was still laughing when she and Jackson reached the table.

"You look like you're having fun," Lydia said as they approached.

"I am," Thea agreed. "I'm glad Jackson convinced me to dance."

Lydia raised an eyebrow. "How did you do that? When I told her no one would mind, she wouldn't listen."

"He threatened to have Travis lock me in the jail." Thea gave Jackson a mischievous smile, daring him to contradict her.

"That's right, ma'am," he said solemnly. "I can be mighty persuasive where dancing is concerned. Only problem is, we worked up a powerful thirst for lemonade."

"I thought I'd regret not dancing," Lydia said as she poured them each a glass of the cool beverage, "but the little one is doing a jig tonight. He's wearing me out."

Though Lydia looked uncomfortable, that wasn't uncommon at this stage of her pregnancy. The summer heat didn't help, either. "It won't be long now," Thea said, trying to reassure her patient.

"Travis keeps saying the same thing. When I get cranky, I tell him he's going to carry the next baby."

"And I agree, don't I, sweetheart?" Travis appeared behind the table and slipped an arm around his wife's waist. "Opal's on her way over to give you a break."

Lydia leaned back in her husband's embrace and smiled. "Travis is the perfect husband."

But Daniel had been far from perfect. Thea forced the unhappy thoughts away, determined not to let memories of Daniel spoil her evening. Tonight was her chance to create happy memories, memories she would create with Jackson.

22

Jackson wiped his brow, then settled back in the saddle. The heat was more intense than he'd expected, and that had slowed him. As annoying as it was, he had no choice but to go slowly. He wouldn't risk pushing Blaze, despite his eagerness to reach Leakey and learn what he could about Helen Bradford.

Being away from Cimarron Creek gave him time to think. Too much time. His brain continued to whirl with memories of Saturday evening and how good it had felt to be with Thea. She had been radiant—that was the only word he could find to describe the way her face had glowed—while they'd danced, and later when they'd strolled around the perimeter of the park, she had seemed more relaxed than he'd ever seen her.

They hadn't discussed anything special while they'd walked, but the simple fact that they'd been together had made the time feel special. Jackson hadn't analyzed his feelings then, but today as he rode toward Leakey, he realized that what he'd felt on Saturday had been happiness.

If only it could last, but the fragile happiness had been shattered by worries. Though he hadn't said anything to Thea, because he didn't want to disturb her further, Jackson was concerned by many aspects of Helen Bradford's death. She and Stuart had obviously been apprehended on their way to

Cimarron Creek and taken somewhere else. Where they'd been taken didn't matter as much as why, and the only reason that made sense to Jackson was that whoever had killed Helen Bradford had mistaken her for Thea.

The undeniable resemblance between Thea and the murdered woman had worried Jackson from the beginning. Hearing about Violet Baker's slit throat had only reinforced his concern. While he told himself there was a chance that there was no connection between Helen and Thea, Jackson knew it was small. What he learned in Leakey would either validate or disprove his fears.

"Helen Bradford." The burly sheriff who'd introduced himself as Matt Driscoll gestured toward the chairs in front of his desk. When Jackson was seated, he continued. "Sure, I know her. She and Hiram are good folks. Guess I should have said 'were.'"

Sheriff Driscoll leaned back in his chair and clasped his hands behind his neck. "It sure was a shame about Hiram dying the way he did. As far as anyone knew, he was as healthy as a man could be, but one day he just dropped dead."

That was the story Thea had told Jackson, a simple matter of a heart giving out before its time. There was no reason to suspect foul play, but Jackson had to be certain.

"Did either of them have any enemies that you knew about?"

The sheriff didn't bother to mask his surprise. "Enemies? The Bradfords? I can't imagine anyone would wish them ill. They didn't come into town much except for church, but when they did, they always had a friendly word for everyone."

That was what Jackson had feared. If the Bradfords had no enemies, whoever had killed Helen had done it believing she was Thea. That was the only explanation that made sense. But Jackson wouldn't tell the sheriff that. Not yet. He wanted to see the man's reaction to the rest of the story.

"It seems someone wished Helen ill. She was murdered when she was on her way to Cimarron Creek."

"Helen left Leakey and was killed?" The sheriff shook his

head as he rose to his feet. "Now you've shocked me. I can't believe Helen left town without a word, especially since she had a new baby. Let's see if the parson knows anything about that."

But he did not. Like the sheriff, he hadn't known that Helen was leaving, and he couldn't imagine anyone wanting to harm either of the Bradfords.

"I hadn't heard she'd had the baby," the minister said, his expression perplexed. "I would have expected her to come into town to have the baby blessed and its name entered in the church register. This is mighty strange."

Mighty strange indeed.

"I'd like to take a look at the Bradfords' ranch," Jackson told the sheriff as they left the parsonage. Not only had he promised Thea a sketch of Stuart's first home, but he wanted to see if there were any clues to Helen Bradford's life, anything that might disprove Jackson's supposition that Thea had been the murderer's target. "Can you tell me where to find it?"

"I can do better than that. I'll take you out there myself. I'm curious about what happened to Helen."

As the two men rode west, the sheriff peppered Jackson with questions about his life in the Rangers, seeming as curious about that as he was about the death of one of his neighbors. "I always wondered if I should have joined," he admitted.

"It can be a good life, but it's not for everyone." The past few weeks had shown Jackson that.

Trying to deflect the sheriff's interest, he turned the subject back to the woman who looked so much like Thea. "Did you have any strangers in town around the time Helen left?"

The sheriff shook his head. "None come to mind." He stared into the distance for a moment, then nodded. "Wait a minute. Charlie said something about a couple coming into the mercantile asking about our midwife. When they learned she was getting up in years, the woman seemed upset. She claimed she wanted a young woman."

Sheriff Driscoll scowled. "Charlie couldn't figure out what all the fuss was about, but then the man showed him a watch with a picture of Helen and claimed she was a cousin. Charlie thought it was strange that they didn't know her name or where she lived, but they had some story about losing the directions to her place."

Questions about a midwife, a watch with a woman's portrait, even the fact that the couple had made their inquiries at the mercantile—this had been no innocent visit. Jackson thought he'd steeled himself for it, but his stomach churned at the realization that Sheriff Driscoll had just confirmed his worst fears.

The watch had to be the one that had been stolen from Daniel Michener's body, and that meant that what Jackson had surmised was true: Helen Bradford had been killed because of her resemblance to Thea.

"You don't look too happy about that."

"I'm not." That was an understatement. "It appears that Mrs. Bradford was killed by the Gang of Four. I'd venture to say that the couple who came to your mercantile were two of the members."

The sheriff's eyebrows rose. "You don't say! You tracking them?"

"Yeah, but so far they've been careful to hide their tracks. I suspect they split up between heists to make it harder to find them."

"That's smart."

Jackson gave a grudging nod. "They're a wily group, but I'm going to capture them." He wanted justice for Micah and Leander and Helen Bradford, but even more than that, he wanted to keep Thea safe, and the only way to do that was to capture the Gang. The sole good thing he could say about this couple's having come to Leakey was that now he might get a description of two of the remaining members.

"I want to talk to Charlie, see if he remembers what they look like."

The sheriff nodded. "Charlie'll talk your ear off, but he's got a good memory. He'll probably tell you more than you want to know."

Jackson doubted that was possible. Even the smallest detail might prove helpful, but first he needed to see the Bradford homestead.

Half an hour later, the sheriff turned off the road. "Here it is," he said, pointing toward the modest house nestled in the shade of two live oaks. Though the flowers that Helen Bradford had planted around her front step had wilted in the summer heat, the house itself appeared well cared for, and there was no sign of anything being amiss. Jackson filed away the details for the sketch he'd promised Thea.

"We might as well go inside." Sheriff Driscoll flung the door open, then stopped abruptly. "What do you make of this?"

The parlor chair cushions were slit, the stuffing thrown onto the floor, and the contents of the kitchen cabinets were now in a heap on the floor. Jackson strode to the bedroom, not surprised when he discovered that the dresser drawers had been emptied onto the bed. What did surprise him was that the robber had gouged chunks of wood out of both the headboard and the dresser top.

Anger, pure and simple, was the only reason he could imagine for the destruction. The same anger that had been unleashed on Helen and that might be directed at Thea.

He turned to the sheriff. "Looks like someone was searching for something, but they didn't find it." And because they didn't, Helen Bradford was dead. Jackson had gotten his answers, even though they weren't the ones he wanted. Now there was only one thing to do.

He extended his hand. "Thanks for your help, Sheriff. What I saw here tells me I've got to get back to Cimarron Creek right away."

Matt Driscoll appeared disappointed. Perhaps he wanted more time to discuss a Ranger's life.

"What about Charlie? You could talk to him and then spend the night with us. My wife makes a mighty fine apple pie."

On another day, Jackson might have agreed, but not today. "I can't stay, but I'd appreciate it if you'd talk to Charlie and telegraph the descriptions to Travis Whitfield. He'll make sure I get them."

"Sure thing."

The sheriff waved as Jackson mounted Blaze and headed toward Cimarron Creek. It would be a long ride, but this time Jackson would take no breaks.

Thea needed him.

"Never . . . ever . . . again." Lydia's breath whooshed out between the words, and she punctuated the sentence with a moan. "That was the worst one yet."

Thea kept her face schooled in the placid expression she'd been taught. Lydia had been in labor for over twelve hours. No wonder she was exhausted and ready to give up. Though Thea would not admit it to her patient, she was concerned by the length of the labor. First babies often took their time, but Thea had never seen a labor with such fierce contractions sustained over such a long time, and that made her worry about the safety of both the mother and the child.

Please, God, keep them safe, she prayed silently, unable to bear the thought that Lydia might know the heartbreak of losing a child or that Travis might face a double tragedy.

"It'll be over soon," Thea said, her voice filled with what she hoped was not misplaced confidence.

"It better be. I don't know how much longer I can do this."

That was what Thea feared, that Lydia would lack the strength to birth her baby. Thea wiped the sweat from her patient's face, then moved to the opposite end of the bed to check the progress. A wave of exultation pulsed through her when she saw that the baby's head had started to crown. If all went well, this would be the beginning of the end.

"One more good push." It would take more than one, but Lydia wasn't ready to hear that right now. "Push, Lydia. Push."

The expectant mother did.

"Perfect!" Thea made no effort to hide her relief. "The head's out. Keep pushing." As Lydia obeyed her commands, Thea caught the infant and smiled. Though red and wrinkled with a misshapen head, it was the most beautiful thing she'd ever seen. A baby. A live baby!

"You did it, Lydia. You've got a daughter." *Thank you, Lord.*

Thea gave Lydia's abdomen an appraising look and smiled. It seemed she'd been right. Knowing her work was not yet finished, she cleaned the baby as quickly as she could, wrapped her in a soft blanket, and showed her to Lydia.

"Let me hold her. Come here, Virginia." Lydia had told Thea that she and Travis had finally decided on names, Virginia for a girl, Vernon if it was a boy.

"Not yet." As much as she wanted Lydia to be able to cradle her daughter, it was too soon for that. "You've got more work to do. You're having twins."

"Really?"

"Really."

Ten minutes later, Virginia's brother made his appearance, his angry squalling suggesting that he had not liked being left behind. If she hadn't been so tired, Thea would have laughed from pure joy. Her first delivery in Cimarron Creek had been successful. Mother and baby—babies, she corrected herself—were healthy.

"It's a good thing you have two arms," Thea told Lydia as she laid an infant in each.

Lydia stared at her children, her face radiant despite the exhaustion. "Thank you, Thea. I couldn't have done it without you."

Thea's heart overflowed with joy as she brushed Lydia's hair before summoning Travis. This was why she'd become a midwife; this was why she'd come to Cimarron Creek. But she hadn't done it alone.

"Thank you, God."

23

"Twins. That's wonderful." Aimee pulled out the plate of food she'd kept warm in the oven and placed it in front of Thea.

"It is, although you should have seen Travis's face when I told him. I thought he might keel over."

Thea took a bite of the savory roast chicken. She hadn't eaten while she was helping Lydia through her labor, hadn't even thought about being hungry, but now that the babies were safely delivered, she discovered that she was famished. Famished, almost limp with relief that Lydia's lying-in had been successful, and filled with the inexplicable wish that Jackson were here to share the experience.

It made no sense. Thea shouldn't consider discussing childbirth with a single man, particularly one who was not related to either her or the parents, but she wanted to tell him how fulfilling it had been to place Lydia's babies in her arms. Though being a Ranger was very different from being a midwife—Jackson worked to protect life rather than bring it into the world—Thea's instincts told her he would understand the satisfaction inherent in completing a difficult job.

But Jackson was not here, and Thea owed Aimee a better explanation. "I don't think Travis was ready for two children, even though I'd told Lydia I thought it likely she was carrying twins."

Aimee refilled her glass of tea and took a seat across from Thea, her expression making Thea believe she was thinking about something other than Lydia and her babies. "Men can be so silly, can't they?"

"What makes you say that?" *Silly* was not a word Thea would ever associate with Travis or, for that matter, Jackson.

"It's Nate."

Of course. That explained why Aimee had seemed distracted. As a blush colored her cheeks, Aimee dipped her head.

Thea cut another piece of chicken, wondering what had happened between Nate and Aimee to make her believe he was silly. "Don't tell me he's back to being silent around you. I thought that ended at the square dance."

Aimee and Nate had been partners for almost every set, and when they weren't do-si-doing, they'd had their heads together, obviously engrossed in conversation. Ever since, Aimee had reminded Thea of the wildflowers that had invaded her childhood secret garden. Some years they barely stayed alive, but when there was a heavy rain at just the right time, they would burst into bloom, covering the ground with a riot of color. Aimee was in full bloom now, watered by Nate's attention.

"Oh no." Aimee shook her head so vigorously that a curl escaped from her chignon. "He comes into town every day so he can walk me home from the apothecary."

"That's less than two blocks." Aimee hardly needed an escort for such a short walk, but if it made her happy, Thea would be the last person to criticize. After all, she looked forward to the conversations she and Jackson had when he came to pick up or drop off Stuart. They might be brief, but they were the highlights of Thea's day.

Aimee gave her a mischievous grin. "It's more than two blocks the way we go. Nate takes the longest route possible."

"And that's what you find silly?"

"No. That's nice. It gives us time to talk."

"Then what's silly?"

"He called me a princess. Can you imagine that?"

A shiver made its way down Thea's spine. "I can." When he'd known her only a few days, Daniel had said she reminded him of a rose. And when she'd laughed and reminded him that roses had thorns, he'd nodded, claiming that she used them to guard her heart but that he would be the one who'd strip the stem of its thorns and capture the beauty.

Though another woman might have called that silly or at least fanciful, Daniel had been so earnest and Thea so entranced that she'd believed him. It hadn't been the *coup de foudre* that Aimee claimed had struck her the day she'd met Nate, but it had been close.

"That's the kind of thing a man says when he wants to woo a lady," Thea told Aimee. "It looks to me as if you have a suitor."

Aimee's color deepened. "I hope you're right, because you know how I feel about Nate. I've never met a man like him. He makes me feel beautiful, even though I know I'm not." She paused to take a sip of tea. "I know it's happening quickly, but my heart tells me Nate's the one for me, and yet . . ."

Thea finished the last of the mashed potatoes and tried to tamp down her concerns while she waited for Aimee to continue. This was different, she reminded herself. Aimee wasn't making the same mistake she had, rushing headlong into marriage with a virtual stranger. They weren't even officially courting yet, and if Nate continued the way he'd begun, it would be a leisurely courtship. Furthermore, while he had been a stranger to Aimee, everyone in Cimarron Creek knew Nate. They could vouch for his integrity.

Nate wasn't Daniel. He wasn't hiding horrible secrets, and yet something worried Aimee.

"Yet what?" Thea prompted her friend.

"I worry that I'm not the right woman for him. What will he think when he learns the truth of my birth? He comes from a respected family."

"So do you." The Hendersons were one of Cimarron Creek's two founding families, whereas the Kentons had come to town later.

"But it's different."

Aimee was right. The fact that she'd been born out of wedlock meant that some residents might condemn her. Thea couldn't predict how Nate would react. All she could do was tell Aimee what she'd learned.

"If he loves you—really loves you—it won't matter." She hadn't cared that Daniel knew nothing of his family, and he hadn't been bothered by her parents' tragic deaths. They'd both agreed that what their parents had done was of no importance, that what mattered were the present and the future they'd create together.

"I hope you're right."

So did Thea.

Jackson frowned when he saw lights on in the kitchen. He'd thought his late arrival in Cimarron Creek would mean that Warner would have gone to bed. Not only was it clear that he had not, but that looked like Nate's horse tied up in front of the house. So much for Jackson's hope that he could avoid a discussion of his trip and simply get some rest before seeing Thea in the morning. After what he'd learned in Leakey, he was not in the mood for casual conversation.

Biting back his frustration, he entered the house by the side door and found both Nate and Travis sitting at the table with Warner, glasses of sarsaparilla in front of them. Nate was no surprise, but why was Travis here? He didn't normally frequent Warner's house this late in the day.

"Glad you're back," Warner said as he registered Jackson's arrival. The smile that accompanied his words told Jackson that whatever the reason the trio had gathered, it was a happy one. "You can celebrate with us. Grab yourself a glass."

Though it was the last thing he wanted to do, Jackson pulled one from the cupboard and filled it with the fizzy beverage, then sank onto the empty chair. He'd drink the sarsaparilla as quickly as he could, then excuse himself.

"What are you celebrating?" He had nothing to celebrate.

"Fatherhood." Travis's face shone with a combination of pride, relief, and deep-seated happiness. "The babies came today."

Jackson stared at the man. He shouldn't have been surprised. After all, Thea had said that Lydia's confinement was imminent, and he'd heard a rumor that she'd predicted twins, but he'd been so caught up in thoughts of death and danger since he'd left Leakey that Travis's announcement startled him.

"Babies, as in plural?"

"Yep. I've got a son and a daughter."

Jackson rose and clapped the sheriff on the back. This was good news, a happy ending to a difficult few days. "Congratulations, old man."

"What do you mean 'old man'? You're older than I am."

Though Travis's grin took the sting from his words, Jackson simply nodded. On days like this, he felt more than old. He felt ancient, but he wasn't going to say anything that would diminish the festive atmosphere in the kitchen. His friends—and he counted these men as such—deserved an evening free from worry.

Travis let his gaze roam from one man to the other before he spoke. "You fellows may not like my advice, but I'm going to give it anyway. Lydia's the best thing that ever happened to me. She changed everything—made me happier than I thought possible, and now with Vernon and Virginia, my life is complete."

It was the longest speech Jackson had heard the sheriff make. Was this what fatherhood did to a man?

"So, here's my advice," Travis continued. "If you find a woman like Lydia, don't let her slip away. I want to see you all as happy as I am."

Jackson stared at the wall as a picture snuck into his brain. He was riding up to what had been the Goddard ranch, knowing that it was now his home. And as he approached the house, a woman emerged, a toddler clutching her skirts, an infant in her arms.

He closed his eyes, taking in the details of the image. This was no faceless woman, no unknown toddler. It was Thea who greeted him, Stuart who clung to her, and the baby nestled in her arms was theirs, a tiny girl with Thea's brown eyes and a shock of hair the same shade as Jackson's.

The warmth that flooded him startled Jackson with its intensity. He might not deserve it, but this was what he wanted: a family of his own. Was this what God had in mind for him, or was it nothing more than a dream? There was only one way to find out, but first he needed to tell Thea what he'd learned.

*　❧　*

"It's bad news, isn't it?"

Jackson hadn't had to say a word. The wariness in his eyes when he'd climbed the front steps had signaled that something was wrong. He didn't bother to deny her assumption, though he'd insisted it could wait until she returned from her appointments, but since Thea had finished checking on Lydia and the twins and had nothing else scheduled for this morning, she'd invited Jackson to stay.

For the sake of propriety, they remained on the front porch, a coffeepot on the table between them, a solemn expression on Jackson's face. Thea had left the door open so that she could hear Stuart if he stirred, but the infant normally slept for an hour or so at this time of the day.

"I wish it were otherwise," Jackson said, "but yes, it's bad news. All the way back from Leakey, I tried to find a way to make this easier to bear, but there's no way to sugarcoat it. I believe someone mistook Helen Bradford for you, and that's why she was killed."

It wasn't a total surprise. Jackson was simply confirming what Thea had feared. She shouldn't have been shocked, and yet she felt as if she'd been bludgeoned. As the blood drained from her head, she whispered the word that reverberated through her brain. "Why?"

"Why do I think that Helen was a victim of mistaken identity, or why was someone looking for you?" Jackson asked.

"Both."

He leaned forward, the coffee cup clasped between his hands. "A couple came to Leakey, asking about the town's midwife. When they didn't like what they heard, they showed the owner of the mercantile a watch with a woman's picture. The owner thought it was Helen."

Thea closed her eyes, trying to subdue the sorrow that threatened to overwhelm her. Inquiries about a midwife, a watch with her portrait. This was no coincidence, and as a result an innocent woman was dead, a baby motherless.

"It was Daniel's watch."

"That seems likely."

More than likely; it was the only plausible explanation. Even if Helen Bradford's husband had once carried a watch with her portrait in it, there was no reason strangers would have it. Daniel's watch, on the other hand, had been missing since his death.

Thea forced herself to open her eyes, wishing there were another explanation, wishing she did not feel so guilty. "That poor woman was killed because someone wanted to find me." It was almost unthinkable, and yet everything pointed to that conclusion.

The September morning that Thea had greeted with pleasure, basking in the satisfaction of her successful delivery, had lost its luster. Though the sky was still as clear, the breeze as soft, it might as well have been gray and foggy for all the joy the day gave Thea.

Jackson nodded slowly. "I'm afraid so. I can't imagine any other reason, especially since the people were obviously looking for you. The first thing they asked about was the midwife."

Thea took a sip of coffee, trying to settle her nerves as well as her stomach, and as she did, the memory of Sarah's letter resurfaced.

"I should have told you about a letter my sister sent me." It wouldn't have changed anything. Helen Bradford had been killed before the letter was written, but it might have been some help to Jackson. "A couple came to Ladreville a few days after I left. Sarah didn't say anything about them having Daniel's watch, but they asked about me at the mercantile. One of the customers told them I'd come here, but the owner was suspicious of them, so she claimed I'd changed my mind and gone to Austin."

As she'd expected, the news did not please Jackson. "The Gang is obviously not giving up."

"The Gang?"

"It's the only answer that explains why your husband was killed and someone's searching for you. The Gang is looking for something, and they believe you have it. That's why they ransacked Helen's house."

Thea shuddered. Another awful thing to happen, all because Helen had the misfortune to resemble her.

"What are they looking for? I don't have anything." The most valuable thing Thea owned was a pair of earrings that had been her mother's, and those were safe in her jewelry box. She'd worn them to church just last week.

"There've been rumors that one of the Gang took off with

all the gold from the last heist instead of splitting it with the others. Based on everything that's happened, I'd say the rest of the Gang believes Daniel had the gold and refused to tell them where it was. That would explain why they killed him and started looking for you. They obviously believe you either have the gold or know where it is."

Jackson placed his cup back on the table and waited for Thea to respond.

"I don't have any gold, and Daniel didn't either. He was always worried about having enough money to support us once the baby was born. He wouldn't have been like that if he'd had a lot of gold, would he?"

Though she'd hoped that Jackson would reassure her, he did not. "That would depend on where he'd hidden it and how secure he thought it was." He was silent for a moment. "It was two months between the last robbery and when he was killed. Did Daniel seem different during that time?"

Thea tried to remember something—anything—that might have changed, but she could not. At the time, she'd been caught up in the wonder of her pregnancy, becoming more inwardly focused. It was a stage she'd noticed in many of her patients, particularly as they awaited the birth of their first child.

If Daniel had done anything unusual, she hadn't noticed it. But that was a time when she'd also been preoccupied with the perfume she'd detected on his shirts, despite his stubborn denial of any wrongdoing. Perhaps the fact that she had been questioning Daniel's love and whether their marriage had been a mistake had blinded her to changes in her husband's behavior.

"I don't know. I don't remember anything special." Thea closed her eyes for a second, remembering the sight of Helen Bradford's body. "I'm still reeling over the fact that I was responsible for Helen's death." While she had lost a few patients and had mourned their deaths, Thea had always known that they'd died despite her best efforts, that she'd done everything in her power to save them. Helen was different.

Jackson reached out and clasped both of her hands in his. "Look at me, Thea. It wasn't your fault. You had nothing to do with it. You didn't even know Helen, so how could you be responsible?"

He was trying to reassure her the way she'd tried to tell him that he had not been responsible for Micah's death, but it wasn't working. "Helen died because she looked like me. You said that yourself."

"I did, and I'm going to be honest with you. That worries me. I don't want to frighten you, but everything I've learned tells me you're in danger until I catch the rest of the Gang."

Thea knew he felt her fingers tremble as the implications of his words registered. "What should I do?"

He tightened his grip on her hands. "You're probably safe here in town, but you shouldn't leave Cimarron Creek alone."

"I'll take a shotgun with me. I'm a good shot."

Jackson frowned. "I don't care whether you can hit the bull's-eye every time. You'd be one person against two or three of them. Those are not favorable odds, especially considering that the Gang are all crack shots."

She knew he was trying to protect her, and Thea appreciated that, but Jackson didn't understand the reality of her profession. "I can't stop calling on my patients." No one knew how long it would take him to find Daniel's former partners, and babies were notorious for their poor timing. Thea had to be ready to travel to an expectant mother's bedside on a moment's notice.

For the first time since they'd begun the conversation, Jackson's lips started to curve into a smile. "I didn't ask you to stop. I'll go with you."

24

Jackson studied Thea as he settled back in the buggy. Once again, she'd surprised him, this time by agreeing so readily to his accompanying her whenever she left Cimarron Creek. Though he'd expected an argument, despite the fact that she had obviously been shaken by what he'd discovered in Leakey, she'd simply nodded, her face white with shock. And now, four days later, he'd helped her into the buggy as if it were an everyday occurrence for him to travel to a patient's home with her.

But it was not normal, not yet, and today's destination was anything but normal. This morning she was calling on Ethel Harris, Helen Bradford's cousin and the woman who might become Stuart's adoptive mother. Though it had to be difficult, Thea gave no sign of nervousness. She was a strong woman, stronger than she realized.

"Are you certain you don't mind my driving?"

Jackson smiled as he looked at the woman who occupied so many of his thoughts. She might be strong—and she was—but she also had insecurities. Not for the first time, Jackson wished Daniel Michener were still alive so he could take him to task for what he'd done to Thea.

"I consider this a luxury," he told her. "It isn't often I can relax."

The truth was, he wasn't relaxed. There was no possibility of relaxing when he knew Thea might be in danger, so he kept a lookout for anything unusual. Not having to control the horse let him do that as well as admire his companion.

Today, dressed for work, Thea had her hair pulled back in a chignon and wore a simple white blouse and deep green skirt. While he preferred the loose curls and pretty dress she'd worn the night of the square dance, Jackson knew she could never be anything but lovely. Lovely, strong, and ever on his mind.

He shifted his position so that he could look in both directions without alerting Thea to what he was doing. As he'd ridden back from Leakey, Jackson had worried about how to break the news of what he'd discovered to Thea and how she would react.

Anyone would be distressed by what had happened to Helen Bradford, but for a woman already dealing with a number of shocking revelations, the knowledge that another woman had been killed simply because of her resemblance to her must have been almost overwhelming. Yet, Thea hadn't fainted. She hadn't even cried, though he'd seen tears hovering on her eyelashes, waiting to be blinked away. She hadn't surrendered to fear. Instead, her expression had become determined, as if she refused to let the Gang change her life.

Jackson did not believe that she had underestimated the threat—Thea was too smart to do that—but she would not be cowed by it. What an amazing woman!

His smile broadened as he remembered that Thea had once called him amazing. She was wrong; he was an ordinary man, but she was an extraordinary woman. She'd survived tragedy and disillusionment and appeared to be thriving. Amazing!

Jackson looked down at the boy in his arms. Though he'd fussed for a minute when Thea had picked up the reins, Stuart now seemed to be entertained by the sight of his hands, which he was waving furiously in front of his face. "Stuart seems to enjoy riding in your buggy."

A sweet smile crossed Thea's face as she darted a glance at the baby. "I think he likes any kind of motion. That's one of the reasons either Aimee or I take him out in his carriage most nights."

"So that's why Nate has been spending so many evenings in town instead of out with those goats of his."

Jackson was still embarrassed by the memory of how he'd mistaken the object of Nate's affections. The first few times Warner had teased Nate about his ladylove, Jackson had merely gritted his teeth, not wanting to think about Thea being courted by another man. Now, in hindsight, he knew he should have realized it was Aimee who'd caught Nate's eye, not Thea. Instead, Jackson had let his own attraction to Thea cloud his judgment. He'd tried to deny it, but the truth was, he'd been attracted to Thea from the day he met her.

Forcing his gaze away from the woman who dominated his thoughts, Jackson glanced in all directions. When he'd reassured himself that there was no danger, he turned back to Thea.

"I probably shouldn't say this about my friend, but Nate seems besotted with Aimee."

"I probably shouldn't say this about my friend"—Thea chuckled as she repeated Jackson's words—"but it's mutual. Cimarron Creek's matchmakers must be gloating about their success: Nate and Aimee, and Warner and Patience."

"Whoa!" When Thea's horse stopped, Jackson shook his head. "That wasn't meant for Maggie. I was telling my brain to stop whirling. Did you say Warner and Patience?"

Thea's smile widened as she flicked the reins. "According to Aimee, they're on the verge of becoming a courting couple."

"And he never said a word to me."

"Do men talk about things like that?"

It was a good question. Jackson couldn't remember ever hearing his brothers discuss the women they married, but perhaps they'd confided in each other. "Nate did, but he might be the exception." After all, Jackson hadn't said anything about his growing feelings for Thea.

To his way of thinking, she should be the first to know, but even though the image of Thea as his wife seemed to have been indelibly etched on his brain and even though it popped into his thoughts when he least expected it, Jackson knew Thea wasn't ready to hear that he harbored tender hopes with her as their centerpiece.

First steps first. Thea needed to recover from the wounds Daniel had inflicted, and Jackson needed to capture the remaining members of the Gang. Only then could he move on to the next stage of his life.

At least now he knew what the Gang members looked like. Matt Driscoll's telegram had confirmed the description Thea's sister had shared. The couple who'd visited both Ladreville and Leakey were brown-haired with brown eyes. That would have made them unremarkable, but the woman was taller than normal, and the man had a jagged scar on his forehead. When Jackson came face-to-face with them, it would not be difficult to identify them. But first he had to find them.

The silence that followed his assessment of Nate was broken when Thea pointed toward a creature waddling across the road. "An armadillo. I didn't know they came out during the day."

"They don't normally. Maybe this one is hungry." Jackson looked around, studying the countryside, searching for any other reason that the armor-plated critter might have left its burrow. Nothing seemed unusual, and he had no sense of danger. As if to confirm his assessment that the armadillo simply wanted to eat, Stuart began to whimper. It was, Jackson knew from experience, the predecessor to the "I'm hungry" cry that frequently came at this time of the day.

"It looks like the armadillo isn't the only one who wants to eat. What do you have for Stuart today—pot roast with carrots and onions or chicken with green beans?" It was a silly question, designed to make Thea laugh, since Stuart was too young for solid food.

As Jackson had hoped, Thea chuckled and inclined her head toward the bag she'd placed on the floor between them. "We ran out of pot roast, so he'll have to make do with milk. There's a bottle in the sack."

When Stuart latched on to the nipple, Jackson shifted the child so he could drink more easily. "Stuart's a better eater than Micah. We had to give him goat's milk."

The instant the words were out of his mouth, Jackson regretted them. Why had he brought up Micah today? He'd wanted this to be a happy day for both of them, and speaking of Micah was not the way to ensure that. Sorrow mingled with guilt rose up to ambush him.

For a moment, Jackson thought Thea might let his comment pass without a reply, but he was not so fortunate. "That's happened with a few of my patients," she said. "They can't tolerate human or cow's milk, but for some reason, goat's milk agrees with them."

She turned her gaze from the road to Jackson. "Do you mind talking about Micah?"

To Jackson's surprise, he shook his head. As much as he'd avoided speaking of his brother, somehow it felt right to discuss him with Thea. "What would you like to know?"

She gave him a reassuring smile, as if she knew he hadn't planned to agree. "Why did your parents name him Micah? It seems that the rest of you were named for presidents."

"You're right. Quincy, Jefferson, and I owe our names to presidents my parents admired. Micah did not like being different. At one point, he demanded that we call him Washington. That didn't last long."

"Why not?"

"Our father, who's a no-nonsense man, informed Micah

that he had a perfectly good name and that was what everyone would use."

Thea winced as if she shared Micah's unhappiness over the decree. "I can't imagine that he liked that."

"He didn't, but then our mother told him she knew he would be a special child, and that's why she gave him a special name."

"Did that satisfy him?"

Jackson nodded. "The real story is that my mother was studying the book of Micah when her labor began, and that's how she chose his name."

"It's a good story." Thea glanced at Stuart, then returned her attention to the road. "What was Micah like when he was growing up?"

That was an easy question to answer. "Micah was the most curious person I've ever met. It seemed he was always getting into trouble. Not deliberately, but because he wanted to discover something."

Thea raised an eyebrow, seemingly unconvinced. "Give me an example."

"He was fascinated by our windmill and decided to climb it, because he wondered what it would feel like to touch one of the blades while it was spinning. You can guess what happened."

"He fell off."

"And broke both arms." Jackson shook his head, remembering how worried their mother had been when she'd seen what Micah had done to himself. "Can you imagine what that was like for an active five-year-old? He couldn't even feed himself."

"Were you the one he turned to then?"

"Yes. How'd you guess?"

The smile Thea flashed at him said the reason should be apparent. "You once told me you'd cared for him when he was an infant. I assumed you'd continued being more than just a big brother."

"You're right. I did."

She gave him a look so filled with admiration that it made Jackson's heart swell. It had been months since thoughts of Micah had brought him anything but pain, but Thea's questions had resurrected happy memories, reminding him of all that he'd shared with his younger brother.

"Micah was lucky to have you. Not all brothers would have been so kind, especially given the age difference."

Jackson nodded, acknowledging the truth in her observation. Quincy and Jefferson hadn't been particularly sympathetic when he'd sprained an ankle and couldn't compete in the three-legged race at the fair. Perhaps that was part of the reason he'd volunteered to help Micah.

"Don't make me out to be a saint. There were times when I considered him a pest and did everything I could to shake him, but he was like a sand burr and wouldn't be shaken off."

"But you loved him."

"I did."

Seeing that Stuart was no longer interested in eating, Jackson placed the bottle back in the sack and stared at the road ahead. Micah was not what he'd wanted to talk about, and yet he couldn't deny that these memories of his brother were pleasant ones that left him feeling more at peace than he had since Micah's death. It felt good to remember and even better to share that portion of his past with Thea. If she was going to be part of his life—and Jackson hoped she would—she needed to understand what had made him the person he was, and he needed to learn more about her.

"Tell me about your childhood," Jackson urged Thea. She did, entertaining him with stories of Sarah and Clay and how they'd taken the place of her real parents, and before he knew it, they'd arrived at the Harris ranch.

Thea's carefree smile changed to apprehension as they approached the farmhouse, reminding Jackson that she was not looking forward to what might transpire here. She had told him she felt duty-bound to ask the Harrises to consider adopting Stuart, but her heart ached at the thought of giving up the baby she'd grown to love.

"Would you watch Stuart for half an hour?" Thea asked as she stopped the buggy. "After my appointment with Mrs. Harris, I'll come for him. I want her to meet her cousin's son."

"You sure this is Helen's boy?" Ethel Harris stared at the infant in Thea's arms, shaking her head when Thea asked if she wanted to hold him. "He don't look like her."

Taking a deep breath, Thea willed herself not to let her frustration show. The official part of her time with Mrs. Harris had gone smoothly. The expectant mother's pregnancy was proceeding as expected, her size and symptoms confirming Thea's belief that the baby would be born in approximately four weeks. It was only when she told Ethel that she had brought Stuart that her patient had started to frown. Though she'd said nothing when Thea had announced that she wanted her to see the child, her frown had deepened when Thea returned to the house with Stuart in her arms.

"He's still a baby," Thea said as calmly as she could. "At this age, it's hard to tell what he'll look like when he grows up. And, of course, it could be that he resembles his father."

Ethel gave Stuart another glance, her lips thinning as she said, "I tole Angus about him. I know it's our Christian duty to take him in if'n nobody else wants him. 'Course, I gotta tell you I ain't gonna be nursin' him. I gotta save my milk for my son."

She shouldn't have been shocked, not after the way Ethel had treated Stuart so far, but Thea was appalled by the woman's cavalier attitude. There was nothing Christian about it. This baby—this wonderful little boy—should have two parents who loved him the way Jesus loved the children who gathered around him.

Thea took a breath and tried to calm herself. She owed it to Stuart to find him a good home.

"Don't worry, Mrs. Harris."

"I tole you to call me Ethel. Did you fergit?"

"I'm afraid I did." That wasn't all she'd forgotten. Thea had almost forgotten her manners and had been tempted to shriek that this woman didn't deserve a boy like Stuart. "What I started to say was that you don't need to worry about feeding Stuart. He's accustomed to a bottle."

Though she'd expected Ethel to show some relief, her patient pursed her lips again. "That's more work, ain't it? I gotta wash them bottles."

"Yes, you do. And heat the milk too."

The woman frowned. "'Pears that my cross just got heavier."

Feeling as if her heart were about to break, Thea rose and turned toward the door. "I'll be back next Monday. Now that you're this close to delivering, I want to check on you every week." And next week she wouldn't make the mistake of bringing Stuart with her.

"What happened back there?" Jackson had given her an appraising look when she'd emerged from the house but had waited until they'd reached the main road before he spoke.

Thea turned to face him, hoping she could keep her tears at bay. Though she'd tried to control her emotions, not wanting to add to the burdens Jackson was already carrying, it seemed she'd failed. "Oh, Jackson, it was horrible."

As tears began to stream down her cheeks, he reached over to take the reins. "Whoa, Maggie." With the buggy stationary, Jackson extended his other hand to clasp Thea's.

Even through her driving gloves, she could feel the warmth of Jackson's hand, and it reassured her as nothing else had done today. Jackson, she knew, would never look at a baby the way Ethel Harris had. He wasn't Stuart's father any more than Thea was his mother, but Jackson lavished love on the orphaned boy.

"Tell me what happened," he urged.

"She called Stuart her cross to bear." Anger and sadness melded into outrage. "He's not a cross. He's not a burden. He's a little boy who's lost his parents." Thea brushed the tears away as she shook her head. "I can't let them take him."

"I agree." Jackson's voice was so calm, so matter-of-fact, that it startled her. Whatever she'd expected him to say, it wasn't that.

"You do?"

He nodded. "While you were inside, I talked to Mr. Harris. The way he looked at Stuart told me this wasn't the right home for him, but he didn't wait for me to figure that out. Harris made it clear that he didn't agree with his wife's suggestion that they adopt Stuart. He said he planned to talk her out of that nonsense—that was his word."

Thea reached over to stroke Stuart's head. "I don't know what to do. My head tells me children should be with their family—if not their parents, then with someone who's related. I can't imagine what my life would have been like if Sarah and Clay hadn't wanted to raise me. I was blessed."

Thea raised her eyes to meet Jackson's, hoping he'd understand. "That's what I want for Stuart, but no matter what my head says is best, my heart tells me the Harrises are not the right people for him."

Jackson loosened his grip on Thea's hand, then threaded his fingers through hers. "I understand, and I agree with you that that's what Stuart deserves, but I'm a little confused. I thought you said you'd adopt him if you couldn't find his family or a couple who wanted him."

Thea nodded. Oh, how she wished everything were black and white, not shades of gray. "I did, but once again my head is warring with my heart. My heart tells me I love Stuart as much as I did Aaron, but my head says that children—especially boys—need a father."

She was silent for a second, composing her thoughts. "There are times when I wonder if the reason Daniel turned to crime was that he had no men to serve as good examples. He told me that the only adults at the orphanage were women, the matron and her assistants, and it doesn't sound as if they gave him much love. I don't want that to happen to Stuart. I want him to have both a mother and a father."

Jackson's expression had grown progressively more solemn as she'd spoken, but now his frown cleared and his eyes shone like blades of grass after a spring rain. "There's a solution to the problem." He paused for an instant, then tightened his grip on Thea's hand. "You could marry me."

25

Aimee looked up, surprised to see a schoolboy entering the apothecary. While children sometimes accompanied their parents, it was unusual for one to come alone. The towheaded boy whom she guessed to be no more than ten years old looked around the store, his eyes widening at the sight of a row of bottles decorated with a skull and crossbones. Then, seeming to recall the reason he was here, he handed her a piece of paper. "This is for you, Miss Jarre. Miss Kenton asked me to wait for an answer."

The two sentences, while hardly a speech, sounded carefully rehearsed, making Aimee wonder whether this was one of Patience's special children. She had mentioned that several of her pupils were unusually shy and that she was trying to coax them out of their shells. Perhaps asking him to deliver a message to the pharmacy was Patience's way of making this boy feel important.

As she unfolded the sheet, Aimee noticed that it was wrinkled, undoubtedly the result of being clutched in a nervous child's hand. The contents were simple: Patience wanted her to come to her house once the store closed. It would have been easier to send the message verbally, but for some reason Patience had chosen the written word, perhaps because handing it to the boy in front of his classmates conferred esteem on him. Aimee was going to try a different tack.

"Please tell Miss Kenton that I'd be happy to accept her invitation." She gave the young messenger a conspiratorial smile. "I know I don't have to write that down, because you can remember that."

His chest puffed with importance, the boy nodded and scampered out the door.

For the rest of the afternoon, Aimee tried to imagine what had precipitated Patience's invitation. Normally if she wanted to talk to Aimee, she came into the shop, which had the advantage of giving her the opportunity to spend time with Warner. Something was different today. Though she said nothing to Warner, Aimee hoped he was not the reason Patience chose to meet in her home.

As she walked toward the modest house that had once belonged to Catherine Whitfield, now Catherine Goddard, Aimee's thoughts took a different turn, and she wondered as she did each day where Catherine and, more important, Grace were. Had they reached Le Havre? Had they found passage on an ocean liner? When would they be back in Cimarron Creek? And when they arrived, what would Grace do when she learned that Aimee was already here?

As much as she longed to meet her mother, Aimee could not dismiss the fear that she would fall short of Grace's expectations and that what Aimee had hoped would be a joyous reunion would become a disappointing and distressing moment for both of them. What would Grace think of her?

There were no answers to those questions, but as Patience opened the door to admit Aimee, she provided one answer.

"I'm so glad you came." Patience extended her hands and drew Aimee into the house. Though her smile was as bright as ever, Aimee detected a hint of concern in Patience's blue eyes.

"I need your opinion on something. I'm making a new dress and don't know which trim to use."

Try though she might, Aimee could not imagine why Patience was worried about trimming a dress. Judging from the clothing she normally wore, she had an innate sense of fashion.

Patience led Aimee to the spare bedroom that was now being used as a sewing room and pointed toward a length of sapphire-blue poplin stretched across the bed. "Which do you prefer?" She laid first a piece of white lace then one of a pale blue grosgrain ribbon on the poplin. "Jacob Whitfield was no help," she said, referring to the man who owned the mercantile. "He told me either one was fine."

Aimee studied the two trims. "I agree with Jacob. They're both nice, and either one would complement the poplin. I'd say it depends on where you plan to wear the dress." She raised her eyes to gaze at Patience. The normally unflappable teacher ducked her head like a schoolgirl, trying to hide her flaming cheeks.

"I'm hoping Warner will invite me to the church social." Aimee had been right. Warner was the reason for Patience's unusual behavior.

When Aimee did not reply, Patience continued. "It used to be an annual event, but I heard the congregation wants to have another one this fall."

Aimee had heard the same rumor when she'd taken Stuart to Widow Jenkins's home. According to the widow, the square dance had been such a success that the townspeople wanted another excuse to gather.

"In that case, I'd use the ribbon. It's not as fancy as the lace, so you won't look as if you're trying to outshine anyone. You'll also be able to wear it more places."

Aimee fixed her gaze on Patience, her instincts telling her there was another reason her friend had asked her to come here. While she may have wanted Aimee's opinion of the trims, the way she'd blushed when she'd spoken of Warner indicated that Patience had more than clothing on her mind. "Why don't you tell me why you really wanted to see me?"

"We need a cup of tea and some of Lydia's chocolates for this." Her face still red with embarrassment, Patience led the way to the kitchen, then remained uncharacteristically silent as she busied herself making tea.

It was only after the tea had steeped and they were both seated at the table that she spoke. "You've probably already guessed that it's Warner. I know he cares for me—he's told me that—but I don't know how to convince him that he's the right man for me."

Aimee wasn't surprised that Patience wanted to talk about Warner, but she was surprised that Patience believed he needed convincing. The woman was clearly besotted with him, and Warner seemed equally smitten. As far as Aimee could tell, they were an ideal couple—well-matched and in love with each other.

"Why won't he believe that?"

Patience set her cup down with so much force that tea splashed on the saucer. "He has some notion that he's not good enough. He believes what happened to his parents and his brother makes him unworthy."

Aimee struggled to keep her expression neutral. While they'd never discussed it, it appeared that a feeling of unworthiness was one more thing she and Warner had in common. He worried about Patience's acceptance of him, and she was afraid that Nate wouldn't want to marry or even court her if what she feared about her father was true. Though Thea had tried to reassure her, telling her she was not responsible for the circumstances of her conception, it was a fear that wakened Aimee in the middle of the night and disturbed her daydreams of a life with Nate.

She wouldn't tell Patience that, but she owed her a response. "Do you feel that he's not good enough for you?"

Patience's shock seemed genuine. "Heavens no! What Warner's family may or may not have done doesn't change who he is. He's an upstanding, honorable man, and I love him."

A feeling of relief swept over Aimee. That was how she hoped Nate would react if they ever reached the stage where she felt comfortable telling him about her birth. She nodded briskly, more pleased than she could say that her friend had responded this way.

"Then tell him."

"Are you certain?" Patience could not hide her reluctance. "It sounds so forward."

It was. Undoubtedly, some of the matrons would be shocked if they heard Aimee suggesting such a thing and horrified if Patience followed her suggestion. Women weren't supposed to make the first move where matters of the heart were concerned. Aimee knew that, but she also knew that sometimes a man needed a nudge.

"If you love him, do it."

Patience gulped, but then she nodded, and her eyes became misty with happiness. Her embarrassment disappeared, replaced by the glow of first love. As she watched Patience's transformation, Aimee's heart filled with hope. Perhaps there could be a happy ending to her own story.

Thea stared at Jackson, not certain she'd heard correctly. They'd been talking about the Harrises' reaction to Stuart and how he deserved more than Ethel and Angus Harris had offered. Thea knew that Jackson had been trying to comfort her, but then he'd said . . .

"Did you just ask me to marry you?"

Jackson nodded, his expression one she'd never seen before. If she'd had to describe it, Thea would have said that he looked sheepish. He'd obviously had a chance to reconsider, and in reconsidering, he'd realized that he'd made a mistake. A huge mistake. He'd had no intention of marrying Thea, not even to give Stuart a good life.

Jackson's momentary chagrin seemed to have faded, for when

he spoke, his voice was as even as if they were still discussing the hungry armadillo. "It was more of a suggestion than a formal proposal, but yes, I did say that. It seemed like a good idea to me. What do you think about it?"

Thea pulled her hand from his grasp and stared into the distance, trying to make sense of her thoughts. She didn't know what to say. Her brain was still whirling from the horrible way the Harrises had spoken of Stuart and her fear that she would be unable to give him the upbringing he needed. As much as she loved him, Thea could not ignore her inadequacy. She had thought Jackson might have a suggestion, but never—never!—had she expected him to suggest marriage.

She blinked as she tried to corral her thoughts. On the surface, Jackson's idea was a good one, at least for Stuart. There was no question that he loved the boy and would be a good father. Thea loved Stuart too, and she believed she would be a good mother. But a marriage simply to protect Stuart was more than Thea was ready to consider.

She looked around, her eyes focusing on a large prickly pear. It was too late in the season for it to be blossoming, and this year's new growth had lost its pale green color, only the smaller size of the pads announcing that they'd not been there a year ago. It was an ordinary sight on a most extraordinary day.

Marriage! The thought made Thea's stomach clench.

Though it was true that she admired Jackson, even that she was attracted to him, it was too soon to be speaking of marriage. She'd rushed into matrimony once, believing she knew the man who'd become her husband, only to discover that she'd been mistaken and that Daniel's words of love had been as false as the name he'd signed on the marriage certificate.

Shakespeare was correct when he said, "Hasty marriage seldom proveth well." Thea was living proof of that. She wouldn't risk making a mistake like that again, especially since there were two other people's lives at stake.

Knowing Jackson was waiting for an answer, Thea looked at the infant nestled in the crook of his arm as she tried to make sense of the thoughts that were tumbling through her brain.

Stuart deserved two parents, but he also deserved parents who loved each other and could teach him about love through their example. She shifted her gaze to the handsome Ranger who'd suggested joining their lives. Jackson deserved a wife he loved the way Clay loved Sarah, not a wife he'd chosen for the wrong reasons.

Swiftly, Thea turned away, lest he read her thoughts. She knew that Jackson had suggested marriage to give Stuart the future he deserved and possibly to protect her from the Gang. Those were good reasons, but they weren't enough.

Marriage should be based on true love, nothing less. And that was the problem. If Jackson loved her, Thea would have proposed a formal courtship to give them a chance to be certain they were meant for each other, but Jackson had not mentioned love.

Swallowing deeply, Thea turned back to the man who'd somehow captured her heart. "I'm sorry, Jackson, but I don't agree. I think it's a bad idea."

26

At least it wasn't raining. Jackson wasn't looking forward to the next few hours, but they'd have been worse if he'd had to deal with rain or hail as well as a possibly displeased captain. Fortunately, the rain had ended before dawn, leaving the air fresh and cooler than usual for mid-September. Under other circumstances, he would have enjoyed the ride. As it was, when he'd received the coded message, insisting that he meet his superior officer the next day, Jackson had scowled.

He hadn't wanted to leave Cimarron Creek, especially since it meant leaving Thea alone, but he'd had no choice. An order from Captain Rawlins was an order. The man had a right to expect him to report what he knew and what he suspected. And so, once he'd extracted Thea's promise that she wouldn't leave town unless Travis or Edgar could accompany her, Jackson had headed to the rendezvous, grateful that it was close enough that he'd be back in Cimarron Creek by nightfall.

A wry laugh escaped from Jackson's lips as he thought of how his life had changed since the last time he'd seen his captain. He'd thought tracking down the Gang was difficult, but it was nothing compared to understanding Thea. He'd believed he'd offered her a good solution to the problem of giving Stuart the family he deserved, but she hadn't agreed. Instead, she'd seemed shocked, and not a happy kind of shock, either. He'd thought she cared for him as more than simply a friend, but when he'd suggested marriage, Thea had looked almost fearful. So much for what he thought he knew!

Though Jackson knew that he, like most Rangers, inspired fear in many criminals, he hadn't expected the woman he wanted to marry to fear him. Women! He would never understand them.

An hour later, he stood under the spreading oak that the captain had designated for their meeting place. Well off the road and far from any houses, it was the ideal place to talk without being observed. Jackson's captain was famous for demanding complete privacy when discussing strategy with his men. Even when they were based at camp, he'd often ride a few miles away with key members of the company to plan their next move.

As Jackson had expected, his superior officer was waiting for him, his expression inscrutable. Wasting no time on social niceties, he asked for Jackson's report.

"So you believe there's no reason to continue the search for the Gang," Captain Rawlins said when Jackson finished outlining what he'd discovered at the orphanage and in Leakey. The man was several inches shorter than Jackson but weighed a good fifty pounds more. While some might see the gray hair, lined face, and extra pounds and underestimate his strength, that was a mistake Jackson had never made. Gideon Rawlins was a formidable man, strong and determined. He'd won Jackson's respect the day he'd joined the Rangers.

"Yes, sir, that's true. In my opinion, it would be a waste of manpower to keep looking for them. Leander and I did our best, but we could never find them between heists, and since they don't seem to be robbing trains or coaches anymore, there's no way of knowing where to look."

Jackson met his captain's gaze and was pleased by what he saw. His commanding officer accepted his assessment. "The Gang appears to have changed since Michener was killed."

Though he knew that wasn't the man's real name, that was still the way Jackson thought of him. "I think they'll split up once they find the missing gold. I also believe it's simply a matter of time until they come to Cimarron Creek looking for it."

That was one of the reasons Jackson had chafed at this meeting. As much as he trusted Travis, he wanted to be the one to guard Thea. "I don't know how long it'll take them to track Thea, that is, Mrs. Michener," Jackson said, correcting himself quickly, "but they appear convinced that she has the gold."

The captain leaned against the tree trunk, his position seemingly relaxed, although Jackson knew he was ever vigilant. "Your reasoning makes sense. Do you need any backup? I imagine Leander told you he's mustering out, so I'll need to assign you a new partner, anyway."

He gave Jackson an appraising look before he continued. "Unless Leander's right and you're thinking about leaving too."

Jackson knew he hadn't mentioned that to Leander and wondered just what he'd said that had led his former partner to that conclusion. He looked directly at the captain, willing the man to see his sincerity. "Yes, sir, I am leaning that way." He wouldn't tell the man who'd devoted his whole life to the Rangers that he'd grown weary of the nomadic life.

Captain Rawlins nodded as he gazed into the distance, searching for anything unexpected. "I hate to lose you, Jackson, but I know this life isn't for everyone. My missus keeps saying she'd like to have me around all the time."

Jackson's shock must have been audible, because the captain's lips twitched as if he were trying to suppress a smile. "You seem surprised."

"I didn't know you were married."

"More than twenty years now. I won't say it's been easy, but if we've made it this long, I reckon we'll make it for another five. By then I'll be ready to hang up my holster and settle down with Beulah."

This was more personal information than the captain had shared in all the years Jackson had known him, and while he wondered what had triggered the confidence, Jackson decided to take advantage of the man's candor. Perhaps he could help resolve Jackson's other problem.

"How you'd convince your Beulah to marry you? Thea turned me down."

Jackson's captain stared at him for a long, uncomfortable moment, as if he were trying to see through Jackson's skin to his heart. Whatever he saw must have amused him, because he chuckled. "Don't tell me you just up and asked her."

Though Jackson refused to admit that that was exactly what he'd done, something in his expression must have betrayed him, because Captain Rawlins's chuckle turned into a full-fledged laugh.

"That's not the way, son. Ladies aren't like bandits. You can't ambush them. You've got to woo them. Flowers, candy, things like that—that's the way to lasso a gal."

Was he trying to woo her? The question that had been hovering at the back of her mind popped to the foreground as Thea walked to the livery. It was Monday, time for another call on Ethel Harris. Today, though Jackson would accompany her, Stuart was remaining in Cimarron Creek with Widow Jenkins. Both Thea and Jackson had agreed that the baby did not need to be exposed to people who considered him a burden, but Jackson was also adamant that Thea not go without him. She wouldn't argue with his desire to protect her, and yet she couldn't deny that the thought of being alone with Jackson for an extended time made her uncomfortable.

She knew she'd shocked him with her refusal of marriage, but it had been the right answer—the only answer she could give. Not even for Stuart could she marry a man who did not love her. Jackson had never mentioned the word "love," nor had he sought to hold her hand or touch her in anything other than a friendly way, but Thea had to admit that he'd changed since the day she'd refused him.

Was he wooing her? Aimee claimed that was the reason he'd brought her a box of chocolate creams from Cimarron Sweets.

"I thought of you when I saw them," Jackson had said as Thea opened the box to reveal half a dozen of Lydia's most popular candies.

That he'd thought of her might be true, but it wasn't the whole story. The tiny buggy that decorated the top of each candy told Thea this had been no casual purchase. Lydia and Opal piped flowers on the chocolate creams they sold to most customers. Only special orders received a different decoration. And the fact that the buggy looked very much like the one Thea owned told her this was definitely a special order.

"The man is courting you," Aimee had announced when she saw the candy. "When he asks, I hope you accept."

Thea wouldn't admit that Jackson had already proposed and that she'd refused him. Instead she'd said simply, "It's too soon for me to be thinking of marriage."

"That's nonsense. I've seen the way you two look at each other. You're both smitten." Aimee's retort had come without hesitation.

Smitten? Was that possible? It was true that Thea was attracted to Jackson. It was true that she often dreamt of him. It was true that the thought of a future with him and Stuart grew more appealing each day. All those things were true, but Thea didn't know whether that was love or merely a passing fascination.

With each step she took, the questions continued to bounce through her mind, along with the puzzle of why Jackson had arranged to meet her at the livery rather than at her home. If he were courting her, wouldn't he have wanted to spend every possible minute with her? Wouldn't he have wanted to walk with her, her hand nestled in the crook of his elbow, even though it was only a short distance? That's what Nate seemed to want from Aimee.

As she approached the livery, Thea saw that Jackson had already arrived and was standing next to Maggie and the buggy. Surely it was her imagination that he looked more handsome than ever today. There was nothing special about his clothes; he still needed a haircut; and yet something about him made her pulse race as if she'd run the length of Main Street.

"You're right on time," Jackson said with a wide smile. "That's one of the many things I admire about you: you're punctual."

Thea's pulse returned to normal with the realization that he couldn't possibly be wooing her. She'd been courted before, and she knew what men who sought a woman's favor said. Daniel had complimented her hair and eyes; he'd never praised her for being punctual. Punctuality was not romantic.

"My patients deserve nothing less," Thea said. Her flight of fancy was over. It was best to remember that she was a working woman.

"I wish everyone felt the way you do. Mrs. Higgins was so late today that I didn't think I'd get here on time."

First punctuality, now Mrs. Higgins. Thea felt as if her head were spinning. "What does Mrs. Higgins have to do with our trip to the Harris ranch?"

"This." Jackson pointed to the basket he'd lashed to the back of the buggy. "I asked her to make us a picnic lunch. I was hoping I could persuade you to take a detour on the way back. I heard there's a nice spot by the creek and thought we could eat there."

A picnic lunch. A pretty spot. Maybe he *was* trying to woo her.

Jackson could not remember the last time he'd been so nervous. It was silly to feel as if the future of the world depended on a simple meal eaten in the shade of a live oak. He knew it did not, but that didn't stop him from wanting everything to be perfect.

"How was it?" he asked when Thea emerged from the farmhouse. Though she was smiling as she approached the buggy, her shoulders were tense, and she gripped her bag so tightly that the seams of her gloves strained.

"It was what I expected. Mrs. Harris didn't even mention Stuart. It was as if she'd never met him."

Though Jackson could not condone the woman's heartlessness, he gave a silent prayer of thanksgiving that Thea would not have to fight the Harrises for custody of Stuart.

"That's for the best." He settled back in the seat, choosing a position where he could watch Thea. "We both know this isn't the right home for Stuart." Jackson knew or at least believed he knew what the right home would be, but he would not discuss that today. Today was a day for him and Thea—no one else.

"I have a proposal for you."

The instant the word was out of his mouth, Jackson knew he'd made a mistake. The way Thea's head swiveled toward him, her eyes wide with shock, told him he'd chosen the wrong word. Would he never learn? He could apologize, but that would only make matters worse. The best approach was to pretend it had not been a mistake, that he'd meant to talk about proposals.

"Here's what I propose." He kept his voice as even as if he were trying to coax a frightened cat out of a tree. "I propose that we spend the rest of the day getting to know each other. We can talk about anything you want other than Stuart and the Gang. What do you think? Does that sound like a good idea?"

This time his choice of words was deliberate, echoing the day he'd proposed marriage, but this time Thea's response was different.

"It sounds like a very good idea. Here's how I propose we begin." She gave him a mischievous grin after she emphasized "propose." "My friends and I used to play Twenty Questions, where we'd ask each other anything we wanted to know. The only rule was that all answers had to be honest. Shall we try that?"

"Sure. You can start."

Thea paused for a second, as if debating what to ask, and Jackson braced himself for a difficult question, but she surprised him. "What's your favorite color?"

They continued in that vein, learning each other's favorite and least favorite foods, which books they'd read more than once, their views on the effects of Reconstruction on Texas, where they'd go if they could travel anywhere in the world, and with each question, Jackson felt the tension that had been coiled up inside him release a bit. Thea, he knew, was having the same reaction, because her smiles came more easily, and she'd even laughed a time or two.

When they reached the spot he'd chosen for their meal, Thea sighed with pleasure. "This looks like a slice of heaven."

While Jackson might not have been that exuberant, he had been drawn to the small meadow near one of the creek's many bends. The presence of an old oak tree to provide shade had only added to the place's appeal.

"Sun or shade?" he asked as he lifted the basket of food from the back of the buggy.

Thea laughed. "Sun, but you've already asked your twentieth question."

"And I'm not allowed any more?"

She answered with a shrug and another laugh. "I don't see why not."

Jackson busied himself spreading the blanket and pulling the containers of food from the basket. Though Thea had offered to help, he'd refused, telling her she was his guest, and guests did not work. The truth was, he enjoyed seeing her so relaxed. Normally when he was with her, she was doing something, even if it was only pouring him a glass of buttermilk. The sight of Thea sitting on the blanket, seemingly at peace, filled him with joy. This was the kind of life he wanted her to have, a life free from worry and fear.

"This is delicious," Thea exclaimed when she tasted the peach pie. It was the same thing she'd said about the fried chicken, potato salad, and fresh rolls. According to Thea, everything Jackson had brought was perfect.

From his perspective, what was perfect was Thea. With her cheeks flushed with pleasure and her eyes sparkling, she was the prettiest thing he'd ever seen. Even the lock of hair that had escaped from her chignon only added to her appeal. Thea was the woman—the only woman—he wanted to share his life, but it was too soon to tell her that, just as it was too soon to declare his love. He had to do everything right so that the next time he asked her to marry him, she'd give him the answer he wanted.

Thea swallowed the last bite of pie and brushed the crumbs from her fingers, then smiled as she looked at him. "This was the best meal I've ever had. I wish I knew how to thank you for it."

"Well," he drawled, "there's one way." Before his sensible side had a chance to tell him to wait, Jackson leaned forward and pressed his lips to Thea's.

27

He was kissing her! Thea felt shivers of pure pleasure make their way down her spine, and her pulse began to race at the sensation of Jackson's lips on hers. What a wonderful day this had become. First, the laughter they'd shared as they'd asked and answered questions, then the delicious meal they'd enjoyed, accompanied by the soft murmur of the creek behind them, and now this, the sweetest kiss she'd ever had.

She closed her eyes, savoring the delight of Jackson's embrace. It felt so good—so very, very good—to have his arms around her, to let his woodsy scent tantalize her senses, to hear the pounding of his heart. It was wonderful, but it was wrong.

Though it was one of the most difficult things she'd ever done, Thea broke away from him and scrambled to her feet.

"What's wrong?" Jackson's face mirrored the confusion she heard in his voice. "Did I hurt you?"

"No." She couldn't let him believe that. "It was my fault, Jackson. I should never have allowed that to happen. Please promise you won't do it again."

He looked as if she'd slapped him. "Didn't you like it?"

Though this wasn't one of his twenty questions, she wouldn't lie. "Of course I did, but it was wrong. Even though being a widow gives me more freedom, it was still wrong."

Furrows formed between his eyes. "Help me understand why it was wrong."

Because you don't love me. That was the reason, but she couldn't tell him for fear that he'd claim he loved her simply to get another kiss. That was what Daniel had done, and while Jackson was not like Daniel, Thea wouldn't take the chance that he might lie.

"It's not proper," she said, hating the fact that she sounded like a sour spinster.

Jackson threw up his hands. "My pa told me women were impossible to understand, and it appears he was right. I don't understand what was improper, but I guess I don't have to. You were upset, and that's what matters."

He stared at the creek for a long moment, then nodded. "All right, Thea. Have it your way. I can't promise that I won't kiss you again, because there are few things I want more than that, but I can promise that I won't kiss you until you ask me to." He turned toward the buggy. "Now, let's get back to town."

"You're a lucky man." Nate clapped Jackson on the shoulder before he settled into the porch chair next to him. It was early evening, and once again Nate had remained in town. When Warner went out walking with Patience, Jackson had thought he'd have the porch to himself and his turbulent thoughts, but he hadn't counted on Nate, who'd apparently taken a shorter-than-normal stroll with Aimee.

"How'd you figure that?" Jackson did not feel lucky. He'd proposed to Thea, and she'd refused him. He'd kissed her, and she'd rebuffed him. That was not what he would call lucky.

"I heard you took Thea on a picnic. I told Rachel I was going to invite Aimee on one, but she said it wouldn't be proper unless I took a chaperone. You—you lucky man—didn't need one."

Nate's lips curved into a frown. "I don't understand all these things, but Rachel said that being a widow gives Thea more freedom. She claims folks would get the wrong idea if Aimee and I went off on a picnic, but it sure sounded like fun to me."

"Picnics are nice," Jackson agreed. The one he'd shared with Thea had been pleasant. More than pleasant. It had been wonderful until he'd spoiled everything by kissing her. He should have listened to his inner censor, but he hadn't, and as a result, he'd upset Thea. The worst part was, though he regretted causing Thea so much distress, Jackson did not regret the kiss itself. It had been the best moment of his life.

"That's what I figured."

A tremor of shock ran through Jackson. Had Nate been reading his mind? He relaxed when his friend continued.

"Picnics are good, but since Rachel would have my head if I tried to take Aimee on one, I wondered if you had any other ideas. This courting business is taking too long."

Though Nate had come to the wrong man for advice about courtship, Jackson empathized with his friend. He'd once believed he was a patient man, but that was no longer true. What had happened today had made him eager to have the courting, wooing, or whatever it was called finished.

It wasn't only the kiss, although that had given him a taste of what marriage to Thea would hold. The whole day from the time they'd left the Harris ranch had been special. Jackson had enjoyed their game of questions, trivial as some of them had been, and the opportunity to learn more about the woman who fascinated him. They'd been making progress, getting to know each other, until he spoiled the day.

Given the mess he'd made of his relationship with Thea, Jackson was hardly a source of wise counsel, and yet he wanted to help Nate. Perhaps he should adopt Thea's tactic of asking questions.

"What do you want to do?" It seemed odd that the man

who'd apparently tried to court several other women was at a loss for the next step, but perhaps he'd bungled matters as badly as Jackson had.

Nate glared at Jackson, as if the answer should be self-evident. "I want to marry Aimee. I know she's the right one for me."

As far as he knew, Nate had not progressed beyond walking home from the apothecary with Aimee. There'd been no flowers, candy, or other gifts. If Captain Rawlins was right, Nate had a long way to go before he was ready to ask for Aimee's hand in marriage, and yet Jackson wasn't convinced that the captain was right. As a Ranger, he knew that sometimes you had to take bold action.

"Then tell her you love her and ask her to be your wife."

Nate's eyes widened. "That simple, huh?"

"That simple." Or that difficult. For a man as tongue-tied around the woman he loved as Nate was, even a two-sentence declaration might be close to impossible, but Nate did not seem intimidated.

He grinned and rose to his feet. "Step 1," he said, holding up a single finger, "'I love you, Aimee.'" He extended a second finger. "Step 2: 'Will you be my wife?' Two easy steps. I can do it!" He bounded off the porch and headed toward his horse. "Thanks, Jackson. I'm gonna be a married man before you know it."

As his friend mounted the bay mare, Jackson slapped his forehead. What a fool he'd been! He'd made it sound so easy to Nate, but he hadn't followed his own advice. He'd skipped the first step.

Jackson groaned at the magnitude of his mistake. He'd never told Thea he loved her. No wonder she'd refused to marry him. No wonder she had found their kiss improper. Jackson was hardly an expert on courtship, but even he knew that kisses were reserved for couples whose affections were firmly engaged. Wasn't that the phrase Ma had used when she'd talked to him about the birds and bees? She'd said that some couples even waited to share their first kiss after the wedding ceremony.

Jackson didn't want to wait that long for another kiss. There was no reason to, because his affections were firmly engaged. They couldn't get much more firmly attached than love.

The problem was, he hadn't told Thea he loved her, not when he'd asked her to marry him or today when they'd shared that unforgettable kiss. Instead, Jackson had made it sound as if the reason for their marriage was to protect Stuart. Admittedly, that was part of it, but it wasn't the whole reason—not even the most important one. The reason he wanted Thea to be his wife was that he loved her.

Would her answer be different once she knew that? Jackson hoped so. He hoped she would give him another chance, that his past two mistakes had not destroyed their hope of happiness.

One thing was certain: this time he wouldn't rush. He wouldn't simply blurt out his feelings. He'd find the perfect setting, the perfect moment to declare his love. And then . . .

28

"As much as I don't like the Harrises' attitude toward Stuart, I'm glad Ethel's your patient," Jackson said as they climbed the hill out of Cimarron Creek, headed toward the Harris ranch.

It wasn't the first time he had surprised Thea with something he'd said or done, but this announcement seemed to come from nowhere, just like the kiss that she could not forget. To his credit, Jackson had made no attempt to kiss her since then, although there had been times when she'd caught him looking at her lips, his expression reminding her of Clay when he looked at Sarah.

The memory of those moments watered the tiny seed of hope that had lodged deep inside her until it began to sprout, making Thea wonder if maybe, just maybe, Jackson harbored tender thoughts toward her. She wouldn't call them love—it was too soon for that—but her heart sang at the possibility that he might view her as more than a friend.

Wrenching her thoughts back to the present, Thea responded to Jackson's statement with a simple question. "Why?" There were days when she was not particularly happy that Ethel Harris was her patient. The last time Thea had called on her, the woman had complained about every ache and pain and was disgruntled when Thea explained that they were normal parts of pregnancy.

"Why?" Jackson echoed Thea's question. "Because it gives us an excuse to spend more time together. Speaking for myself, I enjoy our rides."

"So do I." Each time he accompanied her to the Harris ranch, Thea uncovered new aspects of the man whose kiss had flummoxed her. She'd known from the beginning that Jackson was courageous—Rangers had to be—but she'd discovered that he was also kind. Not only did he lavish love on Stuart, but after he'd heard Angus Harris grumbling about their milk cow no longer producing, he'd brought a large can of fresh milk to the ranch.

Thea wasn't certain who'd been more surprised by that, she or the Harrises. She wasn't sure she could have been so thoughtful, especially since Ethel Harris had not shown the slightest interest in Stuart.

"Having company makes the ride pass more quickly," Thea added. So quickly that, instead of being eager to be home, she found herself wishing the Harris ranch were even more distant. Today, though Maggie seemed eager to trot, Thea kept her at a walk simply to extend her time with Jackson.

"So just anyone's company would do?"

He was teasing. Thea knew that, but rather than reply in kind, she decided to be honest. "No, it's your company I enjoy." And, oh, how she enjoyed it! Each day she found herself more fascinated by the Ranger with the crooked smile. Not even in those first heady days after she'd met Daniel had she been so eager to be with a man.

"I'm glad to hear that, because you're likely to be stuck with me for a while."

Though the prospect made her smile, her smile faded at the memory of the reason Jackson was in Cimarron Creek. "Do you think it will take a long time to catch the rest of the Gang?"

Jackson shook his head. "I'm surprised they haven't already tracked you to Cimarron Creek and made a move. I know you said someone in Ladreville sent them to Austin, but it wouldn't take too long to discover that you're not there. By now they must be worried that you've discovered the gold and are spending it."

The gold. Thoughts of it were like a cloud blocking the sun's radiance. "I still have trouble believing Daniel took that gold." Thea had grown accustomed to the idea that the man she'd married had been a thief, but though she could imagine him stealing from strangers, she couldn't picture him taking his partners' share of their stash. Wasn't there supposed to be honor among thieves? But, then again, wasn't a man supposed to honor his marriage vows?

"It's the only thing that makes sense." Thea blinked, then realized Jackson wasn't responding to her thoughts when he continued. "Are you sure you don't remember any place he talked about that might have been a hiding spot?"

It was her turn to shake her head. "Daniel didn't talk about his past very much, and then it was only to say how miserable he was at the orphanage and how he couldn't wait to escape. When I think back on it, I realize he didn't tell me much at all. He just swept me off my feet with his pretty words."

Jackson feigned a scowl. "You don't need to worry about pretty words from me. My parents raised me to speak my mind."

"And I appreciate that." Jackson might not be one for pretty words, but Thea knew he would tell the truth. Not only was that knowledge reassuring, but it emphasized the differences between Jackson and her husband. She had been wrong to believe Jackson would claim he loved her just to get another kiss. That wasn't something he would do. He was an honest and an honorable man.

Thea placed her hand on the buggy's brake as they descended a hill. While Maggie knew better than to run, there was always the possibility that something might spook her. Thea's lips curved in an ironic smile as she realized that while Jackson was worried about her safety, she worried about his.

"You're an interesting man, Jackson Guthrie."

"Because I tell the truth?"

"That's part of it."

Jackson seemed pleased, but he still raised an eyebrow as he asked, "What else?"

"You're honorable."

"I can see where that would appeal to you, but make no mistake, I'm not a saint. I've done my share of things I'm not proud of."

"But you regret them. That makes a difference." Thea suspected that Daniel had had no regrets about his life.

It seemed strange to realize she'd been acquainted with Jackson almost the same amount of time as she had Daniel before they married, but she already knew so much more about the Ranger than she ever had about Daniel, even though she'd been Daniel's wife for over seven months.

While she'd been fascinated by Daniel, because he'd been unlike any of the other men she knew, her feelings for him had not had a firm foundation, perhaps because she'd known so little about him. Like a house built on sand, her fascination had crumbled under the adversity of real life.

What Thea felt for Jackson was different. She didn't idealize him. Instead, she knew that he had his flaws, just as she did. Thea had no doubts that he'd shown her the real Jackson. The question was, could she trust her judgment or was she making another mistake in believing he might be the man God intended for her? She'd been certain that Daniel was the right man for her, but she'd been wrong. So very wrong.

Jackson was silent for a while, then when the sun disappeared behind a cloud, he rolled his shoulders as if to release a cramp. "I know you've been here less than two months and it might be too soon to know, but do you think you'll stay in Cimarron Creek?"

Thea had almost forgotten that they'd been talking about

how long his search for the Gang would keep Jackson in Cimarron Creek before they veered off on tangents. "I don't have a formal contract, but I told Travis I'd stay for at least a year."

"And after that?" Though his words were casual, when Thea glanced at him, she saw an intensity in Jackson's expression that made her think her answer mattered.

"I'm not sure. I know my sister hopes I'll return to Ladreville, but . . ." She let her voice trail off, not knowing how to complete the sentence.

"What do you hope?" Once again Jackson was being persistent. It was one of his strongest traits, and one that Thea suspected had served him well as a Ranger.

She stared into the distance as she considered how to answer. She couldn't tell him of the tender hope that had sprouted and continued to grow, the hope that she could make a home for herself in Cimarron Creek. A home that would include Stuart and a husband like Jackson. Oh, why mince words? She dreamt of a life with Jackson.

It was the sweetest of dreams, one that left Thea with a smile when she wakened, but she couldn't tell him that. That was not something a woman should do, especially not a woman who was as unsure of her convictions as Thea. What if she'd misjudged her feelings for Jackson? What if they faded the way Daniel's professed love for her had? She wouldn't risk inflicting that kind of pain on Jackson.

"I hope to stay here," she said slowly. There was no harm in sharing that much with him. "What about you? What are your dreams for the future?"

"They depend."

The look he gave her was so intense that it left Thea breathless. What did he mean? Was it possible that his dreams were similar to hers? Perhaps the reason he'd asked her to marry him hadn't been simply to give Stuart a family. Perhaps the reason he'd kissed her had been because he loved her.

Thea broke off her thoughts and gazed at Jackson. When he said nothing more, she realized she must have been mistaken, and so she completed the sentence for him. "On catching the Gang."

He nodded. "That's the first step. I can't leave the Rangers until I've done that."

"Then you've made up your mind." He'd talked about it before, but this time he sounded different, as if he'd made a decision and was comfortable with it.

"Yes." Jackson's lips curved into a wry smile. "I didn't realize I'd made the decision until my captain and I spoke. It seems my former partner knew me better than I know myself. He predicted I was ready to leave more than a month ago."

"Are you sure you won't regret it?" It would be a major change for a man so used to being on the move to settle down in one spot. Thea wondered whether he would miss the excitement of tracking outlaws or whether he'd grown tired of it. Lawrence, the sheriff of Ladreville and a former Ranger, had once told her that the nomadic life took its toll on a man.

Another nod was Jackson's first response. "A month ago I would have said I wasn't certain, but now I am. It's time for me to build a life of my own. I want a ranch and a family. The reason I said you would likely be stuck with me for a while is that I'm considering staying in Cimarron Creek."

"You are?" The thought made Thea's heart leap.

Jackson nodded. "It depends on—"

He broke off abruptly, his head swiveling to look behind them, his hand moving swiftly to grip his revolver.

"What's wrong?"

Jackson continued to scan the horizon before he responded. "I thought we were being followed."

Thea took note of his verb tense. "You said 'thought,' not 'think.' Is someone behind us?"

"Not that I can see. It must have been my imagination."

For the next few minutes, they rode silently, Jackson scrutinizing their surroundings, not relaxing until they arrived at the Harris ranch. It was then that Thea realized she didn't know what he'd meant to say, that he hadn't finished his explanation of what needed to happen before he would move to Cimarron Creek permanently.

"I'm sorry to have kept you waiting," Aimee said as she emerged from the back room. "A shipment came this morning, but I haven't had a chance to unpack it. I was hoping there might be more calamine."

"Was there?"

Aimee shook her head. As much as she hated to disappoint Rachel, the new supply of calamine had not arrived. "I'm afraid not. The only thing I can suggest is to make a paste with baking soda and see if that helps. *Maman* used that when I had a bee sting. It might work on chicken pox."

Rachel looked as harried as Aimee had ever seen her, her normally immaculate shirtwaist wrinkled, the ends of her bonnet ribbons frayed, a button on her right glove loose. Aimee wished there were something she could do for her friend, since it was clear that the strain of caring for a second adult patient was overwhelming her.

"Poor Nate." Rachel shook her head in dismay. "I haven't seen him this upset since that awful business with his goats last year. He's acting like something horrible is going to happen just because he caught chicken pox. He won't listen to me when I tell him that they'll go away. He just keeps muttering, 'I don't want to wait. I don't want to wait,' but when I ask him what he means, he won't answer." Rachel waited until Aimee met her gaze before she asked, "Do you know what he means?"

Aimee did not. All she knew was that she felt as if she'd done nothing but wait for the past few weeks. Her days, which had once been filled with anticipation of the time she would spend with Nate, now dragged. He couldn't help it that he'd caught a particularly bad case of chicken pox and hadn't left his farm in over two weeks, but knowing that didn't make waiting for him any easier.

She was waiting for Nate to be well enough to resume their daily walks and waiting for word of when her mother would arrive in Cimarron Creek. When would the waiting end?

"Would you like a glass of buttermilk?" Thea asked as she and Jackson walked from the livery to her house. They'd had no picnic today, and though they'd both taken drinks from the canteens they always carried in the buggy, she was still thirsty. That was part of the reason for offering him a drink, but it was far from the most important one. The truth was, she didn't want Jackson to leave, not when there were still unanswered questions.

As they'd ridden home, they'd talked about his exploits with the Rangers and Thea's more amusing episodes with her patients, but they'd never returned to Jackson's plans to settle in Cimarron Creek. Though she was reluctant to ask him directly, perhaps if they relaxed on the porch, he might speak of it.

"That sounds mighty good."

Thea nodded, pleased that he sounded as eager to stay with her as she was to have him there. "I'll be right back."

She pulled the key from her reticule and started to fit it into the door but stopped when she realized the door was no longer locked. Aimee must have returned earlier than she'd expected.

"Aimee?" Thea called as she opened the door. There was no answer. She stepped inside, then screamed.

The parlor had been torn apart.

Thea looked down at the baby in her arms. Stuart was contentedly drinking his milk, unaware of the turmoil that still caused her stomach to clench. Though the house had once again been restored to order, she could not forget the chaos that had greeted her yesterday.

As soon as he'd seen the destruction in the parlor, Jackson had summoned Travis, and the two men had walked through the house, cataloguing the damage. Every room had been searched. The contents of the kitchen cabinets had been flung to the floor; wardrobes had been emptied, bureau drawers overturned.

"At least they didn't rip the cushions the way they did at Helen Bradford's house," Jackson had told her.

Though it was a small mercy, Thea still felt violated, knowing that strangers had been in her home. It was no coincidence, she was certain, that Jackson had believed someone was following them yesterday. In all likelihood, that person—or persons—had realized she would be gone for a while and had returned to Cimarron Creek to search for the missing gold. The gold that they were unable to find, because Thea did not have it.

No one knew what they would do next, but Jackson was taking no chances. He'd told Thea he doubted the Gang would strike again during daylight, but he, Travis, and Edgar had taken turns keeping watch overnight. No one had come, and though they'd questioned several of the townspeople, no one had noticed any strangers.

"Be extra careful," Jackson had cautioned Thea this morning when he announced that he was going to search the perimeter of the town, looking for traces of the Gang.

She would indeed be careful, particularly because she had this precious child in her care. No one was going to hurt Stuart. Though she would normally have sat on the porch as she fed him, today she'd remained indoors. And while keeping a watchful eye on the street was not something she'd ever done, today she found herself doing exactly that. That was why she saw five people approach Travis and Lydia's house.

The travelers had returned.

Thea smiled for the first time all day. There was no need to be suspicious of these newcomers. The way Lydia greeted them left no doubt of their identity. The young couple were Catherine and Austin Goddard. Their children, Hannah and Seth, marched a few steps behind them, each holding the hand of an older woman. The children seemed exuberant, perhaps because they were finally out of the stagecoach and could release pent-up energy, but their companion was far from happy.

Thea's smile faded at the sight of the slumped shoulders and hesitant gait that telegraphed despair. This was Grace Sims, Aimee's mother, the woman who'd traveled so far to find her daughter and who had yet to learn that her quest would have a happy ending.

Thea studied the older woman, wanting to see whether the resemblance to Aimee was as pronounced as Lydia had claimed, but Grace's hat shaded her face. Thea would have to wait until they were formally introduced to have her question answered. Right now, it was time to put Lydia's plan into motion.

Lydia hadn't known the exact date of the travelers' arrival, but she'd told Thea that she would insist Grace spend the night with her rather than returning to the ranch with the Goddards. The ostensible reason would be to help Lydia with the twins, when in actuality she wanted Grace to have private time with Aimee.

Since the stagecoach arrived in the afternoon when Thea was rarely with patients, she and Lydia had arranged that once Catherine and Austin left, Thea would fetch Aimee from the apothecary. No one wanted Grace to wait a minute longer than necessary for the reunion.

"C'mon, Stuart, you're going for a ride," Thea said half an hour later when the four Goddards had departed. Though it would take less than ten minutes to go to the pharmacy and return, she had no intention of leaving the child alone. There was no telling what the Gang might do to get the gold.

Jackson could say what he would about the outlaws not returning during daylight, but Thea would take no chances. Once Stuart was bundled into the buggy, she pushed it as quickly as she could without breaking into a run.

"I hate to inconvenience you," she told Warner as she entered the pharmacy, "but I need Aimee at home now."

"More trouble?" Like the rest of Cimarron Creek's residents, Warner had heard about the ransacking of her house.

Thea shook her head. "No. Just something only Aimee can do."

Though she said nothing, Aimee's eyes lit with happiness. A second later, the happiness was gone, replaced by what appeared to be fear. Poor Aimee. No matter how much she'd longed for this moment, she could not help but wonder what it would be like to be face-to-face with the woman who'd given her life.

Oblivious to his assistant's conflicting emotions, Warner nodded. "Certainly. Some of our customers will be disappointed, but we'll all survive."

"Thanks, Warner." Aimee offered him a weak smile as she followed Thea outside. "They're here?" she asked in little more than a whisper.

"The others have left, but Grace is still with Lydia."

Apprehension caused Aimee's face to stiffen. "Oh, Thea, what am I going to do?"

"You're going to meet your mother."

29

I don't recognize them." Though he'd tried to convince himself that the Gang would not strike during the day, Jackson could not stop himself from keeping watch. He'd stopped in the sheriff's office to see whether Travis had learned anything about the people who'd searched Thea's home, but rather than take one of the chairs in front of the desk, he stood by the window so he could watch the street.

The unfamiliar couple did not look suspicious, but that meant little. Jackson doubted that the Gang appeared to be anything other than ordinary citizens until they masked their faces and pulled guns on their victims. As Jackson studied the couple and wondered if he should attempt to talk to them, he realized these were not his quarry. The man had blond hair, not brown, and the dark-haired woman who sat so close to him that Jackson surmised they were man and wife was not tall enough to be the female member of the Gang. When two children sat up in the back of the wagon, the newcomers' innocence was confirmed.

"That's Austin Goddard and his family." Travis had abandoned his chair and come to stand next to Jackson. "Lydia and I've been expecting them to arrive any day now. I imagine they're tired from traveling, but if you're interested in that ranch of theirs, you might want to go out there in the next day or two."

Jackson nodded. "I'll do that."

Aimee knocked on the door, her heart pounding so fiercely she feared it might break through her chest. This was the moment she'd dreamt about, the one she'd been waiting for. She shouldn't be so nervous; she shouldn't have so much trouble breathing; but she did.

Only seconds after she'd knocked, Lydia opened the door and ushered her inside. "I'm glad you're here."

"Does she know?" They hadn't rehearsed the details of the meeting. All Lydia had told Aimee was that she would give them time alone.

"Not yet." As if she sensed that Aimee's legs were about to give way, Lydia wrapped her arm around Aimee's waist and led her toward the parlor. "Don't worry," she whispered. "Everything will be fine."

If only Aimee could be so confident. She wanted to meet Grace—after all, she was the reason Aimee had traveled so far—but now that the moment had arrived, she had no idea what she should say or do.

"Smile," Lydia advised as she opened the door.

The room was empty save for a blonde woman perched on the edge of the settee. Aimee's breath caught as the woman raised her head and looked at her, revealing a face that was an older version of the one Aimee saw in the mirror every morning.

The woman gasped and started to rise, but Lydia shook her head. "You'd best stay seated, Grace, because I don't want you to faint. This young lady is Aimee Jarre, your daughter."

The blood drained from Grace's face, leaving her so pale that Aimee thought she might indeed faint. She stared at Aimee for a moment, clearly not believing what she'd heard, even though her eyes confirmed the truth.

"You're here? This is where you came?" A smile wreathed Grace's face, giving her an almost ethereal beauty. "Oh, my child, I can't believe it! This is the miracle I prayed for."

Ignoring Lydia's admonitions, Grace rose and rushed toward Aimee, enfolding her in her arms, leaving Aimee surrounded by the delicate scent of toilet water and the warmth she'd longed for her entire life. This was her mother. Despite the years and the secrets that had kept them apart, they were together now, and if Aimee had her way, they would never again be parted.

Though she left her hands on Aimee's shoulders, as if she were as unwilling as Aimee to break the contact, Grace took a step backward and stared at her. "You've grown up to be a beautiful woman."

"*Je ne suis pas belle.*" Aimee shook her head. "I'm sorry. Sometimes I forget the English words when I'm excited. I'm not beautiful."

Grace raised one hand and traced the outlines of Aimee's face, her fingers moving slowly down her cheek, then cupping her chin. "Yes, you are. To a mother's eye, you'll always be beautiful. Now sit down here." She gestured toward the settee. "I want to know everything about you."

And Aimee wanted to learn everything about her.

When Aimee and her mother were seated next to each other, Lydia spoke. "I'll bring you some tea and a few sandwiches."

Grace gripped Aimee's hand and kept her gaze fixed on her. "I've dreamt of this moment every day since I left you in Ladreville, but I never truly believed I'd see you again. Oh, Aimee, I love you so much."

A little laugh punctuated her words. "Your parents chose the perfect name for you. When I first heard it, I thought it sounded pretty, much better than Bertha, which is what I would have named you."

Aimee's heart swelled with happiness at the evidence that despite having been sent away from Cimarron Creek, Grace had loved her parents enough to want to give her daughter her mother's name.

"It was only when Catherine explained that Aimee means 'loved' that I realized how well they'd chosen. You are loved. So very much."

Aimee nodded, momentarily unable to utter a word. She could feel Grace's love in the hand that gripped hers. She could see it in her eyes and hear it in her voice. This was what had been missing from her life: a mother's love.

Perhaps it was too soon to ask, but Aimee could not stop herself. "If you loved me, why did you give me up for adoption?"

"I didn't want to. You need to believe that, Aimee. No matter what my parents said, you were not a problem or a burden. You were my child." As emotion choked her voice, Grace paused to clear her throat. "I wanted to raise you. I knew I couldn't do it here, because there would always be cruel whispers about you, so I thought about moving to a town where I could pretend to be a widow."

As she fixed her gaze on Aimee, Aimee realized that while she might be a younger version of her mother, they did not share the same eye color. Grace's were emerald green, while Aimee's were hazel, perhaps a legacy from her father.

"I would have done it," Grace continued, "but my heart told me you deserved more than that. You deserved two parents, and that was a problem I couldn't surmount. I wouldn't have married your father even if he'd been free to offer for me, and I doubted any man would want to marry me after what he'd done to me."

Though she gave no detail, Grace's words confirmed what Aimee had feared: her mother had been attacked, and it appeared that the man had been married. No matter how fervently she wished it were otherwise, Aimee was not the result of an encounter between two young people who'd been swept away by their emotions.

Aimee nodded slowly, encouraging her mother to continue.

"As much as I loved you and wanted to keep you with me, I couldn't let you suffer because of what had happened to me, so when the family I was staying with offered to find a couple to adopt you, I agreed. Perhaps it was cowardly of me, but I knew it would be impossible to hand you to another woman, so I left before they reached Ladreville."

Everything she'd said confirmed what Aimee had thought. "The Russells told me how worried they were about you."

Surprise brought a flush of color to Grace's face. "You've met Ruth and Sterling? You went to Ladreville? How did that happen and how did you know to come here?"

Lydia knocked on the door, deposited a tray laden with food and beverages on the table in front of them, then departed without a word. As she watched her mother sip tea and savor a sandwich, Aimee told her about her childhood in France, how she'd always felt different from the other children at school but hadn't known why, how the letters she found after her parents' deaths had revealed that she had been born in Texas and adopted by the Jarres.

"I wanted to find you or at least learn more about you," she told Grace, "so I came to Texas. When I arrived in Ladreville, Pastor and Mrs. Russell took me in, but they couldn't tell me anything other than that you'd once lived in Cimarron Creek. Coming here was my last hope."

Tears filled Grace's eyes, but whether they were tears of sorrow or joy, Aimee didn't know. "When did you arrive?" her mother asked. When Aimee told her, she brushed an errant tear from her cheek. "Two weeks. If only I'd waited two weeks longer to leave." There was no doubt that the tears that now streamed down Grace's face were tears of regret.

"You're here now, and we're together. That's all that matters."

Though she meant the words to comfort her mother, Aimee wasn't certain she'd succeeded.

"Do you understand why I did what I did?" Grace asked. "I thought I was doing what was best for you when I let them adopt you. I thought they'd love you and that you'd be raised in America. Even though I didn't know their names or that they were from France, the Russells said that the couple had longed for a child and were planning to settle in California. I believed that would be good for you."

"I know that." Aimee patted Grace's shoulder, the gesture almost identical to the way she soothed Stuart. "I'm not sure what I would have done in your situation, but I know it's important that a child have two parents. Thea's been struggling with that."

"Thea?"

As Aimee explained what had happened to Thea and how Stuart had come to be part of their lives, Grace's tears dried. "That poor woman! It must have been horrible, losing both her husband and her baby. At least I had the joy of holding you in my arms for a few minutes. I knew you were alive."

She stared at the floor for a moment, then returned her gaze to Aimee. "Every time I'd see a girl about your age, I would wonder where you were and what you were doing. I wondered if you were in a big city or a small town or living on a ranch, but during all those years I never dreamed that you were in France." She shook her head, as if chastising herself. "My daughter is a Frenchwoman."

Aimee didn't want to talk about herself, not when there were so many things she had yet to learn about her mother. "What did you do when you left Ladreville?"

Grace explained how she'd fled to San Antonio, where she'd met an older couple and become a companion to the woman. "When Marjorie died, Douglas insisted that we marry," she told Aimee. "I was as happy as I could be under the circumstances."

She pursed her lips for a second, as if trying to control her emotions, before she said, "I'll always regret that I didn't see my parents again, but I thank God that I found you."

As they consumed the plate of sandwiches and drank the tea, Aimee and her mother shared stories of their past. "Is there anything else you want to know?" Grace asked when she'd drained her cup of tea.

Aimee nodded. "Who was my father?"

30

He was anxious to see Thea again. Jackson could tell himself that he was worried about her now that the Gang had found her. That was true, but it was only part of the reason his boots were pounding the boardwalk as he rushed from the sheriff's office toward Thea's house.

"How are you?" he asked as she opened the door. She looked as beautiful as ever, although the circles under her eyes told him she hadn't slept well—if at all—last night.

He wasn't surprised. Even if he hadn't been keeping watch, Jackson knew he would have had trouble sleeping. He'd spent the night thinking about the destruction he'd seen in both Thea's and Helen Bradford's homes and feeling as if something important had eluded him. Even daylight, which normally cleared his thoughts, had not helped. He was as perplexed as he'd been last night.

Thea placed a finger on her lips and whispered, "I just got Stuart to sleep. He's been cranky all day, which isn't like him, but come on in."

Jackson kept his voice low as he followed her into the house. After the break-in, he and Thea had agreed that keeping her safe was more important than adhering to the town matrons' ideas of propriety and that Jackson could come inside even when Aimee was not there to serve as a chaperone.

"He probably senses that you're upset." Jackson looked into the parlor, where the sleeping baby lay inside his buggy. Other than a few scratches on the table, the room appeared much as it had before the intruders' visit. There was nothing here to trigger that elusive memory.

He turned back to Thea, hoping she hadn't realized that he'd given the room a professional scrutiny. "Babies are good at sensing our feelings, and you certainly have a reason to be upset. It's not every day that someone breaks into your house."

Thea's lips tightened. "I hope not. I hope it never happens again. As it is, I feel uncomfortable being here." She gestured around the hallway, then led the way into the kitchen. Like the parlor, it had been restored to normal. "Does it seem foolish to you that I wish I had somewhere else to live?"

"Not at all. I'd say that's a normal reaction." A glimmer of hope settled deep inside Jackson. As terrible as the break-in had been, the fear it had engendered just might work to his benefit.

"Would you and Stuart like to take a ride with me tomorrow? I have somewhere I need to go, and I'd like your company as well as your advice."

Though Thea appeared intrigued, she seemed to be pondering the invitation. "Won't you tell me where we're going?"

He shook his head. "It's meant to be a surprise."

"A surprise?"

The way she was acting made Jackson wonder if once again he'd chosen the wrong word. Was "surprise" like "proposal," fraught with hidden meanings? As Thea's gaze darted around the room, he realized that finding her home in shambles had been a surprise, an unpleasant one. He couldn't retract the word, so he continued. "A nice surprise."

This time her eyes lit with pleasure, and she smiled. "Then I accept."

"Are you certain you want to know?" Grace's eyes, almost as deep a green as the Ranger's, clouded as she looked at Aimee, revealing more clearly than words that her memories were painful.

Though she hated to cause Grace more pain, there was only one answer Aimee could give. "Yes, I am. I don't want there to be any secrets."

"It's not a happy story."

Aimee didn't need the warning. She already knew that. Instead of retreating as Grace seemed to hope she would, she reached out and stroked her mother's cheek, wanting to give her whatever comfort she could. "I know that he forced you."

A short nod confirmed Aimee's fears. "I was only fourteen when it happened. I didn't see his face at the time, and I never thought I'd know who he was, but I believe God knew how important it was for me to confront the man who'd changed my life so dramatically."

Grace poured herself another cup of tea and reached for one of the chocolate creams that Lydia had included with the light repast. "After an almost unbelievable sequence of events, I finally came face-to-face with my attacker."

She raised her eyes to meet Aimee's. "It may seem hard to believe, but forcing him to admit what he'd done left me free. It was an immense relief to realize that I no longer hated him. Of course, I still hated what he'd done, but I could separate the sin from the sinner."

"Just last week Pastor Dunn preached about forgiveness and said that was the first step."

Grace sipped her tea before she spoke. "He didn't ask for forgiveness, and everything happened so quickly that I couldn't give it to him, but I want you to know that no matter how I felt about him, I never felt anything but love for you." Her eyes glistened with unshed tears. "Being here with you is the best thing that's ever happened to me."

"I love you too." Aimee wondered whether Grace was deliberately not answering her question about her father's identity or whether her thoughts had simply taken a detour. Determined to get an answer, she asked, "Is he someone who lives here?"

"Lived." A nod accompanied the single word. "He's dead now."

Aimee took a shallow breath, not certain whether she was disappointed or relieved that she wouldn't encounter her father. While Grace might have been able to offer forgiveness, Aimee did not know if she could be so generous to the man who would attack an innocent young girl.

"If he's dead, no one will be hurt if you tell me who he was." It seemed important to know that, even though Aimee would never carry her father's name.

"It's not that simple. His son still lives here."

"His son?" Aimee blinked in momentary confusion as the impact of the words registered. Though she'd guessed that the man was married, she hadn't thought about his having a child. "I have a half-brother?"

Grace nodded. "Yes, you do." She remained silent for a moment, giving Aimee a chance to absorb the fact that had rocked her to her core. She'd always wanted a sibling, and now it appeared she had one.

"I was shocked when you told me you were working at the apothecary and how much you enjoyed being with Warner," Grace continued, "but I shouldn't have been. You see, your father was Charles Gray. Warner is your half-brother."

"Let's go, Blaze." Jackson urged his horse into a gallop. Perhaps the wind in his face would clear his thoughts. One thing was certain: walking had not accomplished that. He'd strode briskly around Cimarron Creek after he left Thea, but the memory that hid just out of reach refused to budge. Riding was his last hope.

He headed Blaze along the road he'd traveled the day he first came to town, hoping that would shake something loose, and it did. Jackson was only a few miles outside of Cimarron Creek when the rank smell of decaying meat assaulted him. Something, perhaps a rabbit, had been killed and left to rot on the side of the road. While normally scavengers would have found the animal and cleaned the bones, somehow they'd missed this one.

Jackson raised his bandanna to cover his nose and mouth, and as he did, the memory he'd sought resurfaced. When he'd walked through Helen Bradford's house and seen the destruction, he had noticed a faint residue of perfume clinging to the sliced bed pillows, as if they'd brushed against the intruder's body before being flung to the floor. There had been no perfume in Thea's house, nor had anything been slashed. In both cases, the search had been thorough, but only Helen Bradford's belongings had been destroyed.

Jackson remembered the gouges in Helen's furniture and the way the pillows had been left in shreds. Whoever had searched her house was looking for more than gold. He wanted revenge. No. Jackson shook his head. *She* wanted revenge. The person who'd invaded Helen's home had been a woman, and if his instincts were correct, she was the same woman who'd killed Helen, first torturing her with a knife, then slitting her throat.

Charity James.

Jackson had no doubt that Charity James had murdered Helen Bradford, just as he had no doubt that she'd been the one who'd killed Violet Baker. But, if his reasoning was accurate, she had not been the one who killed Daniel Michener. Michener had been shot. The question was, had Charity played a role in his death?

Wrinkling his nose at the odor that permeated his bandanna, Jackson knew there was no reason to ride any longer. He'd accomplished his goal. And, if he was right, Warner might be able to help him ease Thea's worries.

Half an hour later, he strode into the pharmacy. "Do you sell perfume?"

Warner appeared startled by the question. "Does this mean the gossip is true and you're courting Thea?"

Jackson shook his head. All he wanted was to identify a scent. If his hunch was right, this perfume was the last thing he would consider giving Thea.

"As strange as it may seem, this is connected to an investigation."

Raised eyebrows met Jackson's statement. Then Warner said, "I'm sorry to hear that. I thought you might have taken Travis's advice to heart." He resumed grinding the tablets with his pestle. "If you're looking for perfume, check with Jacob at the mercantile. If he doesn't have something you like, he can order others."

Two minutes later, Jackson had his answer.

"Mrs. Allen?" Jacob Whitfield nodded when Jackson asked whether she bought her perfume here. "She's the only woman in town who wears that scent—it's too strong for most of them—but I always keep a bottle on hand."

"May I smell it?"

"Sure."

As the shopkeeper unstopped the bottle and waved it under Jackson's nose, Jackson nodded. There was no doubt about it. This was the same scent he'd smelled at Helen Bradford's house.

He wanted to shout with triumph. It wasn't coincidence. He was certain of that, just as he was certain that the other woman, the one who'd caused Thea so much anguish, was a member of the Gang. And, though he had no proof, it was possible that Daniel Michener had not been unfaithful but that his shirts bore Charity James's scent because he'd been close to her during a robbery.

Though he wanted to tell Thea what he'd learned and what

he surmised, Jackson didn't want to give her half a story. He would wait until he'd captured the whole Gang and had their confessions.

"Warner?" Part of Aimee was shocked by Grace's revelation, but part was not. "No wonder . . ." She paused, thinking of the time she'd spent with the man who'd been both her boss and her friend.

"No wonder what?"

Though Grace had refilled their teacups, she had pushed hers away after she named Aimee's father. Aimee took a sip from hers, hoping the hot beverage would help settle her thoughts. She had expected to learn her father's name, but she had not expected to discover that she had a brother.

She replaced the cup on its saucer and looked at Grace. "No wonder we seem to have so much in common. I told you that I work for Warner, but I didn't tell you that we often think alike. There are even times when we finish each other's sentences."

Grace smiled. "When I was growing up and used to see siblings do that, I'd envy them. I even envied them when they squabbled, because although they were angry with each other at the time, I knew they'd make up and be friends again." She sighed. "My mother never explained why they hadn't had a second child, but I always wished that I had a sister or brother."

"So did I." Aimee thought of the years when she'd created make-believe sisters and had had endless conversations with them. Though her fantasy world had entertained her, it could not compare to a real sibling.

"Now I have a brother." The smile that had crossed Aimee's face faded as fears assailed her. "Do you think he'll welcome me?"

Knowing that she was related to Warner seemed wonderful to Aimee, but he might feel differently. It was possible he'd resent her, seeing her as proof of his—their!—father's wrongdoing.

"I don't know how he'll react." Grace laid a hand on Aimee's, as if she sensed how much Aimee needed reassurance. "Warner's aware of what his father did to me, but Travis, Lydia, and I didn't think it wise to tell him about you, especially since we had no way of knowing whether I'd ever find you. His life had been turned upside down for the second time in less than a year, and it seemed cruel to add to his pain."

Grace turned Aimee's hand over and threaded her fingers through hers. "I've told you what happened. I've answered your questions. Now the decision is yours. Do you want Warner and the rest of Cimarron Creek to know that you're my daughter?"

Aimee nodded. It was something she'd thought of many times while she'd waited for Grace to return to Texas. Once she'd learned that her mother loved her enough to search for her, she'd known that she wanted to acknowledge their kinship and—if possible—build a true mother-daughter relationship.

"I crossed an ocean to find you, and you did the same to find me. Now that we're finally together, I want to tell everyone that I found my mother."

Though she appeared pleased by Aimee's declaration, Grace's expression was solemn. "The older people will remember that I left suddenly and will know that I wasn't married when you were born. Some of them may be cruel to you." Her eyes misted. "I hate the idea of someone hurting my daughter. You did nothing to deserve condemnation."

"Neither did you." Aimee fixed her gaze on Grace. "Would you prefer that no one knows we're related?"

Grace shook her head. "Anyone who sees us together will know that we share the same blood. It won't take long for them to piece the story together. I'm actually surprised no one guessed before this."

Lydia had said the same thing, then had speculated that since Grace had worn widow's weeds for most of her time in Cimarron Creek and since no one would have expected a

Frenchwoman to have a connection to anyone in town, they'd ignored the resemblance.

Aimee shrugged. "I'm an adult now. I believe I can handle whatever they say or do, if you can."

Her mother pursed her lips. "I can, and I don't doubt that you can, but we're not the only ones who might be hurt. There's Warner too. People might shun him and his store if they realize what his father had done."

Unfortunately, though she wished it were otherwise, Aimee could imagine that happening. Warner had told her that business had slumped after his parents' deaths. Though customers had gradually returned, needing the items he sold and being unwilling to travel to another town to buy them, many had seemed wary of him until he hired Aimee.

Somehow, having an assistant had turned the tide of opinion. But, Aimee knew, it could reverse just as easily. How she hated the thought of her boss, her friend, her *brother* suffering for something that he hadn't done.

"C'est difficile." She bit her lip at the realization that she had once again lapsed into French. "It's difficult," she told Grace. "I don't want Warner to be hurt, but I want him to know that I'm his sister."

She paused to take another sip of tea, then nibbled a chocolate, smiling faintly as she recalled Lydia saying everything looked better after a piece of candy. There had to be a way to resolve this without hurting anyone else.

Aimee swallowed, giving Grace a long look before she spoke. "Maybe the best thing is to tell everyone I'm your daughter but let Warner be the only one who knows that we share a father. What do you think?"

Grace nodded her approval. "I think my daughter is wise and caring as well as beautiful. Do you want to talk to Warner today?"

There was no reason to delay. "I'll send him a message, asking him to come here when he closes the shop."

31

The meeting with Warner went better than Aimee could have hoped. Although he was shocked initially, that shock soon faded, and a look of wonder lit his face.

"I hate what my father did," Warner said when Grace explained why they wanted to see him, "but I can't hate the result." His blue eyes, so different from both hers and Grace's, filled with warmth when he smiled at Aimee, and in that instant, she realized that while the colors differed, her eyes were the same shape as her half-brother's.

"I've always wanted a sister," he told Grace, "and you've given me one." Though Warner's face had been contorted in pain when he'd heard about Grace's search for her daughter and the fear she'd had that she would never learn what had happened to her, he chuckled. "Wait until Nate hears. He used to say that he'd marry my sister if I had one. Now he has the chance."

Warner grinned at the prospect. Aimee did not. Though she cherished the hope that Nate loved her, she wasn't as certain as Warner seemed to be. Even though there had been times when his expression had been warmer than she would have expected from someone who considered her nothing more than a friend, Nate had never mentioned courtship or marriage. Everything was different now. Even if he did harbor tender feelings for her, he might not want to wed a woman with her history.

"Do you want to tell Nate?" Aimee asked her newfound brother.

When Warner shook his head, her heart felt as if it had plummeted to her toes. She couldn't—she simply could not—be the one to talk to Nate. Though women had more freedom here than they did in France, there were still subjects an unmarried woman did not discuss with a man.

As if he sensed her dismay, Warner nodded. "I don't *want* to tell him or anyone what my father—our father," he corrected himself, "did, but he needs to know."

And Aimee needed to know whether what had happened twenty-two years ago would change the way Nate felt about her.

"What a beautiful day!" Though yesterday had been gray, the sun had emerged this morning, making it the perfect day for a ride. And today Thea was riding. Declaring that he wanted Thea to relax, Jackson had rented a horse, since Maggie still balked when he tried to drive her, giving Thea the unusual experience of riding in her own buggy. She cradled Stuart in her arms while Jackson steered the carriage toward his mysterious destination. And, thanks to Jackson, she had begun to relax.

While she still felt uncomfortable in her house, the fact that there had been no sign of the Gang in over two days had helped her sleep better last night, but the real reason for her peaceful slumber had been Jackson's invitation. When Thea had dreamt, it had been of spending the day with him, not fending off masked outlaws. That was why she'd chosen to wear the apricot-colored gown.

With its lace collar and cuffs and the thirteen buttons closing the bodice, it was fancier than most of her clothing but not so fancy that she couldn't wear it for a daytime excursion. Jackson's pleased expression when he'd seen her and his softly murmured "pretty" had confirmed the wisdom of choosing this particular gown.

"The town's buzzing with the news that the travelers have returned." Though his hands were relaxed on the reins, Jackson's eyes moved constantly, scanning the area for any sign of danger. That was another reason Thea's tension had faded. She knew that Jackson would keep her and Stuart safe.

She was not surprised by the grapevine's speed. "What most of the townspeople don't know is that Grace Sims is Aimee's mother." When she'd returned from Lydia's house, her face glowing with happiness, Aimee had told Thea the whole story, including her relationship to Warner. An hour later, she'd taken Thea across the street to meet Grace.

"Aimee and Grace look so much alike that everyone's going to realize they're related once they see them together."

Though they hadn't finalized the decision, Grace had suggested that they ask Pastor Dunn to introduce Aimee as her daughter following Sunday's service. "We know everyone will speculate, so we might as well satisfy their curiosity," Grace had said.

But Jackson's curiosity appeared to have taken a different turn. "What will you do when Aimee marries Nate?"

"I don't know." The thought had crossed her mind more than once, but now the situation was more complicated. It had been difficult enough remaining in the house and remembering the damage the intruders had wreaked on it when she had Aimee with her. Though last night had been better, Thea couldn't imagine what it would be like with only Stuart for company. He couldn't reassure her the way Aimee did.

Thea smiled at the infant in her arms, grateful that he was continuing to amuse himself with the rattle Widow Jenkins had given him. "I'm not sure there will be a wedding. Nate hasn't proposed." And, though Aimee had once believed he might be on the verge of doing exactly that, now she was worried.

"He will. The man is boots over hat in love with her." Jackson flashed Thea a smile. "I've had to listen to him tell me how wonderful she is. Trust me. It's just a matter of time before Aimee and Nate are hitched. What will you do then?"

For some reason, Jackson was persistent in wanting to know her plans. The problem was, Thea didn't have any firm plans. "I'll probably try to find a house where I feel safer." She paused before adding, "The problem is, I'm not sure that moving will help."

Jackson nodded as if he understood, but, though a smile teased the corners of his lips upward, his words were solemn. "You'll be safe as soon as I put the Gang behind bars. I'll admit that they've been cleverer than I expected. Even though we did a thorough search, Travis and I couldn't find any signs of them." His voice remained sober as he said, "I know they were the ones behind your break-in, but I can't figure out where they're hiding. What I can tell you is that they're not following us today."

And that was reassuring. "Where are we going?" Jackson had refused to tell Thea anything more than that he wanted her advice.

"We're almost there." A minute later, he turned the buggy off the main road.

"Austin Goddard's ranch?" Thea had ridden past the entrance several times when she'd visited patients, though she'd never seen the house.

"Yep. I heard he might be interested in selling it and wanted your opinion. I can tell if the land is good and the barn is large enough, but I don't know much about houses. I was hoping you'd look at it and tell me whether it would be a good home."

Jackson gave a deprecating shrug as he continued what was for him a long speech. "I saw it from the outside once and thought it looked all right, but I'm no expert. When my ma used to say there's a difference between a house and a home, I never could figure out what she meant. I'm hoping you can help."

Thea shared that hope. Jackson had helped her in so many ways, never once asking anything in return. The least she could do was give him an opinion of this house. Perhaps it would turn out to be a home for him and not simply the building where he lived.

As they approached the sprawling ranch house with its wraparound porch, a frisson of excitement made its way down Thea's spine. Though she was here to evaluate it for Jackson, she could not deny her own reaction to it. To her surprise, she was filled with a sense of homecoming, though the building bore little resemblance to the house where she'd grown up.

After a tragic fire had destroyed the original house, Sarah and Clay had rebuilt their home with stone, eschewing the half-timbered style that was common in Ladreville. Unlike Thea's childhood home, this house was a simple frame structure, one story high with green shutters providing contrast against the white walls and black-shingled roof. While there was nothing distinctive about it, the building that Austin and Catherine Goddard now called home seemed to be welcoming Thea.

The feeling was so unexpected, a bit like the *coup de foudre* that Aimee had felt when she met Nate, that Thea wasn't certain what to do. Rather than blurt out her feelings, she busied herself with Stuart, adjusting the cap Widow Jenkins had knitted for him so it would shade his face when they left the buggy.

As Jackson helped her and Stuart out of the buggy, the couple Thea had seen at Lydia's house the previous day emerged from the house, their faces wreathed with smiles.

The man pulled out his watch and smiled. "Right on time, just like you said in your note." He gave Thea an appraising look. "I see you brought someone with you."

Austin Goddard matched Jackson in height, but that was where the similarities ended. His hair was blond, not auburn, his eyes blue rather than green, his chin distinctly square. While the town's new doctor was a handsome man, he didn't compare to Jackson.

Jackson nodded. "This is Thea Michener. I wanted her opinion."

Although Thea could see nothing amusing about Jackson's words, Austin appeared to be fighting to hide a smile.

His wife stepped forward, her smile as welcoming as her husband's. "The men are going to worry about boring things like barns and corrals. Let me show you the inside, Mrs. Michener." Her smile broadened as she looked at Stuart. "I have just the right place for him to stay while we look around." The assurance with which the pretty brunette spoke reminded Thea that she'd once been Cimarron Creek's schoolteacher.

"Please call me Thea," she said as she climbed the porch steps.

"All right, Thea. And I'm Catherine."

Instead of opening the front door, Catherine continued around the porch to what Thea surmised was the entrance to the kitchen. When she'd escorted Thea inside what was indeed a nicely appointed kitchen, Catherine pointed to a wicker basket filled with freshly washed towels. "Just give me a second to get the towels out. I think the little one will fit inside."

And he did. Stuart appeared intrigued by his new surroundings, batting the sides of the basket with his fists while he chortled his approval. Thea knew from experience that Stuart would remain entertained for a while, giving her a chance to explore the rest of the house.

As Catherine led the way around the house, showing Thea the parlor, separate dining room, pantry, and five bedrooms, she said, "It's not fancy, but everything is in good condition. We find it comfortable."

"It's more than comfortable. It's charming." The house where she was living was larger and some would say more stylish, but it paled compared to this.

The sense of homecoming that had settled over Thea as they approached the house had only increased when she'd entered the house that Jackson was considering buying. He might not know the difference between a house and a home, but Thea did. This was a home. It was a place she could easily picture herself spending the rest of her life.

She swallowed deeply, unwilling to voice those thoughts. Instead, she settled for, "It's bigger than I expected."

Catherine nodded as if she'd had the same reaction herself. "The people who built it kept adding rooms as they had children. I understand they had twelve."

Thea gasped. Though she had encountered large families in her practice, the most she'd seen were ten children. "It'll take Jackson a while to fill all those rooms." They had never spoken of children other than Stuart, but Thea knew instinctively that Jackson would want at least three or four.

"A few years, anyway." Catherine turned back toward the kitchen. "I imagine the men will be another half hour or so. Would you like a cup of coffee or tea while we wait?"

"Tea would be wonderful, if it's not too much trouble." It might help settle her thoughts, which were whirling at the realization that she did not want to leave this house.

"It's no trouble at all." As the tea steeped, Stuart began to fuss. Catherine smiled at him, then turned back to Thea. "Would you mind if I held him? I want to practice a bit."

The almost hesitant tone in the formerly confident schoolteacher's voice caused Thea to give her an appraising look. "Any particular reason?"

A laugh was Catherine's first response. "Exactly the one you're imagining. I believe I'll be having a baby of my own next spring. That's one of the reasons I'm glad you came today. I have a million questions for you."

They were still talking about babies when Jackson and Austin entered the kitchen.

Austin laid a protective hand on his wife's shoulder but directed his question to Thea. "So, what do you think?"

"I think you're going to be a father next May."

The look Austin and Catherine exchanged warmed Thea's heart. This was how parents ought to react to the news that a blessed event was in the offing. They were eager, excited, and full of love for each other and their unborn child.

"That's the best news possible, but that wasn't the question I was asking." Austin turned toward Jackson. "Maybe you'd better do it."

His face reddening as though he hadn't anticipated this, Jackson swallowed, then said, "What do you think about the house? Can you picture yourself living here?"

32

As the bell over the door tinkled, Aimee looked up from the shelves she was dusting. She hadn't expected to see Nate, especially not Nate looking the way he did. Dressed in his Sunday suit, his hair freshly cut, a bouquet of slightly wilted flowers in his hand, this was a Nate she'd never seen.

"Hello, Nate." Her mouth suddenly dry, those were the only words she could force out. Not sure what else to say or whether she would be able to speak at all, Aimee looked around for Warner, but he'd disappeared. A moment ago, he'd been in the back room; now the store was empty except for her and Nate.

She laid the feather duster on the counter and stared at the customer who did not look like a customer. Why was Nate here hours before he normally joined her, and why did he look like a man who'd come courting? Aimee's heart pounded at the thought that that might be exactly what he was doing.

As the door swung shut behind him, Nate turned the sign from "open" to "closed" and took a step toward her, and as he did Aimee realized that the farmer who'd once been afraid to talk to her had disappeared, replaced by a man who exuded confidence.

"I was going to wait until the store closed, but I couldn't

wait another minute. Those two weeks with chicken pox were the longest of my life. But what am I doing? I almost forgot."

Extending his arm, Nate handed the flowers to Aimee. "These are for you. Rachel warned me that they would wilt, and they did. I hope you like them anyway."

Aimee buried her nose in the bouquet, smiling at both the fragrance and the realization that this was the first time a man had brought her flowers. Grace had told her that if Nate's love was true, it would not be altered by the story of her father. If these flowers were any indication, Nate's love was indeed true.

"They're beautiful." Some might believe that the simple wildflowers could not compare to the roses that bloomed in what had been her grandmother's garden, but to Aimee nothing could be better than the bouquet she held in her hands. Not only had Nate given them to her, but he'd picked them especially for her. "Thank you, Nate. They just need a little water."

She started to turn, planning to fetch an empty jar and some water from the back room, but Nate stopped her. "That can wait. There's something I want to say first."

He looked at the wilted flowers and frowned. "I don't know what kind of flowers you like. I don't know a lot of things about you, but I want to. I want to know your favorite flowers, what you like to eat, which authors you prefer—everything about you."

For a man who'd once been tongue-tied around her, it was quite a speech. Aimee didn't know what had caused the change, but she liked it. Oh, how she liked it!

Nate smiled at her, and the expression she saw in his eyes made Aimee's heart leap with joy. Nate was looking at her the way Clay looked at Sarah, the way Travis looked at Lydia.

He took a shallow breath, then straightened his shoulders and smiled again. "What I'm trying to say is, I love you, Aimee. I want to marry you."

"Oh, Nate. *C'est ça que j'ai esperé.*" As happiness washed

over her, Aimee found herself unable to find the English words to tell him that that was exactly what she'd hoped for.

Seemingly unconcerned by her inability to answer, Nate continued. "Rachel told me a man's supposed to ask his gal's father for permission, but since I couldn't do that, I did the next best thing. I asked your brother, and he said yes." Nate's grin confirmed that Warner's sudden departure was no coincidence. "Will you marry me, Aimee? Please."

"Are you sure?" Though he'd spoken to Warner and now knew the truth behind her birth, she had to give him a chance to reconsider.

Nate nodded so vigorously that a lock of hair came loose from the Macassar oil he'd used to tame it. "I've never been so sure of anything. So, will you take your chances with this goat farmer?"

"Yes, Nate. Oh yes!"

As he opened his arms, she raced into them. What a wonderful, wonderful day!

"What do you mean?" Thea stared at Jackson, wondering whether he had somehow guessed how much the house appealed to her.

Catherine rose, lifted Stuart from the basket, and nodded at her husband. "Let's give them a little time alone."

When the trio had left the kitchen, Jackson took the seat next to Thea. "I didn't mean to blurt it out that way. The truth is, I've been looking for the perfect time and place, but I haven't found it. Somehow, the words just popped out."

He leaned forward ever so slightly, but it was enough that she could feel the warmth of his breath as he asked, "What do you think about the house?"

Thea chose her words carefully. "I think it would be an ideal place to raise a family." She could picture Stuart chasing another child or two from room to room, then hiding behind the settee in the parlor to avoid detection. "I know Austin wants to be in town and closer to his patients, but I can't imagine ever wanting to leave here if this were mine." Jackson remained silent, as if waiting for her to continue, and so she did. "It's what you said you wanted—a home, not just a house."

Thea hoped Jackson wouldn't repeat his other question, because she wasn't ready to tell him that she could indeed picture herself living here, that the instant she'd stepped inside the front door, she'd felt as if she belonged here. She wasn't ready to tell him that she'd imagined herself dusting the mantelpiece in the parlor and pulling a roast from the oven, placing it on this very table in front of her family—Jackson, Stuart, and a little girl with Jackson's red hair.

Jackson appeared satisfied with her assessment. "That's what I thought. I rode out here a couple weeks ago when I heard that Austin might be willing to sell it, and I haven't been able to get it out of my mind since. I keep picturing us living here."

Us. "Oh!"

He shook his head. "There I go, getting ahead of myself again. The first time I asked you to marry me, I did it all wrong, and it seems I'm not doing any better this time."

Thea shivered with anticipation and apprehension. This was what she wanted, and yet . . .

Jackson's expression remained solemn as he said, "I know it's probably too soon for you. Folks tell me a person needs a whole year to get over a death, and you had two to deal with. If you want to wait, I'll try to be patient, but I don't want to wait another day to tell you that I love you. That's why I want to marry you."

He loved her! One of the doubts that had plagued Thea began to fade.

"But you said Stuart . . ."

Jackson clenched his fists and relaxed them in a gesture she'd seen him use when he was frustrated. "I told you I did it all wrong the first time. I probably left you believing the reason I was talking about marriage was because Stuart deserved two parents."

Thea nodded. She wouldn't tell Jackson how much that had hurt, how she'd felt as if he were rejecting her the way Daniel had.

His eyes clouding as if he understood and regretted her pain, Jackson continued. "It's true: Stuart does deserve that, but that's not why I want to marry you. I love you, Thea, and I know that you're the only woman who can make my life complete."

Those were the words Thea had longed to hear, the words that made her heart sing. The man she loved loved her. He wanted to marry her as much as she longed to marry him. And yet the fears were still there. It wasn't only her happiness that hung in the balance. So did Jackson and Stuart's. She couldn't make another mistake.

When she didn't respond, Jackson reached out and took her hands in his. To Thea's amazement, she felt the slightest of tremors in his. "Do you love me even a little? If you're not ready yet, can I hope that one day you'll marry me?"

Thea swallowed deeply, trying to dislodge the lump that had taken residence in her throat. How was it possible that this strong man, this fierce warrior, was practically pleading with her to marry him? What had she done to deserve a love like that?

"Oh, Jackson, I'm so confused. I care about you." She saw disappointment shadow his eyes and regretted her choice of words. "I care about you a great deal." The disappointment began to fade. "I think what I feel is love, but I'm afraid."

The hope that had filled his eyes turned to confusion that mirrored her thoughts. "Afraid of what?"

"That I'm wrong. That what I feel isn't love. That it'll fade the way Daniel's feelings for me did." She'd begun to bare her heart. Though she wanted to stop before the pain became too intense, she could not. She owed Jackson a complete explanation. "It hurt me. It hurt me terribly to know that his love had died. I can't do it, Jackson. I can't take the risk of hurting you that way."

He was silent for a moment, as if he needed time to digest what she'd said. "What if Daniel's love didn't die? What if he didn't break his vows?"

"What do you mean?" Thea couldn't imagine why Jackson was asking those questions. He'd never met Daniel, and nothing he'd learned at the orphanage would have led him to that conclusion. "I smelled the perfume on his shirts. Every time Daniel went to San Antonio, he came back with another woman's scent on his clothes. What other explanation could there be?"

Jackson tightened his grip on her hands, perhaps fearing she would pull away. "It's possible that he met a woman when he bought things for the store, but I believe that was just a pretext and that the real reason he traveled was to meet the rest of the Gang for another heist."

"You said that before, but how does it explain the perfume?"

A gust of wind rattled the windows, reminding Thea that there was a world outside the kitchen, even though Jackson remained focused on the story he was telling.

"We know one of the members of the Gang is a woman. I believe it's her perfume. It's possible she and your husband worked together to load the booty onto their horses. If so, they could have been close enough to each other that her scent would have transferred to his shirt. Jacob Whitfield told me that particular perfume is too strong for most women."

And that raised another question. "Why would someone wear perfume when she was robbing stagecoaches? I thought you said that she dressed like a man and that your brother was the first to notice that she was a woman."

Jackson shook his head. "That doesn't make any sense to

me, either, but I can tell you that whoever ransacked Helen Bradford's house wore the same scent as Mrs. Allen."

"How do you know what perfume Belinda Allen wears?" It was a silly question. What Jackson had just revealed had challenged Thea's beliefs about her husband, and all she could do was ask how he'd learned the name of a perfume.

If Jackson thought the question odd, he gave no sign. "Jacob Whitfield at the mercantile ordered it for her. He let me sniff it, and it was definitely what I smelled at the Bradfords' house. I may be wrong, but my instincts tell me your husband loved you and that he didn't break his vows."

Jackson managed a small smile as he said, "My parents told me true love doesn't die. I know they had their share of problems, but even during the rough times, their love didn't fade. I don't believe yours would, either."

Thea tried but failed to match his smile. "I want to believe that." Her thoughts were whirling faster than leaves in a storm as she considered everything Jackson had said. There was no question that Daniel had lied about many things, but if what Jackson said was true, and she had no reason to doubt it, it was possible Daniel's love had not wavered. If that was true, then maybe her fears had been unfounded. Maybe Jackson's parents were right and love did not die. Maybe what she felt for Jackson would endure. Maybe. Thea's head spun with the possibilities.

"I need more time," she said slowly. "Until I'm sure about my feelings, I can't let you risk your heart."

Though he made no effort to hide his disappointment, Jackson nodded. "Then I'll wait."

33

How do you know if you're really in love?" Thea gulped as the words emerged from her mouth. She'd spent the last twenty minutes with Lydia and her babies, ensuring that all three were doing well and that the twins' progress was normal for their age. This was supposed to be a professional visit, not a discussion of the questions that haunted Thea: Was she in love with Jackson, and if she was, would that love last?

It wasn't a question she would ask Aimee. Her friend believed in the *coup de foudre* and that you'd know love, because it came like a lightning strike. Lightning had not struck Thea—not the day she met Jackson, nor any day since then. Instead, what she felt for him had been more like a newly planted flower seed, invisible at first, then emerging as a tiny seedling, growing almost imperceptibly each day until it opened in a glorious blossom. What worried her was that flowers faded and shed their petals. Would her feelings do the same?

She had lain awake last night, memories of the day tumbling through her mind like the designs on a kaleidoscope. The feeling of homecoming she'd experienced at the Goddard ranch, Jackson's disappointment when she'd refused his proposal, the undeniable happiness on Aimee's face when she and Nate had returned from the apothecary to announce their engagement.

It had been a day of extremes—extreme happiness contrasted with the heart-wrenching knowledge that she had caused Jackson pain.

"It seems that everyone's talking about love." Lydia's blue eyes glistened as she cradled her son. While his sister had fallen asleep once Thea had completed her examination, Vernon was wide awake. "Just last night Travis told me having children made him realize how much he loved me and that it was more than he'd dreamt possible."

She raised her eyes and glanced toward the room where Grace was still asleep, exhausted by her journey and the drama of the past few days. "You should have seen Grace when Aimee and Nate shared their news with her. I've never seen such unbridled love on a person's face. She was positively glowing."

Thea nodded. Though Aimee had said that her mother was happy, she had not shared the details of the time she and Nate had spent with Grace.

Lydia chuckled. "Love is definitely in the air, but I'm not the one to tell you how to identify it. The person you should be asking is Catherine. She's the one who explained stolen hearts to me."

"Stolen hearts?" What did they have to do with love?

Lydia's expression was serious as she placed Vernon back in his bed. "Did you know that I was engaged to someone else before I married Travis?"

Thea gasped at the unexpected revelation. Though she had known her only a few months, it was almost impossible to believe that Lydia had loved another man. "If you were trying to shock me," she said after she'd caught her breath, "you did. It's obvious to anyone who spends more than a minute with you that you and Travis are deeply in love. I never would have imagined you loving someone else."

Lydia looked up from her sleeping daughter. "It wasn't the same kind of love, but I didn't realize that at the beginning. I was so confused, trying to make sense of what I felt for Travis. That's when Catherine shared her mother's wisdom. She said that sometimes you give your heart to a man. That's one kind of love. But sometimes a man steals your heart. That's the kind of love that endures."

"And Travis stole your heart."

"He did indeed, and if I'm not mistaken, Jackson has stolen yours."

Had he? Thea wasn't certain. All she knew was that what she felt for Jackson was very different from her feelings for Daniel.

Jackson took a quick breath as he strode from the livery after grooming Blaze. His horse was fine, but he was not. How could he be when the woman he loved was still in danger? He'd told Captain Rawlins that he expected the Gang to make another move and that it was simply a matter of waiting. The problem was, he wasn't good at waiting, especially now that he was also waiting for Thea to sort out her feelings.

When Pa had told him a man would never fully understand how a woman's mind worked, Jackson hadn't paid much attention, because there'd been no special woman in his life. Now there was, and the truth of Pa's words hit him with the force of a speeding freight train. He might not understand Thea, but Jackson knew that he needed to find the Gang, because only then could he devote himself to wooing Thea properly.

That was why he'd spent the day searching for the remaining Gang members, a task at which he'd failed. Even though he now knew that at least one of the Michener brothers had a jagged scar on his forehead, that hadn't helped. No one in Cimarron Creek or any of the nearby towns had seen a man like that or a tall female stranger.

As he entered Warner's house, Jackson faced the unpleasant reality that he had no leads.

"I wondered when you'd get back." Unlike Jackson, Warner seemed to be in a good mood. He was standing next to the stove, stirring something that smelled delicious, a broad smile creasing his face, his eyes no longer radiating sorrow.

"Did I miss something?"

"You sure did. Rachel Henderson's been running around town, handing out invitations. She was mighty disappointed that she couldn't give you yours." Warner pulled an ivory envelope from his pocket. "Here you go."

Jackson stared at the envelope. Though his parents had been invited to numerous events when he'd been growing up, not once had they received a written invitation. "What's she inviting me to?"

"A party. Rachel's tickled pink that her brother is getting married, so she's throwing a big shindig at her house. She says it's going to be almost as fancy as the party my great-aunt had for Lydia and Travis. That's why she wrote out all those invitations instead of just telling folks when it was going to take place."

Jackson didn't care about parties, especially fancy ones, but he did care about the first part of Warner's speech. It was the best news he'd heard all day. "Nate finally did it? He asked Aimee to marry him?" After weeks of watching Nate dither, Jackson hadn't been certain he would ever muster the courage to open his heart to Aimee, even though he clearly wanted to.

"Yep." Warner nodded. "And she said yes."

"I've got to admit that I'm surprised, but I'm happy for both of them."

Warner replaced the lid on the saucepan and turned back to face Jackson. "I hope you'll be happy for me too. Patience agreed to be my wife."

His face wore a look of wonder, as if he couldn't believe his good fortune. Though he hadn't said much, Jackson knew that Warner had feared his family's history would make women wary of him. Jackson was glad that Patience had seen beyond the tragedies and recognized that Warner would be a good husband and father.

With two quick steps, Jackson reached his friend and clapped him on the shoulder. "Congratulations, Warner. She's a fine woman."

The words were sincere—he *was* happy for both Nate and Warner—but Jackson could not ignore the fact that while all his friends in Cimarron Creek were either married or engaged, the woman he loved had turned him down. Twice.

"'Bout time you got here." Angus Harris made no attempt to hide his displeasure as Jackson helped Thea dismount from the buggy. "Ethel needs you. Her pains done started."

Forcing herself to keep a smile on her face despite the man's obvious disgruntlement, Thea nodded. It was true that she was later than normal today. Stuart had been fussy all morning and had screamed when she'd tried to leave him with Widow Jenkins, although he'd quieted the instant Thea held him.

Realizing that he had reached the stage where he craved the security of being held by the woman he considered his mother, Thea had kept him in her arms as she and Jackson headed for the livery. And, because he'd thrown a tantrum when Jackson tried to hold him, she'd relinquished the reins to Jackson and had spent the ride to the Harris ranch holding Stuart.

Fortunately, Maggie had either sensed the gravity of the situation or had grown accustomed to Jackson's presence and had responded to his commands. Within minutes, Stuart had fallen asleep. His tantrum must have exhausted him, because even Angus Harris's angry words did not wake him.

"I'm here now." Thea doubted the words would placate Angus, but they were all she could offer. He wasn't her patient; Ethel was. She grabbed her bag from the back of the buggy and rushed into the house. While first babies normally took their time arriving, Thea had no way of knowing when Ethel's pains had begun.

She found her patient lying on her bed, her face contorted with either pain or anger. "You gotta help me," the expectant mother shrieked. "Them pains hurt somethin' horrible."

First-time mothers, Thea had found, fell into two categories—those who were shocked by the intensity of their contractions, and those who'd heard tales of excruciating pain and were pleasantly surprised when theirs were not so severe. Ethel was definitely a member of the first group.

"When did the contractions begin?"

"About a half hour ago."

Thea wouldn't tell Ethel that this was just the beginning and that the pain would increase exponentially before it ended. "Let me check you. I want to see how far along you are."

"Gonna be any minute now."

"Mmm." Thea made her voice noncommittal. As she'd suspected, Ethel was in the first stage of labor. It would be more than a minute before her baby made its arrival.

"Let's get you up. Walking will help."

Ethel's eyes widened in what appeared to be shock. "Walkin'? I ain't never heard of delivering a baby standin' up."

"You won't do that," Thea assured her. "Your baby isn't ready yet. Come on. I want you to walk back and forth. It'll help the pain." And give Ethel something to think about other than her contractions.

As the woman reluctantly complied, grumbling with each step she took, Thea turned toward the door.

"Where you goin'? You gotta stay here with me."

Thea nodded. "There's one thing I have to do. Then I'll be right back."

When she descended the porch steps, she found Jackson walking around the buggy, a still-sleeping Stuart in his arms.

"How is she?" Jackson asked as Thea approached him.

296

"Hours away from delivery. I'll be surprised if the baby arrives before midnight." She girded herself for what she expected to be an unpleasant afternoon and evening listening to Ethel complain about each pain. "Will you take Stuart home? This is no place for him."

Thea knew how Ethel would react if she put Stuart in the cradle she'd prepared for her own child, and while Jackson could care for him, Aimee would wonder where he and Thea were.

Furrows formed between Jackson's eyes. "I don't want to leave you here."

Though Thea shared Jackson's fears, it was not as if she would be alone. "I'll be safe. Angus will make sure of that."

As if on cue, the man emerged from the barn, a shotgun in his hand.

Jackson nodded, though he was clearly dubious. "I'll talk to him, and then we'll make a decision." He handed Stuart to Thea and marched toward the still-angry rancher. A minute later, he returned. "Angus said he'll keep the varmints away. I hope he's as good a shot as he claims."

"Ethel keeps bragging that he's the best marksman in the county. You haven't seen the inside of the house, but they've got a lot of game heads hanging on the walls, and they never seem to be short of meat. He may not be as good a sharpshooter as you, but Angus is good."

Thea looked down at the child in her arms. "I'm more worried about having Stuart in a familiar setting than I am about staying here."

"All right." Jackson's reluctance was evident. "I'll be back as soon as I can. Don't take any chances."

"I won't, and you don't need to rush." Thea pressed a kiss on Stuart's forehead. "Ethel has already made it clear that she expects me to spend every minute at her side. The biggest danger I'll be in is losing my temper with her."

As Thea had hoped, Jackson cracked a smile as he took

Stuart from her and laid him on the buggy floor. Though the baby wouldn't be able to see anything there, he also wouldn't be in danger of falling if Jackson made a sudden turn or stop.

Thea reached out and touched Jackson's hand before he climbed into the carriage. "Don't worry. We'll all be fine."

34

Don't worry. It was one thing for Thea to say it, another for him to follow through. No matter what he told himself, Jackson couldn't stop worrying, especially when he'd returned to Cimarron Creek and learned that Travis had been looking for him.

"Glad you got my message." Travis rose from behind his desk and reached for his hat. "Ben Fowler sent me a telegram," he said, referring to the sheriff of a nearby town. "Claims someone saw two men and a woman heading for an abandoned ranch about ten miles north of here. Thought it might be the Gang."

And so, though his heart urged him to return to the Harris ranch and Thea, Jackson saddled Blaze and rode in the opposite direction, refusing Travis's offer to accompany him. He'd lost a brother and had a partner severely wounded by the Gang; he wouldn't add Travis to the list of their victims.

It was simple to find the ranch and even simpler to confirm that the Gang had indeed been staying there. There was no mistaking that perfume or the gouges in the wall where an apparently furious Charity James had vented her anger. But the tumbledown house was now empty, leaving Jackson no closer to his quarry than he'd been at the beginning of the day.

Discouraged and anxious to see Thea again, he headed back

to Cimarron Creek. If he was fortunate, by the time he reached the Harris ranch, Ethel would have had her baby and Thea would be ready to go home.

He'd just crossed the bridge when he spotted two strangers entering the Silver Spur. The moon, more than half full tonight, revealed two men of medium height, medium weight, probably sporting medium brown hair.

His hackles rising, Jackson hitched Blaze in front of the saloon, confident that one of these men also sported a jagged scar. This was the break he needed.

"Evening, Faith."

"Evening, Red." The proprietor of the Silver Spur touched her auburn hair, then grinned. Jackson kept his face neutral, but inside he rejoiced at the fact that Faith had given him that nickname, saying that two redheads had to stick together. It was far better that she referred to him as Red rather than Ranger, especially tonight.

"What can I get you?"

"A glass of whiskey." He had no intention of drinking it, but he wasn't going to raise suspicions by ordering sarsaparilla. When she'd poured him a generous portion, Jackson made his way across the saloon, keeping his head down and choosing a seat that would put his back to them as he took a table next to the strangers. He couldn't risk their recognizing him, but the quick glance he'd shot in their direction showed that the two men looked enough alike to be brothers and that one of them had a prominent scar on his forehead.

"We're close," one man said to the other. "I can feel it in my bones."

The second scoffed. "I heered that before. Them bones of yours ain't very reliable."

"But Charity is."

Jackson raised his glass, pretending to drink from it, though he wanted to crow with relief. He'd been right. The fact that these two medium-everything men knew a woman named Charity confirmed his suppositions that Cimarron Creek's latest visitors were none other than Will and Rob Michener.

"Don't know why she wunt let us go out to the ranch with her. You don't reckon she's gonna cheat us outa our share."

The first man scoffed. "She wunt do that. Not Charity. She just don't want you around. I reckon she's afeared you'll kill someone else." The gurgling sound of whiskey being poured into a glass accented his words. "She still ain't forgiven you fer killin' Daniel."

Jackson gave a quick nod at the confirmation that his instincts had been correct. The person who'd killed Daniel Michener had not been the one who'd slit Helen Bradford's throat.

"He was cheatin' us." The second man sounded defensive.

"Mebbe, but Charity coulda gotten him to tell her where he hid the gold. She's good at gettin' information out of folks. We'd all a' been rich if you'd kept your hand off the trigger."

"He had it comin' to him."

"And we got gold comin' to us. Charity done figgered it out," the first man continued. "She's gonna take care of Daniel's widow tonight. She tole me the Ranger that's been protectin' her done come back alone. I tell you, Rob, she's gonna find that gold for us."

Jackson shuddered. His worst fears had just become reality. Charity was the leader of the Gang, and she knew where Thea was.

***

"He's a handsome one, ain't he?" Ethel beamed with pride at the infant in her arms.

"That he is." In reality, he looked like many newborns—red, wrinkled, and bewildered by his new surroundings—but he was alive and healthy, which was far more important than physical beauty, at least to Thea.

Ethel's labor had progressed more rapidly than Thea had expected, with the youngest Harris making his appearance at 8:03. Thea wasn't certain who was more relieved—she because Ethel's wailing had ceased or the mother herself—but she could not deny the sense of wonder she felt over the successful delivery. If there was one lesson she had learned from her own experience, it was that life was both precious and fragile. This child did not appear fragile, but he was indeed precious.

Thea smiled as she looked at the baby. It had taken a while to clean him and perform all the tasks that Ethel had declared were essential before the new father could enter the room, but now they were finished.

"Are you ready for me to call Angus?"

Ethel touched her hair, which Thea had just rebraided, and fussed with the ruffles on her bed jacket. For a woman who'd never before shown signs of vanity, she had been insistent that she look her best before her husband saw her again. She had even demanded that Thea bring her her perfume and the pot of rouge that she'd hidden in a corner of a bureau drawer.

"I reckon I am."

"All right. I'll get him." Though her work was not complete, for she would spend the rest of the night here, checking on the newborn and his mother every hour, Thea was looking forward to a brief respite from her demanding patient. She was also looking forward to seeing Jackson again. Though she'd told him not to rush, she had thought he'd be back before now. Perhaps Aimee had had trouble soothing Stuart, and Jackson had stayed to help her.

Thea closed the bedroom door behind her and headed for the kitchen, expecting to find Angus waiting there. To her surprise, the room was empty, as was the parlor. It was later than she would have thought he would be outside tending to the livestock, but perhaps he'd decided to wait on the porch rather than remain indoors and have to listen to his wife's screams.

Thea couldn't blame him for that, especially since Ethel had cursed him more than once, claiming he cared more about his dogs than he did about her.

Thea opened the front door and stepped onto the porch, expecting the dogs to come running or at least bark at her, but the night was eerily silent. "Angus," she called. Surely the man would not go too far away when his child's arrival was imminent. "Angus."

When there was no response, the uneasiness that had begun when she saw the empty kitchen grew. Where was he? Her eyes moved slowly, searching for the father, then stopped abruptly at the sight of a body slumped on the porch floor.

"Angus, what's wrong?"

"Nothin's wrong, Mrs. Michener. Everythin's just right."

Before Thea could register what was happening, a tall woman emerged from the shadows and grabbed her, wrenching her arms behind her.

"You and me's gonna have a nice talk about that husband of yers and what he done with my gold," the woman announced as she tied Thea's wrists.

"I don't—"

"Save your breath. You're gonna need it where we're goin'. Now, you stand right there." She shoved Thea against the house, then reached into her pocket. Within seconds, she had gagged Thea with a bandanna, a bandanna scented with the same perfume that she had smelled on Daniel's shirts.

35

W e're goin' to the barn." As the woman put her hand on Thea's shoulders, propelling her down the steps and toward the outbuilding, Thea realized it wasn't only the bandanna that bore that horrible perfume. The woman had dabbed it on her wrists, sending waves of it wafting through the air as she moved.

Jackson had been right. The female member of the Gang did indeed wear the perfume Thea had smelled on Daniel's shirts, and now she was here, threatening Thea.

Thea stopped abruptly and swiveled, looking up at her captor. The almost full moon revealed medium brown hair, brown eyes that flared with anger, and a form that—despite the masculine clothing—was distinctly feminine.

Almost gagging at the perfume that had once tainted Daniel's shirts, Thea shuddered. Though she wanted to resist, there was no way she could overpower this woman who was more than half a foot taller and whose muscles rivaled any man's.

A feeling of impending doom settled over her. If only she had insisted Jackson stay, she would have been safe, but she had not. She straightened her shoulders and lifted her head in the only gestures of defiance she had at her disposal. There was no point in regretting might-have-beens. She needed to find a way to escape.

"Get movin'." The woman pushed Thea forward. "You and me's gonna talk, but don't get no ideas about screamin'. Ain't nobody gonna hear you out there," the woman taunted.

Even if she could have spoken through the bandanna, Thea saw no need to mention that there was no one to hear her anywhere. Jackson had not yet returned. Angus was unconscious or worse. If Ethel wondered where Thea and her husband were, she wouldn't search for them, because Thea had impressed on her the necessity of remaining in bed for at least four hours. All that meant that Thea was on her own, and yet she wasn't alone.

Taking comfort from the fact that, while there might not be any humans nearby, God would always hear her, she offered a silent prayer. *Dear Lord, I know you see and hear everything. I know you're watching out for me, and I pray that you will give me the strength to get through this night*. Feeling strength flow through her veins, Thea marched forward, determined that whatever happened, she would not give this woman the satisfaction of seeing her cower.

"Well, that's more like it." Apparently, her captor mistook Thea's newfound courage for acquiescence. "Inside."

They'd reached the barn, the structure that sheltered the ranch's milk cow during the worst of winter's cold. Thea knew that at this time of the year it held only a few bales of hay and a small supply of feed corn. With no windows and only one door, it was the ideal place to hide a captive.

The woman shoved Thea inside, lit a lantern, then closed the door behind them. "Sit down." She pushed Thea onto one of the bales. "Like I told you before, you and me's gonna talk."

As she pulled something from her pocket, Thea felt her eyes widen with recognition. One of her questions was answered when the woman flicked open Daniel's watch and stared at the portrait.

"Yep. I got it right this time. Yer the one what made Daniel change." Though the lantern provided little more light than the moon had, there was no mistaking the fury in her eyes. "We had a good life, but you had to go and wreck it. Well, Mrs. Michener . . ." She spat the words. "You're gonna pay fer that, but first you're gonna tell me where Daniel hid the gold." She yanked the bandanna, pulling it down onto Thea's neck. "Start talkin'."

Thea inhaled deeply, savoring the partial freedom of not being gagged, even though it meant smelling the woman's perfume. The relief was temporary. Thea knew that, just as she knew that the woman had no intention of letting her live. Her only hope was to stall.

"Who are you?" Thea wanted confirmation of what she suspected.

The woman's eyes narrowed, and her face contorted with anger. "You mean Daniel din't tell you? Shame on him. It don't seem fair that he din't tell you about me, 'specially when I had to listen to him talk about you." She deepened her voice, attempting to imitate Daniel. "'I'm goin' straight now, Charity.' That's my name," she said in her normal voice. "Charity James."

Thea nodded slowly. That was one of the names Jackson had mentioned when he returned from the orphanage. He'd believed she was the fourth member of the Gang, and he'd been correct.

Charity James deepened her voice again. "'No more robbin' for me. Gonna make a life for my wife and baby.'"

Despite the gravity of the situation, Thea's heart leapt at the realization that Daniel had cared enough for her and their unborn child to want to abandon his criminal activities.

Charity James's laughter held no mirth. "Well, that's where he went wrong, thinkin' me and the others would let him leave. The four of us been together for too long to change, but Daniel figgered he was different. He figgered we'd never find him, but he weren't as smart as he figgered. We found him and we found you." Charity smiled, a smile that sent a shiver down Thea's spine. "Now we're gonna find the gold, 'cuz you're gonna tell me where it is."

The gold. Everything centered on the gold that Daniel had apparently stolen from his partners. Had he thought Thea wanted or needed it? If Daniel had told her about it, she would have insisted he turn it in to the authorities, but Daniel had never mentioned any gold.

Thea looked directly at Charity James, willing her to believe her. "I don't know where it is."

Charity did not believe her. Her lips curving in disgust, she raised her arm and slapped Thea's face. "Yer lyin'."

Though her face stung from the blow, Thea kept her voice steady. "I am not lying. Daniel never talked about gold. He told me he was a traveling salesman."

"He was. When he weren't helpin' me rob folks, him and me pretended to be upstanding citizens." This time Charity's smile was genuine, as if she found the thought amusing. "Daniel would tell folks he was a salesman. I pretended to be a missionary, collectin' money for orphans in China. Can you imagine that? Me, a missionary." She laughed.

"Well, by the time folks figgered out what was goin' on, Daniel and me had planned our next heist. That's why we done what we did, to figger out when rich folks would be travelin' or when a payroll was comin' through. You can learn a lot by listenin'."

Thea doubted that Charity recognized the irony in her words, but she was learning a lot by listening. The woman's story confirmed Jackson's theory of why he and Leander had been unable to find the Gang between robberies. Jackson had suspected they'd pretended to be ordinary citizens, but he had been looking for four people together, not realizing that they'd gone in different directions.

"What about the other two?" Charity had only accounted for herself and Daniel.

"Will and Rob?" The curl of her lip left no doubt about

Charity's opinion of them. "Them two are too dumb to plan anything. They hang out on a ranch between heists. Right now they're probably drinkin' themselves silly in some saloon."

She shook her head. "Time's a wastin'. There ain't no point in talkin' about me and the boys. Yer the one what's got the answers." Charity stood over Thea, her lips twisted into a snarl. "Where did Daniel hide the gold?"

"I don't know." Though Charity wouldn't be satisfied, it was the simple truth. Not once had Daniel mentioned either gold or a hiding place. Charity was the one who'd known him for most of his life. Surely she would have a better idea of where he might have stashed the loot than Thea, who had been his wife for such a brief time.

"Well, now, Mrs. Michener, I ain't believin' that. I reckon a man who was head over heels in love the way Daniel was woulda tole you everythin'." Charity's expression darkened with something that might have been jealousy. "I ain't never seen a man so crazy about a woman. The only other gal what caught his eye was Violet, but that weren't nothin' compared to the way he talked about you."

Charity's scowl deepened. "Heaven knows I tried to get him interested in me, even got me the most expensive perfume in the store, but he weren't havin' none of it."

As Charity's final words registered, Thea's heart began to pound. *Thank you, God*. He'd answered one of her prayers. Although she would never have dreamt that the truth about whether Daniel truly loved her would come like this, there was no doubting the sincerity of Charity's statement.

Thea could feel peace settle over her like a warm blanket, chasing away the fears that had hounded her ever since Daniel's first trip to San Antonio. She hadn't been wrong. He hadn't lied. Daniel had loved her, just as she had loved him.

It was a wonderfully liberating thought, erasing the months of pain when she had believed him unfaithful.

On the heels of that epiphany came another. The last of her doubts was gone. Her questions had been answered, her fears vanquished, replaced by the knowledge that her love for Jackson was deeper and stronger than anything she had felt for Daniel. It was a love that would endure for as long as Thea lived.

But that might not be long. Thea closed her eyes as the reality of her situation once again weighed on her. Charity James was an angry and vindictive woman who had no intention of letting Thea live beyond the night. When Thea did not give her the answers she sought, she would probably slit her throat the way she had Helen's. And then Jackson would always wonder whether Thea had returned his love.

She offered another silent prayer. *Dear Lord, let me live long enough to tell Jackson how much I love him.* When she opened her eyes, she was smiling.

"What's the matter with you? You ain't got no reason to be smiling. You're gonna be as dead as Violet and the one what looked so much like you."

It was as Thea had feared. Charity was a woman who thought nothing of ending human life.

"Ain't nobody gonna rescue you." As if to assure herself that no one had arrived, Charity swiveled around to stare at the door, then took a step toward the stall.

It was the opportunity Thea needed, the only one she might have. She jumped to her feet and ran toward the door, but it was to no avail. Before she could reach it, Charity knocked her to the ground and stood with her foot on Thea's right leg. Even if she'd wanted to kick, she would have hit only empty air.

"You ain't gettin' away so easy. Shoot! You ain't gettin' away at all. Once you tell me where the gold is, you're gonna meet up with Daniel agin."

The threats were no surprise to Thea. What did surprise her was that Charity had voiced them. "Why would I tell you where the gold is when you're planning to kill me anyway?"

"'Cuz if'n you tell me, you kin die quick. Otherwise, it's gonna be slow and painful just like that other woman."

Charity spat again. "That durn Daniel. He led me on a goose chase. He tole me you and him was livin' in Llano. Took a while to figger out that he was lyin' and that you were someplace different. Daniel weren't so smart, though. I figgered that the name started with an L." She shook her head in disgust. "You got any idea how many L towns there is?"

She reached down, grabbed Thea's arm, and yanked her up. "Sit," she commanded as she pushed Thea back toward the bale. "Now stick out yer feet."

"Why?"

"Why do you think?" Charity picked up a length of rope that had been hanging over the edge of the cow's stall. "I'm gonna make sure you don't try to escape agin."

Knowing there was no way she could overpower the woman, Thea extended her legs. Though she would be unable to walk, somehow she would find a way to outsmart Charity.

"Well, that's more like it. Seems you learned a lesson."

To Thea's surprise, Charity wrapped the rope around her calves, leaving her feet and ankles unbound. Though it would be difficult, Thea would be able to walk, almost as if she were in one of those three-legged races that had been such a popular part of Independence Day celebrations. Still, it was an odd way to restrain someone. Though Thea suspected there had to be a reason for the woman's action, she could not imagine what it was, particularly since Charity had made it clear that she did not expect Thea to leave the barn alive.

"Now, where's the gold?"

"I don't know." Thea wondered how many times she would have to repeat those words before Charity believed her.

Instead of the scowl Thea had expected, the woman smiled— a smile so evil that Thea could not help cringing. "Well, now, that's a real shame." Charity pulled a knife from one of her pockets and laid it on the bale. The position was deliberate, Thea knew, designed to taunt her with the fact that she could not reach it with her hands tied behind her back.

"I tole you we could do this easy or hard," the woman said as she began to unfasten Thea's shoes. "I reckon you're gonna have a different answer once I start slicing those feet of yers. The last one screamed mighty loud." She pulled off the first shoe and chuckled. "Well, look at that, will you. Daniel's wife has purty stockin's."

Thea closed her eyes, trying not to think about what Charity was threatening to do. She cringed at the realization that Charity had tortured Helen before killing her. It was no wonder Jackson had shown Thea only Helen's head and neck. From the way Charity was acting, she had probably sliced more than Helen's feet.

Thea tried not to shudder, not wanting to give Charity the satisfaction of seeing her fear. Perhaps if she focused on the woman's poor grammar and the way she began so many sentences with "well," Thea would be able to ignore the pain that was bound to come.

Had there been no teachers at the orphanage, or had Charity simply been a poor pupil? As the questions swirled through Thea's brain, a memory began to emerge.

That's it! That's where it was! She knew where Daniel had hidden the gold.

⁂

Jackson gripped the whiskey glass so tightly he thought it might shatter. He'd always believed anger to be white hot, but he'd been wrong. What he felt now was icy cold determination—determination to bring the Gang to justice, determination to save Thea, determination that he would not fail another person he loved.

You didn't kill Micah. Thea's words echoed through his brain.

That might be true, but it didn't mean that he hadn't failed to keep his brother safe, and it didn't mean that he wouldn't fight to keep Charity from killing Thea.

Jackson laid the still-full glass back on the table, then rose and walked toward the bar as if he had not a care in the world, knowing he must do nothing to alert Will and Rob to his identity. As casually as he could, he walked behind the bar, wrapped an arm around Faith's waist, and whispered in her ear. To anyone paying attention, he would seem to be nothing more than an amorous cowboy, but the words he whispered were anything but amorous.

"The two strangers are wanted men," he told Faith. "Get a message to Travis. Tell him part of the Gang of Four is here. Whatever you do, don't let them leave."

Faith shifted her position, turning her back to the room so no one could read her lips. "Where are you going?"

"The Harris ranch. Their leader has Thea."

"Oh!" The word escaped on a whoosh of breath. Recovering quickly, she pressed a kiss to Jackson's cheek. "I could tell you that kiss is for luck, but you don't need luck. You've got God on your side."

The words melted some of the ice that had encased his heart, reminding him that he was not alone in this fight. "Thanks, Faith." He sauntered out of the bar and sprang into Blaze's saddle.

I need your help, Lord. You know what's in my heart. You know that I love Thea and that Stuart and I need her. I pray that you will keep her safe. The prayers continued as he raced toward the ranch, giving thanks that there was enough light from the moon that Blaze would not stumble in a rut.

When they arrived, Jackson saw two dark forms at the side of the house and an unfamiliar horse grazing in the small paddock near the house. The horse was Charity's, he assumed, though there was no sign of the woman, and the silent lumps

. . . Jackson sighed. The absence of barking dogs left little question of their identity.

Please, Lord, let me be in time to save Thea. Where was she? The night was oddly silent, but the lights in the house indicated that someone was still awake. Jackson flung himself off Blaze and mounted the porch steps two at a time, desperate to find Thea before it was too late. He was reaching for the door when he stopped abruptly, his attention caught by the sight of a body slumped on the porch floor. The ordinary work clothes could have belonged to any man or to a woman who dressed like a man. Was it Angus or Charity? There was only one way to know.

Disappointment threatened to overwhelm Jackson as he turned the body over and recognized Angus. The rancher who'd bragged about his ability to kill varmints had been no match for Charity James. Few men were, but Angus had been luckier than most. Though unconscious, he was still alive, perhaps because Charity hadn't wanted to spend the time to kill him when Thea was her quarry. There was no time for Jackson to try to revive him. Angus would live, but Thea was still in danger.

His sense of urgency growing by the second, Jackson strode into the house.

"That you, Angus?" a woman's voice called from the back of the building. "Where you been all this time? Don't you wanna see yer son?"

It appeared that Thea had successfully delivered Ethel Harris's child, but judging by the woman's annoyance, she was no longer with her. Charity must have taken Thea somewhere.

Jackson entered the room, his eyes searching for signs of the woman he hoped would one day be his wife. What he found was what he'd expected: Ethel Harris in bed with her baby in her arms.

"Where's Thea?"

"Don't know." The new mother was clearly displeased. "She went out to fetch my man. She ain't come back, and neither did he. Where's Angus?"

Jackson had no patience for explanations. "He'll be here soon."

He raced out of the house and looked around. Since Charity's horse was still in the paddock, she and Thea had to be somewhere on the ranch. As his eyes adjusted to the darkness again, he spotted a faint light leaking from below the barn door.

Moving silently, Jackson did a brief reconnaissance of the building. No windows. No other door. As much as he hated going in blind, knowing he could be ambushed, he had no choice. Slowly, he slid the barn door open enough that he could see inside. Thankfully, it did not squeak and betray his position.

Jackson's thanks died on his lips, and his blood ran cold at the sight before him. Charity James was bent over Thea's bare feet, a wicked-looking knife in her hand. He didn't need to imagine what she was doing, for rivulets of blood had dripped onto the dirt floor. She was torturing Thea as she had Helen.

"Well, now, looks like I gotta go deeper next time." God was definitely watching over Jackson, because Charity appeared oblivious to him. "Where's the gold?"

Though Thea had been staring at Charity, she glanced sideways and spotted him. Her eyes lit with what appeared to be relief, and the look she gave him was filled with such love that it warmed Jackson's blood faster than the August sun dried morning dew. Without making a sound, Thea mouthed the sweetest words in the English language, "I love you."

And he loved her. God had led him to her and had kept her alive this long. Now it was up to Jackson to save her.

Charity raised the arm holding the knife and prepared to slice. No! He wouldn't let her harm Thea again. Thea would not be a victim. She would not die as Helen had.

Knowing that he had the advantage of surprise and strength, Jackson leapt forward and grabbed Charity's arm. In one swift movement, he wrested the knife from her and tossed it aside. As she spun around, shock blanched Charity's face.

"You!" she screamed.

"Yes, me. The Ranger who's been tracking you."

Jackson yanked her other arm behind her and handcuffed her. Screaming curses, the leader of the Gang began to kick at him. He'd anticipated that and easily sidestepped her, then knocked her to the ground. This woman wasn't going to hurt anyone again.

Though she struggled to rise, Jackson kept his weight on her and pulled out the rope he'd stuffed into his back pocket. Within seconds, he'd bound her feet and tied her to the empty stall. That would keep her temporarily. As soon as he cared for Thea, Jackson would return with the leg irons that he'd left on Blaze, fearing they might clank and alert Charity to his presence.

"You, you—" Words seemed to fail Charity until she turned her attention back to Thea and began to curse her. "Where's my gold?" she demanded.

"There's no more gold in your future, Charity James," Jackson told her, satisfaction at having apprehended her mingling with sorrow over the pain she'd inflicted on Thea. "The only thing you'll be seeing is a hangman's noose. The State of Texas doesn't take kindly to murdering women."

There was not a doubt in Jackson's mind that Charity had been the one who'd killed Helen Bradford. The memory of the woman's bloodied feet had turned his stomach more than once, and now Thea was the one who'd been subjected to the same torture. At least she was still alive. *Thank you, Lord.*

While Charity continued to curse, Jackson picked up the knife and sliced through Thea's bonds, freeing her hands and feet. "We'll get you to the Goddard ranch. Austin will know what to do for your feet."

Thea shook her head. "I don't need a doctor. I have salves and bandages in my bag back in the house. That's all I need. I'm not sure I can walk that far, though."

"You won't need to." Without a sideways look at the outlaw who was still shouting obscenities, Jackson swept Thea into his arms.

36

It felt so good to be in Jackson's arms that Thea could almost forget the pain in her feet. This was where she belonged, her head resting against his chest, her arms wrapped around his neck as he carried her away from that horrible woman.

She was blessed, so very blessed. Not only was she still alive, but God had answered her prayers and given her another chance to tell Jackson she loved him. She knew he'd read her lips when she'd mouthed the words, but that wasn't enough. She needed to say it aloud—once, twice, a million times—as many times as it took so he never doubted how she felt. There would be time for that. First, she had to tell him what she'd remembered.

"I think I know where the gold is."

As he strode across the yard, Jackson looked down at her, his expression one of astonishment. "You are the most incredible woman I've ever met. You were almost killed; your feet must hurt like the dickens; and yet you're talking about gold."

"It's important." Jackson might deny it, but Thea knew otherwise. The gold was more than a fortune that needed to be returned to its rightful owners. For him, retrieving the gold would be the culmination of his career, a way to ensure that Micah's death and Leander's injuries had not been in vain. "You need to find it so you can close this case."

He nodded, accepting the truth of her words. "You can tell me about it while we get your feet bandaged, but I'll say it again, you're an incredible woman."

Thea didn't feel incredible. She felt exhausted and yet exhilarated. While the time with Charity had drained her physically, the revelations that had come to her when she'd faced the woman's madness had buoyed her emotionally, filling her with peace. Though Thea had known it had not been her intent, the outlaw had confirmed what Jackson had suspected, that Daniel's love for Thea had been true. Charity may have bound Thea's hands and feet, but she had set her spirit free, and that, Thea knew, was a gift from God.

Trying to ignore the pain that radiated from the soles of her feet up her legs, Thea smiled at Jackson. "It's almost over. You've got Charity, and I think the other two are at the Silver Spur."

Jackson shook his head. "They were. I saw them there—that's how I knew she was here—but I suspect they're currently warming the bench in Cimarron Creek's jail. They won't be hurting anyone ever again."

"That's good." As horrible as the night had been, it was ending well.

When Thea and Jackson reached the porch, they found Angus sitting up, rubbing his head and looking confused.

"What happened?" he asked, his voice less belligerent than normal.

It was Jackson who answered. "It appears that a woman knocked you out."

Sputtering, Angus pushed himself to his feet, obviously appalled by the thought of having been bested by a woman. Though he kept one hand on the lump that was forming on the top of his head, his expression betrayed outrage. "This one?" He pointed toward Thea. "She ain't big enough to do that."

Jackson shook his head. "Not Mrs. Michener. The woman's

name is Charity James. She's part of a gang that's been robbing stagecoaches and trains, and she's dangerous. I know for a fact that she's killed at least two people, maybe more."

When Angus seemed to doubt that a woman could do all that plus attack him, Jackson continued. "She's almost as tall as a man, and I suspect she's almost as strong."

Angus straightened his shoulders at the realization that his foe had been formidable. If the situation hadn't been so serious, Thea might have smiled at the way he preened like a rooster.

His expression sobered a second later. "What happened to my dogs? They shoulda barked."

Jackson pointed toward two still forms that Thea hadn't noticed before. "The woman who hit you killed them. Sliced their throats."

As Thea shuddered at the further evidence of Charity's cruelty, the anguished cry that Angus let loose confirmed what his wife had claimed: he was deeply attached to the dogs.

"Where is she?" he demanded. "She's gonna pay for that!" Angus looked around, his wide-eyed gaze making Thea suspect he was searching for his shotgun.

Jackson kept his eyes focused on the rancher, perhaps because he feared what the angry man might do. "She's tied up in your barn now."

Angus started to move, but Jackson blocked the way. "No matter how you feel, you can't kill her. A jury'd string you up for that. You can help me, though. Mrs. Michener has been injured. There's a reward in it for you if you watch over the bandit while I take care of Mrs. Michener."

The moonlight was bright enough to see the way avarice blended with Angus's thoughts of revenge. "I'll make durn sure she don't escape." He turned toward the barn, still holding his head, but stopped when a baby's cry rent the evening air. "What's that?"

This time Thea did smile. "Your son." No matter what else had happened tonight, she had the satisfaction of knowing that she'd brought a life into this world.

The new father was clearly torn between his desire for the money Jackson had promised and the need to see his son. "Wait one minute. I gotta tell Ethel about the reward."

As he raced into the house, Thea turned her head to look up at Jackson. "This is the first I've heard about a reward."

"That's because there wasn't one until a minute ago. I need to be sure Charity doesn't escape—she's a wily one—"

"And Angus is just the one to watch her." Thea finished Jackson's sentence, noticing that he'd positioned himself so that he could see the barn door. "His pride was bruised by the idea that he'd been knocked out by a woman, no matter how tall or strong she might be."

Jackson nodded. "He'll forget that part, but he'll stand a little taller when he tells his friends he helped bring a dangerous criminal to justice."

Seconds later, Angus emerged from the house, his shotgun in hand. "You kin stop worryin' now. I'll keep that bandit safe," he announced as he sprinted toward the barn.

Jackson nodded again and carried Thea inside. "Let's get your feet bandaged." He looked around the small house, then strode into the kitchen, placing Thea on one of the chairs and propping her feet on a second.

"My bag is in the bedroom," Thea told him. Now that the euphoria of her rescue and the revelation of the gold's location had faded, she was once again aware that her feet were throbbing with pain. When Jackson had first untied her, she had done a cursory examination of her soles and had discovered that the bleeding had almost stopped, but she would be grateful for the soothing salve and bandages.

"Ethel isn't happy about being alone," Jackson said as he returned with the bag.

"I'm not surprised. She's the most demanding patient I've ever had."

"But you're the patient now." Jackson lifted Thea's feet, settled himself on the chair, and placed them in his lap.

"I can do this," Thea protested as he examined each foot carefully.

"Of course you can," he agreed, "but it'll be easier if you let me do it. Will you let me help you?"

Knowing he was asking about more than simply bandaging her feet, Thea nodded and retrieved the jar of salve from her bag. When the time was right, she would tell Jackson all that was in her heart. "You need to clean the wounds, then spread this on them."

Jackson rose and placed her feet carefully back on the chair while he filled a pan with cool water and found a soft cloth. Then he resumed his seat and began to wash her feet. Thea caught her breath, not at the stinging the water induced but at the thought of what an intimate act this was. No wonder mothers admonished their daughters to never reveal their bare feet to men who weren't their husbands.

"You've done this before, haven't you?" she asked, trying to keep her mind focused on the skill with which he cleansed her lacerations.

Jackson looked up at her, his green eyes bright with emotion. "I've cleaned and bandaged more wounds than I can count. I rarely had salve, though," he said as he opened the jar and began to smooth it over her soles. When Thea winced, he drew back for a second, then said, "Tell me about the gold. Where do you think it is?"

Thea appreciated his attempt to deflect her attention from the pain. "In a well at the orphanage. I'd forgotten all about it until Charity kept saying 'well.' She wasn't talking about a real well. That was just the way she started most of her sentences."

Thea pursed her lips, trying to hold the pain at bay, before she continued her story. "Daniel once mentioned that a couple boys at the orphanage decided to teach him a lesson about something and dumped him into an old well. He claimed they intended to let him die there, but the sides were rougher than anyone realized, with some of the stones protruding, so he managed to climb out. Apparently, that impressed the boys so much that they accepted him into their group."

"I wonder if that's how he and the Michener boys got together."

"I don't know. Daniel never mentioned any names. In fact, that was one of the few times he talked about the orphanage at all. I remember him saying something like 'We all hated that place and swore we'd never go back.'"

Thea winced. No matter how careful Jackson was trying to be, simply having her feet touched was painful. She looked up at him, focusing on his face rather than her wounds.

"At the time, I didn't ask Daniel who the 'we' were, but when I heard Charity say 'well' so often, it struck me that since the orphanage was abandoned, that would be a good hiding place."

Jackson took the bandage Thea handed him and began to wrap it around her foot. "You're probably right. I'll head over there tomorrow morning, once the whole Gang is locked up." He explained how he'd found Will and Rob in the saloon and that he'd asked Faith to alert Travis.

"I'm not worried about them," Jackson said when he finished wrapping Thea's feet, "but much as I hate to leave you here, I want to get Charity into a cell tonight. I don't trust that woman one bit. From everything I can tell, she was the leader, not Daniel."

Though Thea shared Jackson's reluctance for them to be separated, she knew he needed to do his job, and so did she. Ethel and her son still needed Thea. While she wouldn't be doing much walking, she would continue to monitor their condition.

"You're right about Charity," she told Jackson. "She's an evil woman, and she had every intention of killing me. I knew it was only a matter of time unless something brought you back here before morning."

Thea glanced at the clock that hung on one wall, amazed that less than an hour had passed since Charity had dragged her to the barn.

"I kept praying for you to come, and while I did, I kept her talking as much as I could. It was a stalling technique. I think Charity knew that as much as I did, but she couldn't stop gloating about all that she'd accomplished and how they eluded capture for so long."

Jackson's expression said that he wasn't concerned about that right now. "Later. There'll be time for that later. Right now, there's only one thing I want to do." He fixed his gaze on her lips. "The problem is, I made a promise, and my parents taught me never to break my word."

For a moment, Thea had no idea what Jackson meant. Then she remembered the day he had said he would not kiss her again unless she asked him to. Her sister would tell her it was unseemly, that a lady did not ask for a kiss, at least not in words, but Thea didn't care. Like Jackson, there was only one thing she wanted to do.

She looked up at him and smiled. "I think we both want the same thing. Will you kiss me, Jackson? Please."

His smile turned into a grin. "With pleasure." Still smiling, Jackson reached forward, drawing Thea onto his lap, and pressed his lips to hers.

It was wonderful, simply wonderful. Their first kiss had been unforgettable, but it paled compared to this. While Jackson's lips were on hers, nothing else mattered. She was safe; she was loved; she was cherished. Her fears were forgotten, and the pain in her feet subsided.

Thea didn't know how long the kiss lasted. Seconds, minutes, hours—she lost all sense of time. All she knew was that while he held her in his arms and kissed her so sweetly, there was no one in the world except her and Jackson, nothing but this kiss.

When at length they pulled apart, Thea smiled again, knowing that the last barrier between them had been demolished.

"I love you, Jackson."

Pure joy illuminated his face. "And I love you."

37

It had been more than twenty-four hours since Thea and Jackson had returned to Cimarron Creek, but the townspeople were still buzzing with all that had happened. Travis now had the three remaining Gang members under arrest. While the town's sole jail cell was crowded and some residents were questioning the propriety of having Charity locked up with two men, neither Travis nor Jackson was willing to consider any other accommodation. They knew she was the most dangerous of the trio, and so she stayed under constant watch. Travis and Edgar took turns guarding the prisoners while Jackson headed to the former orphanage to learn whether Thea had been correct in guessing the location of the gold.

Others might be out and about, strolling Main Street in hopes of learning something new about the outlaws in their jail, but Thea had not left her home since Jackson had carried her back in Tuesday night. Aimee was still fussing over her, although Thea had managed to walk short distances. Now they sat in the parlor, watching Stuart amuse himself with a gourd rattle.

"He'll be here as soon as he can." Aimee's voice was filled with optimism.

"I know." Though Thea knew that worrying accomplished nothing, she was unable to suppress her concerns. What if something had happened to Jackson? What if something destroyed the future that had seemed so bright?

"I keep reminding myself I shouldn't be anxious, but there's so much I want to tell him."

Aimee, who'd been standing by the front window, turned and smiled. "It looks like you'll have your chance. Jackson's coming up the walk." She scooped Stuart into her arms. "I'll let him in, and then Stuart and I'll be in the kitchen. You two need time alone."

Seconds later, Jackson entered the parlor, his obvious fatigue warring with his shining eyes. The relief that washed over Thea startled her with its intensity. Jackson was safe. Though a Ranger's life was always fraught with danger, he'd returned unharmed, and now he was gazing at her as if there was nothing he wanted more than to kiss her. But he did not. Instead, he simply nodded, though the twinkle in his eyes hinted at pleasures to come.

"You were right, Thea," Jackson said as he took the seat she'd offered. "The gold was at the bottom of that old well. As far as we could tell, it's all there." Thea heard the satisfaction in his voice and knew she'd been right in believing that recovering the gold was almost as important to him as capturing the Gang.

Jackson leaned back in the chair, as if trying to relax. "I was surprised, but it seems Daniel didn't spend any of it."

Thea wasn't surprised. "I think he was saving it for the baby and me." What surprised her was how easy it was to talk about Daniel now. What she'd learned from Charity had lifted the weight that had been a constant burden since the day she'd found the first perfumed shirt. The anger that had simmered for so long had vanished, replaced by a sense of freedom, releasing Thea from the shadows of the past, enabling her to walk boldly into her future. And now that Jackson was here, the future seemed bright.

"The gold is being returned to its owners," he told her. "Normally, I would have taken it, but Captain Rawlins volunteered. He knew how anxious I was to get back home."

Thea's heart began to sing as the word "home" registered, telling her Jackson hadn't changed his mind about living here.

"He accepted my resignation, so it's official. I'm a private citizen, and within a month I'll be Cimarron Creek's newest rancher, if Austin and I can come to an agreement."

Though Jackson had claimed that this was what he wanted, Thea couldn't help saying, "I hope you never regret the decision."

His reply was instantaneous. "I won't—not if what I hope is true."

The way his eyes gleamed made Thea's heart race, but she had warned herself not to jump to conclusions. She needed to be certain she and Jackson shared the same dreams. "What is it you're hoping?"

It was only a second before Jackson replied, but Thea felt as if the earth had stopped spinning while she waited for his response.

"What I hope is that you've realized the love we share won't fade and that you're willing to be my wife."

Her tender hope had become reality. She and Jackson both wished for a life together. Thea gazed into his eyes, hoping he'd see not only love but confidence shining from hers. The last of her doubts had been swept away by the torrent of her love for Jackson.

"There is nothing I want more than to marry you. The minister in Ladreville used to say that God works in mysterious ways, and he certainly did." She gestured toward her feet, which were still swaddled in thick bandages. "What happened with Charity showed me how precious life is and that I don't want to waste another day."

Thea leaned forward ever so slightly, wanting to bridge the

distance between them, but not daring to touch Jackson. Not yet. Not until she'd said everything that needed to be said.

"I love you, Jackson. I love you with all my heart, and I always will. What I feel for you will never fade. I know that now."

Thea took a shallow breath, remembering the day she had left Ladreville. Though she had tried to convince herself that she wasn't running away, she had been. She had tried to escape her past, not wanting to admit that it would always be part of her. It was only when she had made peace with the past that she had freed herself to run again—this time toward her future.

As her eyes filled with tears of joy, she nodded. "Yes, my love, I'll marry you."

Jackson's response was everything she had dreamed of. His smile was radiant, as warm as the summer sun, sending ripples of delight down her spine, and his voice resonated with love as he said, "God has answered my prayers. He brought you into my life, and he's shown me that hopes and dreams can come true."

The crooked smile that Thea loved so dearly reappeared as Jackson said, "I can't wait to see what he has in store for us next."

Thea smiled, for Jackson's words echoed her innermost thoughts. She'd been blessed. They'd been blessed. And this was only the beginning.

Slowly, as if he had all the time in the world, Jackson raised his hand and caressed her face, his palm cupping her cheek, his finger tracing the outline of her lips.

"I love you, Thea. I always will." And then, as he bridged the distance between them and pressed his lips to hers, there was no need for words.

Author's Letter

Dear Reader,

I hope you've enjoyed your visits to Cimarron Creek as much as I have. It's been a privilege to share the town's stories with you, especially since I know how many other things compete for your valuable time. Thank you for investing your time in my stories! Truly, you're the reason I write.

The end of a series is always a bittersweet moment for me. As much as I hate leaving a town and the people who've become so real to me, I'm also filled with excitement about the next set of stories. Here's a hint about what's coming starting next year.

It's 1856, and life in Mesquite Springs, Texas, a rapidly growing town in the Hill Country, is changing. With the influx of new residents come new businesses—an expanded restaurant, the town's first newspaper, and a luxurious hotel—as well as new dangers.

Evelyn Radcliffe isn't looking for love. All she wants is to escape the man who killed her parents and destroyed *her home, and so she flees to Mesquite Springs with an orphaned girl, never dreaming that handsome horse rancher Wyatt Clark will hold the key to her past . . . and her future.*

I hope I've intrigued you. If you'd like a bit more of an introduction, turn a couple pages, and you'll find the first chapter.

While you wait for that story to be released, I invite you to read my earlier books. If you haven't read the first two Cimarron Creek stories, now might be the perfect time. Although you know that Lydia and Travis have married, I assure you that the path to happily-ever-after wasn't an easy one. You'll find the full story in A Stolen Heart. *And if you wondered how Catherine and Austin discovered true love, you won't want to miss* A Borrowed Dream.

I also encourage you to visit my website, www.amanda cabot.com. You'll find information about all of my books there as well as a sign-up form for my newsletter. I promise not to fill your inbox with newsletters, because I only issue one when I have important news to share, but it's a way for us to keep in touch. I've also included links to my Facebook and Twitter accounts as well as my email address.

It's one of my greatest pleasures as an author to receive notes from my readers, so don't be shy.

> *Blessings,*
> *Amanda*

Stay tuned for
Amanda Cabot's next story
COMING SPRING 2020

Revell
a division of Baker Publishing Group
www.RevellBooks.com

December 21, 1855

Someone was watching. Though a shiver of dread made its way down her spine, Evelyn Radcliffe kept a smile fixed on her face. No matter how her skin prickled and how every instinct told her to flick the reins and urge the horse to race forward, she wouldn't do anything to worry the child who sat beside her.

She took a deep breath, then exhaled gradually, trying to slow her pulse, reminding herself that this was not the first time she'd sensed the Watcher. The feeling would diminish when she reached the outskirts of Gilmorton, and by the time she was an hour away, it would have disappeared. It always did. The only thing that made today different was that she was not alone. Today she had a child to protect.

Evelyn took another breath, forcing herself to think about something—anything—other than the danger she'd sensed. It was a beautiful day and an unusually warm one for so close to Christmas. The sun was shining, bringing a genuine smile to her face as she gazed at the now-dormant cotton fields that brought so much wealth to this part of Texas. White gold, she'd heard some call them.

"What's wrong?"

Evelyn turned toward the girl who looked enough like her to be her sister. While Polly's hair was silver blonde rather than Evelyn's golden and her eyes were a lighter shade of blue, she had the same oval face and a thin nose whose tip turned ever so slightly to the right, just as Evelyn's did. What distinguished them besides the difference in their ages was that Evelyn's skin was unmarred, while a prominent strawberry-red birthmark on her left cheek destroyed Polly's hopes of beauty and was likely the reason she'd been abandoned.

"Nothing's wrong," Evelyn lied, wishing the child weren't so sensitive. "I'm just anxious to get home." They'd be safe there. Logansville was three hours away, far enough that the Watcher had never followed her. But Polly didn't need to know about the Watcher. Evelyn tickled the girl's nose. "You know Hilda can't be trusted to heat stew without scorching it."

The distraction appeared to have worked, for Polly giggled. "She's a bad cook. Buster spit out the oatmeal she gave him 'cuz it had lumps. Big lumps."

Lumpy oatmeal was a better topic than the fear that engulfed Evelyn almost every time she came to Gilmorton. Mrs. Fielding had told her she needed to confront her fears. That was one of the reasons she insisted Evelyn be the one to make these trips. But Mrs. Fielding didn't know that even ten years later, Evelyn could not bear to look at the building she'd once called home and that she detoured to avoid that block of Main Street. Mrs. Fielding scoffed at the idea that someone was watching, calling it nonsense, but Evelyn knew better. Someone *was* watching, and it terrified her.

The tension that had coiled inside Evelyn began to release as the town disappeared from view. She wouldn't have come to Gilmorton if she had had a choice, but unless she was willing to be gone for more than a day each time she made a delivery, there were no other outlets for the lace the children made. Fortunately, the owner of the mercantile was honest and gave her a fair price for their handicrafts. Today there'd even been enough money left over that Evelyn had been able to buy a piece of candy for each child. That would make Christmas morning special.

"When you're a little older, I'll teach you how to make oatmeal."

Evelyn laid a hand on Polly's shoulder. The child had become so dear to her in the month since she'd arrived at the orphanage. Arrived? No. She'd been deposited on the front step as if she were no more important than the piles of clothing some parishioners left when their children had outgrown them. Like worn dresses and overalls, Polly had been discarded.

Unaware of the turns Evelyn's thoughts had taken, Polly grinned. "I know how. I watched you. You gotta stir, stir, stir."

"That's right. You're a smart girl."

"My daddy said that too." Polly's smile turned upside down, reminding Evelyn of the story she'd told about her father being put in a box in the ground. Evelyn was all too familiar with those boxes, but she'd been fortunate enough to have her parents with her for thirteen years before the night everything changed. Polly was only six, or so she said.

Think about Polly, Evelyn told herself. Not the night when it had rained hard enough to muffle her screams from passersby. The sheriff had told her he'd arrested and hanged the man responsible. He'd assured her she had no reason to fear, and yet she did. Ten years wasn't long enough to erase the memories, particularly when she could feel someone watching her.

"I miss my daddy." Tears welled in Polly's eyes as she said, "I want him to come back."

Though it broke her heart, Evelyn couldn't allow the child to fantasize. "You know he can't. He's in heaven now."

Despite her nod, tears began to trickle down Polly's cheeks. "Buster said some girls get new daddies. He said people come looking for good little girls." She looked up at Evelyn, pleading in her eyes. "I've been good, haven't I?"

"You've been very good," Evelyn reassured her. But that wouldn't be enough. Three couples had come to the orphanage since Polly's arrival, and all three had been unwilling to adopt a child with such a prominent birthmark. "It's Satan's mark," one woman had announced. When she'd heard that, Evelyn had been tempted to gouge the woman's cheek and give her her own mark.

"I want a new daddy." Polly was nothing if not persistent.

Evelyn made a show of looking in every direction. "I don't see any daddies here. Maybe if we sing, someone will hear us."

As Polly's eyes brightened, Evelyn smiled. Singing would be good for both of them. And so they sang song after song. Neither of them could carry a tune, but that didn't bother them or Reginald. Evelyn imagined the gelding twitching his ears in time to their singing, and her spirits rose with each mile they traveled. Polly was once again cheerful, there was no rain in sight, and it would be another month before she had to return to Gilmorton—three reasons to give thanks.

Her smile was as bright as Polly's until she saw it. It was only the slightest of limps, and yet Evelyn knew something was wrong. Unwilling to take any chances, she stopped the wagon and climbed out. A quick look at Reginald's right foreleg confirmed her fears.

"What's wrong?" Polly asked for the second time since they'd left Gilmorton.

"Reginald's lost a shoe."

Peering over the side of the wagon, Polly grinned. "I'll find it."

Evelyn shook her head. "You need to stay in the wagon." Though the sun was past its zenith, the day was still warm enough that snakes could be out, and ever-curious Polly might reach for one. Evelyn glanced at Reginald's hoof one last time. There was no choice. She wouldn't risk permanent injury by having him pull the wagon all the way to Logansville. "We're going back to Gilmorton." As much as she wished otherwise, it was closer.

"Okay." Polly watched wide-eyed as Evelyn unhooked the wagon. "What are you doing?"

"We need to leave the wagon here." Even though it meant that anyone coming by could steal the contents, she had to take the chance. "Reginald can't pull it until he gets a new shoe."

Evelyn lifted Polly out of the wagon and placed her on the horse's back. "Hold on to the harness."

Normally agreeable Polly turned petulant. "I wanna walk with you."

Evelyn wouldn't argue. "All right, but when you get tired, Reginald will be glad to carry you." The horse was exceptionally good with children, which was fortunate, given the number who called the orphanage home.

"This is fun!" Polly exclaimed as she began to skip down the road. It was no longer fun by the time they reached Gilmorton. Polly was tired and fussy. To make matters worse, the blacksmith was in the middle of shoeing another horse and told Evelyn it would be at least half an hour before he could see to Reginald.

"Whoever shoed this horse the last time deserves to be shot," the blacksmith said when he was finally able to inspect the gelding's hoof. "He didn't know what he was doin'."

Evelyn tried not to sigh. Mrs. Fielding had wanted to give Buster a chance, claiming he had an aptitude for caring for horses, but it appeared that the matron had been mistaken. "Did he do any permanent damage?"

"Nah." The blacksmith scraped a rough edge off the hoof. "Just be sure to bring Reginald here next time he needs a shoe. He may be gettin' on in years, but he's a fine piece of horseflesh."

Evelyn and Polly rode the fine piece of horseflesh back to the wagon. Fortunately, the contents were all still there. Unfortunately, the delay meant that they'd be very late arriving home. In all likelihood everyone would be asleep, even Mrs. Fielding. The matron wouldn't be pleased, but at least Evelyn hadn't lost the supplies she'd purchased today.

Darkness had fallen long before they reached Logansville, and Polly—worn out by the walking she'd done as well as the excitement of the day—slept on the bench next to Evelyn. Though she stirred occasionally, each time she drifted back to sleep. This time, however, she sat up, rubbed her eyes, and pinched her nose.

"What's that smell?"

Evelyn sniffed. "It's smoke." She squinted, looking for the source of the odor, but saw nothing.

"Phew! I don't like that."

"I don't either, but we're almost home." Though it was late, someone must be burning trash. "It won't smell as bad once we're indoors."

Evelyn had already decided to let Polly sleep with her tonight rather than risk waking the other girls. That prospect along with the promise that she could help stir the oatmeal tomorrow morning had buoyed Polly's spirits when the only supper Evelyn could offer her had been the cheese and bread she'd purchased while waiting for the blacksmith. Though Gilmorton had a restaurant, that was one place Evelyn would not enter no matter how hungry she might be. When they reached the orphanage, she'd warm some milk for both of them.

They were almost there. Within half an hour, she'd have Reginald in his stall and Polly in her bed. The horse tossed his head, perhaps disturbed by the smoke that had intensified.

As they rounded the final bend in the road, the cause of the smoke was all too clear. The building that had been Evelyn's home for the past ten years was now nothing more than ashes and rubble. She stared at the blackened foundation, trying to make sense of something that made no sense. Well aware of the danger fire posed to a frame structure, Mrs. Fielding was vigilant about safety. Yet, despite her caution, something had happened.

What? How? And where was everyone? There should be close to two dozen children swarming around. Where had they gone? The questions tumbled through Evelyn's mind, the only answers too horrible to consider. She bit the inside of her cheek, determined not to let Polly see her fears. But she failed, for the child began to tremble.

"What happened to the 'nage?" Though Polly's diction was far better than one would have expected from the worn clothing she'd worn when she was abandoned, whoever had taught her hadn't included "orphanage" in her vocabulary.

Evelyn wrapped her arms around Polly and willed her voice to remain steady as she said, "It's gone." And, if what she feared was true, so were Mrs. Fielding and the children who had been her family.

As she descended the small hill and approached the front drive, Evelyn saw half a dozen men wandering around the yard, their casual attitude belying the gravity of the situation.

"Ain't no one left," one called to the others, his voice carrying clearly through the still night air. "Smoke musta got 'em."

Evelyn shuddered as the man confirmed her fears, and she said a silent prayer that Polly wouldn't realize the extent of the tragedy. Mrs. Fielding, Hilda, Buster, every one of the people that she and Evelyn had seen every day were gone, lost in a terrible accident.

"Can't figger it out," another chimed in. "Who woulda wanted to do 'em in? No mistakin' them cans, though. Somebody set the fire."

Evelyn gasped as the words registered, and for a second everything turned black. It wasn't an accident. Though her heart refused to believe it, her mind knew that the men were not mistaken. Someone had deliberately destroyed the orphanage, planning to kill everyone inside. Including her.

"*Where is she?*" The memory of the voice that still haunted her dreams echoed through her brain, shattering the fragile peace the sheriff's assurances had created. Tonight proved that she wasn't safe. Someone wanted to kill the last of the Radcliffes.

Evelyn closed her eyes for a second. *Oh, God, what do I do now?* The response was immediate. *Leave.*

It was all she and Polly could do. The only question was where they should go. She stared at the stars for a second, then nodded. Gilmorton, the one place Evelyn would not consider, was east. Resolutely, she headed west.

"What happened?" Polly asked again, her voice far calmer than Evelyn would have expected. Either the child was too young to understand the magnitude of what had happened, or she'd experienced so much tragedy in her life that she was numb.

"We need a new home." For the first time, Evelyn gave thanks that Polly had formed no attachments to anyone other than her. That would make the transition to a new life easier.

"Okay." Though Polly tightened her grip on Evelyn's arm, her trembling had stopped. "Where are we going?"

"It'll be a surprise." That was no lie. At this point, Evelyn had no idea where she and Polly would find their next home. All she knew was that it had to be far from here, far from whoever had set the fire, far from the Watcher.

Polly was silent for a moment before she said, "It's okay, Evelyn. You'll be my mama, and you'll find me a new daddy."

In three days and two hours, it would be Christmas. In three days and one hour, Mesquite Springs's stone church would be crowded with people eager to celebrate the birth that had taken place in a stable probably only a fraction of the size of this one. Wyatt Clark knew he should be filled with anticipation by the approach of what Ma had once called the season of miracles. Instead, he frowned as the rank odor assailing his nostrils left no doubt that Emerald had contracted thrush.

It shouldn't have happened. The stable was clean and dry; she'd never been left out in muddy conditions; none of the other horses had developed the ailment. Yet Emerald, the mare who was carrying what he hoped would be the Circle C's finest foal, had a bad case of thrush on her left hind hoof.

The only cause Wyatt could imagine was the shape of her hooves. He'd heard that horses with long, narrow hooves were more susceptible to the disease than others. That was why he'd bred Emerald with a stallion whose hooves were a little broader than normal. Though not everyone agreed, Wyatt believed that characteristics from the sire and the dam blended in foals.

"Sorry, girl," he said as he scraped away the spongy part of the hoof, then reached for a bottle of iodine. "I know you don't like the smell of this, but you need it."

"There you are."

Wyatt looked up in surprise. It wasn't like his mother to come to the stable this late.

The woman whose dark brown hair and eyes were so like his frowned. "I might have known," she said, her voice sharper than usual. "You ought to be asleep, but no—you're out here with the horses." The horses that had been her husband's dream, not hers, and most definitely not Wyatt's.

Honor thy father and thy mother. It was good advice, but sometimes it took more than the reminder of that commandment to keep Wyatt's angry retorts from escaping. He'd spent more than a decade turning the Circle C's stable from a fledgling enterprise into one whose fame stretched far beyond the Hill Country, and yet his mother still begrudged the time he spent with the horses.

Wyatt bit the tip of his tongue before he said as mildly as he could, "We have a lot riding on Emerald. Right now she can hardly walk because of the thrush." He placed the horse's hoof back on the ground and patted her side.

"Oh." Ma's tone gentled. "I didn't realize what was happening. I'm sorry, son. I know you do your best." Though she kept her distance, lest the mare consider her an intruder and lash out, Ma managed a smile for her son. "It's just that I worry about you. It's time you settle down."

Her smile broadened. "You need a wife and children of your own. There's more to life than horses."

Wyatt bit his tongue again as he considered his response to what had become a regular refrain. Ma didn't want a new bonnet for Christmas. She wanted the assurance that there'd be a new generation of Clarks.

He watched Emerald take a tentative step on her cleaned and disinfected hoof before he turned back to his mother. "What you said may be true, but right now horses are what pay the bills around here."

Wyatt didn't want to think about the first year after Pa had been killed. It was no exaggeration to say that if he hadn't taken the two most promising yearlings to Fort Worth for the big sale and encountered men who spent more on horses than slaves, the Circle C would belong to someone else. Fortunately, the yearlings had brought enough money to get them through that horrible year when Ma had . . . Wyatt shook himself mentally. He wouldn't think about that. Not tonight. Not ever again.

Ma straightened her shoulders and gave him the look he remembered from his childhood, the one that both he and his sister soon learned meant that they were supposed to obey. "I'd rather have a grandbaby than a new dress."

It wasn't the first time he'd heard that, and Wyatt knew it wouldn't be the last. Still, he wouldn't tell Ma that the mere thought of a wife and children scared him more than anything else on Earth. What if he married and had children and then a bandit or a snake or a lightning bolt killed him? He couldn't—he wouldn't—put those he loved in the position his family had been in when the Comanche killed Pa. No, sirree. Marriage was not for him.

⚜

"She's dead."

Rufus Bauman looked up from the board he'd been sanding. Though her words were solemn, his wife did not appear distressed. "What are you talking about? Who's dead?"

Winnie fisted her hands on her hips, her expression saying he ought to know. "That girl. The one you thought could replace Rose."

Rufus tried not to sigh. Though he loved his wife dearly, there were times when her obsession with the girl tested his patience. This was one of them.

He laid the sandpaper aside and looked directly at Winnie. "I wasn't trying to replace Rose." No one could do that. He hadn't even been trying to right a horrible wrong. No one could do that, either. When he'd suggested adoption, he'd wanted to give the girl a home and maybe—just maybe—bring some joy back to his own home.

It wasn't natural for parents to lose all their children, but he and Winnie had. While he'd mourned both Rose and Isaac and the tragic circumstances of their deaths, his pain had begun to lessen. Winnie's had not. She'd clutched it to her like a shawl, declaring only another woman could understand. That was one of the reasons Rufus had broached the subject of adoption. He'd thought his wife would enjoy having another female in the house, but she'd been adamant in her refusal. And now it was no longer a possibility. The girl was dead.

"How do you know she's dead?"

"Jeb Perkins told me. Somebody set fire to the orphanage in Logansville last night. Everybody died."

The anguish that had lodged deep inside Rufus threatened his breathing. Not an accident but a deliberate killing, just like the last time. And just like the last time, he hadn't been able to stop it.

<hr />

Basil Marlow watched the man enter the room that was now his office. He'd thought Bart foolish when he refused to conduct business in what had once been their father's office, instead constructing a separate building far enough from the main house that none of the daily noise would bother him. Tonight Basil applauded his brother's foresight. The isolation and the cloak of darkness ensured that this meeting would remain secret.

He narrowed his eyes slightly as the man closed the door behind him. Though the spring in the messenger's step told Basil everything he needed to know, he still posed the question. "Is everything taken care of?"

"Yes, sir. Just the way you ordered." The man straightened his shoulders with pride over his accomplishment, perhaps hoping for an extra reward. He would get it. "It weren't hard to track down the gal once that old slave let slip that she weren't dead."

Rising from behind the massive desk, Basil struggled not to frown at the thought of the woman who'd betrayed him. He'd believed every slave knew the penalty for anything less than total loyalty, but at least one hadn't. The one that Miriam had insisted on bringing as part of her dowry had told Basil the girl died while he was gone. She'd even shown him the grave, but she'd been lying.

Somehow she'd snuck off the plantation and left the girl at an orphanage. The stupid woman thought he'd never learn what she'd done, but he had. One of the other slaves who'd sought to curry favor had told him.

"Did you take care of her?"

"Yes, sir. She won't be talkin' no more." The messenger mimicked a knife slicing across his throat.

"Good work. What about the girl herself?"

"She won't be talkin' no more, neither. The fire took care of that. I done just what you tole me. Ain't nobody coulda lived through that fire." The messenger practically strutted as he took another step toward Basil. "I hung around long enough to make sure nobody was alive."

"Excellent." Though it had taken longer than he would have liked, most of the loose ends were tied up. The man who'd stolen the woman Basil loved was dead, and so was his spawn. He might not have Miriam, but he had everything else. Vengeance was even sweeter than he'd dreamt.

"This deserves a celebration." As the messenger grinned in

anticipation, Basil turned to the cabinet behind him and withdrew a bottle of whiskey and two glasses.

The man's eyes widened in surprise when he saw the label. *Enjoy it,* Basil urged him silently as he filled the glasses. This was the first and last time he would taste such fine whiskey.

As the man raised his glass, Basil reached into his desk drawer, pulled out a pistol, and fired. The last of the loose ends was gone.

Acknowledgments

You may think that writing is a solitary pursuit, and it is, but publishing is a very different story. It takes a team of talented professionals working together to turn a raw manuscript into the book you're holding in your hands.

I am extremely fortunate to have an outstanding team working on my books. Without exception, the staff at Revell are both talented and dedicated to making each book the best it can be. Each one of them cares about their authors, but—more important—they care about you, the reader, and strive to make your reading experience a rewarding one.

There are countless people who work behind the scenes, and if I listed them all, this book would rival *War and Peace* for length. I would, however, be remiss if I didn't single out five women who form the nucleus of what I consider to be the dream team.

It's been more than ten years since Executive Editor Vicki Crumpton bought my first manuscript. I was thrilled then, and the thrill has not waned. Vicki's belief in my stories gets me through the dreaded middle-of-the-book doldrums, while her gentle editing that combines constructive criticism with very welcome humor strengthens each of my manuscripts. I give thanks each day that I have the perfect editor—Vicki.

Few authors look forward to revision letters, but that's because they don't have Managing Editor Kristin Kornoelje on their team. Kristin's incredible attention to detail and her thoughtful analysis of characters' motivation have given me new perspectives on my own work and made me a better writer. She's a true blessing.

Director of Marketing Michele Misiak does so much more than her title might imply. In addition to constantly looking for new ways to promote my books, a job that she does exceedingly well, she serves as my gateway to Revell, answering myriad questions and educating me about the constantly changing world of publishing and social media. I've learned so much from Michele.

I'm convinced that Karen Steele doesn't sleep. She wears several hats, including Senior Publicist. In that role, she's on what seems like a perpetual search for ways to spread the word about my books. Radio and print, interviews and reviews, blog tours, social media—Karen's got them all covered, and not just covered, but covered well. I couldn't ask for a better publicist.

We've all been told not to judge a book by its cover, but if you're like me, you do exactly that. That's why I'm so grateful that Cheryl Van Andel is part of the team. As Revell's Art Director, she's responsible for those gorgeous covers that are your first look at my stories. This is the fourteenth cover she's created for me, and I can honestly say that each one has exceeded my expectations. Somehow Cheryl always manages to capture the essence of each story and to create covers that are both beautiful and unique. What a wonderful talent!

I am deeply grateful to Vicki, Kristin, Michele, Karen, Cheryl, and the rest of the Revell staff for everything they do.

Dreams have always been an important part of **Amanda Cabot**'s life. For almost as long as she can remember, she dreamt of being an author. Fortunately for the world, her grade-school attempts as a playwright were not successful, and she turned her attention to novels. Her dream of selling a book before her thirtieth birthday came true, and she's been spinning tales ever since. She now has more than thirty-five novels to her credit.

Her books have been finalists for the ACFW Carol Award as well as the HOLT Medallion and the Booksellers' Best and have appeared on the CBA and ECPA bestseller lists.

A popular speaker, Amanda is a member of ACFW and a charter member of Romance Writers of America. She married her high school sweetheart, who shares her love of travel and who's driven thousands of miles to help her research her books. After years as Easterners, they fulfilled a longtime dream and now live in the American West.

Bestselling author Amanda Cabot invites you into Texas's storied past to experience adventure, mystery—and love.

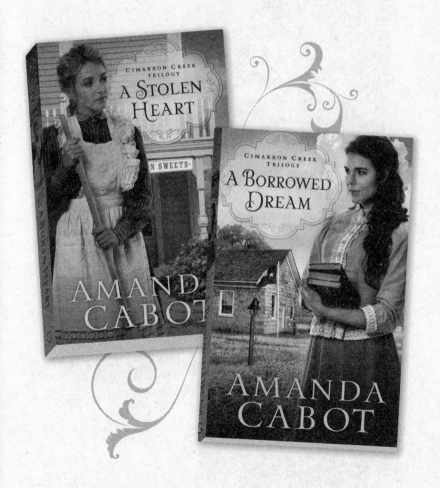

Enjoy a tale of drama, love, and second chances as beautiful as the Hill Country itself.

VISIT

Amanda Cabot

AmandaCabot.com